W9-BQT-223

Time Traders III

Time Traders III

Echoes in Time
Atlantis Endgame

ANDRE NORTON &
SHERWOOD SMITH

SCIENCE
FICTION

ECHOES IN TIME   Copyright © 1999 by
                            Andre Norton, Ltd.
    Publication History: Tor hardcover, November 1999
    Tor Paperback, July 2000

ATLANTIS ENDGAME   Copyright © 2002 by
                            Andre Norton, Ltd.
    Publication History: Tor hardcover, December 2002

First SFBC Science Fiction Printing: November 2002

Published by arrangement with:
Tor Books
Tom Doherty Associates, LLC
175 Fifth Avenue
New York, NY 10010

Visit The SFBC online at *http://www.sfbc.com*

Visit Tor online at *http://www.tor.com*

Tor® is a registered trademark of Tom Doherty Associates,
LLC.

ISBN: 0-7394-3103-X

PRINTED IN THE UNITED STATES OF AMERICA.

Contents

ECHOES IN TIME

With heartfelt thanks to Dave Trowbridge,
tech wizard extraordinaire, for unstinting help.
—S.S.

PROLOGUE

THE DAY'S HEAT had diminished to only a residual shimmer from the cooling earth. The chitter and click of insects in the scrubby green brush formed a kind of musical accompaniment to the laughing and singing of the long, snaking line of children crouched together, one in front of the other, knees up near their chins.

> *"Here is our mother!*
> *Our mother, our mother!*
> *Here is our harvest,*
> *Our fruit, our harvest!*
> *Our mother, our fruit . . ."*

The children laughed as they sang, their bare toes scrabbling forward in the dust as they waddled and hopped. Their dark brown skin was mottled and streaked with painted patterns, some chalk-white, others subtle earth tones. Sweat and dust marred the fine lines of the patterns, not that the children cared. They were only playing. They sang and laughed with the companionable abandon of children who know that the time for real skin painting, when they became adults with adult responsibilities for food and shelter, war and marriage, lay far in the sunny future, after many harvest games such as this.

Saba Mariam, watching from her post beside a jumble of rocks, felt as if she had been wafted back through time. So the children of the Surma had played and sang for countless generations in this sere mountain region of southwest Ethiopia.

She looked down at her hands, the skin dark against the plain khaki of her trousers. She and her recorder were the only jarring notes in this scene out of history, the only intrusion of modernity—though at any time an airplane might roar overhead, causing children and adults alike to pause, like startled deer, before they scampered off to hide.

Saba glanced at her tape recorder, working silently behind a warm gray boulder. The Surma tolerated her strange ways because she did not interfere with them, and she had proved that she was not in fact sent by their age-old enemies, the Bumi. She looked strange to men and women alike, with her ears and lips unpierced. She was, to the Surma, a child walking around in a grown body, for she did not display the ritual markings of a responsible adult, but they dismissed her strangeness with a kind of humorous tolerance.

Saba had learned to sit quietly, patiently, drawing no attention to herself. After her long stretches of neutral observance, she knew that the people would forget her presence. She would become no more interesting than another boulder, or a patch of scrubby grass, and it was then that she turned on the recorder, making a record of music that had been handed down through families over centuries and centuries of time.

It was good work. Important work. Saba was proud to be one of many who quietly went about recording the songs and myths that had sustained human beings since the cradle of civilization. Progress had brought to the Earth untold advantages, but its pervasive growth was choking off in ever-increasing numbers the very old languages, customs, and cultures of peoples who had lived in harmony with the land since humans first crossed the great continents.

It was indeed important work, Saba thought as one very small three-year-old tripped and went rolling in the dust. The song broke up into laughter. The children re-formed into their line; one girl at the front began singing again, soon joined by the others, as in the distance a group of mothers and young unmarried women chattered and prepared food.

Important work—and involving work. It kept one busy, which in its turn prevented one from worrying about those things that could not be solved—

As she thought this, she became aware of a sound that perhaps had warned her subliminally of approaching intrusions.

The faint hum, reminiscent of bees bumbling around flowers, resolved into a battered old motorcycle drawing a three-wheeled side car. The rusty machine was probably older than Saba herself.

The children heard it as well. For a moment they all went still, and then their leader dashed through the dust to her mother. The other children followed, some still laughing, others singing bits of song. The mothers gathered their young and vanished into the sun-dried brush.

Saba climbed up on a boulder and shaded her eyes against the great, bloodred late October sun. The driver of the motorcycle revved the engine and zoomed around brush and scraggly trees, halting two meters from Saba's rocks.

Saba held her breath as the wafting odors of petrol and exhaust blew past, so unfamiliar after her month here in the wild mountainous region. The driver, meanwhile, pulled off sunglasses and a tight baseball cap, shaking free a cloud of curling brown hair. The clothing—tough, anonymous bush garb—had made gender difficult to guess at; a gloved hand pulled out a kerchief and mopped some of the dust and grit from a middle-aged female face as Saba approached.

The driver looked up, shoving the kerchief into a pocket. *"La Professeur Mariam? Vous êtes Saba Mariam?"* she asked.

Saba nodded, adding in French, "Is there an emergency?"

"Oui." French was obviously no more the driver's native tongue than it was Saba's, but Saba had gotten used to polyglot conversations—often in tongues chosen because possible surrounding listeners would not understand the conversation. Not that any listeners were around now.

The woman said, *"Je m'appelle Taski Aleyescoglu. Je suis avec L'Étoile Projet."*

Project Star.

For a moment Saba stood staring at the unfamiliar woman, angry at this breach of promise.

L'Étoile Projet—Project Star—was the bland name for one of the most secret organizations in the world, one for which Saba had given her strength, her spirit, and nearly her life.

Saba turned her gaze on the Time Agent courier. "I was promised a year," she said in French. "A year to recover."

"It is an emergency," Agent Aleyescoglu replied.

"Answer me this first: has Lisette Al-Aseer reported in?"

The Time Agent did not pretend to not know the name. Her lips pressed into a line, and she shook her head. "I am sorry, Professor Mariam."

Saba drew a deep breath. "And they expect me to cut short my recovery time? And return?"

The agent said, "Whatever is going on is classified over my head—as is whatever your former partner is still working on. All I was told was to find you and bring you back. Whatever it is that has them scrambling now, apparently only you can solve it."

Saba turned her gaze to the last limb of the sun, sinking beyond the western peaks. Shadows blended softly now, making it difficult to see the woman's face. If she was to leave, she'd have to go now; they were miles from any road, and driving about at night in Ethiopia in the dark was no simple matter.

She looked back. "Me as a musicologist?"

"You as you. That's all I was told: it must be you, it can be no other person."

Strange. But time travel was strange, that Saba knew. Strange, alien, and even more remorseless than the natural passage of time.

She looked over the distant clumps of trees, knowing that the Surma crouched there, and she smiled sadly to herself. All very well to fancy that she had stepped back in time while recording these people celebrating the year's harvest. Apparently she was to be drawn back into real time travel, in a machine designed and built by beings never born on Earth. How many agents had been lost in the quest to understand this technology from beyond the stars?

She shook her head.

"Can you tell me at least where this emergency is taking place?"

"I wasn't told. Of course," Taski said, settling onto the motorcycle and pulling on her goggles. "But when I was on my way out, I overheard an order for someone to contact the American Embassy for your visa."

"New York! So this new emergency involves the Americans?" Saba shook her head. She knew that Project Star had originated with the United States, but so far her connection with the Americans had been peripheral at best.

Taski grinned as she yanked the baseball cap over her forehead. "Big boss will probably be out here next, and you can ply him with all the questions you like."

Saba sat back on her rock. "If there is so urgent a need," she said, "why did he not come here instead of you?"

Taski revved the engine, which roared, sending some distant birds flapping skyward from the shrubs. Their cries echoed back, faint as the laughter of children, as the motor died down to an uneven growl.

"Might have," Taski called. "But he's still in Mother Russia."

Russia?

Saba mouthed the word, but did not speak. In amazement—and apprehension—she gazed at the courier, who gave her a careless salute, revved the engine once more, then drove off into the twilight, leaving a cloud of light brown dust hanging in the still air.

Russia? And the Americans? Could there be a connection?

She might not have been able to conquer her bitterness, but one thing she had learned was patience.

Saba bent over the recorder, pressed the ON button, then settled back to wait for the Surma to emerge, like shy ghosts, from the shelter of the brush.

"VIKHODITE! RUKE V' VERKHI"

"Like hell I'll come out with my hands up." Mikhail Petrovich Nikulin smashed the butt of his pistol into a corner of window, and stuck the muzzle through the hole. Bitter Siberian air smote his sweaty face.

Two things happened almost at once.

From behind came a shout: "Nikulin! You know the orders!"

From outside the rickety old building came the *klatch!* and *click!*s as two of the half-hidden gangsters dropped bullets into the chambers of their rifles.

Phwup. A large-callibre bullet burrowed into the half-frozen slush just below Misha's window, kicking up splatters of mud.

Footsteps from behind. A moment later a short, darkhaired figure crouched below the level of the windowsill. "Nikulin!"

Misha did not have to look down; he knew that voice, and he knew the expression on the older man's face.

"You *know* the orders. No violence. If we have to, we activate the destruction device on the ship," Gaspardin said.

White hot anger flared through Misha Nikulin. "We are not going to lose that ship," he stated, his gaze staying on the figures in the bulky coats creeping foward from the cars to the old stone fence.

He fired once, and heard a shouted curse. Outside, one of the gangsters flung up his weapon and dropped, rolling in the muddy slush, hand clasped around his wounded knee.

"Misha—"

On the periphery of his vision Nikulin saw Gaspardin reach up for his pistol. "Don't touch me."

The hand vanished. "You will answer to the Colonel for contravening orders."

"If that ship is blown up, she will answer to me," Misha said, and again he fired, winging a second figure in the arm.

The trefoil flicker of automatic weapons fire glowed outside, and all around Misha wood splintered. Glass shattered and rained down in a musical tinkle. He dropped to the dusty wooden floor and bellycrawled, not back to the inner room, as Gaspardin did, but to the kitchen annex, where he'd stashed an old wartime teargas pistol.

As the furious automatic fire stitched across the weatherworn, dilapidated building, Misha loaded the pistol with a teargas cannister, used the butt to knock out a corner of the brittle glass, and then took aim.

He fired into the midst of the attackers. Heard choked, angry cries. A whiff of teargas drifted on the cold air, making him sneeze, just as raking bullets smashed into the antique ceramic oven, sending out a lethal spray of shards.

Warmth creased Misha's ribs. He ignored it. Steadied his grip. Shot a second time, then flung aside the tear gas weapon and picked up his pistol. Dropped the magazine. Checked to see if it still had ammunition. Slid the magazine home and jacked a round into the chamber.

He kept crawling from place to place, forcing himself to make each shot count, until the roaring outside grew louder than the roar in his ears.

The shooting had ceased. He leaned against a window, glanced outside, and realized the gangsters had retreated to their vehicles and roared away.

Misha stared through the window, trying to make sense of the endless gray Siberian sky meeting the distant horizon. But it didn't make sense. Nothing made sense except the fact that the mission was safe. The alien ship was safe.

". . . realize it, don't you?"

Misha looked over his shoulder, made out in the swiftly gathering darkness Gaspardin's anger-narrowed eyes, his mouth white in his grizzled jowls.

"You defied orders," Gaspardin repeated. Then his expression changed as his gaze worked down Misha's shirt.

Misha glanced down, but all he saw were billowing clouds of darkness. He lifted his free hand to his side, and felt the wet warmth there.

"Damn," he said, and slid into the darkness.

████████ ████████ ████████

HE WOKE STARING up at a low sod ceiling. He smelled generations of cabbage and potato meals and unwashed wool. Heard the creak of a chair.

"So you are awake, young man." That voice belonged to Colonel Vasilyeva. Misha turned his head, saw her sitting by a narrow window set into the thick stone wall. Through the window he glimpsed hayricks, and the long white Russian sky. He knew this place; it was the fallback position for their team, in case of disaster. His hand lifted to his ribs, encountered a taped bandage there.

He said, finding his throat dry, "The mission is safe."

"No thanks to you."

The Colonel's face was calm, her gaze unwavering. Like others who had spent childhood under the shadow of Stalin, she seemed to have no emotions whatsoever.

Misha knew that was wrong.

He said, "The ship?"

"It is safe enough. Now." Her voice was as immovable as granite. When she was angry, her demeanor carried all the force of a rockslide. "But that will not be the case if any of your victims die, and the government turns its attention back on us."

Misha fought against blinding anger, and winced as he moved restlessly on the bed.

"If," she stated in a low, soft voice, "I give orders for that alien ship to be destroyed, it will be done."

Misha gritted his teeth and forced himself to sit up against the wall.

The Colonel went on, "They were just a bunch of opportunists, there to take over the energy plant, and use it for some easy piracy by price gouging. They had no idea that we are time agents, and that we have an alien ship. And of course they are going to come back, in bigger numbers. We have to make certain that what they find will be a hydroelectric plant. Nothing more. Nothing less. Nothing," she said in a slow, cold voice, "to raise questions."

"I'm sorry," Misha said at last, though it cost him more effort than sitting up had.

The Colonel sat back, one blunt hand working at her temples as if she had a headache. If one were to interpret that gesture as weakness, that would be equally wrong.

"The Americans have a ship," she said. "We are now allied with them. The Germans have a ship. The French have a ship, as do the Norwegians, and Africans. May I remind you, Mikhail Petrovich, that these are all our allies now? The Time Agency is worldwide. This mission will be carried through, even if one of us loses a ship."

Misha shook his head, then winced as corresponding pain racketed through his skull. "I'm sorry. I just don't believe the Americans are going to help. Or if they do, what their price is going to be."

"None of us know," the Colonel said. "My entire life I have not trusted them, but necessity forces change. You forced it sooner than I would have wished."

Misha winced.

The Colonel said, "Our people should be finishing up at the energy plant right now. Then on their way to St. Petersburg to get ready for the journey." She dropped her hands to her knees. "None of us trust the

Americans. But balanced against that is the reality of our government struggling to survive, and the unrest so very close. No one must find out about these alien artifacts—either the ships or the time-travel mechanisms. You know that as well as I. Rather than let anyone find out, anyone at all, we blow up the ship—we blow ourselves up. These secrets cannot fall into the wrong hands. Every single government who knows the secrets agrees. And so necessity forces us all to compromise. To work together. To solve the mysteries we've been presented, before we find ourselves with bigger problems from outside our gravity well than we're causing for one another within it."

She sat back.

Misha sighed, presing his hand against his side. It hurt. "The mission?"

"The flight to New York leaves tomorrow. We begin the training there."

Lightning flared behind Misha's eyes. He strugged up, made it to his feet. "I'm going," he said, not caring that his voice broke. "Get me on that flight."

"But the doctor—"

"I don't care. I *will* be on that mission, if I have to blast my way across eight time zones to do it. And you know I never make empty threats."

They stared at one another.

"Zina." He relented at last. "Please."

The Colonel's lips creased. Just faintly.

Misha sank down onto the hay-stuffed bed. The effort of standing had made him dizzy. But that no longer mattered. He knew he'd won.

"We will leave tomorrow," she said, "but without you. As soon as your fever is down, you will follow us." She pointed at the bed. "Now get some sleep." The door shut behind her.

CHAPTER 1

THE PHONE RANG. Ross Murdock looked up, startled.

For a moment his eyes met his wife's across the room. Eveleen paused in the act of patting down the folded tablecloth on the basket they'd both just finished packing.

Strange, to hear a phone ring. It'd been days since they'd been so rudely interrupted—long, glorious autumn days there at Safeharbor, on the coast of Maine. No phone, no TV, no newspapers—nothing but seabirds, and the sound of the breakers crashing on the rocks down the hill from the house, and each other. Heaven.

"Let's ignore it," Ross said.

Eveleen shook her head. "This isn't our house, it's Gordon's, and it might be someone who needs to get in touch with him."

"Who?" Ross asked as the phone rang a second time.

Eveleen's expressive brown eyes glanced at him, rounded with amused patience. "Friends? Family?"

"Outside of the Project, he doesn't have any friends," Ross said, half joking. "And I don't think there's any family either. The Project *is* his friends and family."

Eveleen said, "I really think we should answer it."

"Then I'll get it," Ross said. "I'm closer."

On the fourth ring he picked it up. "Ashe residence."

"Ross." The voice was immediately familiar—Major Kelgarries. "I've been trying to reach you. We've got an emergency—"

Ross slammed down the receiver. "Phone sales," he said, forcing a smile. "Let's get going on that picnic before the weather drives us back inside again."

Eveleen smiled back, hefted the basket, and opened the door.

Ross closed the door on the sound of the phone ringing again. "Looks like we might luck out weather-wise after all," he said in a voice of loud, hearty cheer.

Eveleen looked at him with her brows quirked, but she said nothing as he slid his hand next to hers on the basket, and with their picnic lunch swinging between them, the two started up the trail behind the house.

An hour later Ross lay stretched out on the cool grass, staring up at the cloud formations.

Emergency, he thought. Yeah, sure. There *always* was some damned emergency on Project Star, and it seemed to Ross that he'd been stuck in the middle of most of them.

Well, he'd done his time. They'd promised Eveleen and him a honeymoon, and he meant to have it. A honeymoon meant just the two of them, no interruptions, nothing more dangerous than the occasional bumblebee.

He glanced at Eveleen, who had been watching the wheeling seabirds swooping and circling above the Maine breakers. She had turned her attention to him. Their eyes met, and hers narrowed.

"Phone sales?" she repeated.

Surprised, Ross said, "What?"

Eveleen's mouth deepened at the corners. "I might be dense, but it seems odd to me that you'd still be angry an hour after hanging up on a junk sales call."

Ross snorted. "Angry?"

Eveleen reached over and traced her finger over his jawline. "Clenched. Just like some movie hero about to be blasted by twenty machine-gun-totin' bad guys." She tapped his hand, which—he belatedly noticed—had been drumming on the grass. "Not quite white knuckles, but the next thing to it."

Ross gave her a reluctant grin. "It was Kelgarries."

Eveleen whistled. Beyond her, a gull cawed, and far below, as if picking up the sound, came the mews and cries of myriad seabirds.

"This is our time," Ross stated. "I resent like hell their breaking their promise."

"But you know it has to be an emergency, or they wouldn't," Eveleen said. "Did he have a chance to say anything?"

Ross, remembering that same word *emergency*, gave a shrug.

"Darling." Eveleen looked sardonic. "Don't even waste the breath claiming you don't care. Or that they don't care. The fact is, Kelgarries's ghost is sitting right here between us, or you wouldn't be so tense. We might as well go back and find out what the problem is."

"Dammit." Ross got up, and began repacking the basket.

"Does 'dammit' mean that I'm right?" Eveleen asked, grinning. "A spouse likes to be able to decode these little clues."

"Dammit means dammit," Ross said, slinging the basket over his shoulder.

"I'll remember that," Eveleen said, chuckling, as they started back down the trail.

Within half an hour of their reaching Gordon Ashe's house, the phone rang again. Eveleen gave Ross that sardonic look again. "I'll get it this time," she said, and picked up the phone. "Gordon Ashe's residence," she said in a polite voice. "Eveleen Riordan speaking. May I take a message?"

Ross wished—absurdly, he knew—that she would follow that with "Sorry, wrong number," or maybe "No, we don't need any aluminum siding."

But ten seconds passed. Thirty. She still hadn't spoken.

Ross crossed the room to her side and waited in silence.

She finally said, "I understand, Major. And we appreciate the extra time you've allowed us. See you tomorrow."

She gently laid the receiver back into the cradle, and turned her face up to Ross. "Emergency indeed."

"Project Star." Ross swore, then added, "We should have used the damn transfer machine to blast us forward, or back, or somewhere in time when they couldn't find us." He sighed. "What kind of emergency? He say? No, he wouldn't—not over the phone."

"Correct. All he said was that they need us to report to the Center."

"What about Gordon?"

"He's already there."

Ross let out a long sigh. "It was too good to last, I guess," he muttered, biting down what he really wanted to say. But cursing fate, the world, and his bosses wouldn't change anything. So he added only, "Tomorrow?"

"They're sending a copter to pick us up. At least we don't have to drive all million and a half of those windy roads back down the coast again."

"If it meant we could be alone a little longer . . ." Ross started.

Eveleen grinned, and wiggled her brows suggestively. "We have the rest of tonight. Let's make the most of it."

He had no objections to that.

GORDON ASHE POURED a cup of fresh coffee and sat down at the briefing table. He looked up at Major Kelgarries, who gave him a somewhat lopsided smile before saying, "They'll be here tomorrow."

"Was Ross pretty fluent?" Gordon asked, trying for lightness.

Kelgarries—a tall, hatchet-faced man—said, "Ross hung up on me. Ten tries later I spoke with Eveleen. When I mentioned an emergency, she seemed to appreciate our having given them as much time as we have. I suspect Ross might have had a more, ah, characteristic and colorful reaction, but she was the one to hear it—not me."

Gordon Ashe nodded, smiling. Truth was, he was impatient to get Ross and Eveleen back, to plunge directly into what promised to be a tough assignment. He'd never permitted himself to indulge in what he considered to be a dangerous luxury, romance. It was too much like weakness. Yet he had to admit that Eveleen Riordan and Ross Murdock made an excellent partnership.

The catch was that Ross and Gordon were no longer partners.

So would he go solo this time? Or would he, Ross, and Eveleen make a threesome?

Wait. Hadn't Nelson Milliard, the top boss, said something about a later discussion concerning personnel for the mission?

Gordon sipped at his coffee, resigning himself to a day's wait. His years of archaeological study had forced him to learn patience.

AT MIDDAY THE next day, Ross and Eveleen's second copter ride ended outside a nondescript building located on the outskirts of a small town in upstate New York.

They stepped out of the copter, bending low against the powerful blasts of air generated by the slowing blades—and by a cold rain-laden wind.

As if nature had agreed that their honeymoon was over, a powerful storm had swept down from the north during the night, and it had chased them steadily as they transferred from copter to small plane to copter again.

Ross was peripherally aware of his scarred hand flexing and then tightening into a fist as he and Eveleen crossed the tarmac to the front of the building blandly labeled NORTHSIDE RESEARCH INSTITUTE. His danger sense—whether sparked by the storm or by anticipation of whatever news awaited them inside—made him edgy.

He glanced at Eveleen as a security guard opened the thick glass doors for them. She looked neat and competent as always, her brown hair swept up into a chignon, her slacks and shirt attractive but easy to move in. Only someone who had been trained in martial arts recognized in her controlled grace the mark of the expert who was poised for action; though her face was pleasant, even smiling, Ross realized that she, too, was tense.

Just then she glanced across at him, a quick, assessing gaze. He grinned, she grinned.

So they were beginning to read each other's moods.

The elevator opened then, and they passed inside. Instead of going up one floor to what Ross figured were ordinary offices, they went down the equivalent of five or six floors, deep underground.

They did not speak during the short ride down. When the doors slid open again, they looked out on a familiar scene: the main offices of what had been known merely as Project Star, the work of a government agency so secret that there wasn't even any acronym to spark the interest of the curious.

Full-spectrum lighting and lots of potted indoor plants made the best of an underground facility sealed fifty feet below light and air. Ross and Eveleen strode past cubicles and desks, glancing at the busy support staff who researched projects for the Time Agents—and then sorted the data that resulted from the agents' excursions into the past.

How many of these people, most of whom he did not know, had had to read Ross's reports, and write up reports of their own?

He supposed he could find out if he wanted to, he thought as they passed through the double doors at the other end of the big room. But did he really want to know how much work he was making for someone else?

The thought caused him to repress a grin as they reached the outer office belonging to Nelson Milliard, the head boss of the Project.

At their entrance, three men and a woman glanced up. Milliard looked like a typical CEO—big, gray-haired, abrupt in movement, a man to whom time was precious. Major Kelgarries, Ross's very first contact in the Project, could never be mistaken for anything but a military man. But the third man, Gordon Ashe, looked to the uninitiated like an outdoorsman: brown-skinned, blue eyes, brown hair with blond sunstreaks, and very fit. It was not obvious to the casual observer that Ashe was also a doctor of archaeology, and a leader with a very subtle mind.

The fourth person, a woman, was unknown to Ross. Short, middle-aged, and gray-haired, dressed in a plain suit of blue linen, she displayed the same characteristics as Milliard; whoever she was, Ross decided after a second's evaluation, she was important.

"Ross. Eveleen," Milliard said in greeting. "Permit me to introduce you to Colonel Zinaida Vasilyeva."

A Russian?

Milliard turned to the woman. "Colonel Vasilyeva, these are Eveleen Riordan and Ross Murdock, two of our best troubleshooters."

The woman gave a short nod and a brief smile. "I have read much about you." Her English was excellent, if heavily accented.

I'll bet you have, Ross thought grimly. *Question is, our reports—or those written by your spies?*

"Please, sit down," Milliard said, indicating two waiting chairs. "Coffee? Something to eat?"

Just then the smell of fresh coffee registered on Ross, and he rose to help himself. As he poured out two mugs, he looked over his shoulder at Ashe, who watched, smiling faintly. "Russian?" he mouthed the word—knowing the others couldn't see.

Ashe's only response was a slight crinkling of the skin around his eyes.

Milliard went on. "We're still expecting Colonel Vasilyeva's colleagues, and one of our own people, all of whom were delayed by the weather in Washington, D.C. The Colonel came on ahead so that we could begin the preliminary briefings. The Major will give you the general outline of what we're up against." He nodded at Kelgarries, and sat down.

Kelgarries turned to Vasilyeva. "Would you care to begin, Colonel?"

The Russian Colonel gave a short nod, and folded her hands. "We have come to request your aid," she said slowly, in accented but excellent English. "In the past the politics of our governments have made us rivals, and perhaps we Time Agents fostered that rivalry in an intellectual sense even after the political issues were resolved."

Kelgarries grinned, and the Colonel's eyes narrowed in unexpected humor.

Ross found himself grinning as well. Early on during Project Star, the diminishing Cold War had kept the two Terran nations apart, even when they seemed to be fighting the same enemy. Later, after the Cold War was officially considered at an end, the race for knowledge had seemed less political and more of a game to see who learned the most the quickest. Except it had been a game full of danger.

"But you had reason to be wary about approaching us before this."

Milliard's diplomatic statement brought a sour smile to Ross's lips. He hid it by sipping coffee.

"That is so." The Colonel gave an abrupt nod. "In the very beginning, when we encountered the entities you Americans nicknamed the Baldies, we assumed incorrectly that they might be allies of yours. Their actions—destroying our bases without provocation—made investigation into your possible motives seem dangerous. It was deemed better to trust only ourselves."

Remembering those days, Ross felt a twinge in his hands. He nodded grimly.

"I see you agree, Agent Murdock," the Colonel said, comprehension clear in her dark eyes. "These Baldies are dangerous, and even after we discovered that you, too, worked against them, we did not know how far they had penetrated your own establishments."

Ross spoke for the first time. "So what's the score here? Baldies pulling a fast one on you?"

"Fast . . . one?" The Colonel repeated, frowning slightly.

"Baseball slang." Kelgarries turned to Ross. "No—at least not directly. Our target is a world, not a people, though the Baldies might very well be involved."

"But—" Ross looked from the Major to Ashe. "Dominion—"

"Is still safe," Gordon Ashe said quietly. "What this concerns is the world we first visited aboard that derelict, with Travis and Renfry. Remember?"

Ross grimaced, recalling the terrifying journey aboard a ship whose controls were totally alien, the worlds they'd nearly lost their lives on not once but several times. "How can I forget?"

The Colonel said, "When you returned, as you will probably remember, the tapes you brought back were shared among those governments who wished to exploit the knowledge on them. The random draw awarded to us the tapes that focused on that particular world."

"I remember that," Ross said. "And I was just as glad we were officially rid of that planet!"

The Colonel smiled, then continued. "We surmised, as apparently you did, that the ruined city you had visited was once a major starport, a center for many different star-faring species. Our immediate goal was to learn what we could about the Baldies to protect ourselves against another attack like the one that was so devastating to us. Our decoding of the tapes was frustratingly slow, and funding in our country is always an issue. Since we—I speak now of the Time Project—must remain a secret from the general public, and thus we win the government little advantage in the eyes of the citizens, the government wants maximum results for minimum funding."

Kelgarries and Milliard nodded, exchanging glances. Ross felt an unexpected spurt of sympathy for the Russians.

"It is much the same here, then?"

"Much the same," Kelgarries said.

The Colonel smiled again, this time her mouth curving in irony. "Well, you will understand, then, when I tell you that it was decided at high levels in our government to speed our research along by sending a party of scientists back to when the starport was flourishing in order to gather more data."

Ross whistled on a low, soft note.

Colonel Vasilyeva's brows quirked. "Yes, it seemed . . . premature to us as well. We planned what we believed to be a more cautious approach. Our time-travel team jumped back to when the tower you identified as a library was still functional, or at least intact, but after a time when we had adjudged the starport was no longer in use. After all, for all we knew, the starport might be peopled entirely by the Baldies, and we had no faith in their welcoming human beings into their midst."

"We'd probably plan an approach similar to yours," Ashe said. "I take it something went wrong?"

"That's what we need to find out." The Colonel turned to face him, her hands now tightly clasped. "Except for an abandoned Time Capsule, our scientists sent back to the past have vanished utterly, leaving no trace."

CHAPTER 2

"NO TRACE," ROSS repeated. "But wouldn't that give a hint?"

"The Time Capsule's log was ended abruptly, so abruptly that we do not believe that Katarina, the team archivist, had time to add a warning or even a summation," the Colonel said.

"Can you describe your general plan of approach?" Gordon asked, leaning forward, his fingertips together.

"We send our exploratory teams out in doubles, the time-travel team, and the base team. While the travel team of scientists go back in time, the others stay and guard the ship and the transfer apparatus, and gather scientific data while waiting. Our travel teams can't reset the time from the far end—our technology was severely set back by the destruction the Baldies caused us—so time in the past marches parallel to time in the present. Our teams cannot appear moments after they left; that would require resetting the apparatus from the far end, which is impossible, since the far-end equipment is merely a projection, or image, of the present-end apparatus."

Kelgarries said, "Our own practices have brought us to much the same rule, if possible. There are ways to force micro-jumps within a given time: they are incredibly energy-costly, but even more risky, we've found after some disasters, is that they somehow stretch the fabric of time dangerously. We try to keep missions running parallel to current time."

The Colonel nodded in agreement. "We still do not really understand this alien technology—either how it works, or why."

Ross spoke up. "But the Time Capsule?"

"We have a standard schedule," the Colonel said. "Forgive me for what must seem circumlocution, but I believe it is necessary to describe all this in detail."

"We understand," Ashe said. "Please. Continue."

The Colonel paused to sip at her coffee, and then she sat back tiredly in her chair. "We never know if the travel team will execute their orders in hours, or weeks, so we arrange scientific gathering in a priority order. The guard team takes samples of the immediate surroundings, and analyzes them. They set up posts for observing local denizens. In this instance, the orders included finding the tower that you once found, Dr. Ashe, and exploring it, if the indigenous flying peoples permitted. We had included in our equipment items we thought to trade for the ancient spools—if there were any left for us to collect."

"And were there?" Gordon asked.

She gave her head a quick shake. "You and your colleagues had gotten the prime specimens," she said with a nod of approval. "But we wanted to double-check. We expected our travel team to be able to get far better materials from the functioning library—which would correlate with the present. Anything we gathered would, of course, be missing in our portion of the timeline."

Everyone nodded.

"After that, they were to start exploring farther out, excluding only the hostile weasel folk and their territory. Some of our people were to examine the buildings, and others to work in widening circles through the jungle area, taking samples and analyzing them." She frowned down into her coffee cup, her gaze going distant. "We found the remains of one of our travel team on the third sweep."

The room was completely silent.

"On the sixth, we picked up a signal," she continued. "It meant that the travel team had buried a Time Capsule, for whatever reason."

Ross made an impatient movement, caught Eveleen's eye, and controlled it. Major Kelgarries looked over at him, his upper lip lengthened as if he repressed the urge to smile, but he said nothing.

The Colonel, however, noticed the movement, and gave Ross a courteous nod. "You have a question, Mr. Murdock?"

"I just wonder why your team didn't detect their Time Capsule on arrival?"

"If they had, they wouldn't have jumped," Ashe said, grinning.

Eveleen grimaced. "Sometimes this time stuff makes my brain ache."

"Mine as well," Milliard admitted.

"Is same thing as quantum mechanics, Schrödinger's Cat, you know?" the Colonel said, leaning forward. In her intensity to convey her thoughts, her Russian accent was very strong. "The Time Capsule both was and was not detectable until the first team jumped. Then the superposition collapsed. After that the Time Capsule *was*." She shook her head. "Nah! Is easier to say this in Russian."

"Comparable to the Baldies' interference with our station up north, several years ago," Kelgarries said. "We didn't see the evidence of their tampering when we arrived and set up base, until after the events—and we knew what to look for."

Ross realized his surprise must have shown, because Kelgarries went on. "Yes, we've already exchanged detailed briefings on all missions, on both sides. We each need to know everything if there's to be any hope of rescuing that survey team."

How detailed? Ross wanted to ask. He hid his reaction as the Colonel said, "We can explain the specifics this way: where would our team have searched? Should they spend countless weeks searching the entire planet for a possible Time Capsule, which could be anywhere? There was no signal at the transfer site, remember, so our base team had no clue that a search ought to be made. The sixth circle was quite far out."

"Got it," Ross said, still trying to assimilate Kelgarries's matter-of-fact statement about exchanging info. "Sorry about the interruption."

Colonel Vasilyeva gave her head a quick shake. "All questions are important when we deal with the past and present, and how they are interlocked. And I have little more to tell you. The Time Capsule was an almost daily report, ending abruptly after Day Sixty-two—correlating with the present—about three weeks before the Capsule was found. The only common item among them all was a feeling of malaise—an allergic reaction, we judged—but this was also felt by our scientists in the present time, only not as severe. And once they returned to the globe ship, their symptoms disappeared."

"A broad-spectrum course of anti-allergens will take care of that," Kelgarries said.

The Colonel nodded. "We had not taken this precaution as the report made by your team"—she nodded at Gordon—"had not indicated illnesses."

"Nothing serious," Gordon said. "Could be a seasonal thing?"

"This is what we assume," the Colonel said.

Eveleen said quietly, "Any evidence of the vanished team turn up?"

The Colonel shook her head. "At that point, of course, new orders superseded the old priority, and our team searched. Except for the remains of the biologist, there was no forensic evidence whatsoever, not for many miles. Either they were buried on one of the other islands, or they just vanished. Our search team widened their circles of exploration until time and supplies ran out, and they were forced to return home."

"Grim," Ross admitted. "So where do we come in?"

Kelgarries said, "As the Colonel mentioned, the Baldies did severe damage to their bases and equipment a while back. They are still recovering."

"Slowly—too slowly," the Colonel said, her frustration evident in her voice. "Our government does not want to give us funds without results, and we cannot produce results if we do not have the funds to continue our work. So much of our energy has been forced into reconstruction!" She spread her hands, then shrugged. "And so, when the Major contacted us with the proposal to share information, we came instead to ask for help."

"Which we plan to give," Milliard said. "This planet is obviously important—only the treaty, which gave the data to you, according to the division of the spools, has kept us from exploring it further. We, too, would like to learn more about that spaceport, and maybe the Baldies. If we can solve some of the mysteries about them, we might be able to defend ourselves better against them, should their attention come this way again. And we have to assume that it will."

Ashe tapped his fingers on the arm of his chair. "I agree. The only protection we have, and it's mighty slim, is our second-guessing their assumption that in destroying the Russians' bases they dissolved any Terran threat. But they might find evidence of us elsewhere—"

"Or they might just decide to come back here and mess around again with the primitive natives," Ross finished sourly. "I'm with you. So, what's the plan?"

"That my best agents go back with a Russian team to the starport planet, and find the missing Russians—and whatever information you can," Kelgarries said, grinning.

"Three of us?" Ross asked, indicating himself, Eveleen, and Gordon.

"No," the Major said. "Four agents from our agency will join four Russian Time Agents. Our fourth will not be American, however. I've other excellent operatives, from projects you three know little about. One of them seems fated to be assigned to this project."

"Fated?" Ross and Eveleen spoke together, looked at each other, and laughed.

"Fated," the Major said.

He reached behind the desk and carefully pulled out an archaeologist's specimen box. Ross could see Cyrillic lettering on the side.

Kelgarries looked over at the Colonel, as if for permission, and when the Russian nodded, he opened the box. With reverent care he removed a small piece of what looked like dark wood.

"The Russian science team found this in the rubble at the library building. It was buried deeply—they found it after a week of careful sifting for artifacts."

He held it up, and Ross saw that it was indeed wood, carved—ancient-looking. A closer examination showed a woman's face. Human, singularly beautiful, and incredibly detailed. Ross, glancing at it, felt that he'd know the model on sight, were he ever to see her.

Just then a quiet beep sounded in the room. The Major moved to the desk computer and looked down at the message pad at the corner of the terminal. "Ah," he said, "just in time." He looked up. "Ross, you and Eveleen will go back as partners. Gordon, meet your new partner."

At that moment, the door opened, and a tall, well-built woman walked through the door. Dressed in an expensive business suit, the woman moved with grace and assurance.

Ross looked up into her night-dark face, her black eyes, and he swallowed against sudden shock.

"Professor Saba Mariam," the Major went on. "These are Colonel Vasilyeva . . ." He went on with the introductions, which Ross barely heard.

Instead, he tried to process the fact that this woman and the carving had exactly the same face.

CHAPTER 3

GORDON ASHE SIGHED as he sank back into an upholstered chair.

He and Ross were alone, finally.

Eveleen had volunteered to show Saba around the facility; Ross flopped down and idly flicked on a video.

Ashe just sat. The eternal full-spectrum lighting in the den of the suite they'd been assigned gave no hint at the time. Gordon did not need to turn his aching neck to glance at the clock in order to know that it was late. His body knew it, his mind knew it.

The rest of the Russians—all except one—had arrived shortly after Saba, and Milliard had called a break for dinner, saying that they could all get acquainted over a meal.

Gordon hated that kind of gathering, banal chatter between people who did not trust one another, but who were forced by circumstance into the pretense that they did.

He'd managed to exchange half a dozen painfully polite comments with his new partner, and fewer with the new Russians. A poor reward for what had seemed an interminable meal. Boredom and stress combined to give him a headache.

"Okay," Ross said, killing the video with a careless swipe of his scarred hand. "I can feel your mood from here. Spit it out."

"I'm just tired," Gordon said.

"And?" Ross prompted.

"And so what part of 'I'm just tired' is unclear?" Gordon said, knowing that when he resorted to sarcasm, he belonged in bed, asleep.

Ross just laughed at him. "You don't want a woman as a partner. Go on, admit it."

Gordon shut his eyes and leaned his head against the back of his chair.

"You were so polite to Saba at dinner," Ross went on inexorably. "You sure as hell weren't to me when we first met. You only fall back on that lady-and-gentleman routine when you're peeved. Dead give-away, Dr. Ashe."

Gordon sighed. "Not peeved. Not that. Too strong a word."

"So what's wrong with Saba? She's got intellectual qualifications enough to spare for three scholars—Professor of Musicology in Addis Ababa, plays a dozen musical intruments at concert level, knows Western classical music as well as Ethiopian, which, I'm told, is ancient and fascinating both. And she's made a couple jumps on super-secret African missions, one of which involved Baldy interference at about the time we tangled with them, so it's not like she's ignorant of that aspect of our job."

"It's not Saba," Gordon said. "Her credentials are better than mine, and she's probably everything Kelgarries claims, and more. But . . ."

"She's female?" Ross prompted.

Gordon sighed again. "I'm not against women in the Project—despite the way I was raised. The last of my old prejudices was knocked out of me when I first met Eveleen's former boss and thought I'd better go easy on this tiny, gray-haired lady martial-arts instructor, and she proceeded to dry-mop the practice mats with me. I know that our female agents are every bit as bright, as courageous, as capable as we are. But a partner . . . living in such close proximity with one. Especially a highly cultured, refined one."

Gordon remembered the appraisal in those beautiful dark eyes. She'd looked at him with the same intellectual curiosity one might give a fossil, and a not very interesting one at that.

He knew such a judgment might be unfair. It could very well be that she was as reserved as he was; he had no idea what kind of impression his own expression had conveyed. Probably lousy, he decided, grimacing.

Meanwhile, Ross chuckled. "Don't tell me. You think Saba won't be inspired by the vision of you in the morning with a night's stubble on your face and your clothes rumpled and mussed? And then there are the niceties of who gets the bathroom—or what passes for a bathroom on these luxury jaunts to the past—first?"

"All right, all right." Gordon grimaced. "Enough needling."

Ross was still grinning. "It's just that you're being absurd. Believe me, I had all that to contend with on Hawaika and Dominion, and the women managed pretty much like the men do."

"But I'm not used to it," Gordon said. "My experience, even my studies, all pertained to prehistory, when women's movements were largely curtailed, and thus few female agents made the jaunts. It's what I'm used to, good or bad."

"Then it's high time you *got* used to something new," Ross retorted heartlessly. "You won't find any sympathy here, boss. You're the one who told me—on my first mission—that we learn or we petrify. And you know we're going to need Saba's skills too much, from what few hints the Russkis dropped about our mission. She's perfect for this jaunt, and we've got lives to save."

"All right," Gordon said. "I concede."

"And if our positions were reversed, you would have just fed me the very same line," Ross went on. "Okay. I'm done lecturing."

"Then I'll get some sleep," Gordon said, rising from his chair. "What seems impossible at night is often merely improbable by morning."

Ross laughed and flicked the video back on. "Night, Gordon."

ROSS WATCHED GORDON Ashe close the door to his room. He shook his head, then sank back on the couch. There was an action video on, one of the latest releases thoughtfully provided by the Project, but Ross found his mind wandering.

Too much had happened that day. Russians as allies—the prospect of visiting a planet that he'd profoundly hoped he'd never see again—Gordon's dilemma.

Going on a mission, which could be dangerous, with his wife.

He winced. He could talk over with Eveleen all three of the first set of problems, and he'd welcome her fair-mindedness and acute observations. If he brought up his last worry, it would only annoy her. She'd see it as a mistrust of her abilities, but he didn't feel any mistrust on that score. He'd seen her competence proved too many times; in hand-to-hand combat, in fact, she was better than he.

No, having women along as partners didn't bother him.

What bothered him was something he'd never thought to feel—the protective instinct fostered by love. He'd been a loner his entire life, and he'd only had himself to worry about. Now everything had changed, his entire worldview had changed. He still had nightmares about that terrible day on Dominion when Eveleen's mount had fallen on her, nearly killing her. Until he knew she would pull through he'd thought his own life would end.

This, he felt, he couldn't discuss with Eveleen. It was too hard to articulate—too easy to misstate himself, and create a misunderstanding. He didn't really trust words, when it came right down to it. He trusted action.

At the same time he knew if anything happened to her, he wouldn't survive it. He'd rather disaster strike him first. It would be easier to take.

He wouldn't discuss it with Kelgarries or Milliard either; he wouldn't refuse the mission, not when they needed him, and to bring up what seemed like complaints went against his own code of honor. So why bring it up at all?

Instead, just after dinner—when everyone was still standing around outside of Milliard's office, waiting for coffee, and chattering about nothing—he'd checked the computer records that he had access to. He'd found two other married agent teams on the roster. With an idea of talking to them he'd checked on their status, to find out that one team was in Iceland, doing a run that was heavily classified, and the other team was in South America, training for yet another classified project. He hadn't had a chance to send then an E-mail inquiry—thinking out the wording for *that* would take time—but he sure was tempted.

The door slid open, and Eveleen came in, her stride still full of bounce, her eyes clear and sparkling.

"Have a good time?" Ross asked.

She bent to kiss him. "Great!" she said. "Saba's one smart lady. She's going to be a tremendous asset for this mission. She's got a wicked sense of humor, too. Jokes in that soft voice, with that cultured accent, and a totally straight face—she was quite funny about how we have ads everywhere, literally everywhere, in America. And I nearly split my sides laughing at her assessment of the general-issue 'artwork' on the walls in the big data-processing room."

"The people down there are supposed to be working, not living in a museum," Ross protested.

"Work progresses better in congenial surroundings. You know that, I know that," Eveleen corrected.

"It's not exactly a Beaker-trader cave down there," Ross said, secretly enjoying setting her off.

Eveleen's eyes narrowed. "No, but you can just imagine who did the decor. Some government functionary who wanted to save a few pennies on the budget and bought those awful prints at a bargain sell-off from some super-cheap department store. 'Order me artwork in earth tones to match the chairs and cubicle dividers.' And then those pictures are nailed to the walls, as if anyone would even think of walking off with one!"

Ross finally gave vent to his laughter. "All right, all right. So we Americans are cultural no-tastes and upstarts. Come on, let's hit the sack. If we don't get some shut-eye, we'll be sorry tomorrow."

"She's not a snob, Ross," Eveleen said quickly, twining her fingers in his as they walked to their room. "It's just that Ethiopia is such an *old* culture. She can't help seeing us from a vastly different worldview."

"All I know is, we've got a vastly different worldview to start cramming into our brains tomorrow," he said. "Or should I call that universe-view?"

Eveleen laughed.

ROSS WAS STILL thinking about that conversation the next morning.

He rose early, while Eveleen still slumbered, and went straight to the gym. His years of experience with Project Star's routines made the next day's schedule predictable: he and the others would spend hours sitting around and listening to field tapes.

Ross did a lot better riding desks for long stretches after a session with the machines and on the practice mats.

As he worked he wondered about the success of this assignment they'd been forced into. Impatience gnawed at him, the more maddening because there was no single person to blame. Milliard and Kelgarries both had been sincere in their regrets for the curtailed honeymoon. They were both plainspoken men, honest, and hardworking. They did not demand more of the agents than they demanded of themselves.

Yet the truth was, Ross did not want to go blasting across the galaxy in a ship designed and made for unknown beings, to a planet as weird as it was dangerous. He wouldn't want to go again with other Americans he knew; double that a bunch of Russians; and triple that for going with his wife.

"Dammit," he snarled, and sent a punishing roundhouse kick to the padded target. The sound he made was a satisfying *whump!* but the top of his foot stung.

Wincing, he glanced at the clock—and realized how late it had gotten. He was still in a frosty mood when he dashed out of the gym, his wet hair cold.

Down the hall to the main corridor—and at the sight of two people he stopped short.

One, a tall man with long blond hair, had his arms around the other.

And the other was Eveleen.

CHAPTER 4

LIGHTNING FLASHED THROUGH Ross's brain.

He wasn't aware of crossing the hall. Suddenly he was next to them, drawing in his breath preparatory to choking the life out of that yellow-haired sleazebag, but then Eveleen stepped back, her arms moving with calm deliberation.

Somehow she was outside the guy's grip—and somehow she was also between Ross and his target.

"Ross," Eveleen said with determined cordiality. "Allow me to introduce you to Mikhail Nikulin. The last of the Russian team," she added, with just enough emphasis to keep Ross from moving, or speaking. Her head turned, and in the same voice she said to the newcomer, "My husband. Ross Murdock."

Nikulin raised his hands and stepped back, miming surprise. "Now, why is it that the most beautiful ones are always taken first? And I thought it so promising a beginning." His accent was strong, but his English was quite good.

Ross realized his jaw was clenched so hard his teeth hurt. He forced himself to relax. The desire to punch that challenging grin was almost overwhelming, but he had to control it. Nothing had happened.

Nothing had happened.

"I had hoped to meet you eventually, Ross Murdock," the fellow went on. He talked in a lazy drawl that did not fool Ross for a second; the guy's stance, the assessment in his gaze, made it clear he was quite ready for any sort of action Ross might offer.

He knew who she was, Ross realized. And, He did that on purpose.

It made him angry all over again, but at the same time he had to admit it was a fast way of testing the territory.

"We have heard much about your experiences," Nikulin went on, still with the smile and the appraising gaze. "There are questions I have. We shall share a drink and talk, you and I."

Ross forced himself to shrug, and to speak. He was glad his voice came out sounding natural. "We shall sit and listen to a lot of tapes—and sooner than later."

"It's true, we are a bit late," Eveleen said. Ross did not mistake the relief in her eyes. "If you will follow this way, Mr. Nikulin."

"Misha Petrovich," the man corrected. "You must call me Misha."

Eveleen slid her arm into Ross's and led the way. Misha fell in on her other side, his long stride easy. Ross glanced over, still saw that readiness, caught sight of callused palms. This Misha had obviously seen plenty of action. Ross then comprehended what he'd said, and realized that *he* was not unknown to the Russians.

So was Misha Petrovich Nikulin Ross's Russian counterpart?

The thought did not give Ross any added pleasure in the prospect of this mission.

They reached one of the all-purpose rooms where they found Kelgarries and the rest of the team—Russian, Ethiopian, and American—waiting. Ross saw the short Russian woman he'd met at the dinner the night before (what was her name? Irina something?) smile for the very first time. She greeted Misha in fast Russian. As the tall blond guy sauntered over to talk to his group, Eveleen squeezed Ross's arm.

He turned his attention to her.

She whispered, "You let me handle him."

"He knew who you were," Ross said—angry all over again.

"Of course he did," she whispered back. "It's a verbal martial-arts trick—he wants you off-balance. And as long as you come snorting around like a bull before a red cape, he's going to keep pestering me." She grinned. "Think of it as a compliment to your reputation. It is, after all, in a kind of backhanded way."

"If he wanted to compliment me, he could have said, 'Nice work! Glad to have you on the mission.' Or is that unknown in Russia?"

Eveleen gave a soft laugh, but then she whispered more firmly, "I repeat: you let me handle him."

"Please," Kelgarries said. "We need to get started. Everyone, please find a desk."

Ross gritted his teeth again. This mission was already a disaster as far as he was concerned. But he spotted his own laptop waiting, and dropped down behind the desk where it lay. Sitting next to it was a pair of earphones.

Gordon Ashe had the desk next to his. Eveleen had gone over to sit near Saba Mariam.

"All right. We will begin with the tapes found in the Time Capsule. On your terminal, you'll see choices for your language preference. My people: you know the drill," Kelgarries said. "For the benefit of our visitors, let me explain how we usually proceed. We'll listen all the way through just once. Feel free to make notes. When we're done, we'll begin again, this time stopping for questions and explication. But we all need a basis from which to start, so without any further talk, let's proceed."

Ross settled into his chair, yanked his laptop over, and plugged it into the database terminal. As he pulled the headphones on, he stole a look at his wife; she had her head supported in her hands, her favorite listening position. To all appearances she had forgotten the existence of the blond Russian.

Ashe was already making notes, as was Saba. Interesting. The Russians all sat, polite and impassive. They'd heard this before, of course.

The tape began. The translator's voice was a bland, professional actor's voice. "This begins the Record of Exploration Team A, recorded by Katarina Semyonova, team archivist. Day One. We have just arrived . . ."

Ross looked down, saw his hand tapping on his laptop case. He stopped it, and sat up straight. He was restless, but didn't want to show it.

He wasn't just annoyed with that blasted Russian version of Don Juan. He also hated the beginnings of these Project tapes. It was always the same: the recordings went on in great detail about every single thing, most of which usually turned out to be insignificant later, when the team had gathered more data.

". . . what seem to be feathered cats."

Ross grinned to himself. Feathered cats! He remembered those. Now, that was one weird thing. What kind of biological niche would feathered cats possibly fit into?

Ross looked down at his laptop and typed out a quick note. You never know, he thought, what details turn out *not* to be insignificant later.

When he was done typing, he turned his attention to his earphones—and discovered that the Russians had already made their jump into the past. He listened closely—and sure enough, the voice reported that their biologist had gone missing.

The Russians, because of time pressure and a lack of clues so far, had regrouped into doubles and proceeded more cautiously, their priorities being to search for their missing member and to stay hidden.

About a week into their stay in the past, Ross felt his mind wandering again—returning to the feathered cats. Feathered cats—what purpose could they serve? How would they evolve?

The voice changed suddenly, and Ross caught the end of a real surprise.

". . . no evidence of the winged folk, contrary to what we had been led to believe from the tapes of the American Expedition. But this is our third sighting of the beings we call, for lack of data, the weasel folk—as the Americans did. Only at night, and within the great city, have we seen them. During the day, we have seen other beings, but no weasel folk. We have not made ourselves known as yet, though again, unlike what the Americans reported on their tapes, these beings exhibit no signs of aggressive behavior . . ."

Weaslies? No winged beings?

Had someone else gone back in time and caused a major rupture in the timeline? But everything else had checked out—

Ross shook his head, as if to chase away his thoughts. That was the problem with time travel, all the blasted ramifications. It was enough to give any super-scientist a brain sprain, much less an everyday guy.

So Ross decided not to think. He turned his attention back to the tape, and this time he kept his attention on the bland voice detailing a daily load of new surprises.

CHAPTER 5

WHEN THE TAPE was done, the first question was from Ross, which did not surprise Eveleen. "The *Weaslies* are the dominant culture?"

Eveleen bent her head, hiding a smile. Her husband was an acknowledged top agent, brave, intelligent, and altogether wonderful—but he was also impetuous, impatient of rules, and a maverick.

And she adored him for it.

Kelgarries's hatchet face didn't change in expression, but Eveleen sensed very strongly that he was trying to hide a smile. Some of the Russians looked a little startled at the outburst. Only Ashe remained, at least outwardly, unmoved—he and Saba both, she noted belatedly.

"Yes," Kelgarries said. "You are correct."

"But the winged people in the ruined tower were still there in the present," Ross stated. "*Are* still there."

"Yes, they are," the Colonel affirmed.

"And the Weaslies are still feral."

"Again, you are correct."

Kelgarries went on, when the Colonel sat back, "So we can assume that the timeline has not been tampered with—though I guess we'll never really know. But for our purposes, we can assume not."

Ross sighed, clapping down the lid on his laptop. "Weaslies. When I think of that fight we had—well, this is beginning to look like a puzzle where half the pieces are missing. These Weaslies in the past sound like some kind of ancient Chinese culture, only even older and more stratified—so what happened? There was sure no sign of any culture at all when we met 'em."

"The violence is there," Eveleen spoke. "Remember the biologist,

whose only crime seems to have been to enter an enclave without identity or place. How did all that change so drastically?"

"That's one of the mysteries we are going to have to solve," Ashe
spoke up.

Ross groaned theatrically, clutching his head. "I don't think we're
the ones to send. This is sounding more and more like a case for a
regiment of brainiacs. Not a handful of agents."

Kelgarries shook his head—echoed by the Colonel.

"No. These people—we may as well get used to their term, Yilayil—would, to all appearances, not tolerate being studied. We need
skilled agents—yourselves—to adapt to their culture in the ways outlined by the missing team, and work from within."

"But it sounds like we're going to be a cross between servants, and
. . . and house pets!" Ross protested.

A soft laugh and a swift exchange of Russian reminded Eveleen of
the presence of Misha Nikulin. She did not turn her head. Her long
years of martial-arts training had already inured her to certain types of
men—of which Project Star inevitably had its fair share. One sure way
to provoke Mr. Nikulin would be to look at him—a glare just as much
as a smile would be equally challenging.

"Being house pets is an easier assignment than running after mas-
todons in winter, wearing nothing but a wolfskin mini skirt and a coat
of grease," Ashe said, laughing.

Saba smiled slightly. Eveleen caught her glance, and Saba's smile
increased.

The Russians were now deep in conversation, the Colonel illustrat-
ing something. Ashe leaned over to speak with Kelgarries and Ross.

Under cover of the other conversations, Saba murmured softly,
"Your husband. Very like my first partner, Lisette Al-Aseer." Saba's
dark eyes were difficult to read. Humor? Sadness? Eveleen sensed a
little of both.

"Tell me about her," Eveleen whispered back.

Saba gave a little shrug. "She was just as impetuous. Always in
trouble with the authorities—while pulling off brilliant coups. I learned
a great deal from her."

"Where is she now?" Eveleen asked.

"One of the first ones sent off-world," Saba answered, her expression now sober. "I have had no word for over two years. In the data
banks she's listed as 'On Assignment' and whatever that assignment is
has been classified beyond my level."

Eveleen nodded. If anything had happened to Saba's friend, the
other agents might never find out. There was too deep a need for se-

crecy; though the world knew about space exploration, the governments had made a concerted effort to keep all hints of news about time travel from ever reaching the media. The chance of unscrupulous individuals getting hold of a time machine for their own uses was too great a danger.

So the Project was veiled in secrecy, and that meant strict data control even among agents, always judged on a need-to-know basis.

Unfortunately.

As Kelgarries paused to answer a question from one of the Russians, Eveleen thought back over the night before. While Ross had been watching his video, she'd been in the library using the E-mail to query the three teams of married agents that she had found after a quick scan through the data banks.

I'm so used to taking care of myself, she thought as Kelgarries, the Russian with the query, and the Colonel now talked in quiet voices.

Eveleen felt a little sad to have even one secret so early in a marriage, but she hesitated to discuss this with Ross—especially after seeing his reaction at Misha's absurdity.

What good would telling him do, except make him worry? Men had been blithely launching into action for millennia. Women had been equal partners with men relatively recently—but they had been champion worriers since the dawn of time. Better to ask some married couples with more experience in partnerships under dangerous conditions how they coped with the fear of loss of a partner.

She watched Ross typing notes into his laptop, a little frown between his brows.

I'd rather get lost than lose him, she thought bleakly, and then scolded herself for defeatist thinking. The idea was to keep them both safe.

Kelgarries looked up then. "The Colonel suggests that we might actually speed the training along if we split for the language-assimilation portion. We'll get together again when we start training for specific positions on the world. Gordon? Summation?"

Gordon Ashe looked up. "I'll give us all a quick synopsis of what kind of civilization we're looking at, so we can keep the worldview in mind as we crash-learn it in pieces."

He cleared his throat.

"One. The Yilayil people are the dominant culture, a hyper-complex civilization trying to maintain the diversity of an interstellar culture that—for some reason—has no new entries showing up. But the process for assimilation has already begun, through a complex of behaviors that are both cultural and ritualistic, called ti[*trill*]kee—" He whistled the middle part with difficulty. "It seems to mean deportment, but it's more than just that; it's a way of life accepted by all, and deviation, once one has been accepted by the Yilayil, is not tolerated. Since there is no mention in the Time Capsule of the winged people, we must assume they arrived later—"

"From a crashed spaceship, perhaps?" one of the Russians asked, enunciating carefully in English. "Or from one of the islands on the far side of the planet from the spaceport?"

"It is a possibility, though unlikely—not if they have any kind of culture with technical capabilities," the Colonel said. "When our globe ship skirted the planet, we did energy readings. Energy use is uniformly low, except on the island containing the spaceport. There it is exceptionally high."

Kelgarries said, "We assume from the observable drive to conformity that any other race with technical capabilities is eventually drawn to the capital island and conformity in order to have access to data and technology."

"The flyers are not tech-capable in the present timeline," Ross spoke up. "Of course, none of the three races we encountered were. They were a lot more civilized than those feral humanoids or the Weaslies."

"The flyers might be indigenous and hidden, and might be latecomers. We will be looking for clues, of course," Ashe said, nodding. "Second: the Yilayil are the only nocturnal land-living intelligence on the planet, and all the diurnal creatures exist lower in the cultural hierarchy, locked into rigid castes that determine their status and duties. Divergence means ostracism; obedience is rewarded with privileges which translate to various forms of wealth, leisure, etc."

Ashe stopped, looking around for questions. No one spoke, but Ross frowned, flexing his scarred hand. Eveleen bit her lip.

Ashe said, "Ross?"

The scarred hand balled into a fist, and then opened. Eveleen watched her husband force his feelings behind a polite mask as he said, "It sounds a little like we're expected to fit into a society of robots."

"Not robots," Ashe said, smiling. "If they were, there would not be a question of conformity, would there?"

"Conformity," Ross repeated, grimacing. "I have to admit that's what sticks in my craw. Conformity seems another word for—" He looked over at the Russians, and Eveleen saw Misha nod and give Ross a thumbs-up.

It was an unexpected gesture. Eveleen was relieved to see Ross flick a hand up in salute. Then he went on, "I don't know what. Main thing is, I didn't catch who decides if any given race has 'conformed' properly."

"That's because the First Team didn't say." Ashe sat back, scanning his notes. "Until we find out, we can assume that the Yilayil decide. Anything more to add?"

Ross shook his head.

"Then I'll continue with the Yilayil," Gordon said. "They dwell in tunnels and caves, vast spaces underground. At first they had seemed unable to deal with the sudden appearance of the First Team whose place of origin they—obviously—couldn't figure out. This is important to remember: they are, of course, aware of other races—we will apparently meet several—and their way of dealing with them has been to assimilate them into the hierarchy through ti[*trill*]kee. Every race has its enclave somewhere on the world—yet the spaceport on the main island is closed, so no new ones are coming in. We don't know if this is by accident or design. We will have to find out."

He paused. Again, no questions.

"As for interaction, the races are segregated, save for a single exception: the mysterious House of Knowledge—which, apparently, is what Ross and I called the library—where the Russians found that carving."

Eveleen cast another quick glance at Saba. It was clear what her job would be: she'd have to penetrate the House of Knowledge, to learn what she could about the missing Russians. The evidence was already there, if the carving could be believed, that Saba had *been* there. Her visit had already happened—hopefully safely.

What is my job to be? Eveleen thought.

She looked down to hide a grim smile.

She'd find out soon enough.

SABA EXCUSED HERSELF from dinner as early as was polite, and left the common room. Much as she enjoyed watching the impetuous Americans strive to find congenial topics to discuss with the reserved, rather dour Russians—and the way the two male agents, Misha and Ross, watched each other speculatively when the other was not aware—she felt the pressure of time tightening the muscles on the back of her neck.

She'd seen the looks on all their faces when a sample from the language tapes was played. If the stakes had not been so high, she would have laughed at the restrained disgust of the Russians (who had apparently just begun struggling with the Russian version of the tapes) to Eveleen's shock and Ross Murdock's blank despair. Only Gordon Ashe had displayed little reaction, a slight frown between his brows, his head bowed as he concentrated.

She crossed the short hallway to her room, turning on the light and her computer at the same time. Calling up the tapes, she tabbed the sound to the speakers, and paced back and forth in the tiny space as she listened.

Saba was grateful to Katarina, the unknown but gifted Russian linguist/archivist on the missing team, for having done a superlative job on the preliminaries. As it was, learning this language was going to be a terrific challenge.

The translator's voice began.

"The Yilayil language has one component in common with English: it seems to be a tremendously flexible language, adopting words from all the others, altering them and making them its own.

"That is *all* the Yilayil tongue has in common with English."

And next was an example. The sound was strange, midway between a whistle and a drone, with ululations and note alterations rather like a chant, or music, modifying it.

The Yilayil people, with their muzzles that resembled those of earth weasels, were not likely to make the labial sounds of human languages. The humans who were to approximate the Yilayil language would first of all have to know how to whistle—and then would have to learn to hum while doing it.

But harder, much harder, was the prospect of hearing the language and then speaking it. Chinese, often regarded as the toughest language to learn, used to take at least a couple of years for a linguistically gifted individual; now, with the hypno-tape method used by government agencies, it took several months. Chinese seemed easy compared to this utterly alien, bizarrely weird tongue.

Especially since the hypno-tapes she had used until now were complete and these weren't. These tapes left whole levels of expression fragmentary and confusing.

And they had a limited time in which to learn it—the duration of their flight to the planet.

Saba had seen the unspoken reaction in all the others' faces. She knew it matched her own: dread. Everyone was very aware that the First Team's lack of knowledge might have been related to why they disappeared.

Luckily Katarina had taped a great deal of indigenous talk—which her team had been in the midst of studying when they disappeared. Saba, on hearing her tapes, vowed she was going to master it before planetfall. This meant that she had to find the key to the language, its music, even though its speakers had utterly nothing in common with human beings, whose various language-musics carried subtle but definite similarities.

So she'd better get started right away.

GORDON ASHE LOOKED at Saba's closed door. From beyond it came faint sounds: he recognized the weird noises of the Yilayil language. Annoyance and admiration twisted at his guts.

The admiration was easy to acknowledge. He had a lot of respect for any agent who got right to business when a mission was at hand, especially one that carried this much firepower. The annoyance . . . why the hell couldn't she call them all in and share her expertise? Did she have to get ahead, just to show off?

He shook his head, hard. No. Stop attributing competitive American motivations to someone from a totally different culture.

He raised his hand to knock, then sighed. What would he say? Would he just be interrupting her for little purpose?

Better to get busy with his own tapes, he decided. So he retreated to his room and fired up his computer.

He paused the tape after that first Yilayil example, then replayed it.

"Weird, isn't it?" Ross spoke from the open doorway.

Ashe turned around, saw Ross and Eveleen standing there.

"Come in," he said. "I take it you had the same idea?"

"I saw Saba leave," Eveleen said, smiling. "Ross and I made a bet she was itching to get cracking on her tapes."

"Where are the Russians?" Ashe asked.

Ross jerked a thumb over his shoulder. "Finished dinner, Colonel gave them the high-sign, and they vamoosed in a group. My guess is, they're hunkered down right now with their versions of Katarina's tape. Learn fast, make the decadent Americans look bad."

"Be fair," Eveleen retorted, elbowing Ross in the side. "That missing team was their friends. If our friends went missing, we'd do the same."

"I don't want to be fair," Ross said. "I want to be first."

"So much for scheduled recreational time," Eveleen added with a grin.

"We can do recreation on shipboard," Ashe said, and he hit the replay again.

At the end, Eveleen had a faint crease between her brows. "It's like chanting, more than speech," she said.

"Speech sounds monotone after it," Ross added, his eyes closed.

"Mellifluous," Eveleen put in. "That's the word I was looking for."

"Mellifluous—or demented?" Ashe said, and activated the tape again.

The translator's voice filled the room: *"The normal word order is: Speaker identity, status, location, time, verb, subject, indirect object, direct object."*

She followed with a trill/drone in Yilayil, then said, in English, *"This is, roughly translated: 'I, Yeeyee Sight-of-stars, at pathway-meets-water at dawn offer trade of scent-bearers-from-beyond-sun their gili-blossom mat."*

Ashe paused the tape.

"That takes forever," Ross complained.

"The Yilayil statement took half the time the English translation did," Eveleen said. "Are all those flowery things names or noun-identifiers that you have to invent every time you speak?"

Ashe shook his head. "Too little information yet. Let's listen further."

"This is the word order of neutral statements. There are other word orders for different challenges and deferences, for commands, for questions. We will address the matter of questions later, for these constitute another form entirely: briefly, we have questions of challenge, questions of debate, questions of personal consequence—"

"Huh," Ross interrupted, rubbing his chin. "What about 'Are my shoes untied'?"

"That, I imagine, would be a question of personal consequence," Ashe said, smiling.

"If they wear shoes," Eveleen put in. "Now hush, and let's hear this thing through, or we'll never get any sleep tonight!"

Ross subsided with a willingness that he had never exhibited to any of his male partners in the past, and they proceeded through the tape in silence.

At the end, Ashe shut off his computer, and sat back in his chair. "Well?"

Ross pursed his lips, and let out a long liquid trill. "Guess we better practice wetting our whistlers. Think they have beer?"

Eveleen snorted a laugh. *"Will* you be serious?"

Ross sighed. "I think we're going to go nuts trying to learn that mess. I can't hear anything but bird-tweeting. Some cabbie I'll be."

"We'll be," Eveleen said. "Just as well we both are assigned to transportation. One of us is going to have to learn this stuff."

"You learn it. I'll drive." Ross grinned.

Ashe shook his head. "Oh, go to sleep."

CHAPTER 6

"WHAT HAPPENED WITH this new Russian, Misha Petrovich Niku-lin?" Saba asked the next day as Eveleen and she worked out side by side on the stationary bikes. "Something. There was too much tension yesterday that I cannot otherwise explain."

"Oh-h-h-h-h yes," Eveleen said, rolling her eyes. "I was just going down to the training room when I looked up and there was this hand-some blond guy strolling along looking at the door numbers. Before I could open my mouth to ask him if he needed directions he walked up, introduced himself, threw his arms around me, and tried to kiss me."

"No warning?"

"Nothing. Because coming along right behind was Ross."

Saba took her lower lip between her teeth. "Did you know this man?"

"Misha? Never saw him before in my life. But I will wager any amount of money he knew who we were, though he pretended not to. And furthermore it was not my devastating beauty that brought on that excess of affection—it was some kind of crazy challenge, because he wasn't the least surprised to see Ross there."

Saba, to Eveleen's surprise, nodded in agreement. "I know that type. In truth, I think this agency the world over selects for just that sort— both male and female. My former partner was like that. I could see her doing this to your spouse, just to see what would happen."

"And I would probably have decked her," Eveleen admitted. "Yes." She winced. "You know, I *would* have. It's all very well to tell Ross that I can take care of myself, thank you, but instinct is faster than thought, and it does go both ways."

Saba smiled, her dark eyes steady.

"Huh," Eveleen said. "I hadn't thought of *that*. Well. One of those unpleasant little insights that one needs now and again to keep one humble. I'll remember that, in case Misha starts it up again and Ross breathes fire."

Saba put her head to one side, but said nothing.

Eveleen gave a sigh, short and sharp, and forced her mind back onto the job. "Speaking of Russians—and Yilayil challenges. It makes a kind of sense, if what the Russian linguist surmised is correct, in challenge mode one gets very flowery—the more challenging, the more oblique. This would give the other person time to frame a response, and decide who gets preference, who defers. This must mean that everyday activities require relatively simple language—not just with outsiders, but among themselves. Otherwise it just doesn't seem reasonable."

Saba's eyes narrowed as she considered. "I would take care," she said slowly, "in assuming what might seem reasonable to Yilayil culture. Especially given the hints of multiple layers to the language, the odd tenses and sensory aspects."

"I just assumed those were artifacts of a limited data set," said Eveleen. "Just misunderstood."

"I am not so sure," said Saba carefully. "But, yes, otherwise I do agree that far: quick modes of speech for the minutiae of everyday business makes good sense. It does seem, though, that almost every aspect of life involves a challenge of some kind or other—at least when encountering beings outside one's own group."

"If a few months' studies can be trusted," Eveleen said. "I keep thinking of that poor biologist." She winced as she recalled the grief and shock expressed by Katarina when her team discovered the remains of their fellow agent, just after they had made their first encounter.

Saba also reacted, her face tightening, her gaze lowered. Eveleen felt the lance of remorse, and wished she hadn't spoken. She had momentarily forgotten about Saba's first partner. Did the woman lie in some unknown grave worlds and centuries away? Or had something wrenched time out of alignment so that she was forever lost—as had apparently happened to one of Gordon Ashe's former agents?

Eveleen bit her lip, wondering if Gordon or Saba would talk about that. They both had this experience in common, but they were both so very reserved.

Saba looked up, and said in her calm voice, "This has occurred to me as well. Often. The challenge aspect might be emphasized only with newly arrived outsiders."

"We'll be getting that treatment," Eveleen said, relieved that the moment seemed to have passed.

"Perhaps. As for the specifics: most of them sound like they are ritual challenges, and both sides know the question and answer before it's even spoken," Saba said. "It's a kind of right-of-way etiquette."

Eveleen nodded, glad that, so far, her instincts were corresponding with the better-trained Saba's. "And the Russians were still in the early stages of establishing themselves within the hierarchy, so they were exposed to the more formal challenge-speech . . ."

Eveleen thought she heard doubt in the Ethiopian's soft, musical tones. "Except?" she prompted.

Saba shook her head slightly. "It means little to query at this early point."

"I know," Eveleen said. "Just for the sake of discussion—and because, hard as we are working, we're not exactly going anywhere . . ." She pointed at their bicycles.

Saba smiled. "All right, then. It does seem to me that the Yilayils do little that is sudden or impulsive, if what we are learning conveys a true sense of their culture. And yet we come back to the fact that the First Team disappeared—abruptly—without any sign or signal."

"That we've yet discovered," Eveleen amended. "When we get back, we might still find something."

"And, barring that?"

Eveleen bit her lip. "I have to admit it's been bothering me too. I suppose the problem, if problem there was, might not originate from the Yilayils at all—but from one of the other races living on the planet. We don't know anything about these as yet, except for some names and some superficial characteristics. Our Russians didn't have enough time, apparently, to learn much of them between the time they made themselves known and when they disappeared. They spent so much time living in the jungle outside the city, just watching!"

"And?" Saba prompted.

Eveleen sighed. "Well, I know it's not fair to judge, but I can't help thinking about what the Yilayils became down at our end of the timeline—those Weaslies. There certainly was no sign of hierarchy, or structure, or music, when Ross and Ashe encountered them! Just bloodshed!"

"I, too, have pondered this," Saba admitted.

Encouraged, Eveleen warmed to her theme. "So far, in every culture I've studied or encountered, there is at least some trace of the former. But here—we are presented with the Yilayils, whose culture is intricate in the extreme. It reminds me of medieval guilds, only much more complex. Each individual seems to be born into a specific guild, to which they appear to belong for a lifetime. Their name and location indicates their guild, family status, and field of mastery—and everyone has a place. Strangers are not tolerated; they have to be integrated slowly, but integrated they are. No evidence of war, the Russians said. And yet—we always come back to this disappearance."

Saba nodded again. "Since it is my lot to go to this House of Knowledge, I have to hope to find some clues there."

"Except that's another mystery," Eveleen said.

Saba smiled grimly. "When was I there for that statue to be carved? Or am I going to arrive to find a group of women, from some other planet, who look just like me—and if so, where might *they* have come from—and why?"

Eveleen shuddered. "I know it's cowardly to say so, but I'm glad that my 'skill' is just going to be a cabbie. That is, assuming we get *that* far."

The timer went off then, indicating the end of the workout. Saba went off to the showers, but Eveleen lingered. Since this was not officially rec time, she was hoping to find someone for a good workout on the practice mats. There was no better stress reliever, she firmly believed, than sparring and grappling with some feisty martial-arts expert whose skills were as good as her own.

She moved to the gym—but just as she was opening the door, her pager buzzed quietly against her wrist. She peeled back her leotard sleeve and glanced down, then sighed.

Milliard! There was no putting *him* off.

She showered and changed in record time, then raced to an elevator to go to the top brass levels.

When she emerged, she found another surprise—Ross was just getting out of the second elevator.

"Hey," he said, grabbing her hand.

"What's the problem—do you know? Is this meeting an 'uh oh,' or an 'oh yeah'?" she asked, sneaking a peek around the corridor.

"I don't know anything beyond the fact that it's just thou and I, O wife," Ross said, grinning.

"So you haven't pounded Misha Nikulin into paste."

Ross laughed. "I haven't even seen him. Besides, you're the paste-pounder in the family. You could dispose of him faster than I could."

Eveleen nodded, not showing her relief. Especially after her discussion with Saba, she was doubly glad that she hadn't further hassled Ross about that disastrous first meeting with Misha, after they'd retired for the night. Apparently Ross had thought it through on his own. "And don't you forget it," she said, mock commanding.

No one was in sight. She leaned up for a kiss, then Ross knocked at Milliard's door.

"Come in."

The big boss was seated behind his desk, his gray hair disheveled as if he'd just been running his hands through it.

"Something's wrong?" Ross said as he and Eveleen entered and sat down in the overpadded chairs before the desk.

"Many somethings," Milliard said with a twisted smile. "But that's my headache. I called you two in for a last-minute talk. I know it's late in the game, and I'm not sure what to do if there's a problem, but I have to talk to you if only to ease my own mind."

"We're here," Eveleen said, feeling apprehension.

"If its these Russians," Ross began.

"No." Milliard sighed, shuffling a couple of papers on his desk without really looking at them. Then he sat back. "I know we railroaded you two into this project. That's because I desperately want you both there. You're both in tiptop physical shape—the medicos gave you green lights after your evaluations following your return from Dominium. But it's been pointed out to me by several people whose job it is to keep track of these things that we usually keep married pairs at home flying desk jobs for at least a year, until they feel their relationship is stable enough for the intense stress of fieldwork. You two have barely had a honeymoon. How do you feel about rushing off right away?"

Eveleen was so surprised she couldn't think. "Is this," she asked with care, "in reference to specific team members?"

Milliard gave her a quizzical glance. "Not specifically. Has there been a problem?"

"No," Ross said at the same time as Eveleen said, "No."

They looked at each other and smiled.

Eveleen realized that the incident with Misha had in fact stayed between the three of them. Four, counting Saba, but Eveleen did not believe that the Ethiopian woman would have talked about it. So she considered the question in general.

During her single years the emphasis on the Project had always been the work at hand. Of course people did socialize—and match up. She'd dated briefly among the men at HQ during her days as a martial-arts instructor. She'd even briefly dated outside the Project, knowing that she could deflect superficial questions about what she did by just claiming to teach martial arts. Except how could you really get serious with someone you had to lie to if he asked lots of detailed questions about your career?

Nothing—until Ross—had been serious. And her relationship with him had begun off-world, away from therapists, psychologists, and other Project personnel. She'd made her own way, and on her return, had expected to continue making her own way. It hadn't occurred to her that there existed an official policy for such contingencies as marriage among agents.

She looked over at Ross, to find him watching her, and a pang smote her heart. Was he just now beginning to think along the same tracks that had worried her?

She wanted to spare him that. "Oh, I don't see a problem," she said, smiling, infusing her voice with as much confidence as she could. "Remember, we did have a lot of time together on Dominium, so we know we can handle fieldwork together."

Ross sat back, drumming one hand idly on his chair arm. "She's right." He grinned. "And if something happens, I know she can protect me!"

He laughed, Milliard laughed, and Eveleen snorted a laugh as well.

"Are you sure? Any doubts? Because I'd rather pull you off the Project now, and find some other agents, than put you at further risk—"

"No," Ross said firmly, and—

"No!" Eveleen exclaimed at the very same moment.

Their eyes met and again they laughed.

Ross isn't worried, she thought. That's what I want. I *will* protect him, but not in the ways he was joking about.

———

THE DOOR TO Milliard's office opened, and Gordon Ashe almost ran into Ross and Eveleen, who were just coming out. Both of the pair were grinning.

"You too?" he asked.

Ross raised his hands. "We're not in trouble. I promise!"

Eveleen laughed. "Twit," she said, not at all angrily, and the two of them headed for the elevators.

Ashe walked in, to find the big boss looking tired.

"Case Renfry and Mikhail Nikulin took off for Russia last night with the load of scientific equipment," Milliard said without preamble. "You haven't seen Case for a time, but he's been taking intensive training in Russian. With his background—having gone with you on that first run to the Yilayil planet—he's been welcomed by the Russian science team to join their number."

"Good," Gordon said.

"Now. This is the last chance for us to do anything to help you before you take off." Milliard rubbed his jaw. "Anything you foresee as a problem?"

"No," Ashe said. "Beyond the usual range of unforeseen disasters that comes with fieldwork."

"I mean with the personnel," Milliard asked. "Too many untried aspects to this setup. Could spell success—or a major headache."

Ashe nodded. Pairing Russians and Americans was new, and one didn't need to be psychic to see that mutual trust was going to take time. Sending two agents just married was against policy. So was pairing partners of both opposite genders and different cultures. But, at least so far, driving necessity fostered the needed mental readjustments. Except—"Ross and Nikulin might be a problem."

"I suspect that the Colonel was not completely happy with Nikulin either," Milliard went on. "Which may or may not be why he was only here one day."

Ashe waited for an explanation, but Milliard just shrugged. "No, nothing has been said to me. Internal problems, maybe. He's volatile, I've learned that much. There is also the fact that their agent-base is so small that they are perforce thrown together for extended years."

Ashe nodded. "Small because of those successful Baldy attacks. That's got to warp their psyches a little."

"The Colonel says that some of them exhibit what could be called combat fatigue—but what can they do? They can't hire more agents, not until they can show their government positive results. So they cope with the sorts of problems we are able to prevent by reassignment and protracted leaves, when necessary. To get from general comments to specifics, the Colonel thinks Nikulin had some kind of relationship with one of the missing team—and with at least one of the Russians assigned to your team, as well. He's a loose cannon, Nikulin is. Here's his file. You'll have to watch out for him—"

Ashe nodded, picking up the folder. He read rapidly through it, then glanced up. "Right. Or Ross will resolve things his own way. I understand."

"Which brings us to us," Milliard said. "How are you getting along with Saba?" His eyes narrowed shrewdly.

Ashe thought briefly of the tall, handsome woman. "She's like me," he said slowly. "All business."

"Good. I don't require you two to become best friends, but I do need you to work together well. Your lives may be at stake, and you have to be able to depend on each other."

"I believe I can depend on her," Ashe said, with conviction. "And I try to be dependable."

"That's all I can ask," Milliard said. "Anything else?"

Ashe shook his head slowly. Anything else would stay within his skull and not be spoken. It was up to him to solve any problems that arose.

"The Colonel is coming in next; when we've had our interview, if there are no insurmountable problems, we'll start the clock on takeoff."

"Right." Ashe handed back Nikulin's file and rose from his seat. "Then I'll get back to work."

He went out, encountering the gray-haired Russian commander as she emerged from the elevator. She greeted him courteously, then continued to Milliard's office.

Ashe heard the door close behind her. The elevator door stood open, but he paused, his hand on the wall, and looked around.

Silence.

Soon he'd be aboard a ship accompanied by Russians—one of whom, Mikhail Petrovich Nikulin, used to be a major headache to American time agents back in the bad old days—a pair of newlyweds, and a partner who seemed as wary of him as he was of her. And he'd be in command of this jaunt into the past of a planet that was no part of human history.

He'd told Milliard that there were no problems, which wasn't true, but he promised himself that he'd solve them, which was true. The many problems of time, logistics, language barriers, and the rest could indeed be solved. Emotional reactions simply didn't count, not when there were lives at stake.

But the real truth was, with his best friend now married, he'd never felt more isolated in his life.

CHAPTER 7

ROSS MURDOCK PEERED out the window of the airliner.

Russia!

He had to shake his head as he looked over the last of the Gulf of Finland gleaming with gray-green highlights in the weak sun. At home in the northeastern states, autumn meant chilly, rainy days interspersed with mellow warm ones, and driving around to view the glorious changing of the leaves. Here it was already winter—and so it would remain, he was told, until May.

Who would have thought he would ever set foot in Russia?

He looked around the plane. It was full of tourists, and Russian citizens going home. He detected a mixture of languages in the chatter.

The rest of his team was scattered throughout the plane. Next to him Eveleen dozed lightly, a mystery novel in her lap. Two seats behind, Ashe's sunbleached brown hair was visible. By craning his neck, Ross could see that the archaeologist was reading a history of St. Petersburg. Ross had done a little excavation on his own, just before departure. What he'd read was fascinating, and grim in places. He hadn't realized what an ancient land Russia was. But then, Ethiopia was even older, he thought, catching sight of Saba in the next row. She was calmly working away at her laptop computer, headphones on. Occasionally she glanced out the window. At the very end of his row he could make out Renfry's thinning hair. The technical expert was looking down as well, probably busy on his own laptop.

Ross turned the other way, and looked at Ashe again. Why hadn't he sat with Saba? He shook his head silently. Not his place to interfere—anyway, if he did, he'd probably make things worse. But Gordon and

Saba didn't seem to mesh as a team. Ross just hoped this wasn't going to make things tough when the real action started happening.

The engine noise changed; the plane tipped downward, starting to lose altitude.

The seat-belt light flashed on, and people murmured as the plane decelerated, bumping occasionally in the turbulent air currents. Ross thought about launching from the planet again—not in a U.S. spacecraft, but in one of those weird alien globe ships. Somehow a little turbulence didn't seem very scary.

Eveleen woke up, alert within seconds. She clicked her seat belt on, and yawned.

"Great book, eh?" Ross cracked.

Eveleen grinned. "Actually, it's pretty good. But even the most brilliant book is not going to keep me awake after only two hours of shut-eye."

Ross shook his head. "Told you that crazy stunt would be a mistake."

"Wrong," Eveleen said. "Not a mistake. Being tired and headachy is worth it—I really think we started to get to know each other." She nodded toward some of the Russians, three or four rows back.

Ross grimaced. "We'll be doing that, and plenty, when we're all stuck together on that blasted fishbowl."

Eveleen grinned unrepentantly. Ross had been against her going out on their last evening in Washington, D.C., with Saba and some of the Russians to see some folk dance performance. The weather had been wild, and as the hours crawled by, he'd prowled restlessly around HQ, sure they'd met with some accident.

Turned out that they'd gone after the performance to an old dive frequented by Eastern Europeans, and there they'd drunk vodka and slivovitz, and roared folk songs for half the night. When they returned, they'd all been tired, tipsy, but the atmosphere of tension had somehow lessened markedly.

The engines cut in, loud and vibrating, and the plane heeled.

Ross looked down at St. Petersburg, sprawled over the delta of the Neva River. From the air the old section looked almost like a fairy-tale city, and as he stared at those onion domes gleaming in the low northern sun, once again he was struck by a sense of strangeness.

Then the plane touched down, and taxied slowly to the terminal. At once the cabin was full of chatter as people gathered their belongings and prepared to disembark.

Their passports stated that they were tourists, but once they reached the front of the long line, Ross was not surprised to see the official squint at his passport, look at a computer printout, and wave him out of line. He waited; Eveleen joined him a moment later, pulling her suitcase on its wheels.

They were taken to a special room for customs, which was a mere formality. Ashe and Sabe both joined them, both of them looking non-committal as always. Eveleen looked about with undisguised interest as they were led down corridors and hallways, then out into the wintry sun and bitterly cold air. Snow drifted lazily as they were waved to an official-looking car.

The driver loaded their luggage into the trunk, then took his seat without speaking. Pretty soon they were zooming along the handsome boulevards of the Admiralty district. Bridges and canals were every-where in evidence, amid spectacularly beautiful baroque edifices. To Ross the buildings looked heavy and solid—the kind of buildings that would withstand long winters.

"Oh! That's got to be the Hermitage," Eveleen breathed.

"I think so," Gordon said. "The Winter Palace—"

"That is correct," the driver said in heavily accented English. "I give you little tour before destination."

In silence Ross watched the city slide by. The cars all looked strange, and despite the cold weather, there was quite a bit of pedestrian and bicycle traffic about. The buildings really were handsome—most of them—and he found it quite interesting, very different from any Amer-ican city he'd ever seen.

Before long they stopped outside an older stone building with a plain facade. Ross was just opening his mouth to ask where the rest of their team might be when he saw another car pull up behind theirs, and the Russians climbed out, all chattering with a freedom he had never seen them use back in the States.

Before long they found themselves in a big, warm room with high ceilings and ancient plaster, drinking sweet, strong coffee out of little glass cups encased in holders.

Colonel Vasilyeva sat down, smiling broadly. "Welcome to the Rus-sian Federation," she said. "I apologize for the lack of time for a proper tour. When we return successfully from our mission, you can be sure we shall show you everything our city has to offer. Tomorrow morning, early, we will call for you, and a special train will take us to our des-tination. Tonight, we will relax . . ."

Interesting, Ross thought. She doesn't say anything of the mission that could be overheard. A habit of caution or necessity?

Then he thought about how he'd act if they were located in a hotel somewhere in the States. He wouldn't be blabbing either.

". . . supper, and afterward you have free time," she was saying.

Gordon Ashe said, "We'll use that time to work on our studies, if that is possible."

The Colonel nodded soberly. "We will provide equipment with headphones."

"Thank you," Gordon said, sliding a glance from under his brows at Saba, who nodded, her demeanor calm as always.

"Then if there are no further questions, you may establish yourselves in your rooms, and meet back here for supper," the Colonel said, rising.

Five minutes later, Ross and Eveleen stood in their room, which was another with very high ceilings. Ross stared round at the remainders of some unknown Russian's aristocratic past in the moldings at the edges of the walls and around windows. The plaster was old, and the furnishings sparse, plain, but comfortable. A radiator hissed quietly in a corner.

Eveleen went to the window and gazed out over the Russian rooftops. She rocked back and forth on the balls of her feet, silent, looking pensive.

"Problem?" Ross asked, watching her.

She smiled back over her shoulder. "Nothing more serious than trying to decide if I want a workout to stretch the kinks from my muscles after that long plane flight, or if I would rather get a shower."

Ross prowled the perimeter of the room, inspecting the doors. One revealed a small closet, almost a little room; he flicked a low-voltage light on to illuminate a bathroom, complete with tub on feet. "I don't think a shower is an option," he said.

Eveleen appeared at his shoulder, and grinned. "If the water pressure is anything like Vera warned me, I guess my dilemma is solved." So saying she turned on the faucet full blast, and they both watched the thin stream of gently steaming water.

"It's going to take a while for that tub to fill," Ross said.

Eveleen snapped her fingers. "Workout first."

Ross sighed. "I'll turn on the Yilayil tape. We can whistle as we work."

Eveleen groaned and threw a pillow at him.

━━━━━━━━━━━━━━━━━━━━━━━━━━━━━━

DINNER WAS NOTICEABLY different from meals in America.

The food was spicy and interesting, but that wasn't what caught at Ross's attention. They'd been joined by more Russians—but somehow

Ross began to see them in a different light, and it wasn't just Renfry's ability to speak with them that made the difference.

Back in America, Colonel Vasilyeva and these four of her agents had been quiet, polite, and had moved as a group. Except for that damned Nikulin, Ross hadn't really considered the Russians as individuals; he'd looked on them as a kind of unit, and their tight silence had underscored his own lack of trust.

All he'd known about these people was that three of them were the Russian time agents. One, the lanky, bespectacled Valentin Svetlanin, was a scientist.

Back on their home territory, the Russians seemed changed people. Or maybe it was that night out; Ross couldn't imagine Valentin, for example, roaring folk songs—or any other kind of song—but Eveleen insisted he'd in fact been the most lively. He not only knew every single song, but variations on most of those!

Ross wondered if Mikhail Nikulin on his home turf was going to become even more obnoxious—like challenging someone to a duel with pistols at dawn?

Better not borrow trouble, Ross thought, and tried to force Nikulin out of his thoughts.

Instead, he tried to match names with faces.

Vera Pavlova was the redhead who laughed a lot.

Irina Bazarov was short, thin, dark-haired, and subtle-featured. In America she'd moved with a kind of compact neatness that here—on her home ground—Ross recognized as grace.

As the conversation got lively, Ross leaned over and whispered to Eveleen, "That Irina. She into some kind of dance?"

Eveleen's brows arched. "Ballet." She grinned. "About as many years as I studied martial arts. If not more."

Ross awkwardly whistled the Yilayil equivalent of praise.

And from the doorway came another whistle—liquid and pure, and correct in intonation.

"Misha!" the cry went up from the Russians.

Misha lounged against the doorjamb, his coat slung over his shoulder, his shirt open at the neck. Ross eyed the familiar waving blond hair and rakish smile, trying to hide his instant reaction of dislike and distrust.

Misha laughed, said something in Russian, then immediately turned to Saba and Eveleen, bowing debonairly. Ross forced himself to just sit, but inwardly he thought, If that jerk tries to smooch either of them, Eveleen had better paste him one, or else I will.

"So much beauty in my beautiful country! It is poetry for the senses." He kissed Saba's hands, and then, sending a laughing glance Ross's way, bent and kissed Eveleen's as well.

Eveleen snorted a soft laugh, and then took her hands back.

Misha turned to the group and said, "I was sent along, obedient dog that I am, to guard the equipment the Americans contributed. But I assure you I was most diligent with my tapes. So, how far are the rest of you in this accursed tongue?" And he added a fast phrase in Yilayil, whistling and droning expertly.

Ross saw Eveleen whispering a translation to herself; he didn't even try. On the other side of the room the Colonel nodded once in silent approval, and then Saba leaned forward and responded, her intonations correct, as far as Ross could hear. Ashe added a short phrase.

"Chalk one up for us," Ross muttered under his breath.

Eveleen smothered a grin behind her hand. "I wonder if we'll find out if he was sent because he was in trouble or because he's the expert?" she whispered back.

"Somehow I doubt the second choice—despite the grandstanding." Ross leaned forward to sip more of the strong Russian coffee.

"Are we ready?" Misha asked, looking around.

"We leave tomorrow," Vera, the redhead, said. "You timed your arrival close, Misha."

"Ah, Zina said she'd have my ears for breakfast if I was late." Misha dropped into a waiting chair.

Ross glanced over at Colonel Vasilyeva; though she had, at the very first dinner, invited everyone to call her "Zina" he'd found her too formidable for that. But she smiled now, the kind of smile a fond parent would bestow on a favorite child.

Irina leaned over to touch Misha's arm, and she addressed him in rapid Russian.

"English," Vera said quickly, giving Irina a look of challenge.

Misha sat back, smiling. "Not a way to show our gratitude for the technical gifts, yes?"

Viktor Ushanov, one of the other time agents, said something quietly in Russian, and Misha sent an appraising glance at Ashe and Ross, all the irony gone from his face.

"English, English," the Colonel said. "Tomorrow we all begin speaking Yilayil, but tonight, we relax, and we practice the tongue of our guests."

The rest of the dinner conversation was innocuous; after dinner was over, while everyone was milling around the coffee service, Ross made his way to Ashe. "Did you get what was going on when our new boy came in?"

"Nothing bad," Gordon said. "My Russian is pretty rusty, but it was pretty clear that Valentin is coming down hard on our side. He's the young hotshot tech, and I guess Milliard gave the Russians everything they asked for, equipment-wise."

Ross nodded trying for fairness. "No small item, if they're still recovering from what the Baldies did to 'em."

Gordon nodded, his manner approving, then turned away.

The rest of the evening, Ross circulated, trying to get a feel for these new team members. The mission was beginning to take on a sense of reality at last.

The two oldest agents, one man and one woman, spoke very poor English. They were also the quietest and most dour—like Russian agents of old stories, almost, though both were in fact scientists, and would be staying at the base camp in the present, monitoring the time-transfer equipment and making tests. Still, Ross learned their names: Gregori Sidorov and Elizaveta Kaliginova.

The rest spoke English with varying abilities, as they all chatted about scientific developments and some of the problems endemic to secret governmental projects. Nothing classified or politically touchy—just the sometimes funny logistical glitches and exasperating hassles inevitable when dealing with bureaucrats. Those were apparently universal. Renfry became quite loquacious—willingly trading stories with his Russian tech counterparts. From there they moved on to subjects of general interest: movies, television, music, sports.

When the evening ended, Ross was in a good mood.

As he and Eveleen settled into their room, he asked, "So what did you think?"

Eveleen went to the window again, looking out. Then she turned around. "A whole evening of just chatter, but I don't think the time was wasted."

Ross grinned. "That Colonel—Zina. I've got to get used to that. She's no fool."

Eveleen nodded. "The other night, at the folk festival. Tonight. Somehow these Russians seem less and less like aliens, and more like, well, like us."

"Human," Ross said.

"Considering where we're going," Eveleen added, "that's a distinction that might just preserve our lives."

CHAPTER 8

WHEN THE BLEAK sun rimmed the eastern horizon the next day, Gordon Ashe and his Eastern and Western agency colleagues were squeezed onto worn bench seats aboard a rattletrap of a cargo plane that might have seen service during the Second World War.

He looked down through a window at St. Petersburg dwindling rapidly away between two huge bodies of water, then the plane banked and headed north.

Conversation was minimal; the plane was not heated, and everyone seemed to prefer huddling into their coats, sipping at warm drinks. Just as well. Gordon sat back, watching his breath cloud, as he considered the twist their fortunes had taken.

Were there going to be problems with Misha and Ross? Young as he was, Misha had quite a reputation on both sides of what used to be the Iron Curtain. Of course, Gordon knew that Ross had a reputation as well. Gordon knew a little Russian, and he'd overheard some of them talking about Ross the other night. They all knew the story about Ross's burned hand—how he got it, and why.

There were not many who had survived direct encounters with Baldies. Ross was one—and Misha was another. In fact, if reports were accurate, Misha had apparently delighted in acting as a decoy in order to draw the Baldies off. What had happened to the Baldies he'd fooled wasn't clear, but Kelgarries, in a private conversation just before the team's departure, had wondered if the violence of the Baldies' attacks on the Russians had something to do with the kinds of games the humans might have been playing with the inimical XTees.

Apparently Misha had insisted on being included on this mission. It argued not just a dedication to tough causes. Agents on both sides, supposedly, only found out about missions for which they were being considered. Misha's knowing about this one meant either a high status, despite his young age, or an uncanny ability to winnow out secret information.

Was his reckless courage going to be an asset—or a liability? What were his real motivations for wanting to be sent on this mission?

And what caused the almost palpable tension between Misha and Ross?

Misha's sudden laugh punctuated the silence. Gordon lifted his head, listening.

". . . not since I was small. One fall through the ice was enough," Viktor was saying in Russian.

Misha retorted, "Floe hopping was the biggest spring sport in my village."

"It was the only spring sport in your village," Irina said, deadpan.

Misha laughed again. "True!"

Gordon listened to Misha's melodious tenor voice, wavering about what he ought to do. He wanted the team to be safe. Of course. But they also had to work together, and trust one another.

He grimaced, wishing that he knew why the Russian agent had insisted on being included in the mission. Zina Vasilyeva had been noncommittal; it was Milliard who had said something about some sort of relationship with one of the missing scientists. After watching Misha's flirting for an evening, Gordon was convinced Misha had a relationship of some sort with every single female in the Russian agency. Yet whenever Misha had gotten too outrageous, Zina had spoken a soft word, and the blond agent had raised his hands in truce, and subsided.

Gordon glanced over at the gray-haired woman, who was busy with a laptop computer. What kind of internal politics had the Russians been working through?

The engine sputtered suddenly as a buffet of wind hit them hard. The juddering vibration increased suddenly, causing Saba to glance up and Eveleen to look worried. Only the Russians seemed unconcerned.

Gordon sat back, letting out his breath slowly. He was glad when the plane banked again, and started dropping down. Through the window they could see the White Sea, just barely, a ghost outline through thick white clouds. The world this far north was shades of gray and silver and white—definitely the land of winter.

The plane landed without a problem, and silent Russian workers appeared from a rickety shed and began unloading baggage into trucks.

Apparently the scientific equipment had been sent on ahead by train, a precaution against being bumped and banged around in the air.

Someone handed around thermoses of hot, sweet coffee and spicy soup as they piled out of the plane and into the waiting trucks.

Soon they were zooming down a freshly plowed road into what seemed the middle of nowhere. Again, no one spoke much; the truck was unheated. Gordon hunkered in his corner, listening to the growl of the engine and the clash of gears, wondering when he would see the States again. If.

Not if, he thought, angry with himself for permitting even one defeatist thought. And since his own thoughts were lousy company, he turned his attention to the others.

A couple of the Russians murmured softly, their breath clouding in the frigid air. Gordon glanced over—and saw that they were playing cards on a upturned gasoline drum.

He watched idly, listening to the chatter. The Russians were talking about family members, it seemed; after a while he realized they were indulging in the same kind of "what if" he wouldn't permit himself.

He turned his shoulder and glanced at Ross, whose face was grim and stony, his unwavering gaze on his wife. Eveleen had headphones on, running to a portable CD player in her coat pocket. Gordon wondered if it was Yilayil language practice—or something altogether different.

Saba, as well, was listening to earphones. Gordon had no question about what Saba might be doing. Of course she was working ahead on Yilayil nuances. But that was part of her job.

Across from her, Case Renry sat with a laptop on his skinny knees, equally absorbed in his work.

Gordon's attention came back when the truck gave a roar and slowed.

Soon they piled out—to see, sitting out on a barren tarmac launch pad, a globe ship exactly like the one that had inadvertently taken him, Ross, Renfry, and Travis Fox to the other world.

Travis. There was another subject to brood about. Gordon hated to think about Travis lost forever—and he regarded it as his fault, no matter what his superiors said to the contrary. How many would go missing this time—under his command?

As he thought it, he realized that that was his real fear. Not what would happen to him. But the fear that once again he'd lose an agent.

He shook his head; no use brooding. What he had to do was make damn sure that this time, everyone came back. Or he wouldn't.

Making this internal vow, he clambered out after the others.

"Whew," Ross was saying as he tipped his head back and grimaced at the globe ship. "Never thought I'd see one of these things again. Which was all right with me!"

Eveleen walked right up to the ship, and squinted at the dull, pearlescent hull. "Some kind of alloy?"

"Looks like a type of ceramic," Saba said, coming up on the other side.

"You'll have plenty of time to discuss this with Renfry and the other big brains during the trip," Gordon said, forcing an attempt at a light tone. "We'd better lend a hand in getting the gear stowed."

They all joined the line of Russians who were helping the truck driver to load equipment into the ship. Gordon saw Renfry and one of the Russians following a couple of crates with anxious looks—obviously delicate machinery of some type or other.

"At least the Russians seem to have made the inside a little more like home," Ross commented, peering up at the round opening as he muscled his load up the ramp.

"Could hardly be less," Gordon cracked, doing his best to lighten his own mood as he followed Ross inside.

Eveleen snorted a laugh.

"We bunk up here," Zina called down from the level above. "Choose where you wish to sleep. We did not assign."

This globe ship was slightly larger than the one he'd made the trip in before, Gordon noted. The Russians had fitted the big, circular space with movable panels, creating little double cabins that afforded a semblance of privacy.

Gordon hesitated, watching Ross and Eveleen go into one of the small cabins. Out of the corner of his eye he saw Saba hesitate, then she walked with dignity into the next cabin over. Gordon was free to join her—or not.

He looked around, saw that the other cabins were all claimed, and winced. A moment later Ross appeared as if propelled, followed by Eveleen, who whispered, ". . . make it any more difficult than it already is."

Out loud she said in a cheery voice, "How about if we females bunk together, and you fellows do the same? I know you and Gordon are used to each other's habits from old missions."

Ross rather sheepishly beckoned to Gordon, and Eveleen swung her bags into the cabin Saba had chosen.

Gordon did not hear the conversation between the two women, though he could hear the murmur of their voices.

Ross didn't say anything. He just stowed his stuff in a locker beneath the bunk he'd chosen, leaving the other one to Gordon.

Gordon got his stuff stashed neatly inside of a minute, and went out to see where he could lend a hand. He was not surprised to see that Renfry and the weedy Russian tech-whiz, Valentin, had chosen to bunk together. The Russian women had also paired off, the older two together, and the younger, and Misha and the dark-eyed silent Viktor had also chosen a cabin together, leaving the dour Gregori to bunk with the pilot, a quiet man in his forties who was introduced as Boris Snegiryov.

"We do not wait," Boris said almost immediately. "We lift soon. Get into your bunks. Strap in."

Gordon remembered that last trip. "I take it you haven't modified that plus-gees acceleration?"

"Two point sixty-seven gees," Boris corrected. "It is the same. We cannot interfere with the engines—we still do not completely understand them. We can only work around their given function."

"I don't need a second warning," Ross commented, waving a careless hand. "I'm for my bunk."

As soon as the equipment was stored to the techs' satisfaction, everyone retreated to their bunks, strapping themselves securely in.

Gordon listened to the sudden quiet. Neither he nor Ross spoke.

"We are lifting off," Boris reported over the intercom.

The first warning was the vibration. Gordon remembered that; his heartbeat accelerated.

The vibration increased steadily, until it became a low, subsonic moan that resonated through bones and teeth. Gordon shut his eyes— there was nothing to look at anyway—and waited.

The sound changed abruptly, and the cosmic hand swatted them, pressing him into his bunk.

His consciousness receded to a dim awareness of a virulently glowing red eye; suddenly it was the pit of a volcano he was falling into. He struggled against the nightmare, his body spasmed, and the pit dwindled and resolved into the red-lit numerals on a clock mounted near the door of the cabin.

But his inner ear thought he was still falling, so insistently that he barely noticed the aching of his body in every joint and socket. But he forced himself to unstrap and sit up—and immediately he floated free.

Grabbing the webbing of his bunk, he propelled himself toward the door. His stomach fought, but he recognized the zero gravity-induced nausea for what it was, and looked around, forcing his eyes to impose up and down on his surroundings.

It worked. After a few white-knuckled moments his innards settled, and he hit the door tab. "Ross?" He turned his head.

"Give me a minute." The agent gripped his bunk, his scarred hand showing white.

Gordon turned away and watched the door slide silently into the wall.

Somewhere he heard someone being sick; another person moaned, the baffling of the portable walls only muffling the sound.

A Russian voice called out, "Take your anti-nausea meds!"

A deep voice responded unhappily, "I cannot open my eyes."

Misha's laughter rang out. It sounded heartless. But then came his voice: "Here, Valentin. I'll find it for you—get on your bunk."

There was no sound from any of the women's cabins. Gordon hesitated, then tapped lightly at Saba and Eveleen's—grabbing hastily at a handhold to prevent himself from ricocheting back.

"Yes?" that was Eveleen.

"Gordon here. You all right?"

"We're fine."

Gordon handed himself up the ladder into the circular command center, where one of those cardboard-thin viewscreens they'd nicknamed plates on their last journey now showed the blackness of space.

Boris was busy at a console that had been wired to the mysterious guidance console installed by the unknown makers of the ship.

A moment later Gordon was aware of a flicker at his side. He looked up, into Zina Vasilyeva's face. Her chin jutted slightly, but otherwise she seemed composed and calm.

"We are safely launched," she said. "Are your people all right?"

"Adjusting to free fall," Gordon said.

"Shall we turn our attention to making a schedule for our people?"

"Let's," Gordon said.

The mission had begun.

CHAPTER 9

EVELEEN LAUNCHED HERSELF onto the next level, then looked around in delight.

Vera smiled, looking like a kind of cheery cherub with her red curls floating around her face. The other women who had longer hair had braided it and wore it pinned up to keep it from floating in their faces.

"You like?" Vera asked.

"It's great," Eveleen exclaimed. "When we were on the ground, all this space seemed wasted—I forgot about null-grav."

Saba said, "Whoever made these ships must have spent a lot of time in space."

Irina, from behind, said soberly, "That is why we called them scout-craft. We think they were sent out to investigate other worlds. They might have gone long times between actual landings."

Irina, Eveleen knew, was by profession a data analyst—apparently formidably good. Her finely chiseled face was also impossible to read, Eveleen had decided after covertly watching them all. Not so Vera, whose every mood was clear in her expression. Vera was gifted at communication; her missions had involved, apparently, getting people to talk. Eveleen hoped her talents would extend to alien races.

Eveleen turned her attention from the Russian women to the rest of the globe ship. The inner skin of the globe's rec room was lined with recording instruments for the journey, as there was no real cargo space, but it also boasted entertainment—including a pair of VCRs (with a stash of tapes in in English and Russian) and a stereo system with half a dozen headsets so several people could listen to music at once.

In their cabins they also had headsets, but those were wired to the master computer on which the Yilayil language, and other pertinent data, were stored.

Near the Terran entertainment mods were the strange compartments and storage racks of the aliens who had built the ship. Among them were the rectangular boxes that were activated on being handled—and showed pictures of whatever the user wished to see.

Eveleen ran her hands over it, wondering what the hands of the original users had been like. Were they brown, or blue, or rainbow—were they five-fingered, or nine-fingered? What kind of places had been depicted, and what kinds of emotions had been inspired?

She thought about the sonic shower that Vera had nicknamed the Bubble Room. They only had one, but it was enough; she'd stepped out feeling not just clean, but with a sense of well-being that indicated the unknown owners of the globe ship were not so very alien from humans.

"There are two mysteries we have to solve," she said out loud, without thinking.

Saba nodded. "The Russian team—and these people." She nodded at the storage compartments.

They already knew the story of this particular globe ship; like the one Ross and Gordon had found fifteen thousand years ago, the Russians had also found theirs back in the past, the crew dead. Only unlike the American ship, whose owners had been newly killed, the Russian ship's crew had died some time before, of mysterious causes. Had another ship attacked them? Their skeletons had been intact, which argued against local predators. Was disease to blame?

That was still being investigated by teams of XT forensic specialists at home, working under as much secrecy as the time agents.

Meanwhile, the new team had to live together on this ship, and then they had to make it successfully back again after living in the midst of a third alien race.

Eveleen gently put the rectangle back in its place and turned away. Irina was gone; the other two were examining things.

Glancing at one of the clocks the Russians had wired in each cabin, she said, "Our rec time is about over. Shall we get busy?"

Saba nodded soberly, and Vera gave her a quick salute.

They found Irina in the small cabin that had been designated the study area. Zina and Gordon had declared that once people walked into the study cabin, no more English or Russian could be spoken—only Yilayil.

"Here in place of knowledge I—conveyance-motivator—work," Eveleen trilled.

Strange. She was actually getting comfortable with the word order when she used Yilayil—but if she tried thinking in English and translating it over, she got mentally tangled.

Saba added something about repetition, to which the others agreed, then they sat down to the tapes.

A WEEK OF ship's days later found her again in the study cabin, working with the other women. Each had found a favorite place to rest, and a mutually agreed-on method of study: they listened to a segment of tape, then went round in the circle repeating the new phrases. Then they asked one another questions that required answers based on the new material. At the end of the practice session, Saba would explain what they'd be hearing next, so they could either listen in their cabins, or review the old, however they learned best. As they advanced, Eveleen had begun to struggle with the odd tenses and sensory contradictions layered into the more formal challenge language.

"What is a green taste?" Vera asked suddenly. "Are we understanding this correctly?"

"It is correct," Irina said, checking her laptop. "But I do not comprehend it."

They all turned to Saba, who said slowly, "It is possible it means some kind of complicated insult, but that's only a guess. Let's proceed; maybe these contradictions will begin to make more sense."

Eveleen nodded, and reached to flick the tape back on.

Now, as Eveleen worked, her eyes observed the others, and her mind considered her own life. It was the human way, she had decided, to make crazy circumstances into a seemingly normal pattern. One created habits, and habits became customs, if enough people practiced them. When there was a semblance of order, one could function. In a totally chaotic or alien environment, the effect on one's mental health was profound enough to affect the physical self.

During the long days of space travel, the time-travel and scientific teams had all worked assiduously at their language studies, so much so that now and then even during rec time, whistle drones would punctuate chatter, particularly between those whose Russian or English was especially spotty.

The scientific team was also learning it—as Eveleen discovered on a rec shift when Valentin moved too quickly and inadvertently squeezed his bulb of coffee. Eveleen had watched in horrified fascination as the liquid spread into a cloud of droplets.

It was Vera who thought fast, grabbing the weird little device that they'd nicknamed the handvac, and chased after the droplets sucking them up.

As she worked, Renfry trilled, "Make it didn't happen!"

Everyone laughed—or almost everyone. Eveleen saw Saba frown slightly, then purse her lips and repeat the trill to herself.

What was she noticing? Eveleen mentally reviewed the trill. It was deceptively simple. In English it made no sense, but in Yilayil it sounded natural. Could it, she suddenly wondered, perhaps have some religious significance?

She brought it up with the study group later—and as usual, no one was certain. Irina said warningly, "Perhaps this House of Knowledge is a religious cult."

"You think this a bad thing?" Eveleen asked.

Irina's dark eyes flicked to her face for a moment, then down to the laptop that Irina never seemed to be without. "Perhaps," she said. "It depends on what they might worship—and why."

Eveleen thought about this for a time, then decided not to add to her worries—they'd find out when they found out. Meanwhile, there was plenty that she *could* learn.

The ship "day" had been divided into two watches of twelve hours each. The science team had taken the "night" watch, and the time-travel team the "day"—enabling everyone to have a full stint of time at the tapes and people with whom to practice.

Eveleen and Irina had concocted a set of exercises to keep everyone physically fit despite their weightlessness, most of them on a peculiar Russian universal exerciser.

The best time, though, was the overlap when the "night" team and the "day" team shared awake time. They watched movies together, or played cards together (the older Russians in particular seemed especially fond of complicated card games), or—Eveleen's favorite—made music. Not just listened, but made. Viktor played the violin, and Elizaveta could perform on a flute, clarinet, and recorder. Misha played a guitar, and he had a mellow singing voice. Just watching him leaning against a wall, singing ancient folk songs in shivery minor keys, was a distinct pleasure. He looked like something out of one of the romantic Russian films.

Misha. Eveleen grinned privately to herself. The guy seemed constitutionally unable to resist flirting—and not just with Vera and Irina, but with all the women. Saba held him at arm's distance. Nothing provoked her out of her calm dignity. Eveleen herself pretended not to understand some of his ambiguous remarks. So far, Ross hadn't seen any of it—which was just as well. Despite their agreement of before,

Eveleen knew that Ross was not one for hiding his emotions, and the ship was simply too small for feuds.

And it had to be admitted he flirted with her rarely. Most of his attention was equally divided between Vera and Irina, the former of whom showed a very strong interest right back, and the latter of whom responded with a kind of intense coldness that Eveleen could not quite fathom. Misha, of course, seemed to pester Irina the most, to Vera's unhidden (but unexpressed) annoyance. Eveleen felt uneasy about this triangle—and hoped the rivalry wasn't going to translate into trouble later.

Zina turned to her, whistling something—and Eveleen realized she had let her attention wander too long. She dismissed her speculations and turned her mind to the work at hand.

━━━━━━━━   ━━━━━━━━   ━━━━━━━━

FROM THE CIRCULAR accessway, Ross watched the women in the study cabin. They rested on several surfaces, but all their heads pointed in one direction, indicating a mutually agreed-on "up" and "down." What was funny was, the men's customary "up" and "down" was totally different.

How strange it was that the women seemed to have gravitated into one group, and the men into another. No one had set a rule about this—it just happened.

He glanced back at the cabin he shared with Gordon, and sighed. And he had been worried about married life on a mission! Except for that piece of legalese called a marriage license back home, he didn't feel married, not anymore. Most of his time was spent with the men, except for those rec periods at the end of the shift, when everyone got together to watch a movie or listen to music. He could sit next to Eveleen and steal a few minutes for talk, but that was about it for Quality Time.

"Countdown for the first landing just began." Gordon appeared, handing himself down the corridor. "Want to grab some grub now?"

"Sure thing." Ross followed him to the galley. Remembering the weird food he and his three fellow adventurers had been forced to eat on their inadvertent jouney last time, Ross grimaced.

Those areas of the galley were closed and sealed off. The Russians had installed a freezer and microwave unit, with a refrigerator housing drink bulbs.

His hand hovered over the panel of choices. Back in the States, he and the others had filled out a form for the Russians, indicating food preferences and aversions. The result was a selection of choices that took into consideration the highest number of "I like this" marks and the least "Won't eat it on a bet" indicators.

He liked the food—but eating in zero gravity was a hassle. He had realized, while laboring through his first meal, that the aliens had been smart, with their solids and pastes. Rice, mashed potatoes, sauces, were a messy chore. Chunky soup was a dream—and Ross wasn't sure he could swallow it even if they'd put it in bulbs. Food *felt* different going down, when it had mass but no weight. His first meal or two had made him gag, and he'd noted a similar reaction in some of the others.

He'd stuck to the pureed vegetables in juice form, and other liquids, until he trusted his stomach. Now he was used to it, and chose a pita-bread sandwich as well as his usual coffee and vegetable juice. Gordon had the same.

Ross slid his choice into the microwave, then broke the seal on his drink bulb. He took a long sip. The coffee, which was contained in a special unit, was fresh and scalding hot.

"Did I understand Boris right?" he asked. "I know we're going to hit the refueling planet pretty soon."

Gordon nodded.

"But what about that other world in Yilayil's system, the one with the furred critters. Did he say we're going to bypass them?"

"He did indeed. The Russians were able to program that particular landing out of the tape, which incidentally saves on fuel."

"Good."

"Our experiences there were apparently enough to convince them against any investigation of that planet. That will lie on some future team's plate—luckily our mission is definitely on the Yilayil planet."

The microwave light went off, and Ross reached in to get his meal. He shoved himself over to one of the rests, and hooked a leg around a curved handhold in order to anchor himself. He breathed deeply of the ship air—faintly metallic still, reminding him of the taste of the alien water from his previous journey—and then bit into his sandwich. He liked the spices the Russians favored.

"Good cooks."

Gordon grunted, swallowed, then whistle/droned a comment about food. While Ross was cudgeling his brain to make an answer, a perfectly pitched response came from behind them, and both Ross and Gordon turned to see Misha lounging in the hatchway, his blond hair drifting.

With a lazy smile, the Russian time agent moved with expert grace to the food dispenser, chose a meal with a light stab of his finger, and then chucked it into the microwave—all without causing his body to recoil. Ross kept his face impassive, wondering how many had witnessed his own first day or so, when he'd forgotten that any use of force will have an equal reaction, which meant he was left windmilling in the middle of a room until he drifted near enough to a wall to reorient himself. Had Misha seen? Probably.

His food was heated. Misha snagged it, grabbed a bulb of coffee, then pushed himself over to join the two Americans. Gordon made space for him.

Misha waved his bulb at Ross. "Your wife. She is very beautiful."

Ross nodded, instantly wary.

"But so prudish." Misha's brows quirked, and his mouth smiled, but his intelligent gray eyes were direct in their assessment.

Like the first time he'd seen Misha, Ross's instant reaction was a lightning stab of anger. He hid it, though, guessing immediately that he was being goaded. This guy couldn't possibly have the hots for Eveleen—not when he had an equally attractive woman like Vera sitting up and smiling every time he entered a cabin. And he hadn't exactly been ignoring Irina, Ross had noticed.

He's still testing me, Ross thought. And if I take a swing at him, he's just going to see it as weakness, and make a game of needling me.

So he forced himself to shrug, and grin. "I can only speak for myself. And no, I don't think I'm a prude, but I don't find you the least bit attractive."

Misha's laughter rang out—he was clearly surprised, and delighted, at the crack.

Gordon's lips twitched; Ross feigned unconcern, and took a bite from his sandwich.

"She likes to fight, your wife?" Misha continued.

"She's good at it," Ross said. Ordinarily he'd say *Ask her* but he wasn't going to offer this guy what might be interpreted as tacit permission to harass Eveleen.

"Ah, I like to fight. I shall offer her a fall, when we have gravity again."

Ross shrugged. "Be my guest." He knew Eveleen's practice mat persona—all professional. If this clown was looking for a chance to flirt, he'd find a robot more responsive if he planned to try it during martial-arts practice.

The thought made him grin. Misha gave him a speculative look, then turned his attention to Gordon, and he fired several rapid, acute questions about the library they'd found on their last journey, and whether or not the Weaslies had exhibited any signs of even rudimentary language.

By the time Gordon was done talking, Misha had finished his food, and he launched himself out again; they heard his voice floating back from the command cabin.

"Testing you." Gordon pointed with his chin in Misha's direction.

"I'm not an idiot."

"No, but you're the same kind—adrenaline seeker," Gordon retorted.

"Me?" Ross frowned, thinking back. Slowly, almost unconsciously, he flexed his burned hand, then he said, "Maybe. Once. But no more."

"No?" Gordon grinned. "No one, from Milliard on down, would have faulted you for not taking this assignment. Hell, the rules forbid newly married agents from being sent into the field."

Ross snorted a laugh. "Well, maybe a little. Eveleen as well. But not like that guy. What's pushing him?"

"I don't know," Gordon said slowly. "All I know is, he pulled every string to get assigned to this mission. Even to the extent of causing a shootout with gangsters in order to save this ship from discovery."

"You think it's just adrenaline, then? Or there's some other motivator?" Ross asked.

Gordon shook his head. "As yet, I have no clue. The guy willingly talks to everyone, and will even talk about himself, but only what he's done, never what he thinks. And we have to remember what all of them have lived through, finding out about comrades being killed in those Baldy attacks."

"I just hope he's not going to make trouble just to get things stirred up," Ross muttered.

"Zina thinks he's too smart for that. Nevertheless, I'm glad he'll be mostly away from us on his search job."

"Yeah." Ross crushed his empty bulb in his hand.

CHAPTER 10

GORDON ASHE OBEDIENTLY swallowed his anti-nausea meds, and settled gratefully into the webbing of one of the extra seats in the command cabin. Next to him, Zina Vasilyeva waited silently, her gaze on the viewscreen. They'd just endured the hideous wrenching of the transfer from other-dimensional space; centered on the viewscreen was a small, blue-green crescent. A larger black disk with a corona flaring around it marked the planet's primary. The crescent swelled rapidly as the ship followed its programmed course toward the huge, ancient spaceport at which the globe ships refueled.

Gordon's unvoiced worry was that some other ship would show up, and they'd have to deal with the beings—somehow—though the Terrans knew little about how to control the communications of the globe ship.

He did voice one worry—that the reprogramming might somehow interfere with the communications. "When so much of the ship function is automatic," he said. "I wonder if tampering with it might cause some kind of signal to go out?"

"We debated this," Zina replied without taking her gaze from the screen. "There is no way to know if we have sent a signal. We decided to take the chance. The question of fuel, and of defense against the inimical beings on that one planet, made us feel the benefits outweighed the risk."

Gordon glanced at the communication board—still a total mystery. Was a signal going out—or not? There was no clue in the complicated series of lights and buttons.

At least no other ships were in sight, he noted, as the globe sped toward the mysterious refuel planet. Now gees pulled at them, and the ship reacted to floating trash: even after the lapse of millennia, the nameless planet was surrounded by a haze of detritus left behind by visiting starships.

The blue-green crescent resolved into a lush planet swirled with cloud systems. Gordon felt his body pressing into his webbing with more authority. Suddenly his viewpoint changed, though the position of the ship vis-à-vis the planet didn't: his inner ear registered *down*, and vertigo seized him.

At the controls Boris now held his hands ready above his console, watching lights flickering and measurements of various types streaming across his computer terminal as the autopilot brought the ship down toward the apparently endless stretch of white cement that marked the ancient starport.

Gordon swallowed fast, closed his eyes, and tried breathing slowly. They were in flight now, subject to the planet's 0.92 standard gee, which settled his stomach rapidly. The transition from orbit was not as bad as the emergence from the weird hyper-dimensional travel that none of the Terran techs—either Western or Eastern—could duplicate.

Silence gripped the ship, except for the creaks and subsonic groans of entry into a gravity well. All the crew members were in their bunks, on Zina's orders—all except Boris, the pilot, and Zina and Gordon as senior officers.

Gordon and Zina stayed with Boris as a kind of insurance—what kind, Gordon didn't know. He certainly couldn't operate the ship if something went wrong. It would have made more sense to have Renfry on hand—of course, Renfry and Valentin probably had wired up a viewscreen to their terminals, and were following the action from their cabin.

It's probably a political gesture, Gordon thought. Showing us that everything's on the up-and-up, without having to say it. Establishing trust, which we've got to have if this mission is to succeed.

Gordon opened his eyes again.

They were almost down. There was the peculiar blue-green sky again; memory smote him with unexpected force. No moisture was evident in that sky. If the planet had weather, it was all elsewhere. Of course, that would make sense—to locate a spaceport in a desert.

With a gentle bump, the ship settled onto the wide sweep of white cement. There was the rusty red ruin. There were the ghost ships, untouched since their last visit.

The globe ship's position with respect to the nearest ghost ship even looked the same—Gordon wondered if the globes were programmed to set down on the very same landing pad.

They'd have to, he realized belatedly. Or would the refueling bots come out no matter what kind of ship set down—and would they know what kind of fuel to administer?

Fueling bots!

He turned his head; his neck cricked at the unexpected weight. "When we were here, the fuel bot was broken—"

"We saw that, on your mission tape," Zina replied. Her voice was hoarse. "Our first mission was prepared for this problem, and were able to effect repairs on the robot."

Of course. He'd forgotten that first Russian mission—the reason they were here!

Gordon was embarrassed at his own stupidity, but only for a moment. From the way Zina rubbed at her temples, she was having difficulty adjusting to gravity again as well. Thinking was at least as difficult as moving.

"Here he comes," Boris said, for the first time during the entire journey showing some emotion. "Good work, Vasili!"

Gordon watched the viewscreen. The snakelike fuel robot slithered out to the ship and disappeared from view. But a moment later Boris gave a grunt of satisfaction, and indicated one of his measures. "Fuel."

"What type of fuel does this ship run on? Your people figure that out?" Gordon asked.

Boris shook his head. "Our analysis is much the same as yours—a type of slurry encapsulating some of the superheavy elements, triggered by a catalytic environment that we do not yet have the technology to fully understand."

Gordon nodded. All the more reason to take extreme care when using the globe ships. The autopilot tapes might be safe enough—but the only fuel, as yet, was from this ancient starport, and who knew when it would run out?

Boris gave another grunt, and touched a pair of controls. On the viewscreen, the robot hose began its steady retreat.

The globe lifted again, accelerating rapidly. The journey out was far faster, and Gordon realized that some of the inbound maneuvering might be programmed in accordance with planetary defense strictures. Speculation about the gauntlet of ancient weapons they might have faced occupied him until he felt his weight disappear. Soon after came the wrenching transition to hyperspace.

When that was over, he lay in his webbing until he felt recovered. According to that first journey, they now had exactly a week of travel before they planeted on the Yilayil world.

Everyone was progressing well with the language, thanks to assiduous use of the hypno-tapes and keeping to the rules about only using the language in work sessions. They were about as well prepared as they could be, given the incomplete and somewhat bizarre data in the language tapes, and their scanty knowledge of a very complicated culture.

What remained was the Terrans themselves.

Gordon had made a point of trying to get to know each of the crew. Easiest were the younger Russians; at least, easy to talk to, he amended, thinking them over. Misha talked at least as much as Vera, but not about anything personal. He kept his inner self well hidden behind an impervious shield of friendly, joking insouciance.

Hardest were the older Russians. Gordon's instincts told him not to press. He didn't think that Gregori or Elizaveta necessarily hated the Americans and didn't want to work with them, but their younger years had been spent in a rough political climate, wherein one did not reveal oneself easily. That they did talk to him—on such bland, unexceptionable topics as linguistic studies, science, and so forth—meant to him that they were trying their best.

The last one was the toughest—Saba.

Thinking of those intelligent dark eyes, and the smooth, softly accented voice, Gordon decided he'd lain inactive long enough.

Time to get started.

He unfastened his webbing, nodded to Boris, and pushed himself out. Glancing at the time as he sailed through the rounded corridor, he gave the schedule a quick mental review, and headed for the rec room.

The noise of a video made him stop and peek in. Three of the Russians and Renfry were watching some documentary in Russian. He knew that several of the others were in the study right then, which meant that Saba was probably in her cabin.

He stopped himself outside her door, grabbed a handhold, and tapped.

The door slid open. Eveleen was gone; Saba was alone. Gordon saw her laptop terminal lit, the machine anchored down to the little desk. Earphones floated in the air next to the terminal.

"Gordon?" she said politely.

"May I talk to you?" he asked.

She nodded once. "Of course."

"Sorry to interrupt," he said, entering the cabin, which was small and very tidy.

"It is all right," Saba said with a graceful gesture. She swiftly saved her work, then closed the laptop and laid her folded hands on it. "Now. What did you wish to discuss?"

The cabins were too small for visitor space. Gordon had hitched himself over Eveleen's bunk.

"I've been thinking ahead," Gordon began. "We have no idea why that statue of you exists, but we can assume that our mission has something to do with it. It was probably carved as a result of our visit."

Saba nodded; they all knew that.

"Your assignment is to enter the House of Knowledge, about which we only know one thing: that only selected beings are permitted entry, and everyone else stays out."

Again, common knowledge. Yet she exhibited no impatience—she knew, then, that he was establishing the background to his thoughts.

"I might not be able to get in, even as your ******." He whistle/droned the word for *runner/caregiver*.

"I have thought of that," she admitted. "But we do not have any evidence that the inhabitants of the House of Knowledge are prisoners, or how could the First Team have learned even what they did? I must assume that I can come out to visit you if need be."

"No evidence except those anomalies in the language," he insisted. "You yourself noted that the odd tenses seem to deny free will at times, that they might indicate a cultural means of coercion. So I don't think we can count on that. What I'd like to do is establish a code, in both languages—English and Yilayil—that ideally we can use on our radio connection. One code for pulses—for emergencies—and another for spoken communication."

"So you are assuming that we are going to be in a hostile environment, then," she said.

He shook his head. "Given how many pieces are missing from the puzzle, I think it's best. I talked it over with Zina before we strapped down for the refuel, and she says she's had thoughts along the same line."

Saba sighed a little, flexing her hands. Gordon realized she was tense, though she gave no overt signs.

"Look," he said, "I hate to pile on the pressure."

She shook her head, smiling a little. "It is already there."

Gordon smiled back. This was her first admission of real human emotion. And he knew that the same thing could be said of him—that he hid his real reactions. But it would be a mistake to assume that he didn't have any, just as he couldn't assume that she did not feel normal human emotion.

"Well, we can't get around the fact that you are going to be important in some way—if not for us, for them. Let's just hope that this means they think you're great, and give you a cushy position some-where, doing something poetic in one of their rituals. Meantime . . ."

Saba nodded again. "Your code is an excellent idea. Have you de-signed something?"

"I thought that we could do that together," he suggested. "We got a little time before our shift turns in for sleep—how about getting a start on it now?"

Her smile widened, just a bit. "I think that's a very good plan," she said.

THE HOUR AFTER Gordon came into her cabin to speak passed quickly for Saba. Once they'd begun to work, the man's remote coun-tenance relaxed, his slow, careful speech—as if he were reluctant to speak at all—became normal. He was still too controlled for Saba to hear his natural rhythm. Controlled, cautious, but not inflexible. She could be patient.

All people made music of some kind, Saba had discovered when she was a girl beginning her studies in English and French. In Ethiopia, music was very much a part of life for the peoples she had known, traveling about with her father, who was a doctor—the Dorze, her mother's people, and all the other peoples of Ethiopia, from Eritrea to the elusive Danakil, made music all the time, in every aspect of life.

But in listening to the language instructors at her school, she had discovered that there was music in speech. Each language had a different music, and each individual interpreted that music differently.

She'd lost that conviction for a time, when she moved to Addis Ababa to attend university. But after a time life in the large, sophisti-cated city had brought her old convictions back, once she'd gotten used to the noise of technology. There was a kind of music even in modern life. Some people made very little music, but what they had was dark, angry, ugly—jangling with disharmony. Some made the muscle-tightening music of fear. Others made quiet music, repeating patterns they had learned from generations of equally quiet people.

Some—very complex persons—kept their music to themselves until they trusted. At first she'd wondered if Gordon Ashe had any music, but she'd come to realize he was one of these latter. He had a fast mind, and an attention to detail that she appreciated.

In that hour of study that he had come so suddenly to request, they laid the groundwork for a series of signals, ranked according to need, that they could build on.

When the bell toned for the shift change, Gordon seemed as sur-prised as she was how quickly the time had vanished. He said a polite good night—once again careful and remote—and left.

Saba stayed in the open door, her mind ranging over the past hour. As yet Eveleen had not shown up. Saba wondered if she and Ross had managed to find a little time alone, and hoped it was so. Eveleen never complained, but there was a wistful expression in her eyes when she referred to her husband, so newly wed. Her voice, so pleasant, with sunny music very close to the surface, would convey shades of longing.

A flash of long yellow hair caught Saba by surprise, and she looked up to see Mikhail Petrovich Nikulin hanging upside down, just a meter from her face.

With a quick gesture, he oriented himself so that they were aligned in the same direction, then he gave her one of his grins.

"Nice night for pairs," he said, pointing back over his shoulder in the direction Gordon had gone. His own music was exotic, quick with control and unexpected percussive accents. This Mikhail—called Misha by his Russian colleagues—was another complex person.

"Perhaps," she said, feeling a spurt of amusement at his assumption that she and Gordon were romantically involved.

"So do you like old men only, or have you a smile for me?"

"Old? Men?" Saba asked.

"Gordon Ashe might be tough as nails, but I'm younger and much more handsome," came the immediate retort.

"Thank you for the information, Mikhail," Saba murmured.

"Misha! I want two things, and I shall have them: you will call me Misha, and you will smile at me."

"I will give you both, willingly, if I can then retire for rest," she said. "Good night, Misha." And she gave him a very polite smile.

"A challenge!" He laughed. "That's a challenge, Saba."

She closed the cabin door, and heard his laughter echo as he moved away.

Eveleen appeared a moment later. "That guy!" she exclaimed. "Does he ever give up?"

"You too?" Saba asked.

"Ohhh, yes. I noticed him talking to you during rec time, what was it, day before yesterday? It's so easy to lose track—one day so much like another." Eveleen grinned as she wrestled out of her clothes and into her sleepwear. "You know," she added, her head muffled in her top, "I could get used to this nullgrav—all except getting dressed. I feel like an octopus, writhing around in midair!"

Saba chuckled. "You are right. It is difficult."

"So, back to Misha." Eveleen's head popped out, and she fixed her floating hair into its night braid. "He's, what, pressuring you for a date? Or does he just want you to admire his oh-so-fascinating handsome blond self."

"He wants to make me smile," Saba said.

"Well, that sounds harmless enough."

"I have said it wrong," Saba corrected, and she lowered her voice, trying for his characteristic tone of voice—partly humor, partly challenge. "He wants to *make* me smile." She gave the verb a slight emphasis.

Eveleen's brows winged up, and she whistled one of the Yilayil challenge responses. "So. What do you do?"

"Continue to ignore him, and hope that Vera or perhaps even Irina will eventually occupy his attention."

Eveleen hooked herself into her webbing, and fastened it over herself. "Never a dull moment, that's the name for this mission, right?"

"Right," Saba said, giving in to laughter at last. Then she too composed herself for sleep, and doused the light.

AND SO THE last days of zero grav passed. Saba felt the pressure of the imminent landing—they all did. No need to check the schedule anymore. Everyone was putting in as much preparation time as they could, the science team readying their equipment.

Saba continued to meet with Gordon each day, and they rapidly set up a communication code that both could remember with very little prompting. They'd covered as many contingencies as they could invent, leaving room for possible combinations as the mission progressed.

Misha, of course, continued his campaign, but even he seemed rather absentminded—as if he continued out of habit, or to hide how he, too, had emotions about what was soon to take place. She found those emotions difficult to interpret—but she was certain that they were there.

Finally Boris sent the signal for the emergence from the transdimension, and they all retreated to strap into their bunks.

Saba knew that landing on the Yilayil planet was now a short time away. She took her anti-nausea medication. Very shortly thereafter the wrenching weirdness seized her in its grip, making her body feel as if it had been turned inside out and then right again.

When at last it was over, and she had recovered, she opened her eyes to see Eveleen groggily sitting up from her webbing, which was swaying gently from her movements.

She unstrapped and hooked a foot around a hold, working through a series of movements that Saba had learned were very good for restoring circulation and muscle tone.

In silence Saba joined her.

When the two women were done, they left the cabin, and found the others gathered round the command center.

There, on the viewscreen, was the system they were headed toward. A blue-white crescent loomed on one side, slipped away.

"Passing second planet now," Boris reported.

"Good riddance," Ross Murdock cracked.

"Amen to that," Case Renfry said softly.

Not long after, they saw Yilayil—a big blue-green crescent, not unlike Earth at this distance—rapidly growing dead center on the screen.

It swelled, until they could make out the islands thickly straddling the equator, and the white, sere land masses at the poles, all hazed by the atmosphere and obscure under swirling weather systems.

"Back to the bunks," Zina commanded. "We are shortly to planet— our work is to begin."

No one had anything to say to that—even Misha seemed subdued.

In silence the two women retreated to their cabin, and prepared for landing.

CHAPTER 11

ROSS FELT GRAVITY close its fist on his vitals, and he concentrated on his breathing. The ship was now under flight; the globe creaked and vibrated as it arrowed down toward Yilayil.

Ross tried to picture the planet, a series of island clusters belting the brilliant blue ocean that girdled the entire world. The spaceport was not located on the largest island—just the flattest. Most of the rest had active volcanoes on them: not good choices for any kind of city. Ross wondered if they'd be there long enough for the science team to actually explore some of those islands; there had to be tens of thousands of them, if not more.

He hoped not.

It seemed the landing was faster this time than the last, but maybe that was because he knew what to expect. At any rate, they finally set down with a gentle bump, and Ross bounced and swayed in his bunk webbing, stretching his limbs experimentally.

Sounds came from the other cabins. The others emerged, one by one. Some of them had wasted no time in getting their equipment ready for deployment. Gordon was already out of his bunk, overseeing things; Ross listened to the quick American voices as he and Renfry spoke.

"Damn," Renfry was saying. "This stuff is heavy. I sure wish we knew we could safely run power off the ship."

Ross thought about the mysterious fuel, and wondered how they'd power the globe if they suddenly ran empty. They couldn't do it—of course. The idea of floating through space forever, maybe caught in the weird transdimensional plane, gave him the willies.

It was enough to get him to unstrap and swing out of the bunk. He slipped his shoes on and left the cabin.

"Ah. Ross." Renfry hailed him with obvious relief. "Gotta get this generator stuff out first thing, and get us a power supply set up."

Ross nodded, feeling his muscles protest as he lifted a heavy box. After the weeks of weightlessness—despite the workouts—everything seemed to weigh about a ton.

"Misha and Viktor gone out scouting?" Ross asked.

"Soon's Boris lowered the ramp," Renfry said. "That guy Misha acts like he's been in two gees for a month. He was out there with enough bounce to make a Marine drill sergeant happy."

Ross snorted—and then grunted with effort as he started down the ladder after Renfry. He was just as happy not to see Misha lounging around and grinning at his laboring movements under all that weight.

They made it to the outer port, and Ross glanced out. Like before, the rich, scent-laden air hit him at once, and he nearly dropped his burden as a violent sneeze took him.

Renfry sneezed right after, and then sneezed again. He rather hastily set his own box down and sneezed a third time, then sheepishly wiped his nose.

Ross sniffed, trying to get his sinuses acclimated; he looked around as he waited. They'd landed at dawn. Gaudy pink and orange and yellow light filtered through the lush growth at the cracks in the old spaceport paving.

"Phew!" Eveleen appeared next to him, her arms piled with several flat boxes. "Smells like an explosion in a perfume factory!"

"It is just as well we brought a large supply of anti-allergens," Valentin said soberly, appearing behind Eveleen.

"We didn't get sick on our run," Renfry said, "but maybe that was luck. I'm just glad we're immune—at least we can hope we're immune," he amended, squinting around at the unfamiliar varieties of trees and bushes.

"Let's get unloaded, then we can explore a little." That was Zina, behind them on the ramp.

Ross realized he had stopped at the base of the ramp, and was holding up the line. He quickly bent and picked up his box, and the line proceeded with the unloading.

They kept moving until the base camp items were all stacked up and waiting against Misha and Viktor finding a good location. Then they retreated back to the ship, with Gregori and Vera standing guard against the little blue flyers showing up and pilfering souvenirs.

Ross was glad to get back to the sterile ship's air. His sinuses cleared almost immediately—making his nose run. He noticed the others having the same problem.

Gordon was ahead of him in line for the midday meal. "Remember getting the sniffles last time?" Ross asked.

Gordon gave a one-shoulder shrug. "Nope. Maybe it's old age setting in."

Ross laughed, but he wondered if their anti-allergen medication was maybe a tad too vigorous. Last flight—when they'd had, perforce, no protection beyond the alien suits—had produced no such problems.

They each got some food, and Ross hunkered down with his back to a wall, glad to get his weight off his feet.

Zina waited until everyone had food, then she nodded to Gordon, who said, "Listen up, people. We've got to start wearing our communications gear right now. If we set foot off the ship, even for ten feet, we wear it." He gave them an ironic grin. "I don't know about the First Team's visit, but when Ross and Renfry and I were here last, it was me who found himself making an unexpected trip to the local flyers. No problem—that time—but we need to be prepared until we know if there have been any changes."

Ross nodded, and the others made various signs of agreement. It was clear that Gordon and Zina had been talking about general strategy.

Ross was nearly done with his meal when Viktor and Misha appeared in the doorway. "We found a good one," Misha began.

Zina addressed him in rapid-fire Russian, and Misha's mouth tightened. He nodded his head, and spread his hands.

Ross looked at Misha's belt, which was bare, and knew that the maverick agent had left his own com gear behind. Why? Showing off, Ross thought sourly.

Ross also noticed that though the silent Viktor came in for a share of the lecture, it was Misha who caught the full load. Of course it had been his idea to skip off the ship the second the ramp was down, and go out ranging around before the com gear had even been broken out.

Misha kept his head bowed, his lips curved in the merest ghost of a smile, and when Zina finished he said something short and mild in Russian. Then he looked up. "We must get moving now if we wish to get a camp set up before dark," he stated in English.

Ross shoveled his last bite of food into his mouth and stood up. At once his shoulders and arms protested, but he ignored it. "So let's move," he said.

Everyone helped. They formed a long pack train, leaving only Boris and Renfry behind to guard the ship. Each person carried as much as he or she could handle.

Misha and Viktor had done an excellent job of trailblazing, Ross noted as he trudged along behind. Of course.

But—despite his distrust of the blond agent—he was just as glad that Misha and Viktor were as good as reputed. He hadn't really thought about laying camp until he stepped out and looked at this wild land once again. But this was no easy matter. They had to position themselves not just within range of both ship and library tower, but well away from any known weasel or wild-humanoid dens. But that wasn't all. They also had to be in a good position for the transfer equipment—because the time agents would be appearing in the same spot many years earlier. So they didn't want to be where spaceport (if it was being used at all) or city action might be congested, for example.

He knew that Viktor, in particular, had spent a great deal of time with the meticulous recordings of measurement and location reported on the incomplete tape made by the First Team. It was he who had mapped out the probable location of buildings and pathways they might find in the earlier time, and he had to overlay it with the present.

The camp turned out to be in a protected grotto next to a waterfall, with a natural spy-spot on the hillocks above the falls.

Misha stepped into the little clearing first, waving a hand about with the air of a prince offering his palace.

Zina looked around, nodded slowly, glanced at Elizaveta and Gordon, who both made approving sounds.

"We shall set up camp here," Zina pronounced.

And then it was time to really get to work.

"Biomass converters here—" The most bulky machinery they'd brought, squatty olive-green cylinders, took two people to wrestle out of the ship.

"Want the transfer equipment there, or what?"

"Water samples are ready, Zina . . ."

"No, the housing must be here—"

Everyone talked at once. As he worked under Valentin's direction, stacking supplies and equipment whose purpose he could only guess at, Ross listened to the melange of voices. It sounded like some kind of surreal dream—the bits of English and Russian, many of them interspersed with whistles and drones of the Yilayil language. These latter referred to local sights and conditions—it was actually quicker now to think of the world in native terms.

The science team would sleep aboard the ship, but they set up a defensible hut, just in case. Once he'd finished his grunt work, Ross was ordered by a distracted Zina to aid Misha, Viktor, Gordon, Irina, and Gregori in camouflaging the hut.

By the time they'd finished, Ross's body felt like one big ache. His muscles burned, and his lungs labored for breath. Gravity seemed to have converted his body to the weight of granite.

But when he looked around wearily, expecting further orders, it was to see Renfry and Zina—both looking pale and sweaty—standing in the middle of the camp. Renfry finished explaining something, and Zina gave a nod of satisfaction.

"Good," she said. "It is done."

Ross followed her gaze. Now the clearing looked much like it did before. Nothing was immediately obvious unless you stepped close. And the sonic barriers that the science team would set up would discourage roaming predators.

"Were we spotted?" Ross asked.

Vera, atop the hill with her field glasses, nodded. "Six or seven of the little blue flyers."

"Can't be helped," Renfry said, working his neck from side to side. "We'll be contacting the flying people anyway—and they seem to be the only ones the blues communicate with."

Ross dropped onto the ground, wiping his brow. The humid air made him feel hotter and sweatier than a heat wave in the Midwest.

The Midwest. He closed his eyes, all of a sudden feeling a familiar sickening knot in the pit of his stomach. He realized, just as he had on the last journey, how very far they were from home.

A movement beside him caused him to look up, and Eveleen smiled at him as she wiped back a strand of damp hair from her clear brow. "Homesick?" she asked softly.

"Mind reader." He tried a laugh. It was almost convincing.

"Ah, we'll be in action soon, and no time for homesickness," she said with a chuckle.

"At least these guys are all excited." He nodded at Renfy and Valentin. The entire science team seemed to have been infused with some kind of mysterious energy. While all the time agents sat around, either waving broad leaves like fans or just sitting still, the scientists were busy wiring their equipment together, and getting their various systems on-line, while chattering at high speed.

"Excited—and worried," Eveleen murmured softly.

"Worried?" Ross frowned. "What's this? Something new come up?"

"Nothing new," Eveleen said. "Something I guess the big brains all thought of, but no one has said out loud. You know, those feral human creatures . . ."

Ross remembered the desperate fight during his first visit here. He frowned as an idea occurred. "I didn't think of that. You mean, they're afraid that those things might be descendants of the Russian First Team, somehow mutated?"

Eveleen's eyes were sad. "Exactly."

Ross shuddered. "Hell. Hadn't thought of that, but even if it's been centuries—hell." It seemed inadequate, but at the same time appropriate. No one wanted to think their descendants—or their friends' descendants—would be savage monsters. "Let's hope not."

Elizaveta worked at the generator, making sure the biomass converters were functioning smoothly. Ross sniffed; a faint whiff of alcohol seemed to tickle his nose, but maybe that was his imagination. He knew in general how the converters worked—converting organic matter into alcohol, which then burned pure, to power the generator.

As he watched, Elizaveta adjusted something, and that faint whiff was gone, buried in the astonishing variety of scents carried on the heavy air.

"Well, we'll start finding out tomorrow," Eveleen whispered, staring through the open door of the hut, where Gregori worked with steady care on the time-transfer apparatus.

"Maybe we'd better head back and start preparing," Ross said.

He looked up. It seemed the others had had the same idea.

In silence they returned to the ship, a good meal, and a night's sleep.

⸻

EARLY THE NEXT morning, when it was Ross's turn to step into the strange sonic shower, he shut his eyes and let the frothy bubbles work deeply into his skin. Who knew how long it would be until he stood here again? At the back of his mind a voice whispered, "*If* you come back—" but that only succeeded in making him angry, and he closed off the shower controls and got into his transfer clothing.

Eveleen was waiting in the galley, along with the rest of the team. He went to her side. Next to her was his pack of equipment.

The others chattered quietly; when Zina appeared in the hatchway and looked around, they all fell silent.

"The time-transfer apparatus is set up, and runs successfully, Gregori reports," she said. "I suggest we waste no further time."

The others responded with gestures or murmurs of agreement.

Zina added, "I wish that I could be with you on this mission. But my place is here, in the present. And I know that Professor Ashe will carry out command as I would have done." She nodded at Gordon.

The sudden formality underscored the tension in them all—all except, perhaps, Misha. He only grinned. Ross wondered if that mention of command was a reminder to the Russian time agents, Misha especially.

Misha's grin widened slightly, but all he said was, "Let us go. We want to be there at dawn, do we not?"

As they stepped down the ramp into the soft predawn air, Renfry and Boris appeared behind them. "Good luck," Renfry called in a low voice. "See you soon."

Boris added something in Russian, and Vera turned and gave him a cheery wave. Both Boris and Renry stood on the ramp; their job right now was to guard the ship.

There was little talk as the rest of the team marched through the dark forest to the campsite. The faint light of dawn painted the wild growth around them with splendorous color; the sun was just rising.

When they reached the campsite, Elizaveta, Gregori, and Valentin were waiting.

Zina turned to face the time agents. "I have said what is needful." Her eyes were steady in the pale light. "We will await your signal. Good hunting."

The rest of the science team stepped forward to say quick, subdued good-byes, and then Gordon and Saba walked into the hut.

Moments later the ground seemed to shake slightly: an illusion, Ross knew, a response of the mind to the distorted probability waves sweeping out from the apparatus as it catapulted the two agents into the distant past. Other than the slightly acrid scent of ozone, there was no other indication of the time machine's operation.

Misha and Viktor went next.

Then it was his and Eveleen's turn.

She said nothing, only picked up her pack. Ross did as well. They stepped inside the hut. There were the bars, the familiar but weird opaque material for them to step on. He looked down at his feet, thinking about the many jaunts to the past he'd made. Last time, on Dominium, he and Eveleen had come back as heroes. He hoped this time would be as successful but less traumatic.

The platform suddenly seemed to drop out from under him as a million voices shouted inside his head. White light filled him, squeezing out his identity for a moment that seemed endless . . .

Then reality collapsed back around him, a cocoon of certainty, and he opened his eyes. Next to him, Eveleen's breathing was harsh but controlled. She looked at him, her own eyes dark, her lips pressed together.

"We're here," he murmured, and leaned down to kiss her.

For a moment their lips met. Hers were dry, but warm and sweet.

"One more. For the road."

"For the century," she retorted, and gave him a smacking kiss. Then she said, "They're waiting for us." And she opened the swinging metal door of the shed.

They stepped out.

The grotto was surprisingly like the one in the present, but the smells were different. Ross sniffed, finding the air cleaner somehow. He kept sniffing as they rounded a huge shrub, to find Misha and Viktor gazing silently upward, one face puzzled, the other grim.

The Russians turned to face the new arrivals.

"The First Team had reported no flyers," Misha said without preamble, his gray eyes sardonic.

Why state the obvious? Eveleen looked aside, rolling her eyes. They'd known that since the first briefing.

"Right." Ross decided to humor him. "So your job is to search for them as well as for remains. So?"

"So look, American." He raised his hand skyward.

They were looking east at the rising sun. Against the reddish ball, a flight of huge winged shapes flapped with grace—humanoid shapes.

Flyers.

CHAPTER 12

ROSS SAID, "WHERE'S Gordon? Saba?"

Misha pointed up the hill, which was considerably higher than the one up the timeline. Eveleen couldn't see either time agent, but then she knew she wouldn't. They'd be scanning the area under as much cover as possible.

She turned her eyes eastward, and watched the flyers disappear on the horizon. No one spoke. No one moved until the soundless shock repeated, and Vera and Irina stepped out of the shed containing the time machine. Eveleen's mind shied away reflexively from the knowledge of how fragile their link to their own time was: the shed and the machinery it contained were but projections of the apparatus in their own time.

Gordon and Saba appeared a moment later, walking quickly down the steep hillock.

"The perimeter of the port seems to be roughly the same as up the timeline," Gordon said quickly. "And completely quiet. Nothing in sight except robotic maintenance devices of various sorts, either shutdown or quiescent. As for this area, our guess was right. It's a kind of park. There's nothing but vegetation in view. But I can see buildings over that way." He pointed to the southeast.

"No spaceships at the port?" Ross asked.

"Not that I can see," Gordon replied, hefting his field scanners. He turned to Viktor. "And the landing area is full of cracks and brush— indicating nothing has either come down or taken off for many years. So let's get the second phase of this mission complete."

Viktor gave a quick nod. "We are ready. We return as quick as possible."

He and Misha vanished into the undergrowth.

Eveleen exchanged a glance with Ross. He looked grim, and she didn't blame him. Misha and Viktor's first order had been to check the burial site of the Russian biologist to make sure the bones were still there. They would not disturb the body in any way, merely make certain it was just as it would be found up the timeline in the present—to double-check that time had not been altered at this end of the timeline.

Already they had one anomaly: the flying creatures.

As if his mind had been following the same track, Gordon said, "There might be landing sites elsewhere, on another island. We're hampered by our use of the globe ships and the autopilot wire in that we can't go on a scouting trip around the planet."

"That would explain the flying people," Saba murmured. "We know we'll be finding other species who have already assimilated. It could be that the flyers landed and figured out how to assimilate some time during the century since the First Team appeared here."

Eveleen nodded her agreement. "In a hundred years, it's certainly not unreasonable."

Vera frowned. "This could include other humanoids."

Eveleen thought immediately of the feral human creatures in the present timeline—their tentacled bodies and utter lack of any form of civilization. If the Russians had disappeared, how could those feral humans be their descendants? It would mean that either other human-type beings had appeared—or that she and her team would be trapped in this time and place, and those were their descendants. Not the Russians, but hers. Ross's. Gordon's and Misha's and Vera's and the others'.

She turned to Ross, biting her lip. If . . . if it were true, could she bear to have children?

Don't think about it now, she told herself. Keep your mind on the mission.

"Viktor will be fast," Irina said softly. "He and Mikhail Petrovich have been to the burial site twice since we landed, in the present timeline. They will know where to go."

Mikhail Petrovich. Irina never called Misha by his nickname.

Eveleen pursed her lips. When did the men sleep? She had to admit that Misha, despite his attitudes, was a dedicated agent.

Either dedicated, she temporized—or driven.

"Let's grab some eats, shall we?" Ross suggested. "The tough stuff will be starting soon enough—why start it on an empty stomach?"

Vera grinned, and she and Irina cautiously began exploring in the immediate vicintity. Eveleen watched them go. Their job would be food traders, and as such they had mastered all the details about food experiments recorded by the First Team.

Just as the air was breathable, so was most of the food edible. Within a short time the two women returned laden with fruits and some large nutty gourds that turned out to be delicious. Irina had done a scan on a stream just meters away, and the water had nothing dangerous in it, so they each took a turn drinking after the meal.

They'd just finished when Viktor and Misha returned, appearing silently, without disturbing any of the undergrowth. Eveleen privately awarded them points for superior woodcraft.

"He's there," Misha said, his mouth tight at the corners. "We found the body, buried at the Field-of-Vagabonds. It's been left just as the First Team described."

"Then we will assume the timeline is intact," Gordon replied. "All right, ground rules again. Emergency pulses only, at least until we've had a chance to settle in and know that we're not being overheard. Relay everything through me."

He paused, his blue eyes narrowed. Everyone assented.

Gordon lifted a hand. "Then let's go."

Viktor took over, leading them down a pathway. They all knew, in general, the layout of the Yilayil city as described by the First Team. Viktor had memorized every bit of data available—and he would be mapping the areas that the First Team had not reported on, as he and Misha made their methodical search for forensic evidence of the other First Team members.

"The only thing that gives me hope," Ross murmured to Eveleen as they marched single file through the thick jungle undergrowth, "is that the abrupt disappearance of the First Team might just mean that we did rescue them."

Eveleen said, "Except why don't we find anything left by our future selves, to tell us how to do it? I know I'd do that for myself, if I could. There are no signs of any of us—that we've found."

"Not up the timeline, but there might be here. Right?" Ross asked.

"But if there is, we'd have to have left it from the past, not here— because we just got here. And the apparatus doesn't permit microjumps, so we can assume we don't skip back to this day and hide out to leave us little notes to wherever we're going now."

"Unh," Ross grunted, shaking his head. "This time stuff really makes my brain ache."

On the other side of Ross, Saba was smiling. "It's almost easier to discuss in Yilayil. I need to untangle those odd tense constructions."

"Doesn't matter," Ashe said tersely. "From now on, if you speak, speak Yilayil," he ordered. And he added a quick comment in that language that Eveleen translated to herself; leaving out the identifiers and the false origin they'd developed from the First Team's personae, it meant: *We are on their ground, we do as they do.*

No further reminder of the fate of the Russian biologist needed to be made.

Eveleen toiled along, her knapsack on her back. The humid air made her feel damp and hot before long, and the scents of the millions of herbs and blossoms around them were overpowering. She knew they'd eventually be coming to a cleared area; maybe her sinuses would unclog.

As she walked, she heard Saba half suppress a sneeze, followed almost immediately by Irina. Viktor and Gordon began breathing through their mouths. But no one spoke again as they kept walking.

Once they stopped. Viktor lifted a hand, then dashed down the trail aways, followed by Misha. Eveleen watched them move silently and swiftly. She thought she heard a low thrumming, but it was soon gone, and she wondered if it was just the pounding of her own heartbeat in her skull.

Then Misha and Viktor reappeared, and waved them on.

They had to emerge from the jungle within the borders for the foreign enclaves, or *Nurayil*. Yilayil meant "People of the People"; this designation was only for the nocturnal weasel folk. All other races were Nurayil—"People of the Stars."

They descended a hill, and Eveleen glimpsed buildings through the thinning trees.

At once they halted, and Misha and Viktor withdrew into the trees. Ashe nodded at Eveleen, Ross, and Saba, and the four started down the trail, Eveleen walking with Ross, and the other two just behind.

Eveleen felt her palms sweating. She knew her story, she felt comfortable in the simple forms of the question-rituals, but still, her adrenaline was spiking.

A series of round, low buildings were the first things they saw. Each had a round opening, into which beings of several kinds moved in and out. Eveleen felt slightly reassured when she saw those who met one another on the trail make the expected ritual gestures before one or the other stepped aside. The heavy air did not carry the sounds of the ritual responses, at least not at first. As they neared the first building, she could hear the tweets, whistles, and drones of many beings communicating.

It was all much quicker and noisier than she had ever imagined. She saw Ross staring around, his forehead tense. Ashe focused directly ahead of him; Saba, however, gazed around, her eyes narrowed.

Almost at once they encountered three short, heavy-looking bipeds with tough, bumpy hides. Their whistles were so high and quick Eveleen almost couldn't follow, but she recognized familiar notes among them.

Saba whistled in return, and stepped aside. The other three followed. The beings continued on their way without another glance.

Beside Eveleen, Ross let out a long, slow sigh.

It worked! It worked! Etiquette declared that the stranger defer to all; when one met acquaintances, the one who performed a service the more recently took precedence.

If they just deferred to everyone, at least now, they'd manage.

Four buildings in, they found the Transport Center, and Ashe gave Eveleen and Ross a quick nod.

"Here we go," Ross murmured under his breath.

Eveleen watched Ashe and Saba move on. They were going to try to get to the House of Knowledge, and at least see it, even if they couldn't get Saba in as a worker right away. Some time spent in its proximity ought to provide a sense of what was going on there.

In the meantime, Ross and Eveleen had to establish themselves as transportation workers. In private they'd called themselves cabbies, as they memorized the data provided by the First Team on the rail-skimmers the Yilayil and Nurayil used for transport.

The big building was full of beings, the warm, heavy air shrill with whistling, the droning sounding like an orchestra of out-of-tune bag-pipes. Ross and Eveleen made their way to one side, where functionaries sat at a complicated console. Eveleen felt Ross walking tensely at her side, as he scanned the crowds for the familiar shapes of Baldies. Eveleen did not see anyone that remotely matched that description. She did see at the console two of the tall, spidery beings that the First Team had identified as being involved in all aspects of Nurayil tech.

They made their way up the line, and found themselves abruptly addressed not by the spidery beings, but by a tall, imposing creature with six arms. Related to the weasel folk?

Eveleen desperately banished speculation as the being addressed them: "I, Fargag of Nurayil Transport, this morning see strangers here?"

Eveleen wet her lips, and responded with slow care, "I, Eveleen of Fire Mountain Enclave, come to learn ti[*trill*]kee and to work as I learn."

Fargag fired at them a question of challenge: "Fire Mountain Enclave—unknown to me!"

"I, Ross of Fire Mountain, say that our Enclave is known to us," Ross whistled. "Known many generations to us, but we now travel to learn ti[*trill*]kee."

Fargag whistled a liquid phrase that made Eveleen's knees tremble with relief. It was a kind of cautious acceptance of temporary status.

Beings who were anxious to learn "proper deportment" (ti[*trill*]kee) were provisionally accepted. At least, so it seemed, Eveleen thought. She could never forget that the First Team had been provisionally accepted—but they had disappeared.

Fargag instructed them to pass on to Virigu, one of the spidery beings.

They deferred as Fargag passed to the next newcomers, and Eveleen heard his challenging whistle/drone as they waited to address Virigu.

Within a short time they were tested in maintenance of the transport vehicles. They both had studied until they knew the mechanics of the rail-skimmers in their sleep; in fact, Eveleen reflected, as she swiftly disassembled, cleaned, then assembled a series of parts, that she had done this several times during her strange jumble of dreams aboard the globe ship.

They were accepted as maintenance workers—which meant pressing their palm on a square silver measure—and when questioned about their domicile, their second delicate moment came. They admitted that no one from Fire Mountain Enclave was currently in residence among the Nurayil, but they wished to establish a domicile, and once again they were accepted at face value. Virigu put them to work at once, for the turnover was apparently high at this job.

The day's work lasted until the light outside began to fade. At that time, all Nurayil but those formally accepted for service to the Yilayil were expected to withdraw to their domiciles.

Ross and Eveleen followed a number of other beings who didn't have family or clan domiciles. The housing for all the unconnected beings was inconveniently located at the far edge of the Nurayil enclave, but Eveleen and Ross were grateful that it was still there at all. They found that things had changed little in the hundred years since the First Team discovered the place—small round chambers, like cells in a beehive, lined a large round building that Ross and Ashe had found empty and hollow in the present timeline.

No one organized it; Eveleen and Ross poked their heads in at the doors of any unmarked or open rooms as they wound their way slowly up a ramp, until at last they found one—an inner cell, with no window—that had apparently been recently vacated.

No belongings were in it, and the little identity console on the opposite wall from the access gleamed purple, indicating that no one currently claimed the place.

In haste Ross slapped his palm on the metal plate below the light, and Eveleen followed suit, for they could hear feet shuffling out in the corridor, and it was possible that some tired, grumpy being might want to try to claim their place if they weren't formally "in." No one protected Nurayil, unless their families or clans did. This meant that those without either were at the bottom of all hierarchies, and must look out for themselves.

The light gleamed yellow—it was theirs.

Ross hit the door control, and the door slid shut. They were alone.

Eveleen looked around. The cell was just that, smaller even than the cabins aboard the globe ship. A storage compartment opened next to the door, and she shoved her knapsack into it. There were no furnishings; they'd have to scout those out. At least the flooring had some give, and Eveleen felt tired enough to sleep on brick. But she made herself look in the little alcove in one corner of the room. There was a waste recycle unit, and next to it an adjustable frame that vibrated slightly; it was cleaning the air that moved through it. Remembering the instructions from the First Team, she activated it, took off her clothes, then stepped through. It felt a little like pushing one's way through some kind of invisible gelatinous mass, but when she stepped out the other side, all the grit and dead skin was gone from her body. It wasn't refreshing like a good hot shower, or even like the sonic bath on the globe ship, but she did feel clean.

She passed her clothes through the field, and watched the grime in them patter down to the gutter at the bottom of the frame, and slurp away to the recycler.

Dressed again, and feeling slightly better, she went out to find Ross digging in his pack.

"Let's get the sticker on the door," Ross said.

"Oh. Right. Here, I'll do it." Eveleen held out her hand.

Ross handed her a plastic-backed sticker that they'd brought from Earth. The cells of the domicile were all marked in some way by their owners, for there was no other way to tell them apart, unless you counted—and they were at sixty or seventy cells up the ramp.

Irina and Vera and the others also had stickers; this was the only way they'd be able to find one another at night, at least until they had assimilated and could trust using the radios freely.

Eveleen opened the door, affixed the sticker to the outside of it, and closed it again. When she turned around, Ross had gone into the fresher alcove. She squatted down to dig in his pack for food, but before her hand closed on a container a soft tapping came at the door: three short, three long.

She bounced up and hit the control. Vera stood out in the hall, looking tired and sweaty but triumphant.

"Come in," Eveleen said. "Have you found a room yet?"

"Irina is there. She will be here in a moment." The redhead sat down cross-legged, and pulled a substantial packet from her knapsack. "So! We are successful—we are now food gatherers. Here is a meal!" She unwrapped her packet with a triumphant air. "Is good, all of it," she added.

"Shall we divide it into six portions?"

Vera shook her head. "We ate. Save out four only."

Eveleen said, "Have you seen Gordon and Saba?"

Vera shook her head just as another tapping came at the door, the same code.

Ross opened it, and Irina walked in, graceful and quiet as always. She frowned slightly. "No Gordon? Saba?" she asked directly. "It is very dark without."

Ross looked grim, and Eveleen felt her adrenaline spiking once again. No one was supposed to be out at night but the Yilayil and those who had gained their sanction. It had been dangerous a hundred years before, and there was no evidence that it was any safer now.

"Maybe we'd better wait on the food," Ross said, unclipping his radio transmitter from his belt. "I'll zap them once, and see if we get an answer." He looked around.

Eveleen and the two Russians all nodded agreement.

Part of Zina's orders had been to keep actual communications to a minimum, until they knew that it was safe. Various sonic codes were to be used, and those sparingly.

Ross tapped out the "Check in!" code, then sat down—and a tapping came at the door, the usual pattern, but somehow more urgent.

Ross moved fast, opening the door.

Gordon stood there alone, his face tired and grim.

"Saba?" Eveleen asked. "Don't tell me they already took her in?"

Gordon did not speak until the door was shut behind him. "As soon as we crossed into the zone of the House of Knowledge, I knew something was wrong. Everyone we met ignored me, nor did they challenge Saba. They didn't even address her."

"What?" Irina asked. "No questions? No demands for proper Nurayil deference?"

"What happened?" Eveleen began.

Gordon turned to her. "As soon as we got there, she was taken right in, and I was left outside staring at faces carved on giant poles—twenty feet high at least. A different face on each, from various races."

He paused.

"Is this bad?" Vera prompted.

"I don't know," Gordon replied. "I can only tell you this: the one at the very front was absolutely, obviously Saba."

CHAPTER 13

ROSS HAD SEEN that expression on Gordon's face before—when Travis Fox was finally listed officially as "missing in action," and given up by the officials at the Project.

"You tried her on the transmitter?" Ross asked, indicating his belt com.

"I pulsed her," Gordon said. "She did pulse me back. But when I tried voice, all I got was noise. There must be some kind of sophisticated digital jammer operating, forbidding communication above a certain level of complexity."

Ross said nothing for a moment, considering the level of technology needed to jam a spread-spectrum com system, something impossible to Terran science.

"A statue of Saba . . . in *this* time," Eveleen said slowly.

Ross turned to his wife, who paced back and forth along the wall of the tiny room. She looked up. "It must mean that we're going to be making another jump, only farther back."

"To when First Team disappears," Vera said, nodding. "We were all hoping we'd be going back to rescue them, weren't we?"

"If it is safe to do so," Irina said in her precise voice. "We do not go back until we are assured that it will not destroy the timeline."

"Well, I hope to," Eveleen said, then grimaced. "That is, to make it plain, I hope that it transpires that we've already been back there and rescued them and that's why they disappeared. Does that make sense?" She made a face, rubbing her forehead. "Sheesh! I do hate thinking in possible timelines, it scrambles my brain!"

Ross nodded, appreciating his wife's attempt to lighten the tension, but Gordon's expression did not change.

"We're not going backward or forward in time without Saba," Gordon said. "I won't leave her in there."

"You can't get in?" Ross asked.

"Tried." Gordon shook his head. "Tried offers, questions, and even a challenge—and it almost got me lynched. So I beat a retreat, figuring if I pushed it any harder, it might only jeopardize Saba. Came back here, found a room at the top of this Nurayil dorm. It's a long walk up the ramp, but from its window I can see the House of Knowledge."

"Now that was a good idea," Ross said, his mind rapidly developing—and then discarding—possible plans. They simply didn't know enough. But one thing was for certain: being able to watch the House of Knowledge had to be an advantage. "Didn't you and Saba work out some codes on the com, for just in case?"

"We did," Gordon said. "Mostly voice codes, but some pulse ones as well."

Irina sat silently, frowning, her mouth in a straight line. Next to her, Vera smiled and shook her curly head. "It might not be so bad come morning. We know she's alive, at least."

Gordon nodded slowly. "We'll give it a few days. Say, a week, unless there's an emergency. Settle in, gather data. Then meet—all of us, including Misha and Viktor, if we can get them—to review our strategy."

"Sounds like a plan," Ross said. "Come on, let's chow down. No one can rest, or think, with an empty gut. And I don't know about you, but we put in a day of hard work."

He pushed a portion of the food toward Gordon, and was relieved when the professor took it and began methodically to eat.

Eveleen gave them a cheery smile. "Hard labor indeed. You can tell those rail-skimmers are old. Unless today was a real gift from Murphy, they must break down all the time."

Gordon swung his head toward the Russian women. "And you?"

"We are now gatherers," Irina said. "It appears that eating establishments will hire on their preferred gatherers, and one can then get prepared food as well as work credit."

Vera said, "We'll find out which places make the sorts of things we can eat, and zero in on them. No one has noticed our field analyzers, and we're going to be careful to do it when no one else is around. In the meantime, we walk about with our gatherers' tools and listen. A few challenges, but no one took any interest in beings from Fire Mountain Enclave."

"None in us either," Eveleen said.

"Good." Gordon finished his share and got to his feet. "Let's meet tomorrow night and compare notes."

Everyone agreed, and very soon Gordon and the Russians departed, leaving Ross and Eveleen together in the tiny cell.

They looked at each other.

"Alone at last," she said with a tired grin as she held her arms out. "It's not the Yilayil honeymoon suite—"

"Privacy," Ross murmured into her soft hair, "ranks it up there over any luxury penthouse on Earth."

"Privacy," Eveleen said, laughing.

COLD SHOCK NUMBED Saba as she thought of those tall, carved wood statues before the House of Knowledge—and her face on the foremost one.

"This means I've been here."

It was the only possible explanation. She sat in the room that the guardians of the House of Knowledge had brought her to, trying to clear her mind and plan. Except her mind refused to work. So she looked around. The walls were plain, except for paintings that looked very old; she sat on a low couch made of some woven material that felt like flax.

How long had she been here? She glanced at her chrono. An hour and a half.

She sat back, closing her eyes—but then the door opened, one of the green beings, who seemed to be the guardians of the House, entered and beckoned to her.

She said nothing as she rose and walked out of the room.

Fast Yilayil voices exchanged ritual greetings around her—vying, apparently, for the honor of escorting her inside. She knew she ought to be listening, and she caught a few words. Someone trilled something about making a place in readiness, but she lost track of the rest of the statement. Her mind could not veer from that image of her own face, in a time when she supposedly had never been.

When? What had happened?

Someone addressed her: "Saba-music-maker of Far Star is welcome at last to the Yil."

To "the people." Not to any specific ones—Nurayil or Yilayil. They definitely knew who she was. That meant she had already accomplished something.

The first realization banished that earlier image of women from some distant planet that happened to resemble her. The second realization made her heart pound.

If I have been here, she thought, then I know I will have left myself some kind of message. I know it as well as I know myself. Somehow, I must find it, so that I can accomplish what must be done, and protect the integrity of time.

So deciding, she felt inner conviction at last, and with it the ability to think—to assess.

She turned her attention to her surroundings.

Cool, dry air was her first awareness. The second was the glare-free light, from some hidden source. The walls were plain, as had been that parlor to which she'd initially been brought.

Before her stood two robed beings, one tall and spidery, the other feline, with sleek black fur everywhere except the face. The latter spoke.

"We, Rilla and Virigu, teachers of the House of Knowledge, now welcome Saba of the Far Star. We are teachers of deportment."

Saba knew the response to that. "I, Saba of the Far Star, am ready to learn deportment." If nothing else, this would buy her time.

"Saba now come with us." Rilla's voice was scratchy, her whistles weak, but she was understandable.

The Virigu had not yet spoken. Saba gave the spidery being a glance, remembering what the First Team had said about these creatures; they all bore the name Virigu, and they were the highest-ranking Nurayil in that they were involved with all levels of technology.

Saba was led up a curving ramp. "We are females," Rilla went on. "We wear robes which symbolize our dedication to Knowledge."

Saba said nothing. She felt her belt communicator buzzing against her hip, but she did not move her hands to it to acknowledge Gordon's call, not with these two beings watching her. Though so far Rilla and Virigu had behaved with respect, the fact that she had been taken here without being asked indicated she might in fact be in danger.

"We protect you," Virigu trilled, an uncanny parallel to Saba's thoughts. "We teach you."

They paused at a landing, and Saba paused as well. She glanced down, saw a splendid mosaic far below, on the ground floor. It depicted the night sky, and constellations not even remotely familiar.

Rilla moved again, leading the way. Saba was distracted momentarily by the swaying of a long, luxurious black tail among the draperies of Rilla's robe.

They paused before a door. Saba noted that it was alone on a corridor, with a blank wall adjacent. Virigu pointed to her hand with a long, chitinous digit. She then indicated a silver plate next to the door, and Saba pressed her hand against it.

A series of tiny lights rippled, and the door slid open.

All three passed inside a small room furnished with a low couch. On one wall faded paintings made a complicated scene; on the other lines promised some kind of furnishings now folded away.

"You domicile here," Rilla said. She touched a control panel on the blank wall, and a kind of storage enclosure slid out. Saba saw what looked like a stepladder of boxes, each with a tiny light gleaming above a control button at one corner. "Robes," Rilla added, pressing the control on the topmost box. It folded silently out, showing two of the flaxen robes neatly folded.

Saba nodded, unmoving. She was not going to change in front of these others unless she could not avoid it. She did not want to risk exposing, and then losing, her belt com, which she wore inside her overalls.

"We leave, you come to us for eat, we begin to learn," Rilla said, and with a swish of robes, the two left.

Before she did anything, Saba looked around the room. Was she being monitored? She realized that there was nothing obvious—nothing she could identify, so she might as well dismiss that worry for now.

Instead, she explored the room, first touching the controls on each of the storage boxes. Some of the implements she could only guess at; others seemed to be universal—a hairbrush. A toothbrush, though shaped differently. There was a box with a plate and Yilayil instructions. She puzzled out the script, then took off her boot and placed her foot on it. Lights rippled, and a moment later a slipper appeared from a slot in the back of the box, twin in color and material to those she'd seen on Rilla's feet.

She pressed the master control and the boxes all folded neatly away into the wall, leaving only faint lines to indicate where they were. She moved to a control near the corner; this one seemed to control something that extended from floor to ceiling.

She positioned herself directly before the control, touched it, and this time the wall slid back and a tiny alcove appeared, encompassing the corner of the room. She saw a recycle unit, a large frame that reminded her somewhat of the globe ship's sonic "shower," and a sink with a water faucet.

When that slid away, she tried the last control, and found herself with a desk and wall monitor. The keypads were utterly different than Terran keyboards.

But it was unmistakably a computer. Was it her own? Was there protected space on it? This would take exploring—the entire room required careful examination. She knew that if she had any opportunity whatsoever, she would leave herself some kind of message, no matter how brief or crude. Something.

But that would have to wait. They apparently expected her to rejoin them in the House.

First she took out her belt com, and tried to raise Ashe. Nothing but static—inconvenient, but not unexpected. She tried the pulse—and a few moments later she got a return pulse.

So. She tapped out the code for "I'm well" and "I'm investigating." A moment later she got the expected answer: "I received your message,"

Communication! For a moment she felt a strong urge to sit down and fumble her way through the other codes they'd developed—except she still did not know who might be listening, by whatever means. The whole idea behind the codes was quick exchanges, fast enough not to trip some kind of high-tech monitoring system.

Likewise she did not know how long Rilla and Virigu would wait for her without coming back to investigate.

So she changed into the robe, used the alcove to freshen up, and passed her clothing through the "shower" experimentally. It seemed to work on clothes as well as on people. She checked the water with a tool that Zina had issued to each team member; it registered as pure H_2O. She tasted a sip from a cup that she found waiting—handleless, but unmistakably a drinking cup—and found that the water reminded her of pure, almost tasteless distilled water.

Did all the beings here, then, need light, water, and . . .

And harmony?

It was time to find out.

She dressed again in her overalls, but put one of the robes on over them. Her belt com went right back on her belt under the robe, but she stowed her pack—with her laptop—in the lowest of the closet boxes, as she'd mentally named them.

Then it was time to go to work.

CHAPTER 14

THE NEXT FEW days were so much alike that they later blurred in memory.

Each morning Ross and Eveleen left their little cell and walked across the Nurayil district of the port city. Sometime during that first night, a heavy cloud bank had moved in, and a light but steady rain began to fall—without, apparently, surcease.

Ross felt at first that this was a blessing. The rain cooled the humid air slightly, but more importantly it drenched the overpowering scents emanating from the vast jungle bordering the Nurayil area. His sinuses cleared; the heavy smell of wet pavement was preferable to the millions of sweet perfumes.

At the Transport facility, he and Eveleen worked hard, almost continually, alongside numerous other beings descended from a variety of races. Virigu seldom spoke to anyone, but watched continually. Some beings did very little, and no one said anything. Ross and Eveleen kept at their jobs—and by the second day, they saw that good workers would be promoted to other sections.

Their goal was to pilot the rail-skimmers so that they could enable the team to be able to move about undetected, should movement be needed. If they could only become drivers through promotion, then they would continue to work hard.

Most of their fellow workers kept to themselves, or stayed strictly with those of their own kind, but not all. At the one break officially designated, at midday, there was some chatter among a few beings—while little gray Moova circulated through with vending carts, selling an astonishing variety of foods.

Ross noted that the Moova had palm plates on their vending machines: there did not seem to be any kind of coinage or money in other forms. Just the unknown credit as registered by the palm plates.

The mealtime conversation was seldom interesting, but it was good practice in following the language—especially as used by a variety of beings with different types of mouths and vocal structures. Some of the whistles were thin and piercing, others curiously liquid. One set of beings sounded like oboes; lacking a name for them, Eveleen and Ross in private referred to them as the music people.

They both noticed that even among those beings who stayed close to their own kind, no one spoke anything but Yilayil. Ross and Eveleen were careful to do the same, if there was any remote chance of being overheard. It was sometimes frustrating, but at least he was with Eveleen, whose spirits were irrepressibly high. She attacked the work with vigor and interest, and she seemed to regard the world without fear.

As Ross once had. He tried to regain that carefree sense of adventure, but Eveleen's presence triggered that protective instinct. He was always on the watch for danger—something he was careful to hide.

Each evening, Irina, Vera, and Gordon joined them in Ross and Eveleen's room—theirs being the first one of the Terrans along that ramp.

At first, no one had much of anything to report. Gordon had exchanged some brief communications with Saba, who—not surprisingly—seemed to be "learning deportment" as well. He had not heard from Misha and his partner.

The two Russian women were at least as busy as Ross and Eveleen at their jobs. The rest of their time they spent trying to listen to the conversations around them, without trespassing against "proper deportment." Vera did her best to get the beings she encountered talking; Irina listened, and took copious notes on her laptop. She did that at the nightly sessions as well, something that bothered Ross slightly at first, but then he decided it was her way of approaching her own part of the mission, and so he tuned her out. Eveleen didn't seem to mind. She kept up her martial-arts practice every night, whether the others were around or not.

"They all talk so fast," Ross said one night. "And there's so much we hadn't been able to learn about this language. We're still having a tough time at Transport."

"It reminds me of English lessons," Vera said with a grin. "Four years in school, and I thought I was so good with this tongue. But then my schoolmates and I were taken on a trip to England, and—ha! Everyone talked so quick, and with slang, it made my head spin! So much I found that I didn't know."

"A good time, then, to compare notes," Gordon put in. "Here is a challenge I heard today between the guardians of the House of Knowledge and a pair of those gray-skinned beings who look a little like tree stumps with extra eyes—"

"Moova," Irina said. "We found out today. The Moova all take a very great interest in foods."

"Moova," Gordon repeated. "I'll remember. Here's the exchange."

And he whistle/droned, in quick fashion, a long pattern to which they all listened intently.

"What's that tense?" Vera asked. " 'Time-as-was . . .' "

"Sounds like a mixture of time-as-was/to come."

"Conditional?" Ross asked, trying to concentrate.

"No." Gordon shook his head. "Conditional goes like this—" He demonstrated, and Ross remembered the lesson.

"Then what is this new tense?" Irina asked. "Or is it merely some kind of shortcut?"

"We'll have to be on the listen for more of these shortcuts," Eveleen suggested in a grim voice as she moved through a kata. "In case they have a third meaning that the First Team never caught onto."

"Hmmm." Gordon frowned, and Irina looked up, her eyes narrowed.

After they'd thoroughly discussed possible meanings for all the words in the exchange, the group parted to sleep. Ross found himself reluctant to see them go.

As soon as the door was shut, Eveleen yawned, then said, "Weird, how isolation will make a small society into a very intense society."

"What do you mean?" Ross pulled out their single furnishing, gotten the day before. It was a kind of futon that functioned as a couch and as a sleeping mat. The air never seemed to get cool, so they hadn't any need of blankets. At least the sonic shower kept the air filtered.

"Well, we all know how—if one were to try to define a social butterfly—Gordon would be the last person ever named. Irina and Vera are nice, but I never would have picked them as buddies. Yet I look forward all day to seeing them, and I find every word they say interesting. Then, when the evening ends, I'm sorry to see them go. Was it the same when you were stuck in the past with other men, or is this a female thing?"

"No, it was more or less the same," Ross admitted. "Travis, Gordon, Renfry, and I talked a lot about home when we first came here. Those cubes that showed what you valued most had to be hidden for a while, there—it hurt too much to look at them, but we couldn't stay away."

Eveleen nodded slowly. "That was real isolation," she said with sympathy. "You four didn't have any idea if you'd ever go home again."

"Exactly. But it was the same on Earth. I remember hunkering around the fire with some of the other time agents, back in prehistoric times. There was a sense of companionship, though I don't think any of us would have named ourselves particularly social men."

"It's this weird isolation within a crowd. I felt a bit like that when I went with my high school team to Japan to attend a special martial-arts camp," Eveleen admitted, yawning again. "Though there, everyone I encountered was really nice, but I couldn't speak the language, and not everyone spoke English."

"At least you were all humans," Ross commented.

Eveleen grinned. "Yes. At least we were all humans. Here, they don't care, which is a good thing, since too much notice might be dangerous. I can't get it out of my head. Though we're being so careful to follow all the rules reported by the First Team, we still don't know which rule they broke—what caused their disappearance."

"It's been on my mind as well," Ross admitted, feeling that instinct flare again. But he repressed it, just as he repressed the urge to sneak out of the Nurayil dorm and nose around—see just what it was the mysterious Yilayil didn't want the underlings seeing.

This urge hadn't been so bad the first night or so. Then, everything was so new, and he was tired and ready for sleep as soon as the nightly talk session was over. But now, especially when there was no kind of distraction in the little cell—no books, television, music, even—he wished to be out exploring. If he were alone . . .

No. Don't even think that. Not for a moment, he told himself.

He turned to look at his wife, who was seated on the ground, working a complicated yoga step, her face serene. She was content, and he ought to be happy it was so.

As for exploring, that was Misha's job. And if Ross had that guy figured right, he wouldn't appreciate anyone horning in on his turf.

"Ross?"

He looked up, saw Eveleen watching him.

"Anything wrong?" she asked.

"No," he said. "Just thinking—about the mission. You know, those other races. That kind of thing. As for our not being noticed, I'm just as happy to be ignored."

Eveleen smiled, shrugged, and went back to her yoga.

CHAPTER 15

THE VERY NEXT morning the Transport Maintenance Virigu assigned Ross and Eveleen to a new area of the maintenance facility. Virigu seemed to assume that they worked as a pair—an impression that they did nothing to dispel.

They were greeted by a small scaled being who had hands and tentacles, again reminding them of the modern-day savage humanoids. Otherwise there was no resemblance; the creature had a beaklike snout, deepset eyes, and a tail.

"I, Bock of Nurayil Transport Design, this day must accept two Nurayil of unknown enclave and ability. Virigu of Nurayil Transport maligns the Jecc of Harbeast Teeth Islands!"

As Bock spoke, several more Jecc gathered round, their tails twitching. Ross looked them over, noted that they all wore identical garments rather like overalls, but with no pockets. The arms and tentacles were free; front flap of the garments covered the creatures' bulky midsections.

"I, Ross of Fire Mountain Enclave, this day am told by Virigu that our job is here, and so it is," Ross hum/whistled. Annoyance sharpened his tones, but he didn't think that so bad a thing—this groundless challenge was too blatant.

Chirps and whistles went up from all the assembled Jecc. Two or three of them crowded close to Ross; one nudged Eveleen, and she almost stumbled. But she recovered her step, planted her feet, and the next push caused the small creature to squeak and back up a step or two, to the dismay of the others pressing in. Eveleen didn't budge.

Bock riposted with a rapid series of whistle/drones, meaning: "We'll test your knowledge, interloper."

And Ross fired right back the equivalent of: "Be my guest."

The rest of the day, the Jecc did just that. They pestered Ross and Eveleen constantly with questions, demanding to know if they were aware of the functions of various rail-skimmer parts.

The department, Ross discovered, was intended to repair salvaged parts of old rail-skimmers so that new ones could be assembled. The department was not comprised entirely of Jecc, but they were the majority, and they kept Ross and Eveleen away from the others.

Ross had to bite down hard on his temper at least twenty times that day. Each time some Jecc cruised by and pinched a part he was reaching for, or knocked into him from behind just as he was assembling a delicate piece, he was ready to haul off and smack the little beggars across the room.

But he looked over at Eveleen, who was getting the same treatment. Each time she calmly picked up her pieces—taking care that they stayed right on her, or under a knee—and continued as though nothing had interrupted her.

Parts salvaged from rail-skimmers deemed unusable were available to all, but for some reason the Jecc seemed to like to take parts already selected—by someone else. Ross's temper abated just slightly when he saw while walking across the floor to get more parts that they also did this to each other.

One Jecc snagged a connector, stashed it underneath the front flap of its coverall in a movement so quick it was almost a blur. Then the Jecc scuttled away noiselessly, just as the one who'd been robbed started groping around for the connector. That Jecc jerked its head this way and that in weird birdlike movements, whistling a high tweeting sound that Ross couldn't interpret.

At the day's end, Ross felt the grip of tension on his neck as he and Eveleen walked out of the building. Hard rain drummed on the ground and splashed in gouting falls at corners and overhangs. A rail-skimmer whirred by, and Ross looked at it with regret; they had not worked enough, apparently, to earn credit for that kind of luxury. So far the futon, their lunches, and their housing took up their days' accumulated credit, according to the console on the wall of their cell.

Neither spoke until they were safely in their cell. Then Ross went to the wall console and touched the plate. Above it, the flat screen lit with several buttons. Below that was a number, in Yilayil script: they had apparently moved into the black again, though just barely.

"Strange," Eveleen said, looking tiredly at the console as she swung her arms back and forth to work out kinks from her muscles. "We never agreed to a pay rate, or to rent for this place. How does anyone get ahead? Is everything at Virigu's discretion, or is there some big boss over Virigu who sets the prices on work and goods?"

"Maybe we'll find out," Ross said. "Me, I just wish we could kick back with a pot of fresh-brewed coffee, a newspaper—in English—and maybe a good action flick."

"While you're at it, let's have a Jacuzzi and a stereo," Eveleen added, laughing.

Tapping at the door caused them both to fall silent. It was the familiar pattern, and something about the quick sound made Ross think immediately of Gordon.

A moment later he saw he was right. "Saba?" Ross asked as soon as the door was closed.

Gordon shook his head, his blue eyes tired but alert. "Same. She's alive, has a room of her own, and her day is filled with deportment lessons. Nothing more yet—all we have are our codes." His hair was dotted with droplets, indicating he'd just come from outside.

"How's the delivery boy business?" Ross asked as Gordon hunkered down on the floor with his back to a wall.

Eveleen continued doing her kata warm-ups.

Ashe shrugged. "I'm not that high yet. Until I either come up with some prestigious favor I can do for someone, or some seniority, I'm still hauling trash to the recycler."

Ross jerked his thumb over his shoulder at the wall console. "Your pay rate as lousy as ours?"

"I have the same furniture," Gordon said, indicating the futon. "I calculate I owe another day's pay on it."

"How does anyone else without family or connections manage to eat?" Eveleen asked, her voice only slightly husky as her arms arced and snapped through a complicated exercise.

"Probably the same way we do: they scrounge, they get or make friends, they go into debt to someone a little higher," Gordon said. "The current society is not designed to easily accommodate newcomers."

"Conformity," Eveleen said, and finished up her kata with a "Whoosh! This humidity is tough to work in."

"Probably why the Yilayil built underground," Ashe commented. "Think of it—furred beings. Heavy fur like those creatures we saw up the timeline, anyway, would have evolved in cold weather, one would think." He got to his feet and moved to the console. "But you're right, Eveleen. This culture selects for conformity, and does its best to guarantee it. Yet the technical systems all over this city"—he tapped the little wall console with a finger—"are predicated on the fact that each individual is unique."

Ross grunted. "Hadn't thought about that, but of course you're right."

Ashe gave a nod. "Whether by finger, tentacle, tongue, or whatever means one wishes to be identified, apparently one of the few things these beings have in common with us is this one fact: we are all individuals, differing subtly from every other being, or this kind of measure would not work."

Ross looked up at the console, and nodded. It was true. He hadn't been asked his name, or age, or anything else; he was registered in some unknown computer somewhere just by his palm print. And wherever he went in the starport city, if he wished to buy something, or use a transport, or change his residence, he would have to press his hand on a similar silver plate.

"It's also a damn good way to keep track of people," Ross pointed out, wondering if the system had some sinister use.

Eveleen nodded. "I was thinking about that today. Misha and Viktor are existing outside this mysterious registry—but that's because they are not here in the city. How long would they make it in this city without having to sign in? Are some beings trying to exist outside the system in a similar way?"

"And for what reason?" Gordon asked. "We can't be the only ones here with plans of our own."

"Now that's a grim thought," Ross said, just as tapping sounded at the door again, and he went to let in the Russian women.

"News about Saba?" Irina asked, her dark eyes narrowed, as soon as she entered.

"No change," Ashe replied.

Irina grunted a response in Russian, which Ross had learned meant, more or less, *Is good enough for now*. Then she said in English, "She is alive. This bodes well."

"Anything new to report?" Gordon asked them.

"The pollen count is way up," Vera said. "This despite the rain."

Irina sat down, graceful and neat as always. "Nothing new for me to report."

Ross said, "You two pick up anything about some feisty little guys called Jecc?"

Vera and Irina exchanged grimaces.

"Uh oh," Eveleen said, grinning wryly. "Bad news on the horizon, right?"

Vera snorted. "All we know is that they just love to surround a person and rob you blind, unless you can get to a group bigger and tougher than they are."

"They seem to think it a game," Irina added as she passed around some fresh tubers and another dish that looked like chopped carrots, but tasted more like peppered zucchini. "Luckily they tweet these weird little songs when they run about in packs, so you can hear them coming. The first couple times, when we didn't know what the sound was, we got pretty much everything taken. Everything small—luckily none of our important equipment, which we keep zipped up."

"But now we hear that noise and we run like rabbits," Vera put in. "We asked one of the Moova about them, and found out their name—and that everyone avoids them. They don't like anyone—yet they seem to be pretending to learn deportment. I take it you have also encountered the Jecc?"

"They run the department we got assigned to today," Eveleen said. "And if we want to get us a transport vehicle, we're going to have to figure out a way around them."

Gordon said musingly, "Pretending to learn deportment . . . Interesting. Interesting," he repeated, tapping absently at the side of his dish. "You'd think something would happen to them if they are that antisocial. That behavior pattern doesn't fit the conformity paradigm, does it?"

"Not the way I see it," Ross said, setting aside his dish. He felt full—and the food didn't taste bad—but the craving was so strong for a good cup of coffee and something *normal* to eat. He ignored it impatiently, focusing on the problem. "You know what this smells like? Politics. Of some sort. And I am here to tell you I really, really hate that stink."

"Politics would be a problem," Gordon conceded. "At least insofar as we might cross some powermonger or other all unawares." He turned to the Russian women.

"Yes," Vera said. "I know what comes next: more listening. We are doing what we can."

Gordon said, "I know. But the more we can find out, the quicker we can act. I'm limited in what I have access to—but I feel I have to stay close to the House of Knowledge, until I know for certain that Saba is not in danger."

"Right," Eveleen said. "Well, we'll do our bit. We'll work like doggies, and see if those Jecc will back down. We simply have to get a rail-skimmer."

"I suppose there is no opportunity to conceal the parts, build one, and conceal that?" Irina asked. She smiled slightly. "This is what Mikhail Petrovich would do."

Ross hid his annoyance at the mention of the guy's name—and the implication that he wasn't as innovative, if not as smart. "Everything is registered, locked down, and otherwise accounted for—" he began, and then he frowned. "No, that's not really an option. We might manage to build one, but since they follow buried rails, it would have to be registered with the central dispatcher, or whatever the equivalent is, to avoid collisions. At least, that's what we were told. And what we thought. But the Jecc and their stealing . . ."

"Could they be building their own transports? For whatever purpose?" Eveleen asked, her gaze considering.

"And ought we to discuss this with Virigu and let them take their chances?" Ross added. "I have to say, much as I hate squealing in a general sense, after today's fun and games it would give me a hell of a lot of satisfaction."

"It's too easy," Gordon said. "Unless your Virigu is a total fool, surely this has been noticed before."

Ross sighed. "Yeah, as usual you're right. I guess what I need to do is watch these Jecc and see if they actually remove the parts they steal, or if they all get put back again. Which would be crazy."

Gordon got to his feet. "What's crazy to one might be tradition to another. You know that. One of our first lessons as time agents. Meantime, I'm dead tired, and want some rest before another day of trash hauling. It'll be a week tomorrow, so I'm planning to put out the call to Misha and Viktor." He paused at the door, and turned to Vera. "Have either of you heard from them?"

"No," Vera said, looking down at her feet.

"No." Irina's voice was flat.

Ross wondered if it was true, then quashed the thought. Enough problems faced them with possible conspiracies among the Nurayil; he wasn't even going to entertain such thoughts about his fellow humans unless forced into it.

"I'll report on their response—if any—tomorrow. Good night, all."

Gordon nodded at them, and left.

Irina said quietly, "We shall endeavor to discover more about these Jecc, if we can."

"And anything else," Vera added, getting up slowly and stretching. A huge yawn seized her, then she grinned. "A difficult business, this collecting of gossip. If only it were so arduous at home!"

Everyone laughed, and the women departed.

Ross's mind was full of conflicting thoughts—and from the look of Eveleen, who rubbed her thumbnail absently back and forth over her lower lip, she felt the same.

If only he could get out and—

"Come on," he said. "Let's call it a day."

CHAPTER 16

"FOR AN ARCHAEOLOGIST," Gordon Ashe said to himself as he finished loading the recycler-bound wagon, "being a trash man is a golden opportunity."

His tone was somewhat grim, and certainly ironic, but he did believe there was a great deal of truth in what he'd said just the same.

The grimness came of the fact that the recycle transport system had obviously been breaking down for many years, and it was apparently easier to get some unfortunate Nurayil to see to it than to bother with replacement parts or a new system.

The wagon worked, like the rail-skimmers, on the maglev principle: super-conductive magnets floating above buried rails. But it was obviously much older, slow, and it was up to Gordon to pick out the little plants that insisted on taking root all along the track. His unknown predecessor had not bothered.

The loader system had long since ceased to function, leaving the trash to be loaded by hand.

This way, at least, Gordon got a good look at the House of Knowledge's castoffs—everything they did not run through the plumbing recycler. Even if he had had an automated loader, he still would have sorted the trash, partly to examine it, and partly in case there was some way that Saba could get a message to him.

Paper and pen seemed to be out. But he knew she had at least one data disk in her laptop; if her machine had not been confiscated, perhaps she would slip a disk into the waste, which he could then read in his own machine.

Except how to get it back to her? Well, no need to think that out.

She probably had already dismissed the idea; at least no disk had appeared. He hoped because there was no need yet for such a drastic move.

As he grunted a bulky, heavy lump of metal into the wagon, he distracted himself momentarily with speculating what it might have been used for. Nothing came to mind. It looked like an old internal combustion engine block crushed by a four-dimensional waffle iron.

And it weighed a ton.

Clang! Klunk! He paused, breathing heavily, thinking over what really concerned him: the code messages he'd received the night before.

They were all repeats: "searching," "deportment lessons," "well-being," "no danger."

Frustrating. He wanted a real status report—he also wanted to find out what she was learning, and to learn it as well.

He sighed, and stared at the jumble of material on the loading platform. What were these things, and what had they been used for? Among the detritus were what looked like a steel umbrella, half inside-out; an exploded plastic xylophone; and a half-dozen foamed alloy shoe trees made for someone twenty-five feet tall with feet that had toes at both ends. Alien trash.

"Any sufficiently advanced technology is indistinguishable from magic," he muttered. If Arthur C. Clarke had had this job, Gordon thought, he might well have added that such a technology's discards are indistinguishable from art. Well, bad art, anyway. Most of the discards looked like the kind of incomprehensible sculptures that often showed up in public places back home on Earth.

He wondered what the other Nurayil thought of it, or how much awareness they had of the technology that sustained this odd civilization. One thing seemed sure: it was slowly winding down, for down the timeline, the civilization definitely had crumbled.

How long, he wondered, could the ancient Inca, for instance, have kept a twentieth-century city running? Would they have mastered the technology, destroyed themselves with it, or merely ridden it down into ruin as the machines decayed for lack of knowledge? Was that what had happened here?

He sighed as the last of the stuff slid into the wagon.

Already he was wet from the misting rain that never seemed to stop, but at least it kept him somewhat cool. Shaking the rain from his eyes, he slid onto the control seat and activated the wagon.

It shuddered, whining on an excruciating note, then slid forward at a snail's pace. Once he was well out of sight of any of the guardians, he slid up his sleeve and glanced at his watch. Good. He'd calculated well; he'd arrive at the recycle building in plenty of time, then.

The wagon lumbered shudderingly along its route. Occasionally it lurched and almost stopped. Gordon jumped out each time and used a flat tool he'd found to wedge up growing plants whose roots were already fouling the rails. The wagon moved so slowly that he'd only have to run a few steps to catch up.

Back to communication—and the next problem. From Saba there was not enough, but from the Russians there was too much.

He thought over what he'd say to the two Russian men, and how he'd say it. He'd decided against taking the women to task. He wouldn't need to, if Misha was cooperative.

And he did believe the women when they'd said they hadn't communicated with Misha or Viktor. For Vera, though, it wasn't for lack of trying, for she'd been pulsing Misha just about every night. Was she trying to get him to talk real-time? Apparently he hadn't responded—but he'd been pulsing Irina in turn. And she'd been obeying the command to keep silence.

Gordon did not want to have to say anything to Vera. The mission was too important. He did not want to risk bad blood with any of the Russians. Perhaps she didn't intend to talk to Misha, only to get that return pulse—just as Gordon himself did each evening with Saba—but still, he needed to make sure that the orders were kept, at least until they knew they were safe. And it was always easier to remonstrate with men.

He grimaced at the thought, and shook his head.

Slowly the wagon trundled through a tunnel of green growth. He'd be at the recycling building very soon.

His thoughts were abruptly splintered when he heard what sounded like voices—human voices. Children's voices?

He looked around. Nothing.

He forced himself to scan more slowly, each tree and fern. Still nothing. Once the light shafting weakly through the thin rain clouds overhead seemed to darken for a moment, and he looked up, but of course only saw the canopy of jungle growth, and beyond it the gray of clouds.

Now there was silence, except for the quiet *tick* and *plop* of raindrops on broad leaves.

He breathed deeply, wondering if he'd possibly imagined the voices. The heavy scents of the jungle tickled the back of his sinuses.

He was still listening, and watching, when the wagon abruptly emerged into a cemented area. Around the perimeter there were cracks, with rootlings and little plants thriving; it was strange to think that this would all be utterly overgrown down the timeline in the present. Was the science team walking around this very area right now?

He shrugged away the fancy. The wagon slid smoothly now toward the building. Lights rippled above an access door, which then slid up.

Gordon jumped off the wagon, which would finish its job automatically within the building, and emerge empty through the adjacent access.

He started walking around the cement apron, looking for the Russians—or anyone else who might be about.

No one else seemed to be lurking, which was good. He'd deliberately picked noon, having discovered that most of the other beings in the Nurayil part of the city preferred dawn for their recycling, and of course the mysterious Yilayil did their disposal during the night.

He slowed his steps, walking closer to the jungle. No one in sight.

He'd nearly completed a full circle when he heard a quick whistle—not a Yilayil whistle, but a familiar melody, an old jazz tune.

He stopped, his head jerking up, and he saw Misha lounging against a tree, his long blond hair backlit by the weak sunlight. Like a shadow, Viktor loomed at his shoulder, still and quiet as the trees around them.

Gordon finished his circuit, stepped off the cement apron, and joined them. "Is there a reason why we're hiding?" he asked.

"Yes," Misha said, smiling slightly.

In surprise Gordon waited for an explanation.

Instead, Viktor jerked his head toward the shadowy undergrowth behind him, and took off down the trail. In silence Gordon followed, Misha behind him.

They walked for a short time, emerging on a mossy outcropping just beneath the spreading canopy of a tree whose fringed leaves were a deep blue-green. A natural fence of rocks blocked one end, beyond which the cliff fell away three or four meters to a swift-moving stream.

Gordon entered the little area, saw packs and equipment neatly stored, and realized that this was the men's current campsite.

"Welcome home," Misha said. "At least, home for two days. We're almost finished at this end of the district. Coffee?"

Gordon did not know how the insouciant Russian had managed to smuggle it in, but he knew an extravagant gesture when he saw one. "Love some," he said, matching Misha's casual tone—as if they had it every day.

Of course, maybe the Russians did.

Misha snorted a laugh. Even Viktor smiled slightly before he scanned the sky with quick thoroughness, then ran down to the stream to scoop up a pan of water.

When he returned Misha had a small fire going—almost smokeless, Gordon noted. How much experimentation had gone into finding out which deadwood was safe to burn?

No one spoke until the pan was set on a tripod over the fire, then Misha looked up at Gordon. "Questions?"

"How about a report?"

The Russian shrugged, an elegant movement. "In essentials, we have nothing. We have been over the Nurayil burial site twice, sounding for these." He touched his jaw, and Gordon thought of the implants the Russians all had in their teeth. "Nothing."

Gordon nodded grimly. In their first briefing, Zina had told him about the implants, stating that even if the bodies were cremated by normal means, the implants would still give off a signal. This was how the First Team had found their biologist in the first place; scanning for the signal was a part of their regular routine.

"Go on," he said.

"We've been working out in a circle—but our speed has been impeded by these damn flyers we saw on Day One."

Now Gordon understood the cover, and the scanning. "Flyers," he repeated.

Misha and Viktor both nodded.

"They spotted us the morning of Day Two. The rain had started, and there were no shadows. We didn't think to look up," Misha said.

Viktor added, in heavily accented English, "Make no noise."

"Heard nothing, saw nothing. They must have spotted us from above, and they swooped down." Misha demonstrated. "Screaming."

"Words," Viktor added that in Russian.

"We took off for the thickest cover, and outran 'em. They've been circling the entire area ever since. Slow flights. Have to assume they're looking for us," Misha said. "We hid out entirely the second day, and most of the third. By the fourth we saw a pattern: crepuscular hours preferred."

Gordon nodded. "Dawn and dusk. Well, that makes sense, doesn't it? Can't be out at night, not if they aren't sanctioned by the Yilayil, and noontime flying would be hot work when the sun's out."

Misha gave his elegant shrug again. "I do not know. So anyway, we work then, and keep under cover at dawn and dusk."

"And ping Irina," Gordon added drily.

Misha grinned. "Boredom. What is the danger of a single ping? I see you are pinging Saba every night."

Gordon said, "She's locked up in the House of Knowledge. They took her on sight." And he went on to give the Russians a full report, starting with the statue of Saba awaiting them, and ending with an out-line of everyone's activities to date.

Misha listened closely, his challenging smile fading. At the end, he said, "Much to be discovered, then. Your suggestions with regard to these flyers? We know they're searching for us, but not why. Could be that roasted Russki is their favorite appetizer."

"I haven't seen any in the Nurayil district," Gordon said. "But I'm limited in my movements. I can ask the others. If the flyers are not trying to integrate themselves into the society, it could be for a number of reasons, but we'll have to assume for now that their reasons won't advance our goals any. I'd say play least-in-sight for now."

Viktor gave a short, sharp nod.

Misha spread his hands. "You're the boss."

Gordon, looking from one to the other, suspected that some arguing had taken place—Viktor pleading caution, and Misha wanting action.

"Keep searching," Gordon said. "There has to be a sign of them somewhere. I can't believe the First Team was taken off the island, not without leaving some sort of clue."

"Ah." Misha looked down at the water, which was just beginning to boil.

He carefully measured out a small portion of brown powder from an airtight bag, and cast it into the bottom of the pan. A rough-and-ready way to make coffee, but as the delicious aroma rose up, Gordon found himself breathing deeply.

They shared a cup each of the coffee. Gordon drank his right down to the bitter residue.

"Thanks," he said at last. "I needed that."

"We'll escort you back," Misha said with an airy wave of his hand. "Time to get to work."

Viktor had already broken down the firepit and cleaned the pan. Their gear was stowed; they could pick up and move fast at a moment's notice.

The return trip was accomplished in silence. The two men disap-peared into the jungle shortly after Gordon stepped onto the apron and found his empty wagon waiting.

He activated the control, got aboard for the slow ride back. For once he was not impatient of the long trip, for he had much to think about.

SABA WALKED DOWN the ramp to the translation room. If she turned her head too fast, a faint headache throbbed at her temples. She concentrated on breathing slowly, in and out, as she walked the rest of the way.

Everything seemed a little too bright, a little too loud this morning. Yet there was nothing loud, or glaring, in her surroundings. Her slippers whispered on the cool flooring, and her robe swayed gently against her body, one side, the other. The muted lighting seemed exactly the same as it had for the past week; there were no shadows anywhere, no bright lances of light, so it could not have been intensified. But her eyes seemed overly sensitive. All her senses, in fact, seemed heightened, she realized as she listened to the rhythmic swishing of her flaxen robe.

Has to be just stress, she thought as she entered the huge viewing room. I'm fragmenting my focus too much—it has to be that.

As she passed down the long rows of working people, she performed a quick mental assessment.

Her first priority, she still believed, was to find whatever message she'd left herself from the past—if it could be found. That had meant a lot of furtive, desperate searching. Then she had her deportment lessons, which required a desperate mental shift; just the day before she'd found herself utterly lost as they used references to time that the First Team had not even hinted at. And threaded through all this were her doubts about the other beings here, their motivations, their intentions toward her. And of course she had the mission to think about.

On top of it all, the frustration of being limited to pulse code communication once a day.

I have some important task to perform, she thought, trying to gather her strength. I know that I do, or that statue of me would not be out front.

That was another goal: to find out who the other statues depicted, and why they were so honored. But when she asked Virigo or Rilla, they gave her meaningless names, and whistled the traditional phrase for "Nurayil honored as Yil"—which told her exactly nothing.

Perhaps she would find out more in the records. As yet the terminal in her room had not been activated. Just as well; she could barely read Yilayil script. The First Team had only given them the basic consonant sounds, assuming a phonetic alphabet. And superficially it was; foreign languages were diligently reproduced phonetically.

Thinking this, she glanced down at the nearest person, a weedy young Virigu—a male. They were very rare, for some reason; most of the Virigu were female.

He watched a tape on a terminal, his spidery fingers blurring across pads on his console as he translated what he saw.

She paused and looked around.

That's what they were all doing—translating into Yilayil tapes taken from ships. They listened to the voices on the tapes and translated; Rilla had told her that when she had mastered deportment (a term that also included mastery of language, apparently) she would translate tapes as well.

That had both excited and frightened her. Were there tapes from the First Team somewhere? Or would she be trained in some other language, to translate tapes from some unknown world?

Or had other humans come, before or after the First Team?

Her headache throbbed, and she tried to dismiss the thoughts. Instead, she went back to considering the Yilayil script: phonetic for Nurayil, but for the Yilayil it was apparently ideographic—each symbol standing for a concept, and not just a sound.

"Saba of Far Star."

She had reached the far end; Zhot awaited her.

He vanished into the chamber beyond the viewing room, and Saba found that the rest of her "class" was there—both Nurayil, which she found reassuring, and both trying to master the language.

Zhot was an ancient male of a species the name of which had not been mentioned to her. He was shaped rather like a tall, supple seal, but he moved like a reptile. His round body was covered with nubbly sandy-colored scales, except for his face, which was whiskery with tiny antenae constantly waving and vibrating. She had not seen his legs beneath his robe, but when he walked, the motion was sudden and noiseless. The first few times she'd seen him, it had unnerved her.

His voice, though, was like liquid music.

"We begin today our discourse upon the experience of [dis-order-resulting in matter-energy inert/uniform] and its expression."

Dis-order . . . Saba struggled desperately between Yilayil and Terran language. Entropy? she thought, confused.

Zhot gave her no time to consider as he emitted a long trill, most of which escaped Saba at first, and then looked at the class expectantly.

Both the others were silent, Saba noted. Were they as confused as she?

She turned her mind to the trill, as Zhot repeated it more slowly. Grateful, she pounced mentally on each phrase. There was very little information on the concrete layers used in everyday discourse, and the higher-level modulations all concerned the strange tenses and temporalities that they had discussed the day before.

Saba forced herself to relax. It was impossible to translate those levels into any language she knew; they had to be experienced, in the same fashion as music. But the rational part of her mind insisted on scattering phrases across her consciousness.

Consequence-of-act . . . as is-was . . . echo back from will-be . . . conditional termination-of-volition . . .

Her mind refused the rest. She shook her head.

"It is not true for servants of knowledge," a Virigu stated at last.

Zhot nodded.

The second being added, in slow, careful Yilayil, "We speak of what we know/experience."

Zhot turned expectantly to Saba.

She finally felt forced to say, "I don't understand."

He paused for what seemed a very long time.

"Your people tell stories, yes?"

She nodded, but he did not respond, and she suddenly realized that the gesture perhaps had no meaning for him. Hastily she wet her dry mouth, and whistled, "Yes, we tell stories."

"Contrary to fact, and true?"

"Yes."

"Teller of stories sees those-who-live in story all-at-once." Then he fluted another phrase with upper-level modulations, similar to the first. "If story not satisfactory at end, lives of those-within changed at beginning. They will differently, act differently." Another trill, again with the same bizarre tenses.

Was this mode of discourse for storytelling, then?

"We/you live in entropy, struggle against entropy, but not in stories. There we live outside entropy."

"Yes," she said, hesitantly.

"So, too, we/you know entropy on two levels, more. So, too, servants of knowledge speak of entropy on two levels, more."

"But we do not experience it that other way."

"No," said Zhot. "We"—and here she heard the emphasis—"do not. We are servants." Again a complex fluting.

Subject is-was-will-be servant to those who choosing-choices-made dance above decay.

"The Yilayil?"

Zhot emitted the choking snort she had guessed meant laughter in his race. Another trill.

Choices made-making termination-of-volition for subjects.

A thrill shot through her. Down the timeline the Yilayil were savages.

"Then Yilayil . . ." She hesitated, not wanting to give away the fact that she knew anything about time further on. "Decay?"

Zhot trilled again.

Improper transition in mode of discourse.

Saba stifled the urge to groan and hold her head. Instead, she listened as the other two took up the conversation and labored through a painstaking discussion of tenses. Saba had tremendous difficulty following it—her headache was considerably worse at the conclusion of the lesson—but at least she was fairly sure of one thing. The Virigu and the other being were exactly as confused as she was.

CHAPTER 17

EVELEEN LOOKED AT the Jecc swarming about her, all at waist height, and thought, They are like children. They moved fast like children, rammed each other and exchanged buffets and shoves, and their squeaky whistles and drones all reminded her of children. Unpleasant, nightmarish children, to be sure. There was nothing cute or appealing in the stares from those deepset eyes, or the rows of needle-sharp teeth in the coldly grinning beaklike snouts. Or in the little hands—or tentacles—that tried to steal parts from Eveleen's pile if she didn't watch them constantly.

She twisted her head, working her neck as she looked about the cavernous assembly chamber. It smelled of hot alloys and lubricant and a little like burned toast. That was the Jecc. They all smelled a little like burned toast sprinkled with rosemary.

How long would she and Ross have to work among them? As her fingers operated automatically at disassembling a cooling unit and replacing the worn-out parts, she considered the other beings in the department.

No one seemed to make any rules. The Virigu in charge certainly didn't. They merely oversaw, ordering people about when there was apparently a need. People reported for work when they wished to, apparently, and took days off when they wanted.

In this department, as yet no one among the few other species had been promoted—or transferred—which gave her nothing by which to calculate the duration of their probable stay. As for the Jecc, any number of them might have been transferred or promoted, but they looked so much alike that it was difficult to tell.

Not that they were interchangeable. They were all more or less the same size and mass, and they all wore identical plain coveralls, but their gray-green skin was mottled and stippled with iridescent blue dots. She'd realized one morning that the dots made subtle patterns, when a couple of them actually sat still enough for her to scrutinize them. And she memorized the pattern, endeavoring to watch these particular Jecc.

So she did—that day. She saw the one with the snail-shell whorls clip at least three connectors from other Jecc; the one with the braided whorls seemed to concentrate on stealing from other beings.

The next day, though, neither of them was present—at least, as far as she could tell. After she finished reconstructing one directional unit she moved about, on the pretext of getting more parts, and scrutinized as many stationary Jecc as she could—and though she did see that snail-whorl pattern again, it seemed tighter, smaller, with more dots. *Different.*

All new Jecc?

Or was the blue stuff paint?

She asked Vera that night, "Have you found out any more data on the Jecc?"

"No," Vera said, pausing in the act of wolfing down some food. She grinned briefly. "All the others do is curse them. No one likes them. Apparently they don't even live in the city, though how that works is beyond me. But the Moova, everyone else, call them pests." She swallowed, and sighed. "Sorry—no chance to eat today."

Irina nodded her sleek head. She ate daintily, as though she sat in a duchess's formal dining room. "I begin a new labor today." She frowned, massaging her forehead with her fingertips. "Excuse me—my English seems to be regressing. I began a new job today. I work now for Lootignef of the Moova."

"And I for Toofiha," Vera added.

"Moova?" Ross asked.

Both Russians nodded.

"And they don't let you eat on the job?"

Both heads shook decisively.

"They are rivals," Vera said. "We did this on purpose, hoping to find out more information that way. The Moova are very jealous of data, and of their foods."

"Sure is good, though," Ross said, holding up a thin roll of some kind of rice-bread mixed with seasoned vegetables. "Big change from the raw stuff, healthy as it might be."

Vera sighed. "How I dream of coffee! And ice cream. And torte . . ."

Eveleen saw Irina glance over at Vera, her black eyes narrowed. Irina's refined face was largely serene, but that could very well be a facade. Right now, if Eveleen was any judge of character, it seemed that the ex-ballerina was thoroughly tired of her partner.

Of course Eveleen said nothing. She just continued to watch as she worked through her katas. Her stomach was hungry, but her joints were achy and her neck tight. The only remedy, she felt, was to work out, which she couldn't do while full. Her share of the food sat on a napkin next to Ross.

Ross was frowning. "They say bad things about the Jecc? Isn't that anti-deportment? Anti-harmony?"

"Not," Irina said precisely, "if what you say is to point out ways in which the Jecc are anti-harmonious."

Eveleen snorted. "I guess they aren't going to get promoted to the next level anytime soon, eh?"

Vera said, "The Moova say they don't try to harmonize, but I don't know how much of that is just talk. No one has much real data about them, this I can say with certainty. To bring up the subject is to hear, over and over, that they are thieves and pests—stealing things that don't even matter."

Just then Gordon's familiar tap sounded at the door, and Ross moved to open it.

Gordon came in, bringing a swirl of rain-scented air with him. "Big storm out there," he commented.

"Must be," Eveleen said, sniffing for that rain scent. It was already gone, filtered out. The ubiquitous clean, sterile air smelled just as always—and of course there were no windows to look out of. Eveleen fought a sudden surge of claustrophobia and forced up the pace of her kata. "Any news?" she asked over her shoulder.

Gordon shook his head. "Status quo." He sat down and Vera handed him his food. "Pollen count still up?" he asked.

Vera said, "It is. Very high." She smacked her lips as she finished her food.

Eveleen watched Irina, who worked studiously through her food as if the room were silent. Was there another reason why the two had not taken jobs at the same place? Not necessarily, Eveleen thought. Irina, at least, was too dedicated to the mission. She wondered if Vera even knew how irritating she was to her partner.

With a snap and whirl, she finished her last move, then she sank down next to Ross. Gratitude for his presence suffused her. She might be feeling claustrophobic—restless—but at least she had him. And wasn't it better to let the others do their jobs than to think about going out and exploring during the long evenings?

Ross sat back. "Bringing me to what's been bothering me since the first briefing, and that is: who decides? Are the Yilayil watching us when we work? Or do the various Virigu spy on us and send in reports? Or what?"

"Another thing for us to discover," Gordon said equably.

Eveleen noted the tense postures and tight faces in the others. "What I wish," she said, "was that we had TV. I'd even watch alien TV. These nights sitting in this room get a little old."

And she saw an immediate reaction in the two women. Sympathy now flooded her, but she tried to hide it; though the authorities on Earth had been worried about married agents in the field together, they probably hadn't considered what a relief it would be to be penned up with someone you love, rather than someone else with whom you might have little in common outside of the job at hand.

Ross, however, was frowning. "That's another thing," he said. "Deportment—conformity. The Nurayil are kept utterly in the dark, far as I can see. We don't know what our labor is worth. We don't have access to what passes for news, or any kind of data. We don't even get local entertainment."

"I can address that," Gordon said as he worked his neck by twisting his head slowly back and forth. His expression was calm, as always, but his blue eyes were tired. "Every race has its own entertainment—I see it as I pass through the city on my rounds. The Yilayil don't seem to care what beings do in their own space, just as no one has interfered with our laptops or our brief spurts of signal. And someone, at least, has to know. The technology here is sufficiently advanced that it seems safer to assume that they do, rather than the opposite."

Irina nodded. "This is so. I have seen the Moova gathered round their *gyoon*—" And, gesturing with her long hands, she described a round flat plate on a table that projected holographic images. "It looked to me like Moova writhing underwater, but they were very intent."

"Sounds like gargling," Vera put in with a grin. "I have seen this as well." Her round face was briefly serious. "But it is only in private—not when they interact with the rest of Nurayil."

Good spy work, Eveleen thought, and her appreciation for the Russian women increased. They've seen more than we have. Again—stronger—she felt that intense urge to be out and exploring, but she repressed it. If she went, Ross would go—Ross, who always took chances. Thinking about what had happened to the First Team's biologist always cooled her wish to see Ross out taking risks.

She stole a look at Ross—just in time to catch a glance from his narrowed eyes, his dark brows quirked. What was he thinking? For once she couldn't guess at his thoughts.

"I am tired," Irina said suddenly. "I think it is time to sleep."

Vera yawned. "I must admit I have had a headache most of the day. I need sleep as well."

Gordon smiled, said, "Maybe it's something in the air—I've had that headache as well."

Vera said, "The pollens I can measure for we are supposedly immune to. But we have to accept that there might be others that we cannot measure for."

Gordon nodded. "Maybe that's it. Allergies! What a planet! Well, on that note, I think I'll call it a night." He stood, and followed the two women out, everyone wishing one another good night and good rest.

As Ross turned away from the closed door, he said, "Get the feeling everyone is sick of everyone else?"

Eveleen gave her head a shake. "I get the feeling that everyone feels lousy, and no one wants to complain." She decided not to mention that glance she'd caught from Irina—not until she knew she was right. To speculate without facts felt too much like gossip, and even though it was only Ross, what she said might affect how he responded to the others. And Irina, at least, Eveleen thought with sudden conviction, was very, very observant.

"They're not the only ones," Ross said, surprising her. "I have to admit it's hard to think with this headache on me."

"You didn't mention it," Eveleen said, instantly concerned.

He shrugged, an abrupt motion that made it clear how much he loathed any kind of personal weakness. "What can I do about it? Complaining would bore us both."

"Mentioning a headache isn't exactly complaining," Eveleen said wryly. "As it happens, I've been feeling achy all day. Not so much my head as my joints. Neck."

Ross looked up, frowning. "Gordon said allergies, but maybe it's something more than that. Think we're getting sick? Not just us, but the whole team?"

"Oh, lord, I hope not," Eveleen exclaimed. "I don't want to even think about what kind of alien microbes we might be fighting . . ." Horrible scenarios reeled through her mind—the Jecc carrying some kind of dangerous virus, Ross and Eveleen exposed, and exposing the others. Or was it the Moova, through their food?

She shook her head firmly, wincing against a pang in her temples. "No," she said out loud. "I *won't* think about it—not until I have evidence."

"In that case," Ross said with a twisted grin, "let's do what Gordon and the Russians are probably doing right now: let's break some pain reliever out of our packs and get some rest."

———————————

A WEEK LATER, they still felt much the same.

Ross had stopped taking anything but the anti-allergens. He'd already run through half his allotment of pain killers, and though he didn't say anything, his grim thought was if they felt any worse, they'd need them.

They certainly hadn't gotten better. After a couple nights, Gordon got everyone to state their symptoms so he could keep a record, just as the First Team had reported, in detail, their malaise a month or so into their stay.

"I thought the medical brains had decided it was allergies," Eveleen said to Ross one day when they were walking to work. "Didn't they say that at our first briefing?"

"I can't remember what anyone said," Ross admitted, grinning.

The rain was very heavy, and most beings were under the awnings to avoid it. Ross and Eveleen had donned their rain ponchos and walked right through the deluge.

"Ahhh," Eveleen said, taking a deep breath. "It might just be psychological trickery, but I feel like the air is cleaner."

"So you do think it's allergens making us sick?" Ross asked her.

She shrugged, giving him a wry look. Her face was slightly tense, and her eyes shadowed from broken sleep, but she didn't look dangerously sick. She'd better not, he thought. If she did get seriously ill, mission or not, they were going back down the timeline to the sterile air of the ship.

"I don't know," she said. "How could I? I just imagine the air being full of guck that our immune systems don't like. And when it rains like this, I convince myself the air is purified, and I hope this stupid headache will vanish."

Ross said nothing. He'd begun to wonder if he'd live with a headache all his life. Even with the meds, it was never really gone.

"Well, we got every damn anti-allergen in us they could concoct," he reminded her. "And the science team did do an allergen check when we landed, remember?"

Her thin brows furrowed. "Hard to remember anything, except how to build cooling units," she said with a soft laugh. "So you think what's hit us is viral?"

"I don't know," it was his turn to say. "It can't be just exposure to the Jecc or the Moova or one of the other races because Misha and Viktor are apparently sick as well."

Eveleen sighed. "I'd forgotten that. Not that Gordon was exactly gabby with the details."

Ross shrugged. "What's to detail? They feel much like we do, and they haven't seen anyone—despite those flyers chasing them whenever they catch sight of them."

They neared the big building housing Transport, and slipped back into Yilayil. Ross could feel Eveleen's reluctance as strong as his own. It was hard to think in any language when your head continuously ached—and double that for an alien tongue.

Eveleen trilled the equivalent for: "I'll want something hot for mid-day meal."

"A good idea," he responded, and they both fell silent.

Three or four weird purple-greenish beings moved in ahead of them, reminding Ross of seven-foot-tall crosses between teddy bears and sharks. They disappeared in the direction of the rail-skimmer body shop. Apparently they were so strong they could lift most of the big alloy plates that most other beings needed cranes for.

They were quiet, they worked hard, and they didn't give anyone any trouble. Yet here they were, among the Nurayil.

Ross felt a surge of impatience. He hadn't voiced a growing conviction even to Eveleen, but he was wondering if the whole deportment thing was a myth in order to get free—or almost free—labor from all the other races.

The idea of his working so hard, while sick, in what might be a royal scam put him in a thoroughly rotten mood.

The Jecc didn't help. When he and Eveleen got to their workstation, it seemed like there were more of them than ever. He sniffed the gritty, oily smells, and looked at the worn parts they were supposed to retool. When a Jecc rammed against his hip as it scurried down an adjacent corridor, the sudden jar sent a pang through his already aching head.

Annoyance crystallized into the need for action. He watched Eveleen square her shoulders and march off to collect parts for her portion of the day's work—wrapping them tightly in her rain poncho and holding it with both hands. Then she disappeared in the direction of the assembly benches.

Ross smiled to himself.

It was time, he decided, to do a little consciousness raising by showing the Jecc just how it felt to be hassled.

So he shifted a big part into one hand, keeping the other lightly resting against the cool alloy as he paced along a row of Jecc busily retooling connectors and exhaust valves.

And when one reached to alter what Ross called the buffing machine (though it didn't look remotely like any buffing machine you'd find in a mechanic's shop on Earth), he whipped his fingers out and snagged a fine set of data chips from where they stuck out of the Jecc's overall.

The creature didn't even notice, and Ross laughed silently to himself. So his old skills hadn't left him, eh?

He'd given up that kind of life when he was recruited to the time agents—but on this occasion, he was glad he remembered how to pick pockets.

He watched the Jecc at intervals while finishing a piece of work. The one he'd robbed discovered the missing chip, its head moving back and forth, but then it got right back to work. No further reaction.

Ross went walking again, close behind a row of Jecc busy working away. Two of them didn't bother glancing up, and both of them within seconds were lighter of a filter and a measure tool respectively.

And so the day went.

Ross nearly laughed out loud a few times when he watched, from the vantage of his workstation, his victims discover their losses. Ross was careful to put his stolen booty in another location, usually in the parts section, after he got it. He still didn't know why the Jecc stole and hoarded parts that were readily available to everyone, but in case there was some kind of mysterious personal bond with these bits of machinery, he didn't want them to feel deprived. Just . . . warned? Startled?

He examined his own motivations as he finished a last buffing job. At lunch he forebore telling Eveleen about his private game. He wasn't sure she would agree, and she looked so headachy he didn't want to risk making it worse for her.

Maybe it was stupid, but it felt right.

And so he decided to make a couple more five-finger discounts before the day ended—and he'd try it again the next. In fact, the idea of it made him look forward to another day for the very first time since his arrival.

His first pinch was a bigger part, and the victim immediately turned on a neighbor and exclaimed in an excited tongue that was definitely not Yilayil. The neighbor touched the victim's muzzle, and it fell silent. Both looked around in a manner that reminded Ross forcibly of guilty children. He almost regretted his action, but not quite.

No, not quite. One more pinch, he'd promised himself.

He could see that Eveleen needed to quit for the day. Her hands moved slowly, and the angle of her head was expressive of weariness.

He realized that he too was tired—only the adrenaline of his secret game kept him going.

One more.

He saw a Jecc just turning away from a partially disassembled drive unit. He reached, his fingers closed on the main component—

The Jecc's reaction was a blur. A fraction of a second later Ross found his finger pinned to the workbench by a small hand as he gazed down into yellowish-gray unblinking eyes.

CHAPTER 18

SABA PRESSED HER fingertips to her cheeks.

Hot.

It was no longer a matter of tiredness, she was definitely sick. And with something she couldn't sleep off; Virigu had left her alone the day before after twice trying to summon her to work. Did the Yilayil never actully get sick? Or worse, was there some terrible taboo against illness? Saba had realized she did not have the vocabulary to tell her tutors that she did not feel well. She'd only said, repeating it several times, that she had to sleep more. But it had sufficed—they left her alone.

And so she'd slept soundlessly for hours and hours.

Today she'd woken up feeling slept out—yet her body felt no better. She was decidedly feverish, and weak.

She shook her head. Time to stop being stoic and break out the pain relievers in her pack. She had a mission, she was the only one in this particular position, and she was not going to allow some stupid virus or flu to stop the work. Everyone else was doing their jobs, or Gordon would have sent her the signal indicating an emergency.

Well, then. She could do hers as well.

So she rose, walked through the weird glue-field shower, dressed, and took some medication, waiting long enough for it to start taking effect before she left her room.

What I need, she thought as she moved slowly toward the tutorial chamber, is to comprehend the gestalt of this place. Her attention was fragmented, and her perception of the others was fragmented as well.

On Earth, this had always been her initial approach to any new situation, to listen for patterns, for the music of the place. Though sometimes that "music" was hard to hear, it had to be there.

That had been the most important lesson her mother had taught her. From her father, a doctor, she had acquired intellectual curiosity and ambition; from her mother, a wise woman of the Dorze, she had learned that *yets*, vocal music, was in fact a part of human life.

Certainly it was among the Dorze, but her mother had convinced her that all peoples made music, even when they were not necessarily aware of it. To deliberately distort or deny music, as some modern cultures seemed to do, was to dehumanize one, and the healthy person merely sought music in other forms.

These beings are not human, Saba thought. But this language is music. I think, therefore, that among those who can speak and hear, music must be a universal.

And I must find the musical pattern here before I can try to understand these people—and find out what it is I am here for.

When she arrived in the usual place, a breeze of cool, rainy-smelling air drifted across her fever-heated face. She breathed slowly, her eyes closing. It was wonderful, but it only lasted seconds.

When she opened her eyes, Virigu was before her.

"I, Virigu," she began, "take you now to the place where we store knowledge."

Saba wondered if her day of sleep had been misinterpreted, but unless someone said something threatening, she refused to worry. It was going to take all her energy just to follow this new lesson—and to work on the task she had set herself.

The new lesson proved to be with the Yilayil computers. Her delight and curiosity, however, were soon quenched by the stressful task of learning what each keypad meant. They did not correspond with the phonetic letters that the First Team had taught them; instead, they bore idealized keystrokes that were pressed in combination to build up the Yilayil ideographics, which Virigu now made clear it was time to learn.

That meant thinking in Yilayil, and distilling symbols—alien symbols—into meaning for a human being.

Virigu sat next to her at another keyboard, pressing one key at a time, while complicated symbols assembled themselves on the terminal. Patiently, calmly, she described each, then had Saba run through the definitions after which she practiced five over and over, one for each digit on her hand. The groups of five seemed a considerate way of teaching, but Saba wished she could learn this in twos. Or one at a time.

Time sped by. She had the first grouping down and was superficially acquainted with the second group when subtle bell tones, just barely heard, indicated it was time for a change.

They moved down to the refectory and Saba forced herself to drink some of the soup that all the others were taking. She knew that hers was—somehow—deemed appropriate for her biochemistry, for a quick glance in all the bowls showed different colors and consistencies for various races.

But a tiny portion of her mind was afraid that the food might be part of her illness; at any rate she had no appetite. Still, she forced herself to eat the soup.

Afterward it was time for another session with Zhot.

This time the subject was knowledge.

The other two tutorees were not present, only Saba, Virigu, and Rilla.

Again—as it had been for the . . . her head panged as she tried to count up the days, all so alike. Three weeks? Four? As it had been all along, the higher-level modulations all incorporated strange tenses and conditional temporalities that seemed to confuse even Rilla and Virigu, it seemed.

Yet Zhot persisted. After he had asked each to define knowledge, he turned to Saba, his whiskers stiff, his eyes intent.

As always when confronted by differing paradigms, Saba opted for the simple.

"Knowledge," she trilled, "is that which is known."

Zhot droned/whistled a fast, complicated response.

Consequence-of-knowing . . . as is-was . . . unfolding from actions-will-be . . .

Her mind refused the rest. She shook her head, saying, "What I am perceiving is that knowledge stands outside of time."

"What is time?" was the immediate response.

"The . . . artificial measure we apply to the progression of events," she said, again opting for the simple.

"Has time meaning for those who exist all-at-once?"

Saba bit her lip, fighting the urge to retort: *Ask those who exist all-at-once, when you find them.*

She would not get angry. Conditional tenses—hypothetical states of being—the tutoring sessions with Zhot always seemed to involve these discussions. They hadn't yet touched on the other oddity in the language, the bizarre sensory correlations. She wondered what they portended.

No wonder I'm not learning any faster, she thought with a bleak inner laugh. *What happened to teaching language by talking about things beings actually do—like eating, sleeping, reading, working?*

But again she forced her fragmenting thoughts to clear, and concentrated.

"I cannot answer that," she finally said. "But I would surmise that it does not."

Zhot whirled around, his reptilian speed startling.

"Beings outside of time experience those-who-live-in-time all-at-once." Then he fluted another phrase with upper-level modulations, similar to the first. "If beings-in-time not satisfactory at end-of-time, lives of those-within altered at beginning-of-time. Knowledge is—" He trilled the impossible tenses yet again.

Saba fought the urge to hold her head in her hands, and abruptly Zhot whirled to Virigu and Rilla, this time demanding the purpose of knowledge with these givens.

Rilla's answer was almost as difficult to follow as Zhot's, but not quite. From it Saba gathered that the purpose of knowledge was to avert entropy.

When she heard the term, she remembered the discussion during which entropy had been the subject. Was there a connection after all? She'd assumed that the discussion topics were random, formed around various language lessons.

Nothing is accidental, she thought, feeling a visceral sense of warning.

Swiftly she reviewed the topics of discourse before her long sleep. One day the growth of trees and the seeding of new. Another day, the measure of celestial bodies moving through space. Before that . . .

". . . dance-above-decay," Zhot's voice interrupted her thoughts, and again she felt that inner zap.

There was something going on here—something she simply wasn't getting. But she knew it was important.

She forced her mind to clear—but Zhot had apparently finished.

When Saba was back in her room, she found that the terminal had been turned on, and it extended from her wall, with a little bench below it.

She drank some water, then sat down slowly. She traced the key-groupings she'd learned, and watched the symbols flow across the terminal. Then she tried two of the keys, just to see what happened—and the original meaning did not compound. Instead, a third meaning flowed on the terminal, something totally incomprehensible.

She sighed and went to lie down.

Time . . . no, don't think about their time. Her time. Time to stop fragmenting.

Her message to self, Gordon, the mission, sickness, music, gestalt.

Everything must be dismissed except gestalt.

Gestalt outside-of-time?

Don't even think about it. First just gestalt.
She closed her eyes and slept.

RAIN SLASHED THROUGH the jungle growth, a steady roar that covered the sounds of humans making their way at top speed. Gordon followed Viktor and Misha, his mouth open to ease his breathing, his head aching with every step.

Though the two Russians had readily admitted feeling the same symptoms suffered by everyone else on the team, their speed seemed undiminished. Could it be they felt less ill—that maybe living in the city had a deleterious effect beyond whatever it was that had affected them all?

Gordon listened to Viktor's rasping cough, which intermittently punctuated the rain sounds, and decided he'd withhold judgment on relative intensities of illness.

Instead, he concentrated on moving with the same speed, an effort that became increasingly difficult.

Then—just when Gordon was thinking he'd be forced to call a halt—Misha whirled around and said, "Here it is."

Gordon bent over, his hands on his knees, and fought to catch his breath. He noticed that both Viktor and Misha were breathing through their mouths; Viktor had dropped to the spongy moss covering the ground, but Misha leaned against a tree with a deceptively casual air. Gordon watched, amused, as he said, "Here what is?"

"The last camp," Misha said, waving a hand as though producing a magical scene.

Silently Viktor rose, digging in the tangled growth beneath a huge tree, and pulled out a pack—fungus-encrusted, discolored—but still recognizable as the type all the Russians carried.

Misha rummaged around under a semicircle of bright flowers, revealing a ring of stones that had to have been deliberately set. Gordon nodded, impressed with the detective work that had gone into this finding.

Misha dug into one of the packs and pulled out a warped notebook. He carefully opened it, and almost reverently held it out for Gordon's perusal, his manner so far removed from his usual that Gordon knew before he looked at it that this was a major find.

He looked down at the close Russian writing, and puzzled out a few words.

This was definitely from the First Team—one of the agents. Gordon recognized her name.

He looked up at Misha. "Svetlana."

Misha's face was uncharacteristically blank as he took the notebook from Gordon's hands, but before the archaeologist could speak, he gestured to Viktor, who handed him another notebook—and this time neither of them made a move to take it back.

"We find nearby," Viktor said. "I show you his camp as well."

Gordon looked down at the notebook, then up. "This one is Pavel's."

Misha nodded once. "I knew Pavel. I knew them all," he added, his accent very strong.

"Have you read Pavel's notebook?"

Again Misha nodded. "Skimmed it only, soon as we found it. He was the last. Svetlana here"—he indicated the notebook still gripped in his own hand—"disappeared before Pavel did."

" 'Disappeared'?"

Once again Misha nodded, his mouth grim. "We shall have to read these records more carefully, for much is not clear, but this I know. There are no bodies here. And Pavel saw no one die, beyond that first death. They just vanished. One by one."

CHAPTER 19

ROSS LOOKED DOWN into the Jecc's eyes, watching the pupils narrow like a cat's, then widen again.

The Jecc chattered in a hissing language, then altered swiftly to Yilayil: "My progeny will be swift!"

It grabbed for the tool, then scuttled away with a flick of its long tail.

Ross stared after the creature in blank surprise. He'd expected any kind of reaction—anger, fight, outrage—anything but that. And why the comment about progeny, or had he gotten the words wrong?

He'd scarcely had those thoughts when he felt the light touch of fingers against his hip, and he looked down to see another Jecc scurrying off, carrying the calibrating tool he had stuck in his pocket.

Ross gave a laugh, and turned back to his job—for now.

The war was on.

No, not a war. It was a *game*.

All the rest of the workday, Ross and the Jecc carried on this quick, strange interaction. No longer did he find them shoving him out of the way, or bumping him when he was busy—but all his small tools, especially those he tried to hide in his pockets, disappeared. He marked each Jecc who robbed him, and he made certain to get the tools right back again. The calibrating tool must have exchanged hands six times—mostly between Ross and two specific Jecc, one with a star made of purple dots over one eye, and another who was distinguishable by the braided pattern of dots down the back of its skull.

Ross began to see a pattern to the theft game. His calibrating tool, which was in no way remarkable from any other tool supplied by the Transport Department, would be nipped from him, and slid into a Jecc's pouch beneath its coveralls. If he watched closely—without being obvious about it—he could just see the edges of the pouch, though the Jecc kept this portion of their bodies covered. These pouches reminded him of a kangaroo pouch—or of a frog's mouth. After a time, the Jecc would reach in again, with a furtive movement, remove the tool, and use it, or set it nearby—and bingo! It would be stolen again.

That was the pattern: in the pouch, out—steal, pouch, out—disappear, take back.

In the meantime the work progressed steadily. Faster than before. Ross was aware of a change in atmosphere. No one disturbed him, though he saw the Jecc bump up against Eveleen and the other non-Jecc beings, exactly as they always had.

Ross found his job much easier, despite the game.

So he played it right until darkness—perceived through the big hangar at the end of their workstation—began to fall. No more disabled rail-skimmers had been brought in. The outside workers had already left their jobs.

Ross was so bemused by the day's activities he was scarcely aware of the usual headache and scratchy throat. It wasn't until Eveleen fell in beside him, her eyes marked with tiredness, and her lovely voice sounding slightly hoarse, that he remembered he'd meant to quit much earlier.

Sickness had become a part of life, it seemed.

Since there wasn't anything he could do, there was always distraction. "The Jecc have pouches like kangaroos," he said to his wife as they walked out hand in hand.

"Yilayil," she whistled.

Ross grimaced, and repeated his statement in Yilayil. Truth was, he'd been thinking in English all day—not good for the mission, he realized. But so much easier!

The word for pouch he didn't know—he created a compound, which was often done in Yilayil. Eveleen nodded, brushing raindrops from her face as she considered his words.

Ross went on to explain the theft game, and the unexpected results. Eveleen's interest sharpened—he felt it, despite the steady rain pelting against their rain gear. The tale took until they reached the building that looked to him like a giant muffin—home.

Eveleen pushed her hood back from her face. Ross looked both ways; a small, greenish being was just disappearing up the ramp, tentacles swinging rhythmically. He waited until it was gone and bent to kiss the raindrops from Eveleen's eyelashes.

She smiled, but nudged him silently to move on.

They did not talk until they were safely in their cell, and clean and dry. Then she said, "I think it was dangerous to try that—"

"I know," he said, feeling a twinge of guilt.

Eveleen shook her head. "I'm not pointing fingers. It's not like I've done anything for the cause."

Her back was to him. Was that bitterness he heard in her soft voice? She couldn't be angry with herself for not having made any discoveries—how could she?

Unbidden came his wish from the very first week—that he could get out and poke around during the nights. Not get into trouble, of course, just do some listening on his own. He shook his head, as if to banish the thought.

Eveleen took in a deep breath, turned around and smiled. "I was thinking that your instincts have always been good. Maybe there's something for us to learn in this weird Jecc game, with the tools and the pouches and all."

Ross shrugged, fighting a huge yawn. "I don't see how. But one thing for sure: they didn't get in my way. If anything, it seemed easier to do my work. I used to have to wait for what I needed, but after that Jecc caught me everything seemed to be there when I wanted it, and no one rammed against me or upset my balance so I'd have to reconstruct."

"Maybe I ought to try stealing," Eveleen said with a wry smile. "It was business as usual for me."

"I saw that too," Ross said. "And for all those other non-Jecc, stuck way off in the corner."

"I think it's for self-protection," Eveleen said. "I'd been thinking we ought to try to join them, if we can. At least the Jecc don't go there—much. Don't bother them nearly as much as they do anyone directly in their space."

"Maybe, but not yet—"

Ross stopped talking when the familiar tattoo sounded at their door.

"It's Gordon," he said, frowning. "He never arrives before Irina and Vera."

"Uh oh," Eveleen said softly.

Ross sprang to the door and opened it.

Gordon came in, his bright blue eyes looking tired, but his mouth was set in a hard line that reminded Ross of the old days—of impending action.

"A find," Ashe said abruptly, running a hand impatiently through his white hair to shake the raindrops off.

Eveleen pursed her lips. "The bodies—?"

"No." Ashe turned to her. "But new records. Misha and Viktor stumbled onto a camp used by a couple of the First Team." He pulled a warped notebook from his parka, its pages reminding Ross of lettuces. A hundred years buried in a moist environment would do that, even in a supposedly airtight pack; they were probably lucky the books hadn't rotted all through.

"I'll be going through this more closely, comparing it with what records we already have, but Misha and Viktor skimmed it and summarized its contents."

"And the gist is—?" Ross prompted.

"The First Team disappeared one by one. They got sick beforehand, just as we are now. They didn't get sick as early in their mission."

Eveleen and Ross both nodded, remembering the records they'd studied.

"Apparently the illness worsened rapidly for them all, at least according to one of these records. The other one is more cryptic."

Ashe paused. "Thirsty."

Ross moved to the other room. "I'll get you some water."

"Thanks." A few moments later, Gordon took the cup from Ross, drank down the water, then leaned his head back against the wall.

"There's worse to come," Eveleen said wryly, "isn't there."

It wasn't even a question.

Ashe nodded once. "Worse—better, I don't know. It doesn't give us any answers, only more questions. The short version is this: the team members were not together, as we'd surmised."

"But that was orders," Ross protested. "If dangerous conditions existed—"

"Those were orders, and they did apparently pull together, as we have recorded by the records we found at the contact site. However, it must have been after that person disappeared—"

" 'Disappeared'?" Eveleen repeated. "Not died?"

A knock at the door interrupted them, and Ross moved to let in the two Russian women.

Quickly, while Vera passed out the evening's food, Ashe rapidly brought the women up-to-date on the discussion so far.

Neither spoke until he was done. Then Irina said, in her slow, accented voice, "They have disappeared one by one? What means this for us?"

"That's what I'm trying to figure out," Gordon said. "Misha and Viktor have found no human remains, and they have just about covered the entire island. Misha wants to jump back to one of these campsites and watch, of course."

Vera looked up sharply, her lips parted.

Irina shook her head, her fine brows creased slightly. "No. Is not a good idea, not if they sickened rapidly. This disease we all share, it might be more virulent a century ago."

"But if they just got sick and died," Eveleen protested, "then we'd find bodies, right?"

"So we would think," Gordon answered. "Of course, it could be that roving Yilayil or Nurayil scooped them up and obliterated them, although we don't have any indication of this kind of burial custom. But maybe death by illness is treated differently than death by execution, or death by more natural causes."

Vera said softly, "Misha. He had friends with First Team . . ."

Gordon said in a gentle voice, "I know that. He explained—a little. Misha is not exactly gabby with personal details." He smiled wryly, and Vera smiled back, but her eyes remained troubled. "I made him promise to do nothing until Zina is consulted."

Ross felt relief zing through him. "Good thinking. Throw this one in their laps—let the scientists hash out what this sickness is, and all the rest of it."

Gordon nodded. "I'm going to ask you to help me copy Pavel's notebook out—I don't trust it not to disappear," he said to the women. "And Svetlana's, which Misha insisted on keeping and translating himself, will also be copied. He says he has the time when they're hiding from the flyers. As soon as we have copies, I'll send Viktor forward to report, and we'll wait on Zina's decision before we act."

Irina's brow cleared.

"Is good," she said in Russian, and then in English, "very good."

CHAPTER 20

SABA'S DISCOVERY OF the terminal in her room having been activated was a signal to her that she must devote herself to this aspect of the mission.

For two days she forced herself to sit at that terminal in her room, alternately shivering with chills and panting from what seemed stifling heat. She worked at mastering the Yilayil keypads.

Alternating between that and the records of the First Team on her own laptop, her fevered mind constructed dream fantasies that seemed real. When she did not work, she set the audio to play Yilayil music of the Great Dance, the rising and falling voices reminding her somehow of the music of the Dorze, at home in Ethiopia; music that was embedded in daily life, and was heard continually during not just the little customs of each day—waking, sleeping, meals—but during weddings and funerals, and in the festivities occurring throughout the year.

She did not understand the music, not as she did that of the Dorze. She had spent her childhood with Dorze music. As she listened to this music she sensed a kind of kinship, a need—shared by two vastly different peoples—to celebrate the dance of life and death in music.

But true understanding still eluded her. All her goals were still pieces. Shards. It hurt to think, and though she fought the image, her mind persisted in seeing her goals as jagged pieces of glass—or mirror—that must be fit together. But she did not have to touch them, and bleed, for willing ghost hands had appeared to do that: Katarina, the First Team linguist, whose words Saba had perused so deeply for meaning that she had committed them to memory—and began perceiving traces of the personality who had spoken them.

When Saba's tired body forced her to lie down, she began holding conversations with Katarina. She'd seen a photo of the Russian linguist during one of the briefings back in the United States, and now she envisioned that face, broad across the cheeks, wide-set dark eyes, dark gray-streaked hair short and glossy. Katarina's Mongolian antecedents looked out from the shape of her skull, strong and imperturbable and brave.

Saba, from utterly different people, still felt a kinship with Katarina.

The ghost of the Russian woman sometimes seemed real, so strong was Saba's dream state. "Listen," Katarina said, over and over. "Listen outside of time."

More of the strange tenses.

Baffled by the bizarre temporalities of the language, Saba began instead to explore the sensory contradictions. She discovered that one set of keystrokes set up the modulation into the sensory mode, modifying straightforward ideographs into strange little contradictory nuggets of meaning. They were almost like Zen koans. Certainly the feel of a green taste was just as ungraspable as the sound of one hand clapping. Somehow, she began to sense, there was some connection between the strange tenses and the contradictory sensory modalities. But she could not grasp its wholeness.

"Gestalt," she said to her ghost. "I think this is what you were sensing, was it not? You laid out the shards of this mirror."

"It is not a mirror," Katarina said. "It is a window." Katarina smiled, her eyes narrowing to half-moons. "Find the gestalt, Saba Mariam. Find the gestalt—set me free."

Saba dragged herself up from her bed, drank some water, then sat down at her terminal. "Pieces," she murmured. "Pieces."

But again she ran into the mental wall of her own ignorance.

Finally she forced herself to rise, leaning against the real wall until the waves of darkness throbbed through her brain and then died away. Then she donned her robe and walked out in the direction of the translation chamber.

She realized when she reached it that she had lost track of time. It was late.

In fact, it was night, and only the Yilayil were about.

She began to retreat, for she knew the etiquette: not until she had been invited could she interact with the Yilayil.

The sleek weasel-shaped beings ignored her, and she stood uncertainly, until the *wisp-wisp* of a robe upon the floor brought her attention round.

Zhot stood there, still, his eyes unblinking.

"Come. Train," he droned.

Unquestioning, Saba followed him into the chamber beyond, where she saw a terminal. She sank down onto the bench, resolutely dismissing the ache of head and neck, and spread her hands lightly over the key-pads.

They were too far apart for true comfort. Vividly she saw the long, furred, double-knuckled digits of the four-armed Yilayil.

"Now," Zhot said. "Begin."

She tapped out the combinations she had learned, and then, when Zhot said nothing, she went on to those she'd managed to puzzle out.

Moving with his accustomed fluidity, Zhot reached down to tap out a new combination, which caused symbols to flow across the screen.

"See," he commanded. "And let go of the connections you impose . . ."

Again time streamed by, uncounted, as Saba worked under Zhot's direction. Saba's fever slowly increased, noticed only on the periphery of her attention: chills, heat, ache. She dismissed them all. She was aware only that Katarina seemed to stand at her other shoulder, watching in approval.

She remembered a brief discussion of synesthesia from her neurology studies, how some people perceived shapes to have tastes, or colors sounds. The instructor had said that no one really understood the phenomenon, but that it was thought to emerge from the limbic system, where symbols and emotions were correlated.

Where symbols and emotions dance, she thought suddenly. The thought moved her hands, and a new combination of ideographs popped up on the screen.

"You begin to perceive," said Zhot. She started. She had not realized he was still standing there.

Saba did not understand what she had done, so she returned her attention to her hands, and to the symbols scrolling across the screen. Slowly, slowly, she was beginning to make sense of them; or rather, to stop trying to force sense on them and let them speak—dance?—for themselves.

The organization was indeed akin to Chinese writing, something she understood the guiding principles of, though she did not speak or read Chinese.

But finding a familiar structure accentuated the kinship of beings otherwise so far from one another in temporal reality. The miracle of similar structure—of hands, and brain, and mouth to talk and eyes to look—produced similarities in language. It was a bond, a universal bond.

It was exciting to penetrate it.

"I will find you, Katarina," she said to her ghost when, abruptly, Zhot departed and she was left to find her way back to her room.

She collapsed in gratitude onto her bed, dropping immediately into a deep sleep.

Thirst and chills forced her awake again. Groggy and cold, she rose to draw water. The room lights came on as soon as she left the bed. She reached to fill her water glass—then paused, activated the sonic screen, and passed it through a couple times.

The water had registered as pure. She was sure the sonic screen killed microbes . . . so why was she sick?

She sighed, filled the cup, drank thirstily. Then she reluctantly helped herself to another precious dose of her medicine. She'd feel the fever drop soon, and then she could work.

Restlessness brought her to her feet. She tabbed on the computer, blinked at the blurry screen, then decided to wait until the medicine dose had restored her equilibrium.

Instead, the restlessness distilled into a single, strong urge: for fresh air, for light.

Was it morning? She would find out.

She passed her flaxen robe through the cleaner, then pulled it on, sighing with relief as its folds draped softly down her body to the floor. Then she tabbed her door open, and slid out, moving silently.

Not down. That way led only to the grand mosaic—suns and stars— and the chambers of knowledge, more and more of them the farther down one went.

Instead, for the first time, she turned her steps upward.

As she walked, she thought about the Yilayil metaphors and images. One shard was the fact that human and Yilayil idiom evoked opposites: for humans, upward and light meant freedom, opportunity, beauty. Dancing—free—in the sun. How many earth cultures carried just such a potent image?

For the Yilayil, harmony, the Great Dance, meant darkness. Downward and dark were the preferred directions. Saba had unconsciously fallen into the same thought pattern; that was inevitable when one focused one's attention on achieving ti[*trill*]kee.

Upward was undesirable, upward was . . . danger?

She frowned, thinking over the little gestures, the modes of expression she'd unconsciously assimilated while trying to reach for greater understanding.

Was there danger? Her steps up the ramp did not falter. The desire for light, for stillness and air, was too strong.

No one had forbidden her to go upward. Yet she had never seen anyone go there. Still, this space was here, she thought, looking around. There were even rooms.

She paused, laying a hand on a door. The rooms were far apart, but they were there. Rooms—or passages?

She touched the silver control, and to her surprise, the door slid open.

She looked out—not in. This was not a room, it was a kind of balcony, looking out at the morning sun above the tops of the buildings. In the distance she could see the solid green line of the jungle, pressing up against the city borders. And at one end, the edge of the long-abandoned spaceport.

She stepped out onto the balcony, then stopped. Now visible from the door was more space—and on it several still figures.

She saw three beings she did not recognize, but the fourth was Zhot.

He was not wearing his flaxen robe. Saba glanced down his body, seeing the supple seallike muscle structure, the scaled skin. In the strong, clear sunlight his skin had a greenish flush, almost a glow, overlaying the sandy coloration she was used to seeing.

The urge to fling off her clothing—which suddenly felt heavy and confining—seized her. How wonderful just to stand, breathing the fresh air, and feeling the sunlight on face, skin, limbs!

She took a deep breath, then forced herself away.

She had work to do.

The urge stayed with her as she retreated back down the ramp to her room. But duty steadied her, as always. It was morning, almost time for her daily signal to Gordon. Now that she was away from the allure of the sunlight, her eyes ached with the need for sleep, and her mouth was dry, but duty had become habit, and habit steadied her mind. Anchored her to reality.

What to do until the time for the signal?

She turned to her terminal, and touched the control. The screen lit. Sitting down, Saba worked her fingers into one of the patterns she'd recently learned. Without really considering what she was doing, she tested her ability to tranliterate, and traced out Zhot's name.

To her surprise, a new screen flickered into place, offering her choices. On her keypad, several keys lit with subtle color.

She touched the control that she recognized as indicating world-of-origin.

And once again the screen rippled, this time showing a rapidly moving vid of Zhot's people. Two voices whispered from the terminal's audio system: one language she couldn't recognize at all, but the other was Yilayil—someone's translation!

Curious, she watched what seemed rather like one of those travel vids she used to view in school: *Welcome to Kenya!* or *Welcome to Australia!* only this was more like the equivalent of *Welcome to Earth!* because it featured the world's primary in a schematic, and an unfamiliar system, zeroing in on the fourth body out.

Zhot's world was, like the Yilayil world, primarily water, only it seemed to have two very long continents straddling either side of the equator. On it Zhot's people seemed to be the most numerous beings, along with some undersea creatures that might have been sentient, but after the brief introduction, the screen paused and offered choices, this time showing different beings.

History of races?

Saba touched the control that corresponded to Zhot's seal-people, and watched in fascination. This time she listened to the Yilayil, not trying to translate any single words, but letting the whole flow through her.

Zhot's people, the Valeafeh, seemed to have had technology for a very long time. A matriarchy of loosely intersecting tribal families, they fostered young of other races and in turn sent out their young males to learn before coming back to settle down to service; the females stayed in order to learn government.

Opposite from the Virigu? Saba thought, making a mental note to look them up in their turn.

She found lots more information—including data on daily life. But nowhere did she see a glimpse of any of the Valeafeh behaving as she'd just witnessed Zhot behaving. Nor did any of them look green.

Strange! Had she inadvertently stumbled onto a custom that was taboo, or at least forbidden witnesses? Saba decided that must be it, knowing that any travelogue vid made about Earth would not include acts considered private and intimate.

Well, at least Zhot had not woken from his meditation, or nap, or whatever he'd been doing, and Saba decided she would not bring it up. No harm done.

She glanced at the chrono. At last, time for her daily signal to Gordon.

She clicked the communicator on, and her thumb hovered over the little plastic key she had used for so long to send the pulse codes.

For a moment she looked down uncomprehendingly at the walkie-talkie's little display screen. Her vision, though blurry, was clear enough to warn her that the usual pattern of green lights had altered.

She frowned, and held the device up to the light to reread the displays.

Then she identified the single button that had been blank for so long—the frequency for speaking was now clear.

"Gordon?"

"Saba!"

WHEN EVELEEN AND Ross reached the Nurayil dorms, she gratefully wiped her forehead as they passed inside, and let her breath out in a whoosh.

"I don't know whether to be glad it stopped raining or not," she said to Ross as they started up the ramp.

Ross grinned at her. "I'd wanted to see the sun for the past week or three—but now I think I've had enough of it." He squinted upward. "Okay, hear that? You can go back to rain now."

Eveleen laughed. "At least abate the humidity."

"With a jungle a stone's throw away?" Ross retorted. "Not a chance."

"Well, I wish there was a way to get a weather report—either that or to get air-conditioning in the—" Eveleen stopped when she saw Gordon standing outside their room.

She felt Ross tense up beside her. Something had happened.

Nobody spoke until they'd passed inside. Then Gordon said, "The frequency cleared. I don't know why, or what it means, but at least I can talk to Saba."

"And?" Ross prompted in a sharp voice.

Gordon gave his head a shake. "She's sick. Tried to downplay it, but I suspect she's much sicker than we are."

"Damn," Ross breathed. "What do we do? Pull her out?"

Gordon said, "Even if we could—which I doubt—she won't come. Insists she's close to some kind of breakthrough. When I tried to get her to explain, I'm afraid she scared me. Made little sense. Yet it's apparent she's gotten much further than we have in her investigations. She has access to the Yilayil computer system, and she has even been permitted to walk around the House of Knowledge at night."

"Ti [*trill*]kee?" Eveleen asked, amazed.

Gordon shook his head again. "No; the Yilayil ignored her. But she wasn't shooed back by her tutor. She got more lessons."

"How sick is she?" Ross asked.

"That's what I was trying to determine." Gordon looked from one of them to the other, clearly hesitating.

Eveleen felt her heart hammer a warning tattoo. "Oh, no . . ."

Gordon's dark brows furrowed. "You're in her confidence?"

Eveleen nodded soberly, then turned to Ross. "I guess, considering the circumstances, it would be fair to tell you: she was told many years ago that she carries a recessive gene for sickle-cell anemia. Definitely recessive, they said—she probably wouldn't get it, but might pass it on, especially if she ever married someone who carried the same gene."

Ross grimaced.

Eveleen said in a low voice, "It's why she decided she would never marry. Have kids. Didn't want to risk passing on a tragedy."

Gordon looked up sharply, and Eveleen knew that he hadn't heard about that. He'd probably read about the recessive gene in Saba's file, but he hadn't considered what effect it could have on her life decisions.

They're so much alike, Eveleen thought. Each reclusive, solitary, by choice. Only what is in Gordon's past? She would never ask, of course.

Ross said, "So maybe this has weakened her immune system in some way? Made her sicker than we are—if she has the same disease? She's been isolated from us, so it could be something totally different."

"Or it could be something we were all exposed to on arrival," Gordon said. "We're not going to know—at least, not unless Viktor finds out something down the timeline." He glanced at his watch.

"He signaled this morning, then?" Ross asked.

"Yes," Gordon said.

Eveleen bit her lip. Viktor had had his long walk to the transport, and he and Gordon had agreed that he'd spend a maximum of one day and one night there, taking care to arrive in the morning so that the long walk back to the meetpoint would not bring anyone out after dark.

Gordon lived with his walkie-talkie clipped to his belt. Misha's orders had been to signal as soon as Viktor emerged from the transport. If Viktor had to go back down the timeline for more conferences, at least they'd know.

So he was back. Gordon awaited only the second signal, meaning he should get to the meetpoint, wherever that was.

All, of course, before darkness fell. Which would be very soon.

Eveleen opened her mouth to ask how he'd managed to juggle his job so he could accommodate all this moving around, but was prevented by a quick knock at the door.

Ross opened it—and all four came in, Irina, Vera, Misha, and Viktor.

For a moment they all stood there, a silent tableau. Eveleen scanned them, noting the posture of each: Irina graceful and aloof; Misha standing near her, one fist propped on a hip, an ironic smile on his handsome face; Vera standing very close to Misha, unnoticed; Viktor leaning against the wall, looking exhausted, his dark hair lying in sweat-damp strands across his broad forehead.

So many people crowded into a tiny room made the walls close in, and Eveleen was aware of the sharp smell of stale sweat.

Almost at the same time, Misha grimaced and said, "It is very hot today, and in the jungle there are no amenities—"

"Come on," Ross said, gesturing toward the fresher alcove. "It's not palatial, but it's better than what you've been stuck with."

They disappeared inside. Eveleen heard Ross's voice explaining how everything worked as, in silence, Vera passed out the evening's ration of food.

Her eyes were lowered, her generous mouth, almost always smiling, was uncharacteristically somber. Eveleen guessed that Vera had discovered the open frequency and had broken the silence rule—and Misha had taken advantage of it to meet and make his report in person.

Gordon—wisely, Eveleen thought—said nothing. It was apparent from Irina's posture that she had already spoken her mind to her colleague.

The two Russian men emerged then, and everyone sat in a circle to eat.

"Viktor?" Gordon said, once Viktor had taken the edge off his appetite. "You did not report to them ill—"

"I did what you ordered: wrote out a letter stating our symptoms, copied it onto a disk. Sent it forward. Valentin came back to say come forward to report in person."

"They are sick as well," Misha said, saving Viktor from having to frame his report in English. "Same symptoms, came on about the same time."

Viktor then spoke. "Zina. She wants to end the mission."

CHAPTER 21

ROSS REACHED FOR the makeshift calendar that he and Eveleen had begun.

Rapidly he totted up the days, then he looked up at Eveleen and nodded.

Everyone's count was the same: they were on Day 46, and had fifteen days until they reached the same number the First Team had stayed before Katarina disappeared.

Viktor said, "Zina makes order to us. Despite how we know that First Team did not all vanish that day, still, we must be gone by same day. Our time." He frowned, said something swiftly in Russian, then he rubbed his eyes tiredly.

Misha continued for Viktor: "Even if one of us disappears, as did Katarina, it is still too much. We either solve the problems we face in fourteen days—without courting extra risks—or we must just leave, return home, and give our bosses the problem."

Viktor added. "They will withdraw to the ship on Day Sixty, and get ready for takeoff. We must be there by sunset, Day Sixty." He looked up and met Irina's eyes.

Ross, watching idly, felt a spurt of surprise when he saw the man's jaw tighten. He shifted his own gaze to Irina, in time to see a tiny nod, but then she turned her attention down to her laptop—on which her fingers had been steadily typing.

Gordon said, "As long as we have Saba, I agree. But I do not leave without her."

Irina said, "We will not plan to leave without Saba." She spoke in the same kind of calm, flat voice as Gordon used.

Vera said quickly, "Why not right now? We can get her out, and leave now."

Misha struck his hand against the wall, a sharp sound that made everyone jump.

Ross hadn't realized until then how tense they all were. Tired, sick, yes, also tense.

"This mission is not failed," he stated, his accent strong. He gave Irina a cold-eyed stare. "We have time. I *will* find Svetlana."

Irina just stared back without speaking.

Ross slid a glance at his wife. Eveleen watched the two Russians, a sober expression in her eyes.

Misha said, "I have translated all her writings. I can retrace her steps, and if we go back to the day she disappeared—"

Viktor spoke in Russian, gesturing with his hands. Irina also spoke, and Misha produced a disk from his pocket. He handed it to Irina, who took it without comment.

Ross saw Gordon following this action. He said nothing.

When Irina had finished putting away the disk, Gordon said in a quiet voice, "Zina is right. We don't know what this disease is. The fact that we all have it, at both ends of the time line, makes a strong case for the First Team having been afflicted with the same thing. And though we haven't found bodies, we don't know if the First Team died before they vanished—there are too many anomalies. Until we solve at least one, we cannot go back and risk the same thing happening to us."

"Then we find out," Misha said. "You get Saba out, I solve this, my own way."

He turned to the door, hit the control. He went out without speaking another word, and Viktor, with an expressive shrug, followed.

The door closed, its sound loud in the sudden silence.

"Let's go over the facts," Eveleen said in a voice of compromise. "We know we're all sick—but our scientists don't know the cause, or the disease. We know that the First Team were not together, and that they did in fact disappear on different days, but no one earlier than Katarina, the archivist."

Vera said, "Misha won't rest until he finds some kind of evidence. He . . ." She paused, rolling her eyes.

"Mikhail Petrovich," Irina enunciated in her clear, emotionless voice, "is a romantic." Her tone equated *romantic* with *fool*.

Gordon said diplomatically, "He's determined to make the jump up to the First Team's time, and perhaps that is a way to find out what happened." His voice sharpened subtly. "But it might just endanger us without solving anything at all. Until we collect enough evidence to know for sure, let's not end up with the same mysterious fate. And so we're back to our original problem: we must determine, if we can, exactly what happened to them, and why."

Ross nodded, without speaking. Vera made a noise of agreement. Irina shrugged.

Gordon went on, "So let's split up, and do whatever we can to put together the few puzzle pieces we have. See if we can get some sort of picture, something to act on safely. In the meantime, nothing seems to have happened to us—" He gestured to the walkie-talkie clipped to Vera's belt. "So I rescind the silence rule. But let's use good judgment. We still have to assume that someone who can jam can listen in."

"We speak in English," Vera said. "Russian, someone might know, or have on record from a hundred years ago. English would still be new."

Gordon nodded.

Vera gave Irina a questioning look. Irina nodded politely at Gordon, Ross, and Eveleen, then went out, her footfalls noiseless.

Ross thought about that cold, angry glance as he and Eveleen got ready to sleep. Eveleen seemed troubled; Ross glanced over at her a couple times as he rolled out their futon. She was sitting cross-legged on the floor, typing rapidly into her laptop.

When she finished, she closed the laptop and sat back with a sigh.

Ross said, "Any intuition about what's going on in Irina's head?"

Eveleen looked up, slightly startled. "You too, huh?"

Ross shrugged. "I have to admit I'm having trouble figuring these Russkis. I don't know if it's me, or them, or I'm just not a sensitive kind of a guy—"

Eveleen laughed. "Meaning you scent personal gossip behind all the angry looks and so forth. Well, so do I. We do know that Misha has romanced most of the women in the Russian service. We also know he pulled strings to be sent on this mission. I suspect that his relationship with Svetlana wasn't just lighthearted flirtation. How Irina fits into this is anybody's guess."

Ross grimaced. You didn't get this kind of talk on a mission with all men—and, he reflected, you probably didn't get it on missions with all women. Put 'em together, and what do you get?

"Chemistry," he said out loud.

"Hmm?" Eveleen asked, blinking. "Oh! Misha and Irina? Well, either that or politics. I can't pretend to understand them all. Irina especially. All I know is—or rather, all I *sense* is that Irina and Misha are going to be competing in some way, he to solve the mission, and she to get us back to Earth before we end up like the rest."

"So you don't think she wants to solve the mystery."

Eveleen paused in the act of brushing out her hair, and shook her head. "I think Irina has decided it's impossible, and she wants to wrap it up and move on."

Ross sighed as he dropped down beside her on the futon. His thoughts ranged from Misha and Irina to Saba, hidden in the House, and from there to his own situation—the Jecc game. He hadn't mentioned it to Gordon; it seemed so unimportant beside all the other crises.

But as he lay there, his mind drifting, his thoughts came back to that word *chemistry.*

After a little while, the light sensors, detecting no movement, turned the lights off. Eveleen's breathing had already become deep and even; she was asleep. Ross closed his eyes and tried to clear his mind.

Dawn the next morning was again clear, they discovered when they left the Nurayil dorm. Clear, hot, and humid.

"Ugh," Eveleen said, then she cleared her throat and somewhat breathlessly made a comment about the weather.

Ross obligingly forced his mind to switch from the quicksilver ease of his native English to the heavy freight train of Yilayil. Weird, how his brain refused to get used to this language, a problem he'd not had on previous assignments.

He asked—in Yilayil—"Have you trouble with speech in the Yilayil?" He chose the word for thought/mind/speech, realizing as he whistled and hummed the words that this was his problem, the words weren't one-for-one exchanges.

"I concur," Eveleen trilled. "To think/speak . . ." She hesitated, then said quickly in English, "Every word is a paragraph." She looked guiltily at Ross, then went back to Yilayil. "Practice perhaps would take a year."

Ross didn't answer. He knew they were both thinking that they didn't have a year.

They reached their workplace then, and the cool, shadowy building was a distinct relief after the early morning heat.

As Ross took up his station, he considered their performance so far. Back on Earth—what had seemed a thousand years ago—everyone had blithely assumed that he and Eveleen would be able to attain driver status without any problem, thus being able to sneak rail-skimmers out and move the teammates around as needed. At least so long as their destinations matched with the hidden rail system. They'd assumed that Misha and Viktor would of course find the bodies of the First Team, all located in the same place, having been buried on the same day. They'd assumed—

His attention splintered when he felt a dry, scaly hand at his side. The Jecc!

The game was on.

He'd almost forgotten them. Quick as light he imprisoned the small fingers working at the communicator attached to his belt. The Jecc went very still, its pupils contracting as it stared up at him.

Ross spoke without thinking, repeating the same phrase used by the Jecc that caught him stealing, all those days ago: "My progeny will be swift."

The Jecc's gaze seemed to intensify, then fast as lightning it scuttled away.

Ross turned to his work, picking up where he'd left off in a complicated assembly the day before. The Jecc encounter was momentarily forgotten.

It didn't stay forgotten long. Within a very short time he became aware of a change in the behaviors of the Jecc. He'd become the center of their focus—not just the stealing, but they seemed to move about him in busy circles, humming a kind of shorthand Yilayil.

The only time they faded away was at midday break, when Ross went to find Eveleen. As soon as he addressed her, his Jecc followers vanished like a tide receding.

"Something weird's going on," he murmured in an undertone.

"Danger?" She used the Yilayil word.

He replied in the same tongue. "No, I believe not. A change, a transition . . ." Again he felt that the words carried too many meanings, and choosing them was like carrying a mental backpack up a hill, whereas English was like light tiles, easily chosen, enabling him to sprint tirelessly. Frustrating.

He changed the subject to something innocuous as they forced down something to eat. The midday sun was blisteringly hot, and the air outside the transport area was almost overpowering with heavy scents.

When he was done he peered against the sunny glare off walls and roofs, and made out the dark green line of the jungle in the near distance. Weird. It felt as if it encroached menacingly.

"No appetite either?" Eveleen asked—in Yilayil.

He shook his head.

She sighed. "I noticed we are all thinner."

Ross thought back to the night before, and nodded. He hadn't been aware of it, but when he considered the Russians and Gordon—Eveleen was right. Of course, that was to be expected, since they were all sick.

But he didn't *feel* thinner. He felt, if anything, too heavy.

That had to be the heat—and the illness.

He dismissed the thought, and drank some water.

Then it was time to return to work.

As soon as he was alone, the Jecc returned, circling around closer than ever. So it went for the rest of the shift. No one stole anything, but the Jecc stayed close, as if watching him, though they did not stop their work either.

It was when he shut down his workstation that the same Jecc came forward who had addressed him so aggressively on the first day in this department.

"I, Bock of Harbeast Teeth Islands, take Ross of Fire Mountain Enclave to nest for Day of Lamentation."

Ross stared down at the little being. A threat? Or an invitation?

He looked about for Eveleen, then realized that to do so meant that the Jecc would once again disappear.

He hesitated, knowing he should report in. But he also knew what Gordon would say: "Sit tight. Zina's orders."

But they didn't know about the Jecc. And Ross had a hunch that— somehow—this was going to fit into the overall puzzle.

He turned his head, watching Eveleen slowly shutting down her own workstation.

Better she went safely back to their room. If he was doing something stupid, at least he was the only one endangered.

"Yes," he said to Bock. "I come."

CHAPTER 22

"IT'S BEEN TWO hours," Eveleen said, trying hard not to snarl into the communicator.

It wasn't Gordon's fault. It wasn't anyone's fault—except Ross's. Dammit!

"He's signaled the safety code?" Gordon asked.

"Yes," Eveleen said. "Twice. I know he's alive, but I don't know where."

"Exactly what happened?" Gordon asked.

"Nothing. That is, at the end of the workday, I saw him shutting down his work area. He had about six Jecc with him. All of them were quiet, which was unusual for Jecc."

"I don't know any Jecc," Gordon said.

"You're lucky," Eveleen commented, then she sighed. At least their room was cool, but to be in it alone—she shut her eyes against its unwelcoming alienness. "Anyway, I was glad to shut my work down because the heat made my head ache worse than ever. But when I finished and started over to find him, I realized he was gone. At first I thought I might have missed him, and so I walked all over the Transport. Nothing. So I came back here along our usual route. Nothing. So I took out my com. We'd traded off wearing ours, since we work together and could share news. Save energy. He had his on today. I tried to raise him—no answer."

"But you said you got the code for safety," Gordon cut in.

"That was after I raced back to the Transport." Eveleen bit back a comment about the enjoyment of running in the fierce heat. Gordon knew how hot it was. Everyone knew. "He wasn't there, so I tried to raise him by voice, and when that didn't work, I tried the pulse. I got an answer back then—the safety code."

"Could someone have taken it from him?"

"That was my first thought," Eveleen said, reaching for a cup of water. She drank thirstily, then said, "Pardon."

Gordon laughed a little. "I've been drinking gallons myself. Saba as well."

"You've been talking to Saba?" Eveleen asked, diverted for a moment.

"Long conversations," Gordon said, his tone curious. "Back to Ross. You don't think someone took his com?"

"Oh. No. Not unless they also can read minds. You see, back on the ship, we'd also worked out a couple of personal codes. Just in case. Well, he pulsed one of those, too. And an hour ago, when he sent the next safety code, he sent another one—this one meaning 'Can't talk now but I'm okay.' "

She didn't mention that the first one he'd sent was the "I love you" code—not that Gordon probably couldn't guess.

Too bad we didn't work one out for "I love you, but what you did is so stupid I'm going to throttle you!" Eveleen thought grimly.

"This sounds rather like the Ross I've always known," Gordon said next, and Eveleen—though nothing could abate her exasperation—was a little comforted. "Here's my guess. He's following a hunch, something so harebrained he knew we'd all be against it. But his instincts have always been good, so far."

So far. Eveleen sighed. "Right."

"Keep in contact if anything changes," Gordon said.

Eveleen wanted to talk more—for reassurance if for nothing else—but she forced herself to sign off. She knew Gordon couldn't really help. He knew even less than she did about the situation, and it wasn't as if he didn't have plenty to worry about on his own.

He knew less than she did about—

She jumped up, ignoring the pang in her temples. Idiot!

Once again she tabbed her com, but this time—for the first time—she punched in the code for Misha.

His answer came almost immediately. "Nikulin here."

Nikulin? Oh, yes, Misha's last name. Eveleen said, "Misha, have you come across any Jecc on your investigations?"

"Jecc? Yes. They have a, a lair, you must say in English, in a series of caves directly south, near the peninsula."

Eveleen let out her breath in a whoosh. "Any chance you could take me there?"

Misha gave a soft laugh. "Yes, I can. Is there a reason?"

Swiftly Eveleen outlined the situation.

Misha said nothing until she'd reached the end, only, "I will come to you." And the com went dead.

She figured Misha had to be several hours' walk away, and she repressed a wince of guilt at making him walk in the heat. This was too important.

The main thing was to get rest. Until he arrived, she might as well try to catch some sleep.

So she unrolled the futon, trying not to think about lying on it alone, laid out her equipment, and composed herself for sleep. Yet it seemed she'd only just closed her eyes when a rapid tap came at the door.

She opened it to find Misha standing there, alone. She grabbed her canteen and her com, and walked out.

He smiled down at her, his eyes impossible to read.

"Is there a problem?" he asked.

His tone suggested a problem between Ross and herself. She fought annoyance, realizing that it was a legitimate question—that the success of the mission was at stake, and so she answered in an even voice, "No. Opposite, really—" And as she spoke, she *had* it. "He's being chivalrous, I'm afraid. And . . ." The truth almost made her dizzy. "It's stupid, but I think I would have done the same thing."

She had a sudden, vivid mental picture of Ross stumping alongside Misha, cursing at each step as they chased after her, and she laughed out loud, then caught herself up short, choking the laughs back.

Misha gave her a quizzical glance.

Forestalling any more personal questions, she asked, "How long is the walk? All night?"

Misha shook his head. "You will see."

They reached the bottom of the ramp, then, and Eveleen realized it was quite dark outside. This was against the rules—only the Yilayil could be out. Yet Misha had gotten in successfully.

Her heart pounded as she followed him around the side of the building. They walked in a direction she'd never explored. Why not? she asked herself. And the answer came immediately, because she and Ross had spent every waking moment with each other, keeping each other safe. Alone, they probably both would have been a lot more adventurous.

And neither of them had ever spoken a word about this.

She grimaced at the ground as she walked. Well, they were going to make up for lost time, she promised.

But first—a big first—she and Misha had to find Ross, and get him back, all without anyone being caught abroad at night.

Misha raised a hand, and Eveleen stopped. He leaned out, looking in all directions, then he unfolded a small lorgnettelike device and peered through it: an infrared scanner. He did a slow circle, then folded it back up.

"No one," he murmured. "We are at the border of the city. Few come this way."

In silence she followed him at a jogging pace down a curving pathway—a skimmer rail, she realized. They ran past several small, circular buildings, almost none of which had windows. In the distance loomed the black line of the jungle.

Before they reached it, though, Misha made an abrupt diagonal. Eveleen followed, taking care to match the long strides of the Russian agent. He led the way unerringly into what seemed at first to be an overgrown garden, lit with a ghostly glow from the tower of the House of Knowledge.

They passed between two vine-covered walls, then Misha unclipped a flashlight from his belt. A quick look behind, a scan on the infrared, and he motioned Eveleen to follow.

Misha clicked the flash on, revealing a moss-covered ramp leading down in a sharp spiral.

"Careful. One can easily slip," Misha murmured.

Eveleen walked carefully, picking her way over cracked stone and jumbles of small plants that had wedged themselves in the cracks.

They walked down rapidly, passing from the hot, still air into a breezy passageway that smelled faintly like the Transport Eveleen worked at every day. At once she felt alarm, for the rail-skimmers were usually crowded—and at night, of course, they would belong exclusively to the Yilayil.

But Misha seemed to read her thoughts, for he said, "Be easy. This has been closed for centuries."

Attesting to the truth of what he said, the flashlight played over mossy walls and fungus-covered surfaces as she became aware of the musical drip of water seeping down from somewhere overhead.

Down, down they walked, into a dim-lit tunnel. Drier air whooshed softly in their faces, smelling faintly of machinery. An air circulation system?

Misha spoke now in a normal voice: "We found this by accident, when trying to escape one of the recent storms. Apparently one transport was built directly atop the older one."

He pointed down the narrow tunnel, and they walked a short distance along a meter-wide curb.

"This is the very south end of the old spaceport, which must have been abandoned several centuries before the First Team's time. We think this predates the Yilayil. Runs on different principles than those buckets you and Ross repair every day."

"Why didn't they just use this? Why build something new?" Eveleen asked.

Misha shrugged, and then motioned for her to stop, then he reached high over his head and passed his hand in front of something; Eveleen caught a faint flicker, as of lights nearly off the human-perceptible spectrum, and within seconds a hissing noise heralded the arrival of a long, peculiar-looking vehicle, not at all like the rail-skimmers. This looked more like the low, fast cars found in modern mines, only narrow, and it did not run on wheels.

They climbed in, Eveleen behind Misha. The vehicle was damp to the touch, but not full of water. Eveleen sat down carefully.

"Lie back," Misha warned. "Hands and feet together."

Eveleen obeyed. Misha did something. Without warning the car moved forward, at first slowly, then effortlessly gathering speed. The tightening in her stomach gave her the sense of diving down deep underground at a rapid clip; otherwise the tunnel indicated nothing, neither depth nor direction.

Once or twice it swerved, or dove farther, then Misha did something up front. Intersections arrived—brief flashes of light and slight impacts on her ears—then vanished again. At last the craft drove upward again, pressing her back against a hard, ridged seat, then it slowed smoothly to a stop.

"We are at the south end of the island," Misha said as they climbed out.

"Have you been all over, then?" Eveleen asked.

Misha nodded, smoothing back ruffled blond hair from his brow. "There's nothing to be found—nothing for us. But these early engineers were a damned sight better than the weasel folk. No sign of what happened to them, of course."

Eveleen bit back a comment, thinking: If I'd been alone, I would have spent all my free time looking for just this kind of thing. Her head even seemed to ache less. Was it impending action? Or maybe just the clean, filtered air of the deep transport system?

Whatever it was, they were out of it soon, for Misha motioned her into a kind of escalator, which whizzled them to another overgrown tunnel. Now the familiar flowery, warm, humid air clogged her sinuses.

They stepped out into starlit darkness.

"Do the Jecc use these transports, then?" Eveleen asked.

"Yes. We found out purely by accident. They all crowd in at dawn and dusk, and sometimes in between, but never at night. We nearly were discovered by them one morning when we were asleep at the other end."

"Huh." So the Jecc, thieves of everything small and inconsequential, had a secret transport? Eveleen wondered how many other secrets were held by the various races of this world. She shook her head. "We need a year here, not days."

"This I know," Misha said, sounding amused.

Neither spoke for the remainder of the walk, which was up a steep trail. Eveleen was glad that there was no rain—though halfway up, she would have welcomed the moisture, just to cool her off. She was very glad not to be making this journey in the middle of the day.

Once she started to ask a question, but Misha reached, putting a hand to her lips.

She shrugged him off, and nodded. His face, scarcely discernible in the starlight, was unreadable, but she sensed his amusement at her reaction.

Presently he stopped, and motioned for her to drop to her knees. He did also, and they crawled slowly along a narrow cliff, then stopped. Misha pointed over a rocky edge, and she lay flat and stretched slowly out, looking down.

She found herself staring directly down a wide vent. The familiar burned-toast smell of the Jecc was very pronounced, along with a not-unpleasant, slightly astringent scent rather like the herb rosemary.

She inched farther out, looking down into the yellowish light, and caught sight of muted colors. Blinking the sweat out of her eyes, she scrunched forward on her elbows until she had a full view down the vent shaft, into a chamber whose walls were covered with some kind of mural. She saw stars, plants, cavorting figures that, at the steep angle at which she was forced to view, were hard to make out. They seemed to be Jecc, only they didn't look quite right. She wriggled around, trying different angles, but she couldn't really see well; the angle was still too sharp.

The swift rise and fall of voices came then, faint, carried on the currents of soft air.

In silence she waited, listening to the voices, wondering what to do next, when she heard another voice, a lone voice, human.

It belonged to Ross.

Eveleen listened to the familiar timbre of his voice. He was whistle/

humming something in Yilayil, but the distance, the soft whooshing of the air passing up the vent, made words difficult to discern.

One thing, though, for certain: his voice made it clear that he was not in any danger.

She pressed her cheek against a rock, trying to assess the maelstrom of emotions crashing through her mind.

He was safe.

But he hadn't told her.

And they hadn't done any exploring . . .

Once he returned unharmed she knew she had a right to get really angry with him. It was inexcusable, to just take off without warning. Dangerous, *rock-headed*, and inexcusable. Yet she knew she would probably have done the same thing, and for the same reason: she couldn't bear the thought of him going willingly into danger.

They'd guarded each other, without speaking of it, keeping one another from exploring, from taking risks. Eveleen thought of that secret transport so close to the Nurayil dorm. She and Ross should have found it, weeks ago. But they'd guarded each other from doing anything daring—anything they probably would have done were they single.

Single. Now, suddenly, she understood Milliard's real concern about newlyweds on a mission together.

She sighed, listening to Ross's voice among the high chatters of the Jecc. Oh, Ross! She knew she could make a scene. She was his wife, his helpmeet. She had a right to communication! Then she thought of Saba, who had chosen, with intellectual forbearance, never to have a mate. To close herself off from the possibility of this kind of sharing, because of the possibility of genetic-borne tragedy. Oh, sure, there were ways to make certain one didn't have children—and likewise there were plenty of successful relationships that did not include offspring. Eveleen considered for the first time the possibility that Saba's policy was actually the result of a specific relationship. In other words, she had found the right person, but her circumstances and that person's own wishes could not be made to compromise.

That was real tragedy. Next to it, fussing about "rights" seemed just petty.

She looked over at Misha, who watched her in silence.

"Thanks," she said softly. "Let's go back."

Neither spoke as they made the return journey.

CHAPTER 23

"ZINA HAS SET a limit." Gordon's voice sounded quiet and reassuring. "We lift ship before Blossom Day. I'm working on plans for repatriation."

Saba closed her eyes, listening to the calm voice.

"Blossom Day" was their old code for the day of disappearance. If she was reading his oblique words right, the First Team had not all disappeared on the same day, only Katarina. But apparently Zina wanted them to move forward in time well before that day, and it had something to do with the illness they all shared.

"I am learning," she said. "I learn slowly, and there is much to be learned. I think . . . I know there is something important here."

"Continue to learn," Gordon replied. Then he paused, and she heard him drinking water. They were evidently all thirsty, and their appetites had diminished.

Then he went on to talk about his college days, and how much he'd enjoyed discovering archaeology. They buried their real communication in long innocuous talks, but Saba found that she enjoyed these talks just the same.

At first he'd talked generalities, but gradually, as they found similar areas of interest, he'd become more personal.

"It was the discovery of paradigm that hooked me in," he said. "Oh, I'd heard about worldview and 'Weltanschauung' and so forth all during high school, but it was that visceral understanding that other cultures saw the universe through utterly different metaphors that fascinated me."

"Yes," Saba said. "I was lucky—I saw it early, because my parents came from such vastly different backgrounds." She described riding across the plains of Ethiopia with her father, a doctor, to visit the different peoples. And then there came a new culture to learn, when she moved to the capital city to begin her advanced education. "But that is what brought me to my studies, the expression of paradigm through music."

"Music," Gordon mused. "It was on the periphery of my attention when I was growing up."

"It was a part of life for me," Saba said. "Music stitched together the . . ." Inadvertently a Yilayil word came to mind, along with image—color—but she reverted to English. "The fabrics of meaning." As she said it, she frowned. "Fabric"—so inadequate! And so she whistle/hummed her idea, using the outside-time tense she'd been struggling to comprehend, and it came closer to expressing the image.

Gordon drew in a deep breath—she could hear it. "I'm not sure I understand," he said finally. "I perceive each word separately, but the verb—"

"It's part of my lessons," Saba said, thinking that—even if they were overheard, which they must assume to be the case—this conversation could not possibly endanger anyone.

Then she remembered the time, and sat up suddenly, dizzily, staring at her watch. "Ah, I am late," she said. "But I enjoyed our discussion."

"Until later, then," Gordon responded, and clicked off.

Saba rose slowly, testing her strength, her sense of gravity. At Gordon's insistence, she was now using full doses of medication. She worked to time the hours of their strongest effect with her lessons, so she could be as clearheaded as possible when she was trying to learn the alien language in all its nuances.

SHE PULLED ON her robe, and stepped outside her room. Pausing, she looked at the blank wall adjacent. Why did they have her alone on a corridor? The wall, a dead end, intrigued her subconscious mind. In her dreams, Katarina often came through it, like a ghost.

Sometimes Katarina sang, old chants out of Saba's childhood that the Russian probably never had even heard: the polyphonic *edho* of the Dorze; Eritrean songs, echoing two thousand years of history from the long-ago kingdom of Axum; even the songs of the mysterious Afar, who shun all foreigners.

It was the polyphonic *edho* that Saba most often heard, wreathing through the never-ceasing music of the Yilayil. So different to the ears, but the brain insisted on finding connecting points.

She sighed, and walked down to the teaching chamber, where she found Zhot—no longer green—pacing back and forth.

As always, he began without preamble.

"All peoples have part of brain where sensory organs connect, where the senses happen first," Zhot said.

Saba nodded, puzzled at the new direction the lesson was taking. So they would not work on the computer, then?

"We will talk about vision," Zhot continued—again, as if reading her mind. It was eerie, how often their thoughts paralleled—even when she was having the most difficulty comprehending him. "What do your people call the brain part where vision happens?"

That, at least, she could answer, for she had studied neurology for a time in her efforts to plumb the mysteries of music's universal effect on humans. "The visual cortex."

"And if this is destroyed, no vision, yes?"

She nodded again.

"Do you understand****?" Zhot whistle-trilled a complex phrase.

Sight denied but body affirms perception? She shook her head, confused. Her head panged, colors and even tastes flitting through her consciousness. She dismissed them as irrelevant, and grasped at the words that came with them.

"Blindsight!" she exclaimed. "They deny sight, indeed cannot see, but can sometimes grasp objects, tell their shapes."

"Yes! This is true for all sentients with this brain damage. And they do not trust what they perceive, do not believe they perceive, call it guessing," Zhot continued, more excited than she had ever seen him, "for they have no sensations to anchor perception."

Her momentary satisfaction at her understanding him ebbed as she realized she had no idea why they were discussing blindsight. A wave of weakness washed over her, and she swayed in her chair, suddenly dizzy.

"Only a little more," Zhot said, in the first concessions to her condition she had ever known from him.

"I apologize," Saba said. "I discover that I am hungry." She thought longingly of the bluish cheese pudding that was often served, and her stomach growled. She suspected, from its effect on her metabolism, that it was pure protein.

"We talk, then eat," Zhot said. "Your people have legends of those among you who see the future, yes?" he continued.

"Yes. It is very rare, and not to be depended on."

"No more than blindsight," said Zhot, his tail swishing beneath his robes. The sight made more colors flit across Saba's vision, and dizziness dissolved the edges of her vision. She closed her eyes, and concentrated on his words. "For we who live in time have no sensory organ for time, and so no sensations to anchor the perception of time. Do you understand?"

"I—I . . ." She paused, a sudden onslaught of weariness—dizziness—washing through her mind. She fought vertigo, opened her eyes. They stung. The fever was back—already.

"Think, listen, taste," Zhot said. "Now we eat."

Taste, eat. Everything seemed connected by some inner meaning. Saba tried to penetrate it, but the malaise made it impossible, and she gratefully followed Zhot to the refectory to join the other beings for the morning meal.

DAWN WAS GRAYING the gathering clouds when Ross slipped out of the Jecc transport and jogged back to the Nurayil dorm. Now that the adventure was over, his emotions were mixed: excitement at action, at discovery, laced with guilt. He knew he ought to have communicated. Eveleen would be angry. As she had a right to be.

Still, this rational acceptance of his culpability didn't make the prospect of facing the music any easier.

When he reached the dorm building, some of the beings they shared it with were already descending to go off to whatever it was they did during the daylight hours. He moved quickly between them, running up the ramp. He was not even tempted to go directly to work. Better to confront her now, and get it over with.

He reached their cell, and opened the door.

He wasn't sure what he expected to find except an angry wife. What he saw was Eveleen and Gordon sitting cross-legged on the floor, each working at his or her laptop, food beside them. He saw the bluish stuff that tasted kind of like cheesecake, and swallowed a couple times. He was suddenly ravenous.

But he turned his attention from the food to his wife's assessing brown eyes. He met that gaze—and he saw her grin.

"Well," she said, "since I didn't get to share your adventure, how about a detailed report?"

"Of course," he said. "Ah, you're not mad? Not that I'd blame you."

Gordon said nothing, only smiled slightly.

Eveleen said, "Oh, I wasn't mad once I'd made sure you were all right."

"What?" Ross demanded.

Eveleen's smile sharpened a little at the corners. "Misha showed me the way to the Jecc caves. I got a good peek, but not much more."

Ross drew in a slow breath. "You—"

"Went out to make sure you were okay," Eveleen said slowly. "Just as you would have done, had I been the one to skip out. We'll have to talk about that, but later. We all have to get to work. Sit down, have some breakfast. I take it the Jecc didn't feed you?"

"Oh, they tried, but I just pretended. The stuff they like would make a squirrel happy, but it was too close to nuts and gravel for my taste. Or what looked like gravel."

Ashe sat back, his brows lifted slightly. "You thought there was something important to pursue—enough so that you avoided our orders. I'm here to follow up on whatever it was you discovered."

Ross sat down, knowing that Gordon's mild manner was deceptive. It was as much of a reprimand as Gordon was going to make—but it was enough.

"I'm not sure," Ross said, "but I think there *is* something."

"Go on," Eveleen said. "I'll type it up as you talk."

"I didn't put it all together until I got to the Jecc city. Because that's what it is, a little city. They are pretty handy with their fingers for building, and not just thieving. Hot and cold running water—and they like baths just as much as humans. Forget this ecologically sound but unsatisfying glue-field thing." Ross waved behind him.

Gordon gave a faint grin, but his attitude was still one of waiting.

"Anyway, when I got there, I saw Jecc with kids in their pouches. They don't come into the Nurayil town when they are gestating their young. I think they are biologically a lot like marsupials—the young are born helpless, and finish gestating in the pouches. But the Jecc are asexual. All that thieving comes down to the exchange of genetic material."

"That's why our tools feel like they've been dusted with pollen?" Eveleen asked.

"Exactly. And by playing what I thought was a game, I somehow made myself one of the gang. See, it works like this, far as I can figure: it's an honor to be stolen from, because it means someone else wants your genetic material for their offspring. But it's not just stealing, because you're expected to get the thing right back again. And you're not supposed to get caught, but if you do, you make some comment about progeny—though in the past, I think, they used to fight. But that fighting turned to ritualistic dueling by the time they got civilized—developed writing and reached for the stars. They are insatiably curious. I think they feel rejected by the rest of the beings on this world because no one participates in their thieving games."

"But they can't expect to be exchanging genetic material with other races, can they?" Gordon asked.

"No. I don't think it's that all the time with them, either. They also do it with new encounters, so I believe it's a kind of acceptance custom as well. A social exchange. Only no one outside of the Jecc seems to know it—or care."

"Is that why they don't try to become harmonized?" Eveleen asked.

"It might be a part, but here's where it gets weird. They are wary of ti[*trill*]kee because every generation or so, the ones here on this island seem to disappear."

Gordon let out a long whistle—not a Yilayil whistle, but a low, American expression of "Uh oh!"

"Oh, but that's not all of it. They seem to want to fit in, but they want to know what happened to their ancestors. For beings who don't have families the way we have them, they are very involved with their ancestors. They showed me those caves you saw. Each one makes a mosaic about its life, and accomplishments, naming its progeny. They used to have more, but now they only have one, maybe two, if their population drops in number."

"The mosaics looked interesting."

"Not just that," Ross said, feeling for words. "Sad, kind of. Poignant. Their ancestors didn't just stop at depicting themselves. They have special rooms that show pictures from their homeworld, and others showing their journey through space. Jecc have spread over several worlds, and they used to keep in contact—they have things not unlike those picture cubes we found on the globe ship. Remember, Gordon? That showed pictures of home?"

"Yes," Ashe said. "Go on."

"Well, the Jecc have these ancient message cubes, and they revere them. Play them often—I don't know what kind of energy they run off. Solar? Anyhow, here's the kicker. The Jecc in the messages are different."

"Different? How?" Gordon asked.

"Taller. Bigger. But the real change is the tentacles. The Jecc of the past didn't have them. And all of a sudden—if the mosaics are correct—a generation or so after they arrived here, all the offspring were born with them."

"Tentacles," Eveleen said, looking up from her typing. "The Yilayil don't have them—they have four arms—but a lot of the other beings here all have those tentacles."

"Those savage human types did as well, down in our time," Ross said. "Anyway, the tentacles are new, and the Jecc mourn the fact that even if they had a spaceship, because of them they could never go home again. That's what yesterday was, their Day of Lamentation. They seem to have these about once a month."

"Mutation," Gordon said slowly, getting to his feet. "No, more than mutation. Genetic alteration. Tentacles are too much of a change to be a mutation, and on many races, at that. But alteration by whom, and to what purpose?" He frowned as he packed up his laptop. "This requires thought." He shook his head. "But later. For now, we'd better not make any overt changes in our routines, because we still don't know who is watching or listening. I'm off to work."

He left, and Eveleen slowly and thoughtfully shut down her computer.

Ross watched, trying to figure out what to say.

But Eveleen forestalled him. She got to her feet and put her hands on his shoulders. She smiled up into his face.

"How long," she asked, "do you think it would have taken for us to get thoroughly sick of each other?"

"What?" Ross gazed at her in astonishment.

Her eyes were narrowed in amusement—and understanding. "If we hadn't gotten whatever this illness is. How long would we have guarded one another against taking risks—meanwhile getting more and more frustrated?"

"I—" Ross let his breath out in a whoosh. "I don't know."

Eveleen turned away, no longer smiling. "We should have found that old transport system, Ross. You and I—weeks ago. Misha and Viktor stumbled on it only because they were looking for some kind of shelter from one of those rainstorms. That station is right near us. We should have been out, exploring, ages ago. We two are action agents, not Vera and Irina. They are communicators, analysts. But they've been finding out data, much more than we have."

Ross sighed. "I know. It's just—"

"You don't have to say it, because I felt exactly the same. You're used to taking action—taking risks. And when you were risking only yourself, it was perfectly all right. I know because I felt the same way. But when it came to considering your safety, I couldn't stand the thought that something might happen to you, and I meant to stay with you every minute. Keep you safe. Keep you out of harm's way."

Ross laughed a little raggedly. "Hell, Eveleen."

"And we didn't even *talk*. Just heroically did our duty as spouses—guarding each other from doing our duty as agents." She gave him a troubled look. "If we can't work this out, we shouldn't be partners. If we were on our own again, we'd have that old freedom of action. And we're both action people—you have to admit it. That's what brought us together in the first place."

Ross said, "Don't think that."

"But we have to," Eveleen said. "If we can't handle the emotional consequences of our jobs, then we'd be better off working separately. We have to consider it—but later. Right now, we'd better get to work. Gordon said we don't want to alter our routines any."

Ross nodded, forcing himself to grab his share of the breakfast. He would munch it on the way, though he really didn't want to eat. Didn't want to work. Truth was, he felt heartsick. Anger would have been better than that logical calmness.

The worst of it was, he knew she was right.

Outside, the air was slightly cooler, a strong breeze smelling of rain bringing some relief. Eveleen walked beside him, her profile serene, as she made light comments in Yilayil.

Ross didn't talk. He thought about his night with the Jecc—and when they got to work, and the Jecc recommenced their little game, he thought about Eveleen.

On the way back from work, he said, "You're right. And I promise. No more hiding. Half and half, share fair and square, as we used to say on the streets when I was a kid."

"Share fair and square," Eveleen repeated, her eyes steady and bright with a sheen of unshed tears. "That, my dear, is *real* trust."

Ross didn't respond. As always, his deepest emotions were impossible to express. He looked forward to their being alone at last, so that he could at least try.

But when they reached the Nurayil dorm, they found Misha waiting outside their cell, pacing like a caged cat.

A small group of Moova trundled past, but he paid them no heed. As soon as he saw them he said abruptly, "Open up."

In mute surprise, Eveleen palmed the door open.

As soon as they were inside, Misha said, "The flyers. They got Viktor."

Ross looked to Eveleen. She looked back, question in her eyes.

"What are we waiting for?" Ross said. "Let's go get him back."

CHAPTER 24

SABA SPENT THE day drifing in and out of consciousness.

Gordon called her once, and then again. His worry penetrated the strange dreaming wakefulness that she couldn't seem to escape on her own. Patiently, slowly, he bade her describe—in detail—her room, her hands, courses she'd taken in university. Anything to anchor her to reality.

But as soon as they quit conversing, she lay down again, exhausted, and the strange dreams seized her—always punctuated by Yilayil voices singing never-ending chants. Twice she rose to shut down the Yilayil computer, so that the sound would cease and she could sleep, but both times she found it dark. Was the sound coming from hidden speakers? Or—somehow—was she dreaming it, too? Except how could she dream language she only partially understood?

Her mind kept insisting on listening, and trying to parse the complicated levels of verb and modifier until she'd rise again, cram more anti-inflammatory meds into her dry mouth, and wash it down with long gulps of water.

Once she awoke suddenly, and Zhot seemed to be in her room. He demanded definitions for time and space and insisted that she learn the terms for those who stood outside temporal reality . . .

She slept again, and when she woke a second time—now drenched in sweat—she wasn't sure if she'd dreamed the conversation or not.

As soon as she sat up, the sensors flicked the lights on. The lights seemed dim; she felt a sudden longing for the bright clarity of sunlight.

She looked up, about to reach for her medication—and there was Zhot, standing in the shadows of the corner.

"Are your senses one, or many?" Zhot's voice blurred in a scintillation of green-tasting rainbows—Saba knew the thought senseless, but it was the only description that fit.

"Many," she said slowly. Her lips felt dry and cracked. She reached for water, drank. When she looked up, Zhot was still there.

"Different modes of sensation, yes?" he insisted. Now she heard the *wisp-wisp* of his slippered feet on her floor, the quiet hiss of his robe as he walked back and forth in front of her door.

Her muzzy mind jumped to the musical modes, and she worried a moment at the problem of whether the taste of water was Dorian or Myxolydian.

When she looked up again, her vision had gone blurry; in Zhot's place she saw Katarina.

Katarina did not wait for an answer, or maybe it was an hour later. Saba didn't know.

"But you can imagine colors for tastes, sounds for shapes, different modes?" she continued. "Symbolically associate them?" Katarina spoke in Russian, or was it still Yilayil?

Katarina was a warm slurpy column of melted licorice emitting blue bubbles that enveloped her head, each conveying a quantum of meaning.

Now Saba tried to assign the proper color to the modes, until she suddenly, but only for a flashing moment, realized that she was below the words, below the world of symbols, in a seamless unity of sensation. Then everything wrenched back into focus, intensifying her headache, and Katarina was gone.

Synesthesis, Saba realized.

Unable to think beyond that, Saba lay down, and slept.

Urgency bled through her dreams: there was something she had to understand, to learn, to know. Now! Now!

She gasped, woke up, fumbling with trembling fingers for her water.

As she drank, she realized that the sound that had wakened her was that of movement outside her door—not footsteps, but voices. Yilayil voices, chanting.

She levered herself painfully off the bed, all her joints aching. The room spun about her for a moment, then steadied. After some experimentation she found that she could walk, albeit slowly, as long as she did not move her head quickly. It took all her strength for her to pull on her robe, but she welcomed its warmth.

She opened the door, in time to see two weasel faces look directly into her eyes before passing onward. They did not pause in the eerie whistle-punctuated chant, but passed slowly onward, their robes swaying in time to their steps.

Saba turned her head—impossible that they would walk in that direction. There was nothing next to her room but a wall.

An unfamiliar glow lit the corridor. The adjacent wall was gone! In its place was an archway, its ceiling lit from beneath. Was it a stairway?

She waited, but no one appeared, and she became aware of a weird sound, almost like a heartbeat, but with strange musical overtones and harmonics. It seemed to come up through the floor, through her feet, but then she realized that some of the sound, the musical part, was more audible from the open door.

"Is this real?" she whispered, and then she reached for her com—her link to sanity. She clicked it on, and said wearily, "Is this real?"

She held it out, for a few seconds, but her arm could not bear the weight, and so she clipped it to her belt—and then forgot it as she concentrated on the difficult actions involved in standing on her feet.

She groped her way through the door, and stood in dismay. The stairs she had expected to find were apparently endless. She blinked feverish eyes. The perspective was odd, and her eyes wouldn't quite focus on the walls.

Only a few steps before her were in focus. The music crescendoed, echoing in cacophony—then it resolved, each voice, each instrument harmonious, the whole transcending melody into a form of mind-numbing beauty.

The music was more complex than any she had ever heard. It beckoned her downward.

Is this my fever? she thought. Am I really here? Only her trembling legs and pounding head and heart tied her to reality—but those too could be part of her dream.

Again the sense of urgency gripped her. She stumbled on.

Time was fragmented now; she had a vague sense that sunset had passed, that it was no longer Yilayil time. She remembered the two Yilayil faces, so briefly seen.

Sight blurred, and she knew she had to be hallucinating, for now she saw ghosts: the First Team, all lined up along the stairs in a row. And then Gordon. He reached a hand toward her, but she passed through his fingers. When she paused, swaying, on the stairs, she looked back—and he was watching her, his blue eyes mute with appeal, his sun-bleached hair disarrayed as if he had been running. He's sick too, she thought, and she passed downward.

Finally she reached the bottom, and found herself in a huge cavern, glittering with the light of torches, bioluminescent spheres, electric lights, and other sources of illumination she did not recognize.

All the races of the planet were represented there, distributed about the vast space in a complex pattern whose geometry seemed to hold importance, but again the meaning escaped her.

The cavern was also full of stalactites and stalagmites, of fragile webs of rock, arrays of stone cylinders, and other forms, some natural, some obviously shaped, and some whose provenance she could not discern.

The beings danced among them, striking them with various instruments adapted to their sizes and physical nature. Big creatures held huge hammerlike strikers, little creatures carried small rods, or flexible drumsticks. Some struck the rocks, some stroked them, some tapped them. Some were on scaffolding high on the walls, some, the Jecc for instance, even swung on fragile trapezes, the length of the pendulum thus formed determining their rhythm: pulses of complex beats at long intervals.

This was but one aspect of the sound that pulsed in her head, her blood, and impelled her forward. She saw Zhot and stumbled toward him. He turned to her, welcome in his greenish face.

"We thought you too ill. Tonight we see."

"See?" Saba said weakly.

He waved one arm at the activity all around, while still stroking a stalagmite with the filelike rod in his other. It made a grating noise that made her teeth itch.

"Sensation! We anchor perception, achieve the unity of sensation that denies time, and those who dance-above-decay speak, we see, we hear."

Dance-above-decay. Again, he used one of those non-temporal verbs.

A tall Yilayil approached with deliberate step, its elongated body only remotely resembling an Earth weasel. The gowned creature studied her with large eyes that gleamed with intelligence and compassion; another approached on her other side.

The first Yilayil motioned for her to step forward. The second one held out a small rod, about two feet long. Her fingers closed round it. She glanced at the thing in her hand, confused.

Zhot turned back to his stalagmite, while the two Yilayil pressed her forward, gently, to a small fan of rock, so thin she could see light through it.

The first Yilayil pantomimed drawing the rod across the top of the rock-fan; she tried it, producing a melodic glissando. The Yilayil both nodded and whirled away.

For a time Saba stroked the fan at random, and then the pulse of the music penetrated her consciousness once more, sounds and voices rising and falling in a syncopation that caused her to grope for meaning within a context ingrained in memory, deep and abiding, from her earliest years.

The *edho* of the Dorze usually had five components. There was the *yetsu as*, the chorus—the chanting voices. Response, reaction, cohesion. . . .

The Yilayil. They were the *pile*, the highest voices, and limitless in number, at once the most important and the least important of the harmonic pattern.

The *kaletso*—who was that? Was it Zhot? The *kaletso* was the youngest, extending the melodic interventions of the *aife*—

The ban'e. The "belchers," the percussive voices. Those were the ones making music on the stones.

The *dombe*, those who cover. The other races, all singing sustained music to better the cohesion.

But who were the *aife*, the elder, the eyes?

Saba's mind reached, and reached again—

And the pattern changed in her mind, and she abandoned the symbol of childhood, immersing her consciousness in the alien harmonics—

—And the music resolved wholly into beauty such as she had never heard, and she was part of it. Her will fled, and she became one with the music. The sound became color became touch became scent and then all of them and the cavern dissolved into pure sensation for a moment, bereft of perception, then snapped back, and she was somewhere else.

She saw men and women, dark and stern of face, in the ancient dress of the great Ethiopian kingdom of Axum, and others bearing gifts of gold and myrrh and jewels. Then violence, war, men struggling, weapons lifted, chariots sweeping across sandy wastes, the legions of Rome, men in white with scimitars uplifted, women weeping, pale men in pith helmets, swarthy men in uniforms with archaic rifles, an old man dragged from a throne and cast into darkness, the bright line of a rocket traced against a full moon huge on the horizon . . .

Then she gasped as the sneering, hate-filled visage of a Baldy confronted her, but just as suddenly his face became fearful, terrified, and disappeared.

Now she saw the Earth, bright and small, dwindling to a point, and the sun with it, merely another point of light in the glory of the galaxy, but from that insignificance grew a web of light, like sap refilling the veins of a dying leaf, melding with other webs from other stars widely scattered, and to her eyes was presented the destiny of humankind, glory and shame together as humanity reclaimed the ruins of the star-spanning empire that had crumbled so long ago.

Something SomeTHING *SOMETHING* sang in her head . . .
The *aife*?

spoke in her head . . .
spoke in her head.

A vast pressure surged through her mind.
It was too much to comprehend—to bear.
She swayed, dropped the rod, and fell senseless to the ground.

━━

"AS NEAR AS we can tell, they live off the island entirely," Misha said as they trotted through the darkening streets.

Rain tapped against Eveleen's face, cool and pleasant after two days of incessant heat. She ran at Ross's side, her jogging pace easily matching the taller men's strides.

Misha used his infrared scanner to detect body heat. Three times they ducked back behind shrubs or once a low wall, as beings walked by: once the tall green ones that functioned as guardians of the peace, and twice gliding Yilayil, talking swiftly in the language that was so melodic when they used it.

"All in the direction of the House of Knowledge," Ross observed, staring after the Yilayil. "Think something is happening?"

"How would we know?" Eveleen asked, thinking immediately of Saba. "We haven't been outside enough to put together any kind of pattern."

"True," Ross said, but his tone temporized—and Eveleen knew, without asking, that he felt the same sense of danger that gripped her.

"Come." Misha jerked his head, impatient to be gone.

No one spoke again until they had descended to the ancient transport station that the Russians had found.

"We spent three days riding this thing. Finding where it went. Where it still works," Misha said as they waited for one of the flat cars.

When it came up, they squeezed in, lying flat as Eveleen had the first time, and once again commenced a long ride, swooping downward. Concussions of air at intersections testified to the size and complexity of the system. It was miraculous that it still worked—that, somehow, there was still energy to run it.

Finally Misha stopped the car, which hummed beneath them. In the dim bluish light, he looked back at them. "This station here"—he gestured upward at an archway and glowing light—"is on the west coast of our island. As you see, the transport goes on. I think it crossed beneath the bay to a smaller island off to the west. We have seen the flyers retreating there when the sun sets; we think that is where they live. And I assume that this transport goes there as well, but I don't know. Want to test it, or find another way across?"

Eveleen said, "Test it."

At the same moment Ross said, "I'm not in the mood for a night swim."

Misha smiled faintly. "Then we go."

He faced forward again, leaned back—his yellow hair brushed over Eveleen's knees—and activated the car.

Again it dove downward, so fast her stomach seemed to drop. Then, quite as suddenly, it swooped up again, and she had to swallow to keep her ears from popping painfully. There were no intersection concussions this time.

When the car stopped, all three climbed out.

"Here is what happened," Misha said as they walked toward the ramp leading upward. "We circled back for one last check at the Yilayil graveyard—just in case. We were careless—not enough sleep, maybe too sick." He shrugged. "It was clouding up, and we forgot to check for shadows. They came on us quite suddenly. I got under cover, Viktor did not. When I came out, I saw two of them holding him in a kind of net. They flew west, high, fast."

"So it's probable they took him here," Ross said.

Misha shrugged again. "Where else?"

And why? Eveleen thought—but she didn't speak out loud. They were here to find out why.

Cold air fingered their faces, and Eveleen pulled her rain jacket tight against her. Misha paused, checking his infrared and his flashlight.

Ross and Eveleen also had flashes clipped to their belts; in silence, Eveleen gripped hers, but she did not turn it on.

Misha led the way, scanning with the infrared. No warm bodies showed up on the screen.

Ross murmured, "Why do I think that the First Team ended up here?"

"There were no flyers in their time," Eveleen whispered back. "Not in any of the records—or were there, Misha?"

He shook his head. "No. No flyers."

Ross grunted. "Well, it was a nice solution."

"This mission has no easy solutions," Misha retorted in a sardonic voice.

"It's had no solutions at all, so far," Eveleen shot back.

Misha laughed softly, then paused again. They'd reached the entrance to the station. It was nearly overgrown with ferny plants. They tromped over thick moss and scrubby brush, then pushed through the hanging boughs.

Obviously the flyers did not know about the station, or if they did, they didn't use it. The three were the first ones in centuries to step that way, Eveleen could tell even in the darkness.

Misha had fixed his flashlight so that it emitted a thin pinhole of light. He shined it carefully, then clicked it off. Eveleen blinked in the sudden darkness, until her eyes began to adjust; whatever he'd seen was enough to orient him, but he was used to moving about in jungle at night. She was content, for now, to follow.

They found themselves on a rocky ledge that was once some kind of road. Flat portions, broken by hearty plants, made walking easier.

The road was built into the side of a cliff. They rounded a hill, and below them, quite suddenly, they saw dancing lights.

Too late they heard the *swoosh* of great wings beating; Eveleen looked up sharply, to see five long shapes dive down on them.

Misha's hand went to his side—his weapon. He didn't unclip it, though. Eveleen kept her own hands away from her sides, balancing lightly on her feet. Adrenaline flooded her system, temporarily banishing malaise, headache, tiredness.

Ross had gone still. "Wait," he said.

Misha gave a short nod; he'd decided the same.

The five winged creatures surrounded them, and one of them gestured below. The distant yellow light outlined a sharp face with bluish highlights; the creature looked excited.

It opened its mouth, and began to speak. Eveleen heard a stream of non-Yilayil gibberish, and wondered what was being said. It sounded hauntingly familiar.

Then she heard a sharp indrawn breath from Misha.

Ross looked up. Eveleen's heart thumped.

"What?" she croaked.

"This language," Misha said, his voice suddenly hoarse. "It—it is— Russian."

CHAPTER 25

GORDON SAW SABA lying on the ground.

No one else was in the cave. His footsteps hissed and grated as he ran heedlessly down the worn stone steps to the vast floor.

There Saba lay, utterly quiescent, her body, slender and graceful the last time he had seen her, now dangerously thin and frail.

"Saba. Saba," Gordon breathed, and knelt at her side.

He placed fingers to her neck, and gratitude flooded through him when he found a pulse—rapid and light, but steady.

She sucked in a deep, shuddering breath, and opened her eyes.

In the weird glow from the multiple light sources, she stared up at him, her black eyes reflecting the harsh light.

"Saba."

"Gordon? Are you real?" The whisper was the merest ghost.

"I am." A strangled laugh escaped him. "You left your com on. That was quite a concert."

"It was real, then?"

"Well, I heard real sounds, all right—but I don't yet know what you heard that might have been different. Can I help you?"

"Yes. Please." She lifted a hand.

He bent and slid his arm round her shoulders. So light, she was!

He rose, lifting her—and realized that his strength had been sapped as well.

"I can walk. Just help me balance," she murmured.

Gordon let her feet touch ground, and together they proceeded slowly up the steps, each of them soon breathing harshly.

They stopped when Saba made a sign. Both sank down onto the

steps, Saba leaning against the stone wall. Gordon unclipped his canteen and they both took deep swigs of water.

Saba leaned her head against the rough wall. Her face in the dim lighting was drawn, but her eyes were steady and alert. "How'd you get in?"

"Over the last couple weeks I marked at least three ways around those green guards," Gordon said with a grim laugh. "And I found that this building is riddled with enough tunnels to make the New York subway system look simple. I've been exploring them during the early morning hours. I even found your room. And I mean to take you there right now—unless you think my presence will endanger you."

Saba canted her head, her eyes going unfocused. Gordon watched in dismay, hoping she was not about to fade out on him—but then she blinked, and saw him again, and smiled faintly. "No. No trouble."

He didn't ask. He could be patient.

When she was ready, she nodded, and again they moved up the stairs, drunken-sailor style.

"It's not . . . as far . . . as I thought," she panted when they had neared the top—but still she had to stop and rest.

This time, though, it was a short rest. She gulped some water, drew in a deep breath, and straightened up. They continued on, straight to her room.

No one was about. Saba reached, palmed the door open, and they passed inside. Full-spectrum lighting, somehow calibrated to be comfortable for the human eye, clicked on.

Gordon helped her to the narrow bed, and she collapsed gratefully. "I have a lot to tell you," she murmured. "Let me catch my breath."

Gordon looked around the chamber. It looked comfortable; his attention was immediately drawn to the unfamiliar computer system. "Is this the Yilayil terminal? May I turn it on?"

She nodded.

He touched the keypads, noting how different they were from human keyboards. The screen lit, and some of the pads glowed faintly.

Yilayil script flowed across the screen. With difficulty he made out some of the words, then he shook his head. He'd make no sense out of this system. He closed it down again.

Saba said, "First, tell me, please. What did you hear? I mean last night."

"Voices. Whistles, trills, chants, and a lot of percussives that I could not identify. I heard you speak to someone. I only caught a few words, something about you being ill. That was the most distinct voice. Then there was just the chanting, on and on and on, until it either ended or your battery ran low: it faded suddenly into quiet, then silence. I tried to raise you, couldn't, so I reported to Irina, and moved in myself to check things out."

Saba opened her eyes. "The Yilayil are not . . ." She paused, then frowned slightly. "That's not true. They *are* the predominant culture, and all others are shaped to them, but the drive to conformity is not engendered by them merely for the sake of dominance. The issues behind ti[*trill*]kee are a response to yet another, greater . . ." Her voice suspended, and once again her gaze went diffuse.

This time the reverie, or whatever it was, lasted far longer.

Gordon drove his teeth into his lip, fighting for patience. He sat at her side, waiting, and again she blinked and focused on him.

After a few seconds, he prompted, "There is someone else behind the Yilayil ti[*trill*]kee?"

Saba breathed in and out, her brow furrowed in perplexity. Then she said slowly, "The harmony is Yilayil, but it is an attempt to understand the incomprehensible. Almost, I wish to say, the—the ineffable, except that carries spiritual connotations, does it not? And these *are* finite beings, that is ones with corporeal existence, I am quite sure of that—though as yet I am sure of little else concerning them."

"So there is yet another race here, is that it?" Gordon said.

"Yes, but they exist outside of time."

"Impossible."

She shook her head slightly. "It's true. I don't know how, but I know this much: they knew I was coming. They gave me Zhot, and Rilla, and the Virigu I know. The carving out front was waiting for me. From each I have learned many things. Rilla has looked out for my comfort. I believe it is she who programmed my room, turned on my computer. The Virigu, I have come to realize, are in some ways empaths. They sense emotions, and perhaps—in some way—patterns of thought."

Gordon nodded. "Go on."

"As for Zhot, he seems to be the prime communicator. He kept trying to get me to 'taste color' and the like, at the same time as I had to learn to think outside temporal limitations. It's, oh, a little like Zen, I think. Koans of synesthesia, to break apart the unity of the sense that bars the time sense. Perhaps the entities even knew that music would be the metaphor, the catalyst, for understanding . . . It sounds egocentric, doesn't it, to surmise that music has developed here in preparation for my coming?"

"I can believe anything, if you present enough proof," Gordon said with care.

Her slim, dark fingers pressed against his wrist. "Ah, my anchor, my link to reality." She laughed soundlessly. "Here's what I can discern. These entities are not in constant communication with the House of Knowledge, or the beings in it. That would overpower them, remove their free will."

"How do you perceive them, then?"

"Voices, in the mind—through the music," Saba said.

"I heard nothing like that," Gordon said.

She looked at him. "Did you understand everything you heard? Did you taste and feel the music? Did you***?" She trilled a Yilayil term that he did not comprehend at all.

"One of the temporal verbs?" he guessed.

She nodded. "It takes all the senses to comprehend the deepest symbols, and when one is able to do that, one can—partially—hear *them.*"

"And so?" he prompted.

"And there is some event nigh, something important. We are crucial to it."

Gordon thought of the disappearance of the First Team. He did not like what he was hearing. All the clues added up to something drastic— like human sacrifice. And Saba was lying, weak and enervated, in the midst of what might be the enemy.

Gordon repressed a sigh.

His communicator pulsed him then, and he clicked it on. "Ashe here."

"They are returned," Irina's voice filled the room. "All of them. They are all going to Ross and Eveleen's room."

Saba nodded. "Go. I'll be safe enough."

Gordon nodded, reaching to unclip her com. She pointed to the recharger, and he slid it in, and saw the red light come on. There were still charges left in it, he saw with relief. Not many, but enough.

Then he got to his feet, hesitating.

"I will be all right," she said.

"I'd feel better if you could contact me," he said, pointing to the recharging com. "Shall I leave you mine?"

"No," she said. "You're the leader, you must have one. I know I am safe, for now. I need sleep."

Gordon nodded, thinking that if need be he could break in again— and this time bring Ross and the other men.

Sneaking out of the House of Knowledge was strangely easy. He attributed it to the daylight hours—and once he was outside, he did not need to use care.

Once he was outside of the House boundaries, he moved rapidly across to the Nurayil dorm, taking care not to confront anyone who would demand precedence.

The rain kept him cool, though he was thoroughly soaked by the time he reached the dorm.

Inside Ross and Eveleen's chamber, he found everyone on the team—that is, everyone except Irina. They all sat against the walls, looking tired and thin. Everyone had water at hand, and he smelled the cream-cheese-and-lemon odor of the protein food they all seemed to crave.

Viktor was also there. Gordon saw him and sighed with relief.

"False alarm, then?" he asked.

Misha gave him a wry grin. "Not," he said, "even remotely true. We have much to report."

"How's Saba? Do we need to do something?" Eveleen asked, as always quick in her concern for others.

"I found her. She's still there, but she insists she's safe. I'll give you a report on what she said after you explain." He waved a hand at Misha, but he turned to survey them all.

"We think we've solved the mystery of the First Team," Ross said.

"What's this?" Gordon drew in a deep breath, trying to marshal his thoughts.

"The flyers," Eveleen spoke now, her eyes tired but alert. "They speak a kind of Russian. They were fixated on us because they recognized us, sort of, but humans have turned into mythic figures for them."

Gordon felt as if someone had hit him in the head. He sat down, took a long drink of water, then he said, "Go ahead. Talk."

"They took Viktor to *talk* to," Eveleen said. "Viktor heard it all while we were traveling to get him."

The Russian nodded, his eyes exhausted.

"They told it in stories. They live in primitive surroundings, but in recognizable tree huts. They lost technology, somehow, when they gained the wings—"

"Gained wings?" Gordon cut in. "Is that what you're trying to tell me? They all just . . . dropped everything and sprouted wings?"

"That's not clear," Ross said. "They told it in a form of poetry, apparently." He looked over at Viktor, who nodded again. "Their first generation is recognizable—by the names—as our First Team. We still don't know how or why they abandoned all their gear, and the mission, and ran off. How they got to the island isn't clear, and when the wings happened isn't either."

"Babies," Viktor said. "Their babies flew."

"And they stayed there, and built a new culture," Eveleen added. "They seem quite happy—exuberant, even. They really wanted us to stay with them, but when we said we had to go they were willing to let us leave."

"They're blue," Ross added. "Sky-colored. The First Team are the ancestors of our flyers down the timeline!"

"So they all—what, mutated? That's nonsense. Genetics doesn't work that way."

"Of course not," Vera cut in, her voice uncertain. "This is what Irina and I have recently discovered, and what Ross tells us about these Jecc corroborates it. From separate evidence, Irina found out that the Moova practice infanticide—culling out genetic defects. Not by choice. See, a week or two ago, her employer was desolate. The grief was the more profound because it was apparently the third one in the family in a year. At first we thought it was illness, but apparently nobody suffers illness. There are no doctors—as least among the Moova. But I don't think there are any for the other races either."

"*We're* sick," Gordon pointed out the obvious.

Vera nodded, her face troubled. "We will come to that. First, last week. We did not report this, as we had no real evidence, only our guesses. But we decided that desperate measures require quick action. Irina told me to decoy the Moova, and she did some excavating on their computing system, and found out that they, too, have altered from their original form, but it is more slow. They try desperately to halt the changes through this practice. What seems to be happening to the races here is genetic manipulation, on an impossible scale."

"Genetic manipulation?" Gordon repeated.

Ross laughed, a sardonic, unpleasant laugh, quite unlike his usual. "Oh, but you haven't figured out the good part yet. What it *means*."

Eveleen's brown eyes were huge now, and strained. "What it means is, this is what's happening to *us*."

CHAPTER 26

ROSS WATCHED THE news impact Gordon Ashe. As usual, the archaeologist showed little reaction other than the narrowing of his blue eyes and a tightening of his shoulders.

Then he looked up, his mouth grim. "Where's Irina?"

Eyes turned to Vera, who shrugged. "Probably either finishing her work or else following up on something."

"Following up on what?"

Vera shrugged again. "She does not always talk about what she's working on . . . She finished entering Pavel's notebook, and a couple of evenings she sneaked out—"

"Wanted Svetlana's data," Misha interrupted. "I gave her a disk containing what was pertinent to us."

"So is she preparing a report for us all, then?" Gordon prompted.

"I don't know," Vera said. "All I know is, she has been gone some evenings, verifying data was all she said. I asked her twice. More than that, she ignores the question." Vera gave a rueful smile. "As for me, I confess most evenings I am asleep within moments after we leave here. I am hungry very much, I want protein, I need sleep very much." She winced, and shrugged again, this time rolling her shoulders as if her back itched. "Do you think if we do not leave soon we're going to sprout wings?"

Misha laughed.

"No," Viktor said. "Our bones, they are losing mass."

That doused Misha's humor like water on a fire.

"None of us have much body fat left," Eveleen observed, then she turned to Vera. "You two have analyzed all our food. Is that cheesecake stuff we all seem to want made out of protein?"

"Yes," Vera said.

"Fueling molecular changes," Gordon said. "Our metabolisms are working in overdrive. Some of the malaise is probably due to just that." He frowned slightly, then turned to Viktor. "What other data did Irina need for verifying?"

"My maps," Viktor said. "Needs for final report."

Gordon looked down at his hands, then up. "The mission has been canceled. Zina is not going to authorize a trip back to the First Team's time." He did not look Misha's way.

Ross glanced at the blond Russian, who smiled derisively.

I'll bet anything he's already tried to make a jump on his own, Ross thought, and tried not to let it annoy him. He didn't know for certain, and anyway, the Russian had obviously been denied access to the machinery that set the time jumps—to the past.

"So let's end it," Gordon finished. "Let's all put in a regular day—a last data gathering—while I work on getting Saba out, and then we're all out of here."

"Sounds good to me," Ross said.

"I am ready," Vera added, rolling her eyes.

Misha said nothing.

Gordon got to his feet as he unhooked his communicator from his belt. "Saba doesn't answer," he said a moment later, then, as he started out the door, Ross heard his voice. "Irina? Listen, here's the latest . . ."

"Anything else?" Ross said when the others had not moved. He looked at Vera, who bit her lip, but his question was really for Misha.

"Good night," Misha said, and he went out. Viktor followed, sending a brief grin over his shoulder.

Vera left in silence.

━━━

SABA TOOK HER medicine, then went down to the refectory to eat something. When that was done, she went directly to the chamber where Zhot had given his lessons—and there she found Rilla and Virigu waiting, alone, obviously for her.

In Yilayil, Saba said, "I must talk about what I experienced last night, for I have many questions."

Rilla said, "We are here, by your desire."

Saba looked at Virigu, and Rilla forestalled her by saying, "A question about Virigu's knowledge of our motives and desires is best addressed to me, for just as your people do not go before others without garments to conceal the outer being, so the Virigu do not talk of what is not spoken aloud."

Saba parsed that, thinking: So telepathy is a taboo? A brief spark of humor lit her mind, instantly extinguished. She hoped that Virigu did not hear it, even as she acknowledged to herself that one culture's (or race's) taboos almost invariably seem funny to another that does not share them.

Saba said, "I wish to understand what I saw/sensed/experienced last night."

She paused, considering the sudden flowering of sensory images when she used the weighted verb. It had *tasted. Felt.* She had *seen* it as well.

"You joined the Great Dance," Rilla said. "You have found ti[*trill*]kee, and so you are a part of the dance. You must be a part of the dance," she added.

Saba said carefully, "This is why the carving of myself outside the House of Knowledge?" The verb for *carving* tasted of destruction and distortion. Strange.

"Carving?" Rilla repeated, then she made a gesture of negation. "It is always there. It grows there."

"Grows," Saba repeated. "You mean, it's a living tree? Or was?" she amended, remembering that there were no branches on it, no leaves. The carving was a tall pole, the image at the top, recalling totems of various Earth cultures—except where those were rough, this one was remarkably smooth and polished, an almost photographic representation of her own face.

Rilla glanced at Virigu, who said something in a low murmur, and then she faced Saba. "It is not done, to take the trees, kill them, and make them into semblances of something else."

Saba said, "But it was done in the past, right?"

Again Rilla made a gesture of negation. "It is there, always. For all beings to see. For you to come and find your place."

"So you are saying that it grew there, for us to find?"

Virigu and Rilla agreed.

Saba shivered. Again she felt that weird tug at her brain, as if from inside. It wasn't as if someone tried to access her mind—like a computer accessing a disk. It was as if a planet-sized vastness waited outside a small bubble, trying to . . .

The image would not come; she felt vertigo. Even searching for a mental verb did not work, because each one was wrong.

She did yoga breathing, then said, "Who are the . . . entities/outside/

time—" Again, a flash of synesthetic experience almost disoriented her. "There is someone in this world besides the races we see, is there not?"

"Yes," Rilla said. "It requires us all to hear/taste/see/touch/experience, it is important."

This time it was Rilla's verb that sent the wash of synesthesia through Saba.

"Why is it important?" Saba asked. "I too feel it. I need to know why this is important."

"Zhot tells us," Virigu said, "that you are the one who hear/taste/see/touch/experiences the most. All of us are a part, but you translate it for the temporal mind."

"I." Saba knew then that what she had experienced was no dream, despite fever—despite physical debilitation. It was real, and the metaphor of music was the key. For some reason, her own unique capabilities, her lifelong studies of symbol in relation to sound and sense, had made some kind of limited breakthrough. And she was not the only one who felt the sense of urgency.

"Tonight, I will listen again," she promised. "But where is Zhot?"

"There is sun," Rilla explained.

Even considering all the strange synesthetic experiences associated with terms and verbs, this was a non sequitur.

"I do not understand."

"His people, Zhot more rapidly, they become plants," Rilla explained. "It is his race's great change. Your people, they change the more rapidly, become those-who-fly-and-sing-myth." She waved to the west.

A bomb seemed to go off behind Saba's eyes. "Changes. Do all the races change?"

Virigu and Rilla both made gestures of agreement.

Rilla said, "It must be swift, so Zhot says. Until you hear, he hears best. It is because your metabolism fights the alterations, and thus you are made very ill."

Virigu again opened her long, thin fingers in a gesture of concurrence, and Saba thought immediately of her genetic makeup. Was it because of the sickle-cell gene? No way of knowing without tests. The immediate priority was to let the others know—and to get herself away, as soon as possible.

She thought again of the impending deadline. Whatever had happened to the First Team might be happening to them—and apparently it did not necessarily involve death, but mutation.

Yet the Yilayil did kill. Thinking of the Russian biologist, Saba said, "I have not dared to ask. Those who are buried in the Field-of-

Vagabonds. They have been deprived-of-life. Why? For not wishing to attain ti[*trill*]kee?"

"This data can be found in the Knowledge bank," Rilla said.

"Come," Virigu spoke, rising. "We must view the records."

Rilla looked at her. Saba tasted surprise, then wondered how she had done so. Then she mentally gave herself a shake. It did not matter how, right now, or even why. She was on a data search; at last the puzzle pieces were coming together.

But the picture was not clear yet.

She followed the other two into the great computer room, and they settled around one of the terminals. None of the other beings in the room paid them any attention, as always. Though Saba had experienced great change, that apparently did not affect life in the rest of the House.

She sat, and waves of darkness washed through her consciousness, receding. She would not faint; adrenaline was serving her for now. When they finished this session, she must report to Gordon, then sleep, for she had to be physically ready for the great dance that night.

Thinking these things over, she did not watch what Virigu did to the computer, thus when she looked up at the screen and saw a close-up of one of the beings nicknamed "Baldies" by Terran Project agents, she felt shock zap through her nerves.

Virigu looked at her, her attitude one of concern, but then she turned back to the screen and her chitinous fingers blurred rapidly over the pads.

In silence the three of them looked at an ancient record—the space-port, Saba realized. Ships of all kinds sat on the vast field, some lifting, some arriving. The reverberations of power seemed to vibrate through the screen as a great vessel lowered slowly, on a blue-white column of fierce light, to the field.

A voice spoke in a staccato language, but Virigu damped that, and brought up the Yilayil translation.

At once Saba realized she was going to have trouble with the Yilayil language. She wondered, as she grappled with meaning, if this was a very old record—if Yilayil had evolved like human languages do. Of course it would, she thought, if the culture has changed. And the Yilayil in the House would see no necessity of changing it—any more than a modern scholar of literature would change Shakespeare, or the epics of Anglo-Saxon. A scholar would have learned the early forms of the language, just as a human scholar did.

So she did not understand everything she heard, but the visual record made it clear enough: the Baldies' globe ships were among those that arrived, but suddenly they arrived in great force, and the visual record changed rapidly as it recorded a horrifically devastating war.

Great areas of the planet's islands were laid waste as the Baldies and their enemies—in this instance a race that looked like ambulatory turtles—fought viciously.

And then the Yilayil appeared, armed with some kind of energy weapons, and began killing both combatants in the war. The narrator did not give any reason for the war (as far as Saba was able to comprehend). It was enough that they were killing anyone and anything in their way.

It was not the Yilayil who ended the war; the narrator said, in flowery language, that the Yilayil were able to halt the ending of life so that the ✻✻✻ could alter the destroyers into harmless form.

And the rapid flow of images showed Baldies metamorphosing into sea life, and vanishing into the great waters, and the other beings altered into flying insects that settled on the mountaintops above the cloud layers.

The record ended, and Saba watched the blank screen, her mind struggling to grasp all she had heard—and consider the consequences. First, the ✻✻✻ term: the closest she could come in translating it was non-ambulatory-life, singular.

Something—some one thing—had caused the Baldies and the turtle-people to mutate into utterly different life-forms. It apparently had taken many generations; Saba had not heard numbers, or had not understood them if they were mentioned.

But something, some one being, had that power. And this was the same being—or its descendant?—that was changing human beings.

"Field-of-Vagabonds," Rilla said. "Is for those who destroy life. When the Yilayil see them, they end those lives before they can recommence the destruction of before."

And suddenly Saba realized what this implied: that that poor Russian biologist, who emerged so suddenly from the jungle, probably carrying some kind of scientific tool in hand, had been mistaken for a Baldy on the attack. And since he'd not been able to explain himself, the Yilayil had taken summary action.

Now it made sense, in a weird way. To other races, the humans *would* look like Baldies. The absence or presence of hair might be too subtle a difference for other races to see; meanwhile, the similarities were strong. The Baldies stood upright, had the same number of limbs as humans, their coloring could be considered similar. They wore clothing.

They carried weapons.

The Yilayil might still have assumed that the First Team—and the present team—were Baldies, and though they spoke Yilayil, lived peaceful lives, and professed to wish to attain ti[*trill*]kee, the genetic alteration was vastly speeded up—in self-protection.

But it wasn't the Yilayil who caused that, it was this mysterious ***.

They think we're Baldies, she thought as she rose slowly from her seat. A salutory realization!

What do we really know about the Baldies?

Her mind went on its relentless drive to extrapolate to the logical conclusion.

We know they flew about in these futuristic globe ships—and that they have the capability to move about in time through the gates. They are capable of extreme violence.

This, and their humanoid form, would lead anyone to conclude that the Baldies were, in fact, human beings from the future.

Her heart and spirit wished to reject that image utterly, but she forced herself to examine the evidence. What was the likelihood of humanoid races evolving on other worlds? A glance at Rilla—even Virigu—showed that similarities were certainly possible. And biologists argued for bilateral construction and other aspects of Earth life-forms being logical progressions in the chain of evolution.

But she did not want humanity to become Baldies—at least, not like the glimpse they'd had of Baldies so far. Only, was that the whole picture? The Baldies could in fact be far different than those strange beings who appeared and destroyed, as thoughtlessly as humans of the past had wiped out peoples of other races, and today wiped out various species of creatures.

She grappled for a time with vast questions of ethics and morality, and then abandoned them. There was not enough evidence. The question of the Baldies' origin was for some other team to discover—some data analysts, who had the time and resources to plumb the question with the thoroughness it demanded.

Right now she had immediate concerns—ones that must be reported to Gordon, before she prepared herself for the night's work.

She said to Rilla and Virigu, "I must rest now. I thank you for this session."

They both nodded, and moved away.

She retreated to her room, grabbed her communicator, and tapped out the code for Gordon.

He connected a moment later.

"Gordon," she said without preamble—appreciating, as she always did, that she could talk to him that way. "We are being modified at a cellular level."

"I know that," he said. "I have a report for you on the flyers, who are our First Team."

"I just found that out as well," she said, "though I haven't had a chance to think it through. But here's a poser for you: the reason all this is happening to us is because every being on this planet, including the mystery being, thinks that we are Baldies."

Silence, then laughter. It was the kind of poignantly painful laughter that Saba immediately recognized, for her own reaction had been the same.

"Well," he said. "Interesting indeed. Quite sobering."

Saba said, smiling, "I thought you'd see it that way. Now, shall I report first, or shall you?"

"Go ahead," he said, and they took turns summing up the day's findings.

CHAPTER 27

AS EVELEEN MADE her way slowly out of her dreams the next morning, she became aware of a sense of change—of portent, almost before she opened her eyes.

It was a good feeling of portent, that much she was aware of.

When she did open her eyes, it was to see the familiar rounded, bare walls of their Nurayil dorm cell. She turned on her side, listening to the faint scrunchings the futon material made, and she sniffed the familiar dusty-laundry-room smell.

No more, she thought. Then it struck her what the portent was: they did not have to go to work. It no longer mattered. They were going to go *home*.

She laughed. Her ever-present thirst no longer mattered, nor did the weird appetite for protein. Or the headache, or the joint-ache. Home—soon, to fresh strawberries, and luxurious baths, and sanity. Home.

Ross stepped out of the fresher just then, and smiled when he saw her smiling. "Good dream?" he asked.

"No. Good wakening," she said, getting up slowly. "Shall we bother rolling this stupid mat? Oh, Ross, I am so glad we're going home. I hope Gordon got Saba already, because—"

A tapping at the door interrupted her.

"You get that, would you?" Eveleen suggested. "I'll go clean up."

She walked into the fresher, enjoying for the first time in what seemed an eternity the strange sensation of passing through the gunk that felt like plastic wrap. Never again, she thought as she stepped through, and never again, she chortled happily as she shoved her clothing through.

From the outer room she heard excited voices, but no sense of alarm accompanied them, for she recognized the high one as Vera. Vera always sounded like that.

She fingered her hair into a braid, then pinned it up off her neck; the walk through the jungle would be hot, if this day was as sunny as the one previous had been.

Stepping into the room, she saw a brief tableau: Ross standing head bowed, hands on his hips. That posture sent a pang of warning through Eveleen.

She turned to Vera, whose hands were spread wide, her round face haggard—as though she hadn't slept.

"Everywhere," Vera said, her accent very strong. "Everywhere I could think. Each Moova house. Each place we have found food. I hide from Yilayil—I do everything. No Irina."

"What?"

It sounded like someone else's voice. Eveleen grabbed her middle, which cramped suddenly. "What? Don't tell me Irina is missing."

"I won't if you don't want me to," Ross said with bleak humor, "but the fact is, she hasn't turned up—not all day yesterday, or, what is more important, last night."

"Gordon," Eveleen said, thinking rapidly. "He was talking to her when he left here yesterday morning. Does he know?"

"Yes," Vera said. "I reported to him very late last night, when I went to sleep. He was not worried—said she was probably following up on some details. So I did not worry either. But she never came back."

Eveleen nodded. "Did she show up at her job?"

"I do not know that, for we work for different Moova. She was not at our meeting place at midday, but sometimes she would not join me because she was busy. I did not really worry at that point."

"No Moova said anything to you?"

Vera shook her head. "That is not their way. We serve, they take no further interest in us."

Ross said, "I still am inclined not to be too alarmed. You said she sometimes takes off to do her data verification on her own, right?"

"It is true," Vera said, drawing in a deep breath, which she let out in a sigh. "She does not always tell me what she is working on. But this is the first time she did not return at night."

Ross glanced at Eveleen, who shook her head slightly. Eveleen realized they'd both had the same thought: Irina might have gone to see Misha—for whatever reason. But they weren't going to bring *that* one up without more evidence.

"She might even have gone out to see the Jecc place," Ross said slowly. "For the final report."

Eveleen said, trying for lightness, "Good. Then you won't have to write one!"

"Oh, won't I," Ross fired back grimly. "You watch. Milliard and Kelgarries will expect breath-to-breath detail, in triplicate."

Now Eveleen looked from Vera to Ross. "Should we contact Viktor and Misha?" She suggested with what she hoped was delicacy.

"I did," Vera said, for once not smiling. "They do not know where she is. Misha has said they will search the jungle."

Eveleen felt a spurt of worry. So Irina—wherever she was—was *not* with Misha. A romantic tryst—Irina going to spend time with Misha—would have been simple, despite the emotional fallout for poor Vera and her unrequited crush.

"Why she'd go there makes no sense," Ross said.

"To check on the positions of the First Team's camps," Eveleen said. "She always seems to need to see everything herself."

Vera looked wry. "This is true. She thinks no one observes properly." She sighed again. "Viktor is going to check the Field-of-Vagabonds in case she needed to see the biologist's grave for some reason, and Misha said that after he visits the camps, if she's still missing, he would see if he could track the movement of the ancient transport system."

"She knew about that?" Eveleen asked.

"Oh, yes, Viktor showed her when he gave her his maps. She had to see everything, she said, and so he showed her everything he could think of."

Eveleen looked up at Ross, feeling sick inside. "All I can think of is those disappearances. We're not quite to Disappearance Day—"

"But who says that it has to match up exactly with Katarina's? We already know that the others disappeared at different times than she did," Ross finished, his expression pained.

"But *after*," Vera said, her tone hopeful, as she turned from Eveleen to Ross. "All of them. After Katarina. Not before."

"We still do not know why they disappeared so abruptly, though," Ross said softly. "We know what happened to them after. But not what made them drop everything and vanish."

Eveleen asked—afraid she knew the answer—"Viktor thought also to check—"

Vera pressed her lips together. "Yes."

Eveleen finished the statement in her mind: check to see if there are any fresh graves at the Field-of-Vagabonds out loud, she asked, "So what should we do? Search as well?"

Vera said, "Gordon was very specific. He said to meet here, and no one to go anywhere, after I checked my job and hers. This I have just done. She is not there."

As an afterthought, Vera unslung her carryall and pulled out some food.

"I'm not hungry," Eveleen said, sitting down against the wall. She pressed her arms against her middle and brought her knees up.

"We have to eat," Ross said.

Vera nodded. "Must keep up our strength."

Eveleen forced herself to take a few bites, but she kept looking from one to the other, wondering if they were going to disappear next. A firestorm of emotions burned through her. Though she could not claim to have become friends with Irina—not in any sense of the word—she respected the woman as a colleague and as a very fine agent. She did not want her to have been killed, but she also did not want to find out that some—unnamed, unknown—*thing* had somehow taken over her brain and forced her to, what, run to the island of the flyers?

"The flyers," she whispered. "Then maybe that's the next place to check—and we're the ones to check it."

Vera hesitated, then said, "I promised Gordon. We must do this plan only if he concurs. Too many of us missing—" She gave a shrug. "Then the others must search for us."

Unspoken was the implication that the unnamed something would take *them* over as well.

Eveleen gritted her teeth, wondering how she could have felt so wonderful on waking.

Vera's fingers trembled as she unhooked her com from her belt. She tabbed the control, then uttered a Russian curse. "He is using his unit," she said. "We must wait."

"I'll prepare our packs," Ross murmured.

Eveleen sat where she was, hugging her arms tightly to herself as Ross moved efficiently around the little chamber, which felt more like a cell every moment. Vera sat down against the opposite wall, and did not speak as she kept tabbing her communicator every minute or so.

Finally—when it seemed to Eveleen that something must happen or she would run out screaming—Vera's face lit with relief, and she said, "Gordon! We think—what? What's that?"

Eveleen clenched her teeth.

Ross froze in the act of hooking a freshly filled canteen to Eveleen's pack.

Vera lowered her communicator and looked blankly at them. "Irina is back," she said.

" 'Back'?" Ross repeated, and something in Vera's tone must have triggered an idea, because he snapped his fingers. "She went down the timeline!"

Vera nodded. "And Zina has returned with her. She has called Misha, and Viktor. They are coming, they will be here—Zina wants us to go back at once."

———————————————————

GORDON RAN UP the access tunnel, puffing hard. A sharp pain in his side forced him to slow, but he would not stop, not until he reached Saba's room.

She was not in the great cavern; he would tear the place apart, he vowed, if she was not in her room.

But when he pounded on the door it opened almost immediately—and he found himself staring up into the face of a tall creature looking kind of like a sandy-skinned seal.

From beyond came Saba's voice, a little hoarse, but sane—and amused.

"Gordon, this is Zhot."

Ashe gave the being a nod, and a formal Yilayil greeting.

Zhot replied in kind, then withdrew to a corner. His movements were quick and fluid; disconcerting in so large a creature.

"Zina is here," Gordon said—in English. "We are to leave."

"I can't," Saba said.

Ashe faced Zhot, ready to demand her freedom.

"It's not anyone here," Saba said hastily, before Gordon could speak, she cleared her throat and added in Yilayil, "No one is forcing me to do anything. It is I who must do this. Zhot is here to help me to understand what it is I discovered during the Great Dance."

Gordon gritted his teeth, and when he knew his voice would come out steady, he said—in English again, "Please. Report."

Saba stayed with Yilayil. "I cannot express any of the terms in English. Some you might not comprehend; bear with me. Last night I was more ready for the experience, and I went rested. What I found out is that the other entity that I spoke to you about is in fact real, it seems to either be comprised of, or controlled by, all the plant life on this planet. Undersea, above sea, it's all connected."

"A sentient plant," Gordon repeated—in Yilayil.

"Yes. I still do not perceive how it exists outside of time. I mean, I could understand the past—but the future? Yet this is the reality," Saba said.

"Go on."

Zhot remained motionless, listening.

"It is I who was able to comprehend a portion of the entity, just enough to provide an image for the others. It—they—don't really communicate. It's too large, too vast, too *alien*. But I understood this much: what it's doing to us—to all of us on this planet, every race that has come here—is turning us into plants, or harmless animal helpers for the plants. That is perhaps what the flyers are. We've been breathing spores since we arrived, and that's making the change. Rapidly for humans, though there is great danger, but the entity was afraid that our volatility, our violence, would endanger the planet once again."

"But . . . Wasn't that the Baldies?" Gordon said the last word in English.

"Perhaps—or perhaps it hears our innate violence. I don't know."

"So we're being mutated—against our will."

"Yes," Saba said calmly.

Gordon struggled with the inherent moral question.

Saba went on—as though reading his mind. "It is just the same as our terraforming planets."

Gordon considered this, and though he still fought against an instinctive revulsion—as if the jungle outside the city had suddenly turned evil—he said, "No, it's more immediate than that." He thought about how he'd carelessly uprooted plants all along his rail route. "We routinely kill plants for food, for other needs, to make this city, even. Not just us, but the non-plant beings."

Zhot spoke for the first time. "The entity heals the planet."

Saba said, "It knows what I am going to do—apparently what I must do, to protect the timeline downstream. I must warn all the races on this world. Even the Yilayil do not quite know the extent of the changes, or why they are occurring. Whatever they decide to do, they have a right to know. And it must be I who tells them. I cannot leave until I do."

Gordon considered this, then nodded slowly.

"All right," he said. "Understood. Keep in touch. I will inform Zina, and I'll get back to you on the next step. Maybe we can help you with this?"

"Some of it I can do with the Yilayil system," Saba said. "I know how it functions; what I don't know, Virigu can help me with. I will get started right away. But every race must be informed before I can leave. I see that as my own moral responsibility."

Gordon thought about the present timeline—and the flyers, weasel-creatures, and the humanoids, but before he could formulate his thoughts into a question, the com burred against his skin—in the emergency pattern.

He clicked it on. "Ashe here."

Vera's voice blared out, in Russian. "You must come! Irina is back—she went down the timeline—Misha is furious. I think he is going to strangle Irina, for she then *went up the line to the First Team!*"

CHAPTER 28

"SO MISHA AND Viktor are coming here?" Ross fired the question at Vera.

Eveleen felt a wash of sympathy for the tired, confused, frightened woman.

But Vera answered steadily, "Yes. Misha just said so. But they have one stop to make before they reach the transport close by."

Ross snapped his fingers. "Of course. The other spaceport station—that's not far from our terminal site. Misha will probably head right there," Ross guessed. "I would, if I was going to make trouble. The Field-of-Vagabonds is a relatively short hike from that first station." He looked at Eveleen. "Let's meet them there. We might need you to keep something stupid from happening."

Eveleen knew she could prevent Misha from strangling Irina if she had to, but she didn't look forward to trying.

But she kept that to herself. "Right," she said. "Let's."

They left, almost running down the ramp.

Outside, they were astonished and dismayed to see the streets of the Nurayil city impossibly crowded. A huge, spectacular cloud formation loomed to the northwest; the sun, unfortunately, was still in the east, and it bore down with accustomed intensity.

Eveleen ignored it as she, Ross, and Vera dodged around the various denizens of the city. All three avoided confrontations, by mutual and unspoken agreement. They deferred to everyone, though Eveleen could have screamed with impatience when a trio of slow-moving oboe-people maneuvered some kind of complicated machine in front of them and set it to inch forward.

They followed it only until they reached a side street that Vera knew. She pointed, and the three of them dashed into the narrow, less crowded alley. Domiciles lined both sides of the alley. Eveleen glanced through an open door to see some of the green beings just about to emerge, two of them humming a kind of dirgelike chant that set Eveleen's nerves on edge.

What was going on?

They skidded around a corner, cutting across Moova territory. Eveleen had only glimpsed this area, and had avoided it; there were many small, conical houses that all looked alike, and they were arranged in intersecting circles, not in orderly rows.

Vera led them through, threading unerringly between houses.

They emerged, panting, in an area that Eveleen recognized. Less traffic clogged the ways here; mostly the buildings were old, some abandoned, their architecture strange.

Past those, into the area that had been abandoned longest. Here, the jungle had encroached steadily. Now they dodged plants and vines and undergrowth, until they reached the ivy-choked hole that led to the ancient transport system.

Another run down the ramp. At least the air was cooler.

They reached the concourse, just as one of the flat cars arrived with a whoosh and a hiss. The foremost figure had yellow hair.

Ross stepped down directly onto the rails, raising a hand. "We'll join you," he said.

Misha waved them on, his gesture casual, but his face in the dim lighting was tight with anger.

Ross flicked a look at Eveleen, and she interpreted it to mean that she and Vera should board first.

"Come on," she murmured.

Vera followed, glancing doubtfully back at Misha, who ignored her. She settled behind Eveleen. A moment later Ross slid in behind her; he'd stayed on the rail in case Misha decided to leave before they could board.

No one spoke. The car jerked forward, moaning and vibrating, then slowed again fairly soon; the journey to the second stop was not a long one.

The car pulled up behind another one. Halfway up the ramp they saw Irina and the Colonel—the latter's square body also considerably thinner. It seemed strange to see her in this environment.

Both paused, waiting.

Misha disembarked with a vaulting leap, then turned to offer his hand to Eveleen. "Are you here as my guide or my guardian?" he asked.

"We're here," she stated, "to stop trouble before it starts."

"More fool you, then," he said, turning his back.

He was in a hot rage, obviously; his boot heels struck the old tiles as he strode up the ramp directly to Irina, who stood a little way from the Colonel, her arms at her sides.

Misha stopped before her and spoke a short sentence in Russian.

Eveleen didn't understand the language, but the meaning was clear: *Why did you do it?*

Irina answered in English, her voice, as always, clear, precise, and emotionless. "I went alone," she said, "because you would not have permitted Svetlana a choice."

Silence. Eveleen watched the impact of that realization hit Misha— that Svetlana had, for whatever reason, chosen to stay in the past.

She had chosen.

The Colonel looked from one to the other, then said, "We will discuss this. Let us go to a more convenient location."

Ross said, "The signal on the coms won't reach here."

"Then we shall go where they will," Zina said calmly.

Everyone followed, even Misha. He walked still with that tight anger, but his eyes were narrowed, their expression unseeing, almost stricken. Eveleen looked away, feeling that even a simple glance was intruding on his privacy. She slipped her hand into Ross's, and he gave her fingers a reassuring squeeze.

Out in the sunlight, Irina took over the lead. She had found a new shortcut. Eveleen recognized none of the streets, but fairly quickly they arrived back at the Nurayil dorm.

Moments later they were in her and Ross's cell—and Gordon knocked almost as soon as they shut the door.

"Saba?" Eveleen asked.

"I have lots to report," Gordon said. "But it can wait," he added, frowning as he looked round at them. A little louder he said, "Let's sit down, shall we?"

Irina remained standing. Everyone's attention shifted to her.

"As soon as I read the notebooks," she said, "I knew what had happened. I knew that it was I who effected the disappearance. It had to be so. I knew that if I told any of you, then Misha would try to stop me, or to go himself, and he would not consider the timeline, or the consequences."

Eveleen glanced at Misha, who just shrugged.

Irina went on, "I prepared my evidence, and presented it to Gordon."

At that Misha's head came up sharply. "You *knew*, then."

"Yes. We discussed this yesterday morning. I also understood her reasons for keeping her mission a secret until it was completed. Go on, Irina, give them all the details."

Irina sighed, leaning back against the wall as if her energy had abruptly drained. "What was needed were the physical tests," she said. "So I went forward and reported. We needed Valentin and Elizaveta for that; I went back to the First Team and found Katarina, and explained." Her voice suddenly went uneven. She pressed her lips together, hard, then continued, her voice harshening.

"Katarina understood. Together we went forward to the present-day timeline, and there Valentin and Elizaveta performed tests on us. The key one was bone density. The other molecular in nature. I don't understand it even now, but there is this to know: the spore interaction on the molecular level is so subtle that we do not really have instruments to measure it. But the fact is that Katarina's bone density was so dangerously altered that there was no returning. The changes had gone too far. Even removal from the spores would not restore the team to health. The changes were such that any of the First Team who returned would be forever crippled—if they survived long enough to shed the effect of the spores."

"Then we're doomed as well," Eveleen said, not even thinking. Horror seized her.

Irina glanced at her, compassion clear in her gaze. Tears gleamed along her lower lids, but she went on, "No. For they tested me as well. Our bone density is not yet at this danger point. For this we either have Vera to thank—"

Eyes turned Vera's way.

Irina said, "It is she who took responsibility for the food analysis. When we all began to sicken, the headache and joint-ache required calcium, or as near as we could find, this she decided, and she found the foods that would provide the supplement. That is in the cheese dish we all came to rely on, for it also carried a complex protein that again slowed the damage."

Zina spoke now, for the first time. "Valentin does not wish to rob Vera of credit that is due her, but there is the possibility that the spores affecting us are different than those that affected Katarina and the First Team."

Irina sighed again, a shuddering sigh that seemed completely uncharacteristic, and she said, "So when this news was complete—last night—Katarina and I went back. I knew where most were, from Viktor's findings, and Katarina knew the rest. Together we found each team member, and told them. They left their things exactly as we found them. She did not go back to her archive, but left it buried as she had when we first went forward. I showed them the transport, and they went as a group to the island to await the changes there. It was peaceful, it was not bad. They knew that they would have children. They knew that their children would fly. And they knew that someday, their descendants would see us."

Silence met this news.

Irina swiped at her eyes, then she turned to Misha. "You are not the only one to leave someone important. Katarina and I, we were in the university together. We served two missions together. We were close—we were sisters—" Her voice suspended, and she shook her head, hard.

No one spoke.

Irina then dug into her pocket. "As for Svetlana, she chose to go to the island. She did write to you: I brought it with me, so there would be no alteration in time. Here it is."

She handed Misha a paper. He took it, then thrust it into a pocket in his shirt.

Zina said, "Valentin urges us to leave now. He says daily the damage does worsen, and he does not know when the point of nonrecovery would be, but does not want to risk finding out after the fact."

Gordon stepped forward then. "It is time for my report. You probably saw the mass movements toward the House of Knowledge?"

"Is that what's going on?" Ross asked. "All we know is, everyone who could get in our way was out on the streets, just when we were trying to hurry." He cast an amused glance at Misha, who gave him a sardonic smile. Misha's eyes, though, were still somber.

"There is a mass meeting being held right now, for everyone who can cram into the Yilayil caverns. Basically the word is what we already figured out, but not the scale. Apparently the key sentience on this planet is the plant life, a vast interconnected awareness that is trying to heal itself by altering us. It's been trying for centuries to communicate; the Yilayil language and music kept evolving in the direction needed, but none of them, for whatever reason, could make the mental leap outside of time and sensory awareness that it required for even as limited a contact as Saba made last night. A being named Zhot was the closest, but he had only reached the awareness of this other entity. A Virigu, and some of the Yilayil as well. They knew of the entity, but had never been able to communicate."

"And Saba did?" Eveleen asked.

"Yes," Gordon said. "She made the breakthrough. Her musical sense, apparently, was the last link needed, the catalyst. She feels that she is obligated to inform every being on the planet about the genetic alterations. What they do is up to them."

Irina nodded slowly. After a moment, Zina opened her hands. "It is right," she said.

No one else spoke.

"So what can we do to speed it along?" Ross asked. "About all I can contact is the Jecc."

"And I the Moova," Vera chimed in.

Gordon nodded. "Do it. The rest of us will remain here and stay in contact. Saba's colleagues in the House are telling those who came in person. Saba and one of their computer experts are busy on the communications system, letting everyone else know. They should be done about the time we finish here, for it's enough to let each enclave and race know, and spread the news in the way they think best."

Ross turned to Eveleen, who felt adrenaline—the old call for action—suffuse her body. With a clear goal, she found she could move again.

ONCE MORE THEY found themselves following their customary route to the transport station, but once they reached it, not surprisingly they found it completely empty. Even the Virigu was gone; the place was like a vast hangar, completely deserted.

"Jecc city," Ross said. "Up to it?"

"Of course," she replied.

They scarcely spoke as they made their way once again to the ancient transport. Eveleen realized they probably could have taken one of the rail-skimmers—but even after all this time working on them, they never had learned how to operate them. The rail-skimmers might not even reach the Jecc city.

The flat cars whooshed them speedily to the southernmost point of the island. Together she and Ross walked up to the Jecc caves, hand in hand.

They were soon sighted, and a swarm of Jecc came running out to surround them.

At first Eveleen felt a twinge of alarm; too late she realized that the Jecc might consider them interlopers or even enemies.

But the tweets and calls as the Jecc tumbled about Ross reassured her. They largely ignored her—all their attention was on Ross.

At one point one of them must have put a question, for Ross responded in Yilayil, pointing to Eveleen, "My mate."

Shrill tweets rose from all sides. The Jecc obviously found the notion of "mates" an exotic concept.

Eveleen did not try to comprehend all the various Jecc reactions, but Ross seemed to know who to listen to, for again he responded in Yilayil. "Yes, it requires one of each of us to pass on genetic material. One offspring results—rarely two or more—but we can repeat the process, just as you Jecc do . . ."

Eveleen felt a sense of unreality seize her; the biology lesson lasted until they reached the outer caves.

Here, abruptly, they entered civilization—but for totally different beings.

Beautiful colors were everywhere. The catwalks and pathways, the furnishings, everything was child-sized. Jecc swarmed everywhere, on all levels—for Eveleen saw, tipping her head back, that catwalks and cave tunnels were located at several levels. At the very top, she saw tiny faces peeping timidly down—Jecc children?

Then she lost sight of them as they were led beyond, into an even greater cave. Cool air swirled gently across her face as she gazed up at row on row of great murals painted in realistic, glowing colors all round the stone walls. This was what she had glimpsed from the upper vent— but it was far vaster, and more beautiful, than she had conceived.

Sudden silence brought her attention downward.

The Jecc had settled into rings, with old wrinkly Jecc closer at hand, and others outward in widening circles.

One of the Jecc greeted Ross formally, using all the Yilayil deferences.

Ross said back, "I have come to make certain you were aware of the new people recently discovered."

The old Jecc trilled, "We know of the world-being. We know now why we have changed."

A weird, sighing whistle went through the ranks of Jecc; Eveleen felt hairs prickling on the back of her neck. The emotions caused by the sound were intense—loss, isolation.

"Then you can decide what you want to do," Ross said. "This is why I came."

"What do you do, Ross of Fire Mountain?"

"We have a ship, we will go back to our world," Ross said.

Again a sound swept through the Jecc, this time a susurrus of high-voiced whispers.

"We have a ship," the old Jecc said at last. "At Harbeast Teeth Island. It is secret all these generations."

"One ship?" Ross repeated.

Rapidly the Jecc explained—and Eveleen began to understand. That sense of unreality still pervaded her mind. She seemed to be watching from somewhere else, observing this exchange between two utterly different races, using the language of a third race, to talk about spaceships from the past—a technology not yet attained by Earth civilizations.

Comprehension worked its way slowly into her head. The ship the Jecc had was a kind of shuttle, hoarded against the day when they would return to normal. Apparently they had a great ship up in space, circling around. Eveleen nodded to herself; of course it would be unmolested. The mysterious plant entity only controlled what was on the surface.

How many other races might have motherships circling around in orbit?

No way of knowing.

Suddenly the conversation ceased. Ross turned to Eveleen. "Come on, we're done," he said.

In silence they walked past the ranks, and out of the caves.

Neither spoke until they reached the transport.

"So are they going back home?" Eveleen asked. "I confess I didn't follow it all."

"They don't know," Ross said. "Some want to, some don't. Others want to stay—and a fourth group wants to find another world."

"That same debate must be going on all over the world," Eveleen commented.

Ross sat back. "I don't know why, but the whole damn mess makes me sad."

He activated the control, and the flat car zoomed forward, relieving Eveleen of having to think of anything to say.

━━━━━━━━━━ ━━━━━━━━ ━━━━━━━━━━

"LET'S GET OUT of here," Ross said when they reached the Nurayil dorm for the last time, and found everyone gathered—Misha having also just returned from an unnamed errand.

"I am going to need help transporting Saba," Gordon replied, looking relieved that they were safely back. "She's by far the weakest of us all. Her body has—we believe—been resisting the changes, and her immune system is at a dangerously low ebb."

Eveleen watched Ross's face brighten. Now he had orders, impending action—a clear need, one that he could meet, even if it was just to carry a sick woman on a stretcher.

"There's a transport near the House of Knowledge," Misha began.

"Found it," Gordon said. "Everyone needs to get their gear, and meet at the transport near this dorm. Come on, let's move."

Under cover of the sudden springs of conversation, Eveleen heard Misha address Gordon. "So it was a false trail you sent us on—the island, the Field-of-Vagabonds."

"I needed to keep you busy," Gordon said. He hesitated, then added, "You'll have to admit even a needless trip is better than sitting with nothing one can do, counting off the seconds."

"Ah." Misha shrugged. "So you claim empathy as your reason?"

Gordon only laughed. "Go. Get your gear."

Eveleen watched Misha vanish through the open door.

She knew that whatever Svetlana had said in her letter was not going to be shared with anyone; nor would Misha permit anyone to see him reading it. She thought about being separated forever from Ross, and even though the Russians' relationship might not have even remotely been like what she and Ross shared, for the first time, she felt pity for the blond agent.

She kept her thoughts to herself as she packed her few belongings. To her surprise her emotions were mixed at the thought of abandoning forever the little cell.

Ross and she were alone. She was not aware she'd sighed until he said, "You can't be wanting to stay."

"No," she said. "But I hate feeling that I could have done better. That this mission was so strange, so . . . ."

"Nightmarish? Long? Boring?" Ross prompted, looking amused.

"Oh, I don't know," Eveleen said. "Confusing, I guess is the best term. Is it only going to get harder, Ross? Suddenly I feel, well, *old*."

"You're sick. I'm sick. We're going home," he reminded her. "C'mon, help me get our sticker off the door. I hope the next inmate has a better time—"

"If there is one," Eveleen said. "How weird. It could be that we are the ones who caused the evacuation."

"Except we still have three races down the timeline, two of them nothing anyone would want to be," Ross reminded her.

They laid their palms on the screen, then pressed the control that they had learned meant *vacate*.

"Uh oh, we forgot to check our credit rating," Ross joked.

"Oh, I'm sure we had enough for half a ride," Eveleen joked back, trying for lightness.

They kept up the banter as they threaded their way through the crowded street.

This time there was a difference. Unasked, various beings offered them deference. Again and again the other races withdrew, permitting them to go first. No one spoke to them, and expressions were as impossible to read as ever, but somehow their status had changed.

Eveleen was still pondering this when they descended the ramp to find everyone waiting.

Everyone—even Saba, who looked so frail Eveleen felt her heart start pounding. But Saba's dark eyes were clear and smiling, and she held her head at a proud angle as she leaned on Viktor's and Gordon's shoulders.

Together they all rode the last car to the station near the parkland.

Half an hour's hike, through misting rain, and they reached the time apparatus.

Zina stepped forward and worked the controls.

Eveleen watched, waiting impatiently for the doors to open.

Lights flickered on the little console. Zina frowned, and punched the code more carefully.

Impatience turned to alarm.

"What now?" Ross asked, then he cursed under his breath.

For answer, the doors slid open.

And framed there were two Baldies, blasters in hand.

CHAPTER 29

QUICKER THAN AN eye blink, Zina slammed her hand on the door controls and they shut on the Baldies.

She poked at the manual lock, saying over her shoulder, "Fast. Out of here."

Misha led the way.

Gordon picked Saba up; Ross fell in step right behind them, in case Gordon, who was breathing heavily, should falter. Ross glanced down, saw Eveleen at his side.

"They must get that same vertigo right after the transfer," she panted.

Up ahead, Zina turned. "I counted on that." She gave them a faint smile.

Under his breath, Ross said to Eveleen, "She's fast. Give her that."

Eveleen chuckled somewhat breathlessly. "You mean the rest of us were going to stand around like zombies."

From behind came the keening noise of blaster fire.

"They're out," Misha said with mordant humor. "And hunting us."

"Quiet." Zina's word was not loud, but her voice carried command.

No one spoke. Ross's mind roiled with questions—guesses—plans as he plunged along the pathway behind Eveleen.

Viktor took over the lead, and in silence they wound along trails and under hanging ferns, coming to a stop in a deep little grotto.

Gordon bent, and Saba slid to the ground, where she sat with her eyes closed. It was hard to see her expression; the light seemed muted.

Ross blinked, surprised to discover that night was falling.

The rain had ceased, but the sky was covered by a heavy bank of clouds.

Everyone was breathing hard.

Ross said, "If they've got the machine, that means they've got the camp upstream."

Zina gave a tired nod. "It means they might have the ships as well." She turned to Gordon. "Your surmise was my own: that our tampering with the navigational wire must have sent out some kind of signal we were never aware of."

"Where do we go now?" Vera asked. "Back to the city?"

"Then we lead them right to the others, and they'll start shooting everyone," Eveleen protested.

"They will find their way to the city anyway," Zina said. "And they will shoot until they find us. I think we must go ahead, and warn the Yilayil. Now, so they have time to prepare."

Viktor gave a single nod, and plunged into the undergrowth.

A short time later they came to the transport, and both Viktor and Misha checked the area carefully before they emerged from the protective screen of shrubbery and dodged down into the partially overgrown entrance.

"This ought to buy us a few hours," Ross commented as they half skipped, half ran down the steep rampway.

"The lights will draw them," Misha responded.

"Whom do we tell to get the fastest action?" Zina asked.

Saba said, "We must return to the House."

The car was still there from earlier; they all dropped into it, Gordon hovering protectively near Saba. The two of them conferred in quiet voices as everyone else found a seat and leaned back.

Misha worked the controls. The car lurched, then began to pick up speed, pressing Ross back into his seat. He rather enjoyed these things, but he'd always liked roller coasters—the more dangerous the better.

They passed their old station and continued to the House of Knowledge station.

This one, Ross noted with grim surprise, did not seem as dusty and neglected as all the others. Who in that place used it—and why?

Useless to ask now.

When the car had come to a stop, Gordon helped Saba out, and in a group they proceeded up the ramp.

There they found a clean, dry tunnel. At the exit doors, Saba turned. "You'll have to wait," she said. "No one's been permitted inside. Even with all the changes, I don't know what it might mean to break that rule."

Zina said, "We will be much better here. Gordon, go with her. The rest of us will remain here until you return."

Ross promptly dropped his pack to the tiled flooring and sank down with his back to the wall. He pulled out his canteen, took a deep drink, then offered it to Eveleen, who also drank.

Vera sat down on Eveleen's other side, and Viktor beside her. They began to converse in quiet Russian. Zina and Irina had embarked on another conversation, also in Russian. Ross, lifting his head slightly, saw Misha standing at the other end of the tunnel, his back to the group, his body tense. Reading his letter, of course. Ross shook his head, and returned his attention to his immediate surroundings; from time to time, he saw his wife sending covert and compassionate glances Misha's way.

It was not long before Gordon and Saba abruptly returned.

"They know," Gordon said. "And if I understand right, they are prepared."

"Then here our responsibilities end," Zina said. "Let us return to the time-shift apparatus. We have to see if they still hold it."

"We have to take it back," Ross said grimly.

Misha turned around. "You don't," he said with all his old sardonic humor, "want to see what happens?"

"And how can we do that?" Eveleen asked, hands on hips. "I'd as soon not have a ringside seat, especially with blasters providing the special effects."

"No," Ross cut in. "Let me guess: another of these transport stations will give us a perfect view?"

Misha smiled, and Viktor laughed.

"The other tower. The spaceport tower," Misha said. "It was probably a military outpost of some sort. You can see over the entire city from it."

Zina hesitated, then gave a nod. "If it's quick. We'll have a better report, maybe a better understanding of what happened."

Again to the cars, and this time they proceeded farther up the line. Ross realized he was getting a feel for the geography of the transport system; if he was right, the Yilayil city had been much, much bigger in the past.

They disembarked and walked out into an empty street, partially overgrown. All of them used their flashlights, making their way after Misha.

The tower turned out to be one of the ones Ross and Gordon had found in the far future—the tall red one wherein the savage weasel-creatures had built their lair. They had not been able to explore farther.

This time there was an elevator to take them up, silent and slow but still working. Bluish lights flickered in it, faint but still working from some long-term power source.

At the top, there were a number of devices that turned out to be zoom lenses. A central control area with a huge screen above must have been a video linkup of some sort—but age had destroyed that system.

The lenses were manually operated. The one Ross chose had dust and some tiny fungi growing tenaciously in it, but it worked well enough. He could see more clearly down into the dark street than he could with his naked eye. The principle was not infrared—he couldn't figure it out. Everything looked shadowless and curiously flat, but discernible.

"Hey!" Eveleen's voice was sharp. "They're right below us!"

"The spaceport," Zina said. "Of course. They would check there first—"

"What do we do? We haven't any weapons," Vera asked, looking from one to another.

Ross saw his wife in her fighting stance, her face tense but calm. Misha had not moved.

He suddenly looked up. "Watch now." He pointed downward.

Ross pressed his eye to his viewer, in time to see not two Baldies, but a team of ten of them, walking in single file up the empty street, firing at anything that moved. They also shot away any plants in their way, blazing a trail that anyone could follow.

And had.

As Ross watched, the lead Baldy tipped his head back and stared right up at the tower—seemingly at him.

"You think this was *their* tower, long ago?" Eveleen murmured.

No one answered—everyone was watching.

From behind came a group of six tall, four-armed figures, all of them in flaxen robes.

"Yilayil," Saba murmured, easily heard in the silent room.

The lead Baldy swung about, lifting his weapon, but before he could fire, the Yilayil all raised long tubes to their mouths. Ross could see their furred cheeks puff as a cloud of particles that glowed with odd colors streamed out of the tubes; he didn't know if the colors were real, or some effect of the lenses.

The Baldies got off two shots, and two Yilayil collapsed to the street. Then the Baldies stopped firing. Looking around wildly, they slapped at their faces and bodies, tried to run, but moved as though wading through glue. The ground seemed to be sticking to their feet. Involuntary wormlike motions lifted their arms into the air, splayed their fingers, and tipped their heads back. Within a minute, they stood frozen, and horror suffused Ross as he saw thin green tendrils curl out of their ears, mouths, and noses.

He hastily looked away, swallowing rapidly. Whatever had happened, it was no more pleasant a death than the blasters had been.

Zina's voice was flat. "That's enough. Let us retreat."

"Just as well," Ross said tightly, "we don't have to go out there."

Eveleen gave a quick, wincing nod.

They withdrew in ordered haste, glad of the tight air system—for whatever that spore had been that the Yilayil had used might still be permeating the air.

No one spoke on the return—either on the transport ride or during the night hike to the time-transportation apparatus.

Misha and Viktor checked ahead—but they found the transport hut deserted. The rest of the group emerged from the jungle, Gordon still helping Saba, and Zina once again pressed the controls.

And again nothing happened.

Ross felt Eveleen's hand slide into his. It was obvious what had occurred. The Baldies had either changed the codes or else had jammed the apparatus. Either way, unless the team up the timeline figured out what was going on, they were stuck here forever.

"We assume that a signal brought them," Saba said at last. "Why do you think they came?"

"To rescue that scoutcraft," Gordon said in a tired voice. "Remember, the globe ship belonged to the Baldies originally."

"Then . . ." Eveleen said slowly. "Then we are the bad guys here, not the Baldies?"

Silence met this, but Ross sensed everyone's attention turning her way.

They all sat in the dark, forming a semicircle around the transport doors. No one lit a flash—too dangerous a lure.

"Think about it," Eveleen said. "I mean, I'm scared of them, and I know the horrible things they did. But we came here on their ship, and we know that the crews on these globe ships all died. How would we feel to get a signal from one of our craft, and follow it up to find a lot of aliens on it—and our crew gone, presumed dead?"

"They brought the war to us," Ross said.

"We don't know if it was a war. Oh, they seem to be shoot-happy, but then so have we been in the past, and we've always seen ourselves as the good guys."

"So we're the villains?" Misha's voice came out of the darkness, cool and amused.

"To them we are," Eveleen said, her voice steady. "We don't know anything about the Baldies' motivations. Boris—everyone—thought that the globe was a scoutcraft. That argues that at least some of their missions were not war-related. Their encounters with us have involved their deaths as well as our own."

"So their action on Dominium—the old timeline—was self-defense?" Ross asked.

"No," Gordon said. "That was warfare, all right. But we don't know when those Baldies appeared from. Their cultures might vary as much as ours have. All we really know about these people is that they are hairless humanoids, that they have interstellar travel, that some of their foods can be ingested by us, and that they have time-travel capabilities. We don't know what their grand strategy is, we don't know their motivations, emotions, loyalties, or what they consider threats. Nothing."

Just then a hum filled the air, lights flickered on the transport—and the doors slid open.

In the dim light, Valentin stepped out. "Ah! Did we manage well?" he asked.

Voices talked, laughed, whooped, a spontaneous expression of relief—and release. Neither Gordon nor Zina said anything about maintaining silence as they helped Saba in first.

Ross squashed his primitive but urgent instinct to shove his way forward and make sure he was next. Instead, he waited, and Irina and Vera were sent next; after that he and Eveleen stepped inside.

As soon as the doors closed, Eveleen sighed and leaned against Ross. "I just want to go home," she said.

He tightened his arm around her.

The vertigo seized him then, and a moment later the doors opened. He stumbled out, Eveleen with him, and there, in a lit clearing, were other members of the team. The acrid scent of burned vegetation singed his nose; he sneezed as the doors closed behind him.

"What happened?" he asked, finding Case Renfry standing nearby. "Baldies hit you guys first?"

"Wait," Renfry said, sounding as tired as any of the agents. "We'll brief everyone at once—and we'd better hurry, because more of them might show up at any time."

"I take you to ship." That was Gregori.

Ross and Eveleen fell in step behind him, letting him lead—and make all the decisions. Suddenly Ross felt exhaustion grip his head, and he forced himself to walk at a smart pace.

Still, it seemed forever until they reached a clearing, and there was the ship. The Baldy ship. With a weird mixture of emotions skittering through him, Ross walked up the ramp and straight to the galley.

The weird mysteries of the universe could wait—first order of business was some hot coffee.

The welcome aroma of fresh brew made him realize someone had been ahead of him here, too; he looked up to see Gordon pointing silently to a row of mugs, just set out, judging from the steam curling up lazily.

Grateful beyond words, Ross grabbed the nearest and slurped, not caring that his tongue scalded. Tears sprang to his eyes, but the coffee made its warm way down inside him, imparting a sense of well-being that he hadn't felt for an eternity.

He was partially aware of the others crowding in behind, and the row of mugs diminished to just one left over.

"Are we all here?" Gordon leaned in the doorway, trying to count heads. The galley was crowded with bodies, but no one seemed to want to move. "Case, why don't you fill us in on what happened?"

"They landed at the space station, luckily," Renfry said. "Elizaveta was over that way doing a last check to make certain we'd collected all our analyzing gear, and saw them come down. She hightailed back here and we shut the ship down so they couldn't get whatever homing device had brought them. Unfortunately, they must have some kind of signal on the time devices, because they found ours, and of course we had the time set to your year. There was no way to warn you."

"Well, they won't be following us back," Irina said, her eyes wide and dark with strain.

Ross frowned. Eveleen was not looking at him. She stared down at that one last mug of coffee, her lips parted.

Ross realized then that someone was missing.

Quick glance—Misha was missing.

Irina said in her precise voice, "Mikhail Petrovich reset the time to the First Team. He said he was going to destroy it when he got there. The Baldies—those the Yilayil don't get—will be trapped back where we were."

Ross whistled. "He went back? To the First Team?"

Irina's nod was short, her face now blank. "With Colonel's permission."

Zina turned to Boris. "We are here, and since the transport is ruined, there is no need for a last equipment run. Let us take off."

Gordon looked at Zina, his face strained. Then he turned to the crew. "You heard. Coffee break is over—strap down in your bunks."

Ross retreated, taking his coffee with him.

Gordon was apparently going to stay in the control cabin, as Ross found himself alone. He climbed into his bunk and gulped the rest of his coffee before strapping in.

A short time later came the unpleasant sensations associated with takeoff, but this time he thoroughly welcomed them. His mood was so good it must have made him get over the effects faster, because as soon as they had reached nullgrav, he unstrapped and launched himself out of the cabin.

He was not the first, though.

He found Irina at the screen, her face turned away, her shoulders hunched, and her hands gripping her arms as she hung in the air, watching the planet dwindle into a tiny point of light.

Finally she said something in Russian, her voice broken, and Ross hastily pushed himself back, glad he had not made any noise.

He found Eveleen at his shoulder—and Gordon.

"What did she say?" Eveleen asked when they reached the rec room.

Gordon winced. "I have lost them," he said slowly. "I have lost them both."

CHAPTER 30

ROSS WAS SURPRISED when Gordon offered to room with Viktor—and Viktor accepted. This left Ross alone, but only for a short time. Eveleen appeared, duffel floating beside her, half an hour later.

She grinned as she tossed her bag in the direction of the bunk. Ross watched it gyrate in midair, then bump gently against the cabin wall as he said, "Not that I'm not glad to see you, but what about Saba?"

"She's the one who needs the most sleep. We just talked, and although she's so invincibly polite I thought we were going to go around and around forever with the 'Whatever you prefer,' no, 'Whatever *you* prefer' routine, I finally got the impression she'd just love to have the cabin to herself so she can sleep, sleep, and then sleep some more." Eveleen wrinkled her nose, and sniffed. "Your sinuses clear? Mine almost are. When I think of those spores . . . ." She mimed a shudder—and since she wasn't holding on, she accidently began spinning gently in the air.

Ross laughed, and grabbed her in a hug.

A little later, he went out in search of food. He was ravenous almost all the time—and he wasn't the only one, he noted.

After he got his meal (and he was determined to eat as wide a variety as possible, if for nothing else but to get rid of the taste of that one food they'd eaten for weeks), he cruised directionlessly.

Hearing voices from the direction of the old study cabin, he paused. There he heard Gordon—and Viktor.

The conversation was a mixture of Russian and English, with an emphasis on the former, but in it Ross heard Misha's name several times—and once the name *Travis Fox.*

It was Gordon talking. Has he finally made his peace with Travis's disappearance? Ross thought. Because one of the scenarios the big brains back at HQ had come up with was that Travis had not suffered any kind of traumatic death, but had chosen deliberately not to return. Gordon had seemed to take this personally—as if he were responsible, as if he had failed the Apache agent.

Now another agent—a part of Gordon's team—had deliberately made the same choice. His motivations were different, but the effect was the same.

Misha had chosen never to return home again.

MISHA'S CHOICE KEPT coming back to bother Ross from time to time as the ship days slid measurelessly into one another.

He slept, ate, played games, and watched videos. The entertainment stuff brought along had been used minimally on the way out, but on the way back, they all seemed to have the same idea. It wasn't just the lack of a mission to focus on; they were all soul-hungry for scraps of home, even stupid movies. Ross found himself watching action flicks over and over, just to listen to English.

The return trip passed without incident.

They landed, refueled, and no one was waiting to attack them. The globe ship lifted again, obedient to the mysterious tape that unknown minds had designed and programmed, and arrowed them unerringly straight for Earth.

When they landed, it was still winter in Russia—deep winter. The journey back was the same, only in reverse: a truck to the cargo plane, a cargo plane (this time it was heated) back to the landing strip, then a train to St. Petersburg, where they were quarantined until Russian and American scientists had determined that the spores were gone from their bodies. During their time in quarantine they continued to eat voraciously, and their recovery progressed fast. And it was true that Saba had suffered the least alterations; her damage had been to her immune system. About the time that Ross began to feel desperately restless they were released from quarantine.

And Zina came through on her promise of a celebratory tour. They spent a couple of days visiting historic Russian sights. Ross looked at some of those ancient Byzantine mosaics and wall paintings. The strange eyes that gazed down at him from those old paintings somehow reminded him of the Jecc.

What had happened to them? Weird to think that whatever it was had already happened by the time these paintings had been made.

Ross wanted to go home.

He kept his mouth shut. Eveleen clearly appeared delighted with everything; Gordon was interested, and Saba, who still tired quickly, insisted on not missing a single tour. She gazed about her, those intelligent, far-seeing eyes sometimes going diffuse. But she never stopped smiling.

Ross found the baroque palaces and fabulous art collections interesting, but what he really enjoyed was seeing human beings all around him—hearing a human language, even if he couldn't understand it. Normally impatient of crowds, he now welcomed humans all about him.

He did get unexpected reminders, though; seeing children darting about in a snowy park, his thoughts were drawn yet again to the Jecc.

And to the present timeline, which Ross, Gordon, and Renfry had first discovered.

In the present timeline, there were those three races: the flyers, who knew they had to stay. The humanoids, who were probably the Baldies caught back in time. And those Yilayil who—for whatever reason—refused to leave the planet. Or had been forced to stay?

So many unanswered questions! At least for now, he thought one night, after they returned from a ballet. He sat down and opened his laptop, resolving—now that their return to the States was mere hours away—he'd better get started on his report.

The first note that popped up was his surmise about the feathered cats.

Feathered cats.

Who brought the cats? he thought. We never saw any, and we know the two teams never brought any. It argued yet another expedition, for whatever reasons. And the planet's great entity would start altering these little predators into, what, the birds that they hunted?

He closed the laptop, grimacing. No, he'd deal with reports—and memories—when he had to. For now, he was on vacation.

TWO DAYS LATER, they stepped off the plane in Washington, D.C. All around them were people speaking English!

Ross's euphoria lasted well into the expected battery of debriefings, medical and psych tests.

During the interview portion of his reports, he startled himself by frequently resorting to Yilayil to express certain ideas. He realized that one cannot completely shed one's experiences; good and bad, they shape one permanently. In conversations he—and Eveleen, Saba, and Gordon—frequently resorted to whistle/drones for certain words and verbs that really were better expressed in Yilayil.

"It's a habit we're going to have to drop," Ross said to Eveleen as they prepared for bed that night. "Unless we want to be talking a secret code."

"Not in front of other adults," Eveleen said, smiling. "But in case we have kids—so much better than spelling the crucial words out, don't you think?" She grinned in fun.

"Kids," he repeated. "Is that what you want to do?"

"Don't you?" She still smiled, but her brown eyes were serious.

He shrugged, a little helplessly. "I don't know—I hadn't thought. Is this something you want right away?"

Eveleen shook her head. "No. We've invested too much time in our training, and the Project needs us. And the work we do, even when we fail, is good work, I believe. I've been thinking about this a lot, ever since we lifted ship. I think we need to stay with the Project, at least until they don't need us."

Ross considered. "I had such a bad childhood," he said slowly. "I just never considered kids . . . But I do know how I'd raise them, which would be the opposite of how I was raised. Or not raised," he finished, laughing ruefully.

Eveleen grinned. "Well, we have plenty of time to consider our options." Then she narrowed her eyes in that familiar assessing look, and added, "There *is* something. Did I upset you with the idea of kids?"

"No," he said. "Surprised, yes. I was so used to thinking about us being stuck on Yilayil—and if we were stuck there, would we eventually have mutated offspring . . ."

"Yes, me too," she murmured.

"It's Misha," Ross said. "And his staying behind—"

Eveleen waited as Ross struggled to articulate.

"I—am I warped somehow? Has my background done something to me—" He shrugged. "This is stupid. I don't know if I can express it, or even if I should."

"Talking things out is good, we agreed on that," Eveleen said. "You can't shock me—I've seen too much in my own single years."

"It's Misha," Ross started again.

"Misha? Go on."

"Not him, but what he did."

"Ah!" Sudden enlightenment widened her eyes. "Is it that you don't think you could have made the same decision, given the same circumstances, only if I were on the First Team instead of Svetlana?"

Ross grimaced. "If I found out you were prisoned there for the rest of your life I don't know if I could willingly join you, knowing there were no options. Does this make me—"

"It doesn't make you anything," she said fiercely. "Stop it. Stop. You can't torture yourself with 'what if' questions because the circumstances are not the same. For one thing, both Saba and Gordon are convinced he meant to go back and stay, if he found Svetlana, and further that choice was made from the git-go. I guess they talked a lot about it. Not surprising, considering they both lost agents to past timelines."

"How do they see that?" Ross asked. "Because Misha wangled his way onto the mission?"

"That could have just been his sense of adventure." Eveleen laughed. "I don't know all their reasons. One thing Gordon brought up was Misha's own psychological state. He was so much like a man suffering from combat fatigue. Too much violence, too many dead companions, after all those Baldy attacks on the Russian stations. It makes people see life differently."

Ross nodded. That he could understand.

"There were other things, though I didn't ask for them. Here's what convinced *me*. All that flirting before we left, and on the ship. It was so . . . so empty. I really think it was his way of blinding us all to what he meant to do if he could. After all, once we got to the planet, he could have carried on with both Vera and Irina. Each of those women would have welcomed him. But he didn't. He'd closed everyone off by then, and he was angriest when he thought that Irina had closed off his access to Svetlana. But at the end—" Eveleen shrugged. "He finally saw the way he'd looked for, and the fact that Zina let him do it meant not only that she'd seen how the destroyed machine would keep us safe, but that he'd refuse to come back. He'd thought it all out ahead. It was not a moment's decision, made in anguish."

Ross sighed, and cut right to the real issue. "Would you go back?" he asked.

She turned her head away, her brow furrowing slightly. "I don't know," she said finally. Then she smiled at Ross. "It works the same for me as it does for you. Unless I knew all the circumstances—unless they were *real*—I have no idea what I'd do."

He kissed her. "Then let's drop it, and move on," he said.

She grinned, and they finished getting ready for sleep.

Later on, when he thought over the conversation, he suspected that she did indeed know what she would have done, but she was wise enough, and generous enough in spirit, to at least pretend to match his ambivalence.

That's real love, he thought sleepily. She's a couple steps ahead of me—but I can learn. And it will grow, and change, and make new people of us both.

All we need is time.

ATLANTIS ENDGAME

CHAPTER 1

"SURE WE HAVE the new software," Ross Murdock said, scrupulously unaware of his landlady peeping up at him over the tops of her spectacles as she drowned her potted plants for what was probably the fourth time that day. "It's a fine spreadsheet. Plenty of new features."

Gordon Ashe, following him up the stairs inside the hall, looked amused, but said nothing until Ross had shut the apartment door behind him and locked it.

"Nosy landlady, I take it?" Ashe commented.

"The tenants here are better than TV, she seems to think. At least from the gossip she rattles off to Eveleen when she can catch her."

Ashe and Ross both surveyed the plain living room with its garage-sale furnishings. Eveleen had done her best to add homey touches: a brightly colored braided rug on the floor, a few very hardy houseplants, and one or two ancient artifacts brought up from the past—nothing to raise eyebrows, should anyone drop in who knew about such things. But Ross and Eveleen knew the real stories behind them—sometimes even had known the person who had made them, thousands of years before.

Ashe shook his head. "Seems like a lot of trouble to go to, if you ask me. Project Star would be happy enough to issue you living quarters, and the ones married couples get are fairly plush. A lot nicer than this, if you want to know the truth."

"But underground. And it's still there, under their control. I've worked for the Project just about my entire adult life, and I respect everyone in it, but I want my own place. My own space. And so does Eveleen," Ross added.

Ashe opened a hand. "But what happens when you're gone on a mission? It's Project Star that handles your pay and banking, right?"

Ross nodded. "Yeah. They renew our yearly lease when it comes up. They cover the utilities. And they pay the cleaning service that comes through here once a week. Those guys dust and even water the plants." Ross gave the leaves of a spider plant a flick. "So, yeah. They hassle the details, but that's only when we're gone."

Ashe, amused, said, "I confess I don't see the difference. Plus you've got the added annoyance of a nosy landlady."

"But she's not our boss. Maybe it's the street kid in me, but I get itchy at the thought of living under the boss's roof, however benevolent." Ross shrugged, looking sardonic. "Makes no sense, does it?"

"Contrary," Ashe replied. To him, it didn't seem all that long ago when he was assigned the nervy, distrustful troublemaker Ross Murdock, straight from juvenile court. Ross had become one of the best agents in the ultrasecret Project Star in spite—or maybe because—of his readiness to apply action first, and palaver afterward, to unexpected problems.

Ashe dropped down onto one of the chairs, giving Ross a skewed smile. Did the landlady also see the signs of the street kid in him?

ROSS BROUGHT OUT a couple of mugs of coffee, giving his old partner an appraising glance. Why was Ashe so silent, staring through the coffee as if he were trying to scry his future in it? Gordon Ashe was a tough, lean man around middle age, sun browned and fit. His blue-eyed gaze was direct and intelligent, his dark hair worn short. His plain brown suit conveyed a semblance of bland city-civilization, but he looked and moved like someone who preferred being out of doors.

To break the lengthening silence, Ross said, "The landlady doesn't seem to believe I'm a computer software salesman."

Ashe blinked and looked up. "I take it you don't think I played a convincing buyer?" he asked, the corners of his mouth deepening.

"Well, neither of us looks much like the TV version of your standard computer geek. In any case, Mrs. Withan thinks I'm a no-account. It's Eveleen she keeps pestering. A 'real lady karate expert'!" His voice went squeaky on the last words, and he clasped his hands and looked skyward. "We can all sleep well of nights, knowing we have a real lady karate expert in the building!"

Ashe laughed, but it was a quick, absent laugh, and Ross sat down on the couch. Yep, something was wrong. Instinct had become conviction. "Well, you didn't come over to shoot the breeze. What's going on?"

Gordon Ashe hesitated, one hand absently touching his breast pocket, where Ross saw the edge of a folded piece of paper. Then Ashe shook his head. "I take it Eveleen is teaching a karate class?"

Ross nodded. "She likes to keep in shape, and it gives her a perfect cover job." He glanced at his watch. "She'll be back in a couple hours."

Ashe struck his hands on his knees and got to his feet again. "You asked what's wrong. There are so many possible levels of wrongness here I don't really know where to begin."

Ross whistled under his breath. *I knew it.* Their last mission—to another planet and thousands of years into its past—had been tough enough, but when Ashe first told them about it he'd been business-as-usual. What could be nasty enough to get the guy—old Ice Veins, some of the younger Time Agents had nicknamed him—this jittery?

"I have a meeting in an hour," Ashe said. "I'd hoped to find both of you here for a strategy powwow first, but maybe it's for the best, because there would be more questions than I could answer."

"All sufficiently mysterious," Ross said, now feeling that inward sense of tension ignite. Incipient action. He could almost smell it, like the ozone moments before a lightning strike.

Ashe paused with his hand out just before Ross opened the door. "Oh, a request," he said, smiling oddly. "When you two do come, would you ask Eveleen to wear those gold earrings of hers?"

"Sure." Ross snorted a laugh. "Going romantic at last?"

Ashe only shook his head again, so Ross opened his front door. There was Mrs. Withan, sweeping the hall stairs.

Ashe sent one of those ironic looks over his shoulder. But after years of playing an astonishing variety of roles, from a Folsom Culture trader to a garbage collector on a planet so far away there was no meaningful measure of distance, he was obviously capable of dealing with one nosy landlady.

"We'll get those statistical disks next round," he said, descending the stairs. "Remember to send me the new catalogues."

"In the mail tomorrow." Ross lifted a hand, watched the landlady's shadow on the opposite wall as she peeped out after Ashe, and then shut the door, laughing softly.

He moved into the kitchen and opened the fridge. Did all newlyweds develop their own codes, almost a private language? He reflected on that as he gathered together the fixings for chicken salad. What Eveleen had begun calling his Threat-o-Meter had gone into the red zone; he strongly suspected that the two of them would be called in early tomorrow. Maybe even tonight. Better get dinner going right away, or they might not get any.

As the meat sizzled in the broiler, he wandered into the bedroom and fired up the computer. Did an e-mail check. That, too, came coded, if it was from Project Star, sufficiently bland messages that even the cleverest hacker—supposing one could actually slip past the Project firewalls—couldn't make anything of. Of course, as to that putative hacker, Ross suspected anyone smart enough to do that had already been hired by Kelgarries.

Nothing on the e-mail.

His Threat-o-Meter ratcheted up another notch.

EVELEEN OPENED THE door moments before Ross had everything ready. "Just tossing the salad," he called from the kitchen.

Eveleen appeared in the doorway, small, neat, her mouth quirking just so. "Well, in a minute," he corrected, dropping his utensils and crossing the tiny kitchen so he could grab her up and kiss her.

She returned hug and kiss with surprising strength for so small a woman, but, then, a third-degree black belt in four forms of martial arts is bound to be strong.

"There's trouble," she ventured, after he set her down again.

"How can you tell? I haven't said anything!"

"It's your silence." Her brown eyes narrowed as they studied each other. "And—I don't know, this sense I get." She poked his nose. "Threat-o-Meter?"

"Force nine," he admitted. "Gordon came here, said something mysterious, then took off again without another damn word."

She whistled. "Unlike him, you must admit. Force nine indeed. Let me shower and get something weekendy on. If the call comes tonight, we'll be going out to dinner and a flick." She pointed downstairs.

Ross snorted. "And if Mrs. Withan asks what movie we saw, and what we thought?"

"I read all the reviews of the new ones just yesterday." Eveleen chuckled as she leaned back against his shoulder. "I can handle any questions she might ask. And you just say something grunty and mannish like *I love action flicks* or *Geez, another chick flick*."

"Grunty and mannish. Check."

Eveleen gave him an unrepentant flicker of a smile, and then her expression went pensive. "I hope you don't hold a grudge against Mrs. W. You have to remember she's the normal one."

"It's normal to nose into everyone's affairs?"

"Well, she takes it to excess, but my point is that she's more normal than we are. Humans do form social and kinship networks. She likes to think of the tenants here as a little social network, a family, and loves to see them all getting together and doing normal things, like big barbecues and July Fourth celebrations with buddies at work and so forth. All the other people in the building seem to know a little about one another, yet here we are, living like a couple of hermits."

"Well, we travel a lot," Ross protested. He added with a grin, "They just won't find out where—or when."

"It's not that; it's us," Eveleen said. "I was thinking about it at the dojo today. They all ask after one another's families and friends, and if someone has a disaster, they rally. Oh, I know if we have problems the Project takes care of us—that's not it. It's just that I realized so many of our social and emotional networks—kinship networks, almost—were formed with people in the past, some on other planets, and we can never get those back. It's finished, because if we go back again in time, we risk ruining the *now*. We can pretend we live with normal people in the here and now, but we aren't really part of the contemporary world; we can't let ourselves be."

Ross took her face in his hands so he could gaze down into those lovely brown eyes flecked with tiny bits of gold. *I could swim in those eyes,* he thought, but that was sensory reaction. What was she thinking? He remembered some of the poetry he'd tried to get out of reading when he was a school kid, proclaiming eyes as the window to the soul. Very poetic, except they weren't. You couldn't really tell what thoughts went on behind those eyes, even the eyes of one you loved more than anything or anybody. "What're we really talking about here?" he murmured. "You want to quit the Project, is that it?"

She shook her head, smiling. "No. Because it really is our family, in a sense, even though we took this apartment to make a kind of grand gesture, as if we really do have a life outside Project Star. But there isn't one. We do have to admit it and not take out our annoyance on innocent busybodies like Mrs. Withan."

Ross kissed her again. "All right. Got it. From now on, I promise to think of Mrs. W. as a normal, *nice* busybody."

Eveleen laughed. "I give up. Lecture over! I'd better grab that shower, or when Gordon's call comes, I'll be not just hungry but grungy."

"Oh! Almost forgot. He said the damndest thing right before he took off. When we do meet up, he wants you to wear your gold earrings.

Something dubious about those I don't know?" He wiggled his eyebrows.

"If there is something dubious, no one told me," Eveleen said, going into the bedroom and coming out again with the earrings.

They both looked down at the simple beaten gold hoops on her palms. Inexpensive for golden earrings, a style that women—and sometimes men, according to the vagaries of fashion—had been wearing for thousands of years.

"My dad gave me these when I turned twenty-one," she said. "I don't think that exactly registers as dubious, mysterious, or otherwise provocative."

Ross spread his hands. "Crazy."

Eveleen laid down the earrings, and padded toward the bathroom. "But I guess you never know! Watch 'em in case they suddenly start beeping mystery messages."

"With our luck, they're more likely to explode," he said grimly.

She was still laughing when the phone rang.

CHAPTER 2

GORDON ASHE REACHED the restaurant twenty minutes early and was annoyed with himself. He could sit in the bar and brood for what would seem like twenty hours, or he could take his laptop in and look like a pompous fool. Or he could drive around the block twenty times.

With a sigh of annoyance he got out of his car and tossed the keys to the parking attendant. He checked his watch again, knowing it was a stupid impulse. Thirty whole seconds had sped by!

All right, he was in a sour mood anyway; why not go inside and brood.

The restaurant was an old favorite. It wasn't dark as pitch inside— he hated that—and it had decent food without a lot of the pretentious posturing that seemed to go with it in tonier places. He headed for the bar, which was mostly empty, for the hour was early yet.

A woman sat alone at the end. He almost looked away, but something in the curve of shoulder, the angle of her head zapped his memory. Twenty-five years he hadn't seen her, but he knew her immediately.

"Is that you, Gordon?" Her voice hadn't changed.

"Linnea?" His mind fumbled back and forth between two different tracks of thought: memories of their last meeting—a towering argument—and the e-mail she'd sent him just yesterday. A third track superimposed itself: what subtle measures did the mind use to mark a familiar face or form? He'd probably seen twenty thousand women— more—since he last was in Linnea Edel's presence, but he'd immediately known that precise tilt of chin as if he'd just parted from her an hour ago.

"Yes, it is I," she said, getting off her bar stool and coming forward. Neither spoke as they looked at each other. *She's the same,* he thought. Oh, older—and she didn't bother to hide it, either. Her thick cloud of dark hair was streaked with gray, and maybe her contours were softer, for she'd never been fashionably thin (or had shown the slightest interest in fashion) back then. She was still short and round, and though age, and experience, and the inevitable effects of gravity had carved lines in her face, her Mediterranean bone structure was more sharply emphasized now, and he realized she was more attractive than ever.

He tried a polite opener. "How was the drive up from New York?"

"Slow. And then pretty." She gave him a rueful smile. "Gordon, I hope you're not mad at me. I realized after you sent your e-mail about meeting here—so neutral a place, like a truce—that maybe it seemed like I was threatening you, and it wasn't that, not at all."

Nothing like the exigencies of work to snap the mind back to the here and now. Aware of interested ears at the bar, Ashe said easily, "Threaten me all you like. I have just as much back history to bore you with as you could have for me. But how about we get a booth first, and we can play catch-up in comfort?"

Her eyes narrowed in a subtle signal of comprehension. She laughed. "Ah, but I came armed with family photos! Lead on."

They were soon settled into a corner booth near the fireplace. A bar waiter appeared, and Ashe asked for seltzer on the rocks with a twist, just to get rid of the guy; he did not want alcohol clouding his brain now. As the waiter moved away, he looked at the drink Linnea had brought and realized she was drinking the same thing.

"Before we start," he said, striving for normalcy, except what is normal when you haven't seen someone since a fight twenty-five years ago, and then she sends you a sinister letter? "Do you really have family photos? How is J.J.? And didn't I hear you'd had kids?"

"Two." She raised her fingers. "Twins. Mariana is in the navy, doing something arcane with radar, and adores it, when I hear from her, which is about twice a year. Max is in Los Angeles at film school, working about twenty hours a day, which is what you have to do until you break into that business. I hear from him *once* a year."

She had picked up her glass and was gently clinking the ice cubes round and round, round and round. She seemed to realize that she was doing it and set it down again, then tipped her head, that inquiring angle that had reminded him of a bird, and said, "J.J. died five years ago."

"I'm sorry," Ashe said, hating how inadequate it sounded.

"Don't be. It was sudden, over his breakfast coffee. Just like that. I was even there to be with him those last few moments."

Ashe winced.

She laced her fingers together, her wedding band winking with golden light in the reflection from the fire.

"Best way to go, I think. No fear, and the doctors insisted there couldn't have been much suffering. Though it's hard enough on those of us left behind. So I became a hermit for a time, and then that time ended, and I looked about me, and realized that I was still alive, that my children were grown and didn't need me—and that I could, well, have a life of my own."

Again the tilt of the head. "And you were right, by the way."

Right? Was she talking about that last nasty exchange? Ashe's mind wheeled back rapidly, faster than light-speed. He was again on warm, dusty Crete, digging at Knossos. Two on the dig were J.J. Edel, twenty years older, and Linnea, young and earnest and ardent about the archaeology. Gordon swinging between finishing his doctoral work and getting lured by the government into the supersecret Project Star, during the years the Iron Curtain still blocked off the East.

What could he say? He could say—

"Here's your seltzer, sir. Now, are you folks ready to order?"

Ashe accepted the drink, and the waiter launched into a recital of a long list of specials. Ashe took a slug of cold seltzer, fighting the urge to tell the guy to take a hike.

Linnea smiled. "Oh, I'm sorry, we haven't even looked at our menus yet. Would you come back later?"

"Sure. Just wave a hand," the waiter said, and he left.

Linnea leaned forward. "The last time you and I saw one another, if you remember, we were walking along the harbor at Heraklion."

"I remember."

"And you told me, in pungent and specific detail that I can still recall to this day, what a fatheaded doormat I was to do all J.J.'s work at the dig."

Ashe winced and shook his head. "And I've regretted it ever since, though I know that doesn't excuse it."

"Why should you excuse it? You were right. I did do all his work and let him take the credit. A lot of that was the cultural conditioning of the time—that's what ladies did. And you were right about J.J. incidentally: he really wasn't interested in archaeology or in any of the other degrees he almost got. He was just marking time until his father died suddenly and he took over the business, which he ran until the day he died. And I am delighted to say that my son never showed any interest in inheriting it. The new CEO is, in fact, a woman."

Ashe nodded.

"Well, bear with me now, Gordon, because it all ties together." She chuckled softly and again tilted her head. "After you and I had our little talk and you vanished into the ether, J.J. inherited, like I said. And since I was pregnant with the twins—and you know how primitive conditions were at the dig—and J.J. didn't want his little princess working, we both dropped out, moved to New York City, and I became a housewife until the morning I became a widow."

She finished her seltzer and sat back, sighing. "So as I said, my year of being a hermit passed, and then I looked around and realized that I had a life. Not as a mom or a wife, but as me. And I'd always loved archaeology, with a passion. I subscribed all these years to *Archeology* and a half dozen other scholarly magazines. So I decided to go back to school. No hurry and I don't care if I even graduate, because I'd never take one of the rare jobs from some young person struggling to follow his or her dream. J.J. did leave me very well off, so I can do what I want. Which, this last winter, was to go back with some students on a little dig."

She leaned forward, and Ashe did as well. "Not to Crete this time, but to Thera itself. And that's where I found what I sent you."

Ashe now drew the printout from his coat pocket. The picture in itself was nothing of interest to anyone who might glance casually at it: a photo of a hoop earring of beaten gold, somewhat dull, with bits of mud and debris stuck to it, but on the clearest part, quite distinct, was a jeweler's mark. A modern jeweler's mark.

Ashe looked down at it and up at Linnea's face.

She said, "You disappeared that spring from classes, and you kept giving these evasive answers when people asked what you were doing. And a couple of times the department secretary said you got calls from these guys from Washington, DC, which was quite a ways from our university."

Ashe said nothing.

Linnea grinned. "I tried to find you afterward, I have to admit. At first to continue the argument. That comment about doormats did stick in my craw, but as the years went by, and J.J. still called me his little princess, I realized that you were right all along. It stuck because it was true. Oh, I loved him, and he loved me, but J.J. never did see me as an adult in my own right—and I guess the role I got in the habit of playing wasn't exactly conducive to changing his worldview." She waved a hand, as though shooing away an annoying fly. "But we're not here to hash over old feminist issues. The thing is, I did try to find you, as well as some of our old friends, and though I eventually found all of them, you remained amazingly elusive."

She paused, sending Ashe an inquiring look. He said slowly, "Most of my subsequent work was on artifacts here in North America. If you stayed with Aegean studies, of course you'd lose track of me—" He shrugged. He had never minded deflecting people from his real work, but it made him feel queasy to issue these half-lies to a friend.

"Nice try," Linnea said, laughing a little. "I also heard from one of our mutual old friends about a dig in New Mexico, and you'd been in on a find that later vanished. No articles, no papers, no conferences. That, he told me in a letter, spells 'government' and 'top secret.'"

Ashe looked down, fiddling with his drink. What could he say?

She didn't seem to expect him to say anything; she kept on. "Then, a few years back, there was all that news about the alien spaceships, and the tapes, though it all disappeared from the news really quickly when it was discovered that they were old artifacts and aliens weren't coming here in peace or in war. People forgot. But I never did; especially when, it turned out, one of the sites mentioned was New Mexico, and a Dr. Ashe was quoted just once. I put the variables together, wondered if you might be part of the equation, and last winter when I uncovered that earring in a place that had been sealed under volcanic ash since 1628 B.C. and saw that modern jeweler's mark, I decided that maybe it was time to try again to dig you up. Luckily people are easier to find on the Internet these days, even if their jobs aren't."

Ashe let out a sigh. "And you decided to find me because . . . ?"

"I figured if there was anyone who could tell me how a modern earring could get back to the mid-1600s B.C., it was you."

Ashe hesitated. There was one obvious question to be asked, but he didn't think he could bring himself to do it quite yet. So he went to the next obvious. "You were the one who mentioned threats. I take it you haven't shared your find with anyone?"

"And don't plan to, if it will cause trouble. As I said, I am not hunting for a career, or even notoriety. Truth, yes. Insight into the past and how we got here today—the roots of our present civilization—yes. But not at the cost of people's lives. I paid my own way to the dig, so no one owned my time, and if it turns out to be a genuine artifact and I'm wrong, I'll restore it to the Greek government. But I do," she said again, in a low voice, "want to know the truth."

Ashe stared down at the picture again, his mind darting in circles like fireflies in a high wind. Nothing, though, got past that primary question—

"What is it, Gordon?" she whispered. "You look like you'd seen a—oh!" Her voice broke off.

He glanced up, to see her eyes gone round and dark with intensity. He realized he was clammy with sweat. At the same moment he saw a wince of compassion tighten her face, and she murmured in a fast, low voice, "I did not take it from a skeleton. I did not see any remains."

Ashe's breath leaked out, though his heart still hammered.

She gave her head a quick shake. "Of course you know what that dig is like: two more inches, and we don't know what we'll find. But the Marinatos and Doumas teams have not uncovered any human remains so far, and that is still the same."

That leap of compassion, of sudden understanding, was not the reaction of an eager young student desperate to make a mark in the world. It was the reaction of a woman of experience, of integrity. It was the Linnea he'd once known, only grown up.

"I'll see what I can do," he promised.

CHAPTER 3

EVELEEN RIORDAN FELT her gold earrings swing against her jaws as she stepped into the elevator. Why did she feel so self-conscious all of a sudden? How many times had she worn this pair to work and never thought anything of it?

But no one had ever asked about them before. *How odd,* she thought, as Ross tapped a code into the elevator pads. A subtle jerk, a whine of hydraulics, and the elevator did not go up—though the people in the lobby of the Northside Research Institute would think it had. Upstairs a legitimate marketing research company did a thriving business. Down below ground level existed a complex that those busy researchers would have been astonished to discover.

They dropped fast and smooth; then the elevator doors slid open onto spacious hallways with full spread–spectrum lighting and rows of healthy ferns and other plants. Off both sides offices full of computer banks and desk cubicles opened up, people moving to and fro. The designers had made it as pleasant as they could, but to Eveleen it still felt like vintage government-agency ambience, and modest as their apartment was, she was glad to call it home.

"Ah, there you are." Major Kelgarries emerged from an adjacent hallway, three or four disks in one hand and a sheaf of files in the other. *He's been riding a desk for a long time, but he still looks and moves like a man used to being in the field,* Eveleen thought as Ross returned the brief greeting and they followed Kelgarries's broad shoulders the last few paces to one of the conference rooms.

It was one of the big rooms, with a big projection screen on one wall. No one spoke as they entered and set up their laptops. Ross moved straight to the coffee dispenser next to the door and brought them both a cup. Eveleen was still feeling off balance. She smiled at Gordon Ashe, and decided the light touch was the way to handle his odd request. She tapped her earrings and blinked her eyes, as if to say, *See? I remembered!*

He smiled back, but his smile was tight, and perfunctory at best.

Eveleen looked away, troubled, and began seeing the clues she'd overlooked: tension. Tension in Kelgarries, tension in Ashe, tension in Milliard, the big boss, muttering over there into a cell-phone. Tension in the older woman sitting in the corner, laptop open. She talked quietly with the tall redhead whom Eveleen recognized as one of the top computer simulation experts in Project Star.

The redhead gave Eveleen a brief wave.

"Hi, Marilyn," Eveleen murmured. Then wished she hadn't spoken, for her voice seemed oddly loud.

"We're all here," Ashe said then. "Eveleen, if I may trouble you for those earrings, please?"

She no longer felt like laughing as she unfastened and handed them over. In silence she and Ross watched Ashe examine the simple gold loops, then place them on the light-plate of a projecting microscope arranged next to his chair. Eveleen felt Ross tensing up beside her, his gray eyes narrowed.

Everyone watched as Ashe took out a small manila envelope from a file and shook its contents out into his hand: another hoop earring. Then he produced from a pocket a jeweler's eyepiece and bent over the earring, glancing occasionally at the projection screen, where Eveleen's pair loomed as large as basketball hoops, every dimple strike of the jeweler's hammer plain. He reached and turned over the two earrings on the microscope's projection stage.

Eveleen felt tension grip her own neck when she realized she'd heard his breathing stop. In silence he placed the earring from the envelope on the microscope, pushing aside one of the ones already there. There was his hand, big enough for them to see the whorls of his fingerprints as he nudged the earring into the center, next to the other, and then Eveleen realized what she was seeing.

The earring was identical to one of the pair she'd brought, a little more worn, but it had the same little jeweler's squiggle on it and in exactly the same place. It was the same earring.

Cold certainty settled into the pit of her stomach, and Eveleen felt a familiar dizziness; the paradoxical nature of time travel wasn't something anyone ever got used to. She was too experienced a Time Agent to mistake what she and everyone else in the room were seeing: bilocation, the selfsame object existing simultaneously in two places at once.

"Where?" Ross demanded, gazing at Gordon Ashe, his face like granite. "And when? And how long have you known about it?"

Eveleen took her lower lip between her teeth. The truth was, a weird little voice in the back of her mind gibbered and giggled, Mrs. Withan was *scared* of Ross. He had no idea he looked as out of place in her clean, low-key apartment building as a pirate in a swimming pool. Tall, lean, scarred hand, his walk the silent, action-ready walk of someone who was raised on the streets, Ross didn't look even remotely like any sort of software salesman.

The street kid was very obvious in his attitude now. But Ashe had been handling that oblique threat for years.

"To answer your questions in reverse order: I did not know about it until last night. 'When' is somewhere in the middle of the 1600s B.C. We think it might be 1628. And where . . ." He smiled wryly. "Have you ever heard of the legend of Atlantis?"

Eveleen said, startled, "But that's New Age woo-woo!"

Ross then surprised her—surprised everyone—by saying, "Plato, fourth century B.C. Retelling Solon's story."

Kelgarries snorted a mirthless laugh. "Glad I didn't put any bets on that one."

Gordon nodded, giving Ross a brief smile. "Dialogues between Timaeus and Critias. So you did a little reading while you were up at my cottage in Maine?"

Ross grinned back. "Books were on the shelf, and you did say to feel free."

Gordon looked around at them all. "Our so-called Atlantis, as far as we can tell, did in fact exist. But it was not a great continent, and it did not sink. It was a volcanic island—actually an arc of small islands, the very top of a massive undersea volcano—just north of Crete, now called Thera. Which means 'fear,'" Gordon added with a sardonic lift of his brows. "The people of the time seem to have called it Kalliste. And as near as we can tell, approximately in the 1620s B.C. from thirty to fifty cubic miles of it blew into the sky, sending out a tsunami that took out all the ports along the Aegean and sent a black cloud into the atmosphere that ruined crops in China and showed up in tree rings as far away as northern California."

Eveleen rubbed her temples, stunned at what had to have been the magnitude of that volcanic eruption.

Kelgarries turned to the red-haired expert. "Marilyn?"

"For purposes of comparison," she said in a strong French accent, "the explosion at Mount St. Helens in Washington was an explosion of a mere half-cubic-mile, as you Americans would say. Krakatoa was about eight cubic miles."

The woman next to her—short, thick graying hair—listened, taking notes steadily, but as yet she had not spoken, and no one had introduced her.

Ashe tapped the projection stage of the microscope, making the huge images on the screen tremble and bringing their attention back to the earrings. "And this was discovered buried under approximately twenty-five meters—say eighty feet of volcanic ash, undisturbed until just this summer."

Ross looked sick. "A volcanic island?" His mouth tightened. "I suppose our bones were next to it?"

Eveleen felt her heart squeeze at that *our*. No one had mentioned him yet, but she knew that he'd be there beside her, somehow, no matter how.

"No," Ashe said. "Understand that the progress at that dig is barely measured in inches, especially in the past few years, and as yet there have been no remains. Just a few scattered artifacts in the street of a city. The people, as far as we can tell, seem to have been evacuated."

"By us?" Eveleen spoke, her throat dry. That voice at the back of her mind was no longer laughing. *If everyone got away, why was my earring there?* "I mean, it's clear that we were there. That we're going to be there."

Ross tapped a pencil on the edge of his laptop, a militant tattoo. "Why all this background chat? Are you building up to some big idea about the Baldies maybe causing that volcano to blow?"

"Well, we don't know," Ashe said. "The truth is, until yesterday somehow this remarkable incident in Earth's history had seemed a random natural event, albeit extraordinarily spectacular. As a possible site for our investigations, it had been previously overlooked. Probably because as yet there has been so little excavation done, and we know so very little about what happened—and of course there had been no mysterious artifacts found, none of the globe ships or other signs of the Baldies that we've discovered and dealt with in other times and places."

Eveleen's mind worked rapidly through what she knew of history. "Thera . . . north of Crete. Those were the Minoans, weren't they? The bull worshippers? Weren't they supposed to be this sophisticated, peaceful trading civilization?"

"They were," Ashe said. "They were probably the most sophisticated culture Earth had produced until the past couple of centuries—and some will argue about that, considering the wars we've managed to wage against ourselves and the environmental damage our industrial

developments have caused. The Minoan houses that have been excavated so far had running water, possibly hot and cold. Toilets. Showers,
even, in one place. A standard of living, in short, that would not be out
of place today. Only they didn't wage war, they traded, all along the
Mediterranean, for their distinctive artwork shows up in tombs in Egypt
as well as points north and west. Yet right around this time they vanished. Simply disappeared from history."

Ross nodded. "Right. But you said that no bodies were found, and
that they might have evacuated. So how did that civilization vanish?"

"No one knows," Milliard said, pointing to a sheaf of printouts.
"We've pulled up as much research as we can, and most of it is speculation."

Eveleen looked around. Anomalies—events that could have been
caused by outside agency—existed all through the human past, of
course. She and the other Time Agents had certainly experienced
enough outside interference from the hairless, humanoid aliens they
called Baldies to make every incident that did not have clear cause and
effect appear suspicious.

Ross frowned. "What we might be looking at here is some kind of
dirty work, then? Someone deliberately setting back the development of
our civilization a couple thousand years?"

Ashe pressed his thumbs into his eye sockets. "It is one hypothesis,
isn't it? Marilyn and her team have been up all night running sims on
this, and correlating it with what we know. The most accepted hypothesis in my field posits that if the Minoans had survived, we might have
had our industrial revolution at least a thousand years ago—if not more.
We might be immortal by now. Colonies on other planets. But, though
theories are neat, as is usual when dealing with human psychology, it
might not be that simple."

Kelgarries said, "There's apparently even a computer analog in Ath-
ens, made some two thousand years ago." And he looked over at the
gray-haired woman. "Mrs. Edel? What was that you were telling me
about earlier?"

The woman spoke for the first time. "It's called the Antikythera
mechanism. It was pulled off a shipwreck. Layers of interlocking gears,
with readouts to calculate and display astronomical positions." As she
spoke her eyes widened with just that sort of wonder that sometimes
characterized Gordon Ashe when he talked about the mysteries of the
past. *The eternal curiosity of the scholar,* Eveleen thought.

And Milliard said, "Mrs. Edel is our authority on the time and
culture."

The woman gave them a tentative smile. Eveleen met her dark gaze, with its expression of inquiry, and smiled back.

Ross also gave the woman a nod and smile, but it was a distracted smile. He was back tapping his pencil again, his scarred fingers tense. "A computer, eh? So, what, we're going back to see if the Baldies dropped a couple of their equivalent of nuclear bombs down the shaft of that volcano?" He sat back and sighed. "But if they caused the volcano to blow, then it doesn't really matter if it was them or Mother Nature, does it? It already happened. That means if we were there we lost the battle, and it happened. If we'd been successful—if we were to be successful in stopping 'em—then we might destroy ourselves up at this end of time."

"Yes, and no," Ashe said, leaning forward. "As usual, it's not that simple; it's not clear that the Baldies touched off the volcanic explosion by some arcane means." He turned to the computer expert. "Marilyn?"

"There is another hypothesis that projects an unexpected version of what our modern times might have been like if the Minoans had lived," she said, tapping at her computer console.

The light under Ashe's display blinked out, and the power shifted.

Once again the screen came to life, this time with a picture of the Mediterranean world. "This hypothesis, less popular, begins with the obvious statement that our present-day civilization is a direct result of that disaster."

Eveleen frowned, staring at the map.

"The key word, now, is *peaceful*," Marilyn went on. "The Minoans were peaceful and stable. If they had continued to build their remarkable ships and carry goods and ideas around the world, there is a chance we would have developed along more peaceful lines. Most of our technological development has been a side effect of inventions for warfare. Or defense. This second model gives us this picture—" The image shifted. "Had the Minoans continued to influence our development, Earth's population would have grown slowly, engaged more in trade than warfare, giving us—today—a largely pastoral civilization of maybe half a billion people."

The images showed humans in small towns amid great forests and swathes of undisturbed land.

"Our state of technological advance might be the equivalent of the early steam age."

Kelgarries said, "Which would leave Earth open for invasion."

Eveleen sat back in surprise. "So what you're saying is that the Baldies—if they were there at all—might have gone back, or might go back, to *prevent* the volcano from going off?"

"It's possible," Ashe said. "In which case none of us would exist."

Eveleen shut her eyes, struggling—as she always did—with the idea of time and what the higher-math experts termed *superpositions. After all I've been through, you'd think I could get used to thinking in the conditional, nonrelativistic tenses,* she thought wryly. And she noticed Ross rubbing his forehead; he was having just the same trouble.

"The key thing to remember is that we seem to have gone back," Ashe said. He added with a faint, sardonic smile, "I say 'we' even though all we have is Eveleen's earring. But I know Ross won't be kept from going on this mission—"

"Damn straight."

"And I confess I would pull any strings I had to pull to be there as well."

Ross flipped his pencil into the air. "All right, so what we're looking at is a trip to the past. See if we find any Baldies. If we don't, we come back. If we do, then what?"

"Circumvent them, of course," Eveleen said.

Ashe nodded at her. "If they did tamper with Thera's volcano, we have to find out what they intend. We might also be the ones who caused the evacuation—"

"Oh, yes," Eveleen exclaimed. "I was just thinking of that. Those people have no other way of knowing, do they? So do you think we are the ones who got them safely away?"

"We won't know anything until we get there," Ashe said. "And we'll begin training at once; we will have to assume that time is pressing."

"Why?" Linnea Edel asked, leaning forward. "If we can truly travel back to any time—a concept I still have trouble grasping, even with the evidence before my eyes—why can't we just take a few months—years, even—to prepare and go back at our leisure?"

Gordon Ashe indicated the three earrings. "To put it simply, the anomaly of this earring being here twice might be something the Baldies can vector in on. We don't want to find out if your discovering that earring, and our bringing it here to its original self, has triggered some kind of detector; the sooner we go back to 1628 B.C. the better."

"So who is going?" Ross asked, hands on his knees.

Kelgarries said, "You, and our top two Greek Time Agents. Stavros Lemkis is down in the labs experimenting with some of the technology you brought back from your previous mission." He nodded at Ross. "Konstantin Skrumbos, our maritime expert on that time, is flying back from the Aegean right now, so he can join the briefing sessions."

Eveleen felt a surge of excitement. Few women agents went into human prehistory because so few cultures had permitted women to move about. But the Minoans had been different.

Milliard got to his feet. "Jonathan?"

A youngish man stepped forward. He looked tired. Eveleen felt a surge of compassion; had he been up for days and nights? But tiredness wouldn't explain that painful quirk to his underlids, the lines beside his mouth. This man was deeply unhappy.

"As yet," Jonathan said, "no one has established what language the people of Kalliste spoke. Linear B has proved to be an Ancient Greek form, but those tablets date from a later time. The few written artifacts from our time are written in hieroglyphs we call Linear A, which have recently been recorded. They, too, proved to be a kind of proto-Greek, but we have very few words in that language—not enough for your communication needs."

He paused to look around. "There are many archaeologists who still feel that the Kallistans first came over from Anatolia, that they are Hittites or Luvians, or even Amorites, bringing the bull worship with them, though it developed into a much more peaceful form. We've put together a core vocabulary that might enable you to understand some words, or at least to begin to form a vocabulary. You will pose as traders, say from Egypt, and we'll give you some Ancient Egyptian language training as well as some Ancient Greek, since traders in that area did get all around the eastern Mediterranean."

Milliard frowned. "The thing to keep in mind—never lose sight of—is the fact that in this situation, we know, or think we know, the year the volcano exploded, but we don't know the day. So we'll put you where we think you're safe, but you'll have to act fast. There's no time to be digging in and doing linguistic studies, no matter how tempting they might be." He cast a meaningful glance Ashe's way, but Eveleen wondered if the warning was actually for Mrs. Edel, who had been listening with intense focus.

"Yes," Ross said, his wary expression back. "Fast. I like fast."

"Marilyn can show you the sim on what happens when the volcano goes off, based on evidence from St. Pierre early in the twentieth century, and Krakatoa, and St. Helens. It's fairly grim," he said.

No one spoke; Eveleen saw Linnea Edel looking down at tightly gripped hands.

Kelgarries spoke up, looking tense and tired and very serious, "What we can be sure of is that nothing within a hundred miles of the blast—whatever day it occurred on—could have lived through it."

CHAPTER 4

THE AEGEAN SKY was mild as milk, a pale, hazy blue with gauzy brush strokes of high cirrus that reminded Ross of southern California. The cargo vessel now plowing its way through the choppy seas could have been heading for Catalina Island. Strange, how you expect the cradle of civilization to be exotic, to strike the senses with profound or dramatic impact. Not like familiar territory.

"Look there. Just off to the northwest," Gordon Ashe said, coming down one of the steel ladders and pointing off the starboard bow.

Ross turned his attention briefly seaward. Just past a smaller craft, equally nondescript, he saw bumps on the horizon. He heard clunking and clanging on the steel ladder from the bridge. Down came Eveleen and Linnea Edel, the latter with more care. All of them had field glasses. Ross pulled up his own pair and shaded the sun with one hand while he focused with the other.

Thera, at this distance, even looked a little like Catalina. He envisioned yesterday's flyover: an island cluster looking like a half-submerged donut. The center, now a peaceful lagoon, with brilliant clear water and a couple of islands dotting it, was the sleeping caldera of the mighty volcano that had blasted fifty cubic miles of matter into the sky.

Everyone studied it in silence as the cargo ship made its way in a slow circle all round the island cluster. Behind them, glimpsed earlier that morning, lay Crete, a long, thin blade of an island. Way off to the northwest, behind Thera, lay more of the Greek islands, and finally Greece itself. To the northeast lay what was once ancient Anatolia, Turkey now.

Getting a basic familiarity with the island and its surroundings now would save them a lot of time when the beautiful little craft lying shrouded in the cargo vessel's hold was launched through the great time-gate two nights hence. They wouldn't, of course, limit themselves to seventeenth-century B.C.E. technology: the ship had a small, virtually silent engine concealed in its stern, but it was only for emergencies. And there'd certainly be no GPS satellites to lock onto, so they'd be navigating using techniques that differed very little from those of the mariners of that period. Best, as always, to go in with as much information as possible, even though there was no way of knowing just how much the surrounding sea and islands had been changed by the volcanic explosion.

It was hard to imagine this peaceful, sunny scene vanishing under a fireball of steam and vaporized rock, then choking under a pall of volcanic ash as glowing volcanic rock fell like hellish hail. Ross shook his head. He knew the reality was the huge magma dome deep underneath the island, just welling up, shouldering aside the rock around it. . . . Somehow going up against a volcano seemed tougher than facing aliens with laser weapons. You can't even pretend to negotiate with a volcano.

He felt a nudge against his arm, and saw Eveleen at his shoulder, silently studying the biggest island. They were close enough to see striated rock, compressed levels of pumice and ash angling up, indicating tectonic activity no less powerful—only slower.

"I don't care what that lady finds," Ross muttered, glancing over at Linnea Edel. "In and out."

Eveleen grunted in agreement. "What bothers me is that they don't have dates for the Big Blow. It's educated guesswork, but still guesswork."

"I don't mind being put in there a year in advance," Ross said. "I don't want to jet through the gate to find ourselves in the middle of the eruption."

"No." Ashe appeared on Ross's other side, silent of step. "None of us does." He looked amused.

Ross figured he'd complained enough, so he didn't respond. The truth was, he flat-out did not like this mission. There were too many variables. On the surface it looked easy: go in, see if the Baldies are around, and if they are, find out what they're up to. But in Ross's experience, the "easy ones" were the ones that always went screwy. Usually that just meant they had to use their wits, and maybe their fists. But how do you use either against a volcanic eruption?

He said nothing, though, as the cargo ship angled round the western portion of the island and steamed north.

When they had completed their circuit, the team descended aft to the wardroom, which had been made over into a command post. Maps had been pinned up against bulkheads, with labels in English and Cyrillic: the Russians in the other ship were due to come over for the last planning session, over dinner. Stavros and Konstantin were already there.

Ross and Eveleen had just gotten fresh coffee and were sitting down when the ship gave a lurch and muffled clanks and metallic groans announced the skiff grappled alongside.

A short time later three Russians ducked through the hatchway. Without a word the ship's steward handed out the dark Russian tea they all favored, in the little glass cups held in wire frames.

The Russians, two men and a woman, sat down, and Ashe took over to run again through the familiar drill. Too familiar. Ross knew he should pay attention. This launch through the biggest time-gate ever made—stretched between two ships—was a first for both the Russians and Americans. There were too many firsts here, but none of them concerned Ross. Stavros and Konstantin, who would remain aboard their craft, would masquerade as Kallistan sailors. They were actually in charge of the time-gates. Ross couldn't do anything about that, so he scowled down at his coffee. The mission wasn't really real yet, in a sense. Wouldn't be until he and Eveleen went to their cabin for the last time, and pulled on those costumes waiting there.

And she put on those earrings, one of which was lost for over three thousand years.

EVELEEN STOOD WITH her feet apart, rolling unconsciously with the ship, as she stared down at the earrings in her hand. She had never been much of a philosophic type. Action was what she liked and understood. But you can't help picking up ideas as you go through life, and she remembered someone or other talking once about the single flap of a butterfly's wings causing a forest halfway around the world to fall a hundred years later.

How can one ever know for certain which of our movements causes disaster? Well, she wasn't about to test that theory now. She knew that one of these earrings would, somehow, end up on that island. Where its mate would go—where *she* would go—was what she had to discover.

But she wouldn't risk doing damage to history by leaving those earrings behind. Or leaving one behind, and tossing the other one onto a road in Akrotiri on their arrival.

She sighed and put the earrings in her ears, then turned around to find Ross watching her. His gray eyes were wide, and wary, but he didn't say anything other than "Let's get it over with."

Together they exited the cabin, leaving behind all their obvious twenty-first-century trappings: watches, rings, running shoes, machine-stitched synthetic fabrics. Their equipment had all been cleverly disguised.

Eveleen wore a flouncy three-tiered skirt and a short jacket with embroidery along the outer arms and down the sides. Under it she wore a thin cotton garment. Ross wore a brightly colored kilt of mostly red and black cloth, his skin dyed a deep brown with a long-term sunscreen worked into the chemical makeup of the dye. His black hair, which he had been growing, had been crimped and permed into tight curls, which he held back from his face with a thin gold headband. Both of them wore sandals that tied up their calves.

They met Ashe and Linnea Edel down in the hold. Eveleen was startled to see how different they both looked. Of course Ashe was good at taking on attributes of whatever culture he chose to adopt, and now he appeared to be a trader, his blue eyes hidden behind brown contact lenses.

Linnea Edel, however, had loosened her curly hair, and dressed in the flowing garments of a Kallistan. She looked so like a Greek woman she could have stepped from one of the beautiful painted pots or wall frescoes.

Their two Greek agents, Stavros and Konstantin, had donned the plain linen kilts and sandals of sailors of the time. Konstantin looked like a Greek pirate. Stavros, though superficially resembling Konstantin in his brown skin, dark eyes, and curling hair, was thinner, wirier, and he wore the indefinable air of the engineer.

Both of them were waiting beside the beautifully crafted little boat that would be their trading vessel. Its simple lines concealed an amazing concentration of equipment, including, fastened along the bottom, a small undersea sled for scuba exploration.

"Everyone in," Ashe said, waving his hand.

They climbed in, Stavros and Konstantin going down into the hold where the electronics that would synchronize them with the time-gate were hidden.

Linnea Edel looked around, ran her hands up her arms. With a pang of compassion, Eveleen saw that the skin along her arms was rough with goose bumps. She was frightened; that was easy enough to see.

"I think I'll ride this one out below," Linnea said with a faint smile.

Ashe nodded once, and the older woman vanished below as well, to seat herself among the carefully aged wooden barrels that would, if the mission were extraordinarily lucky, return full of volcanic test materials and various Theran goods—

Kallistan goods, Eveleen thought, correcting herself. *The island is now Kalliste.*

Kallistan goods for the scientific brains back home to happily pore over.

"You two going below?" Ashe asked. Eveleen couldn't quite get used to his gaze, suddenly so dark. Even though she knew that the effect was just caused by lenses, they still gave him a faintly sinister air.

Ross shook his head once. "Want to see."

There was no enjoyment in his tone. Eveleen knew that Ross, in fact, hated the translation between one time and another as much as she did. It was too easy, when one saw that glaring light, and smelled the energy-tortured air, to believe that humans were never meant to endure that wrench.

But endure it they would. The Russians had lost an entire base in the Baltic through a misunderstanding of how the big portals worked. They insisted they had mastered it, and supposedly here was the proof.

Eveleen thought, as the cargo bay doors began to widen, that if anything went awry, hopefully they would never know what hit them.

"Sit toward the center," Stavros said in heavily accented English.

"Speak Ancient Greek," Ashe corrected, using the Greek of Linear B, so painfully decoded just within the past twenty-five years.

Why is he being dogmatic? Eveleen thought, looking Gordon's way. Then she thought back to the hasty training, the many sessions prefaced with "As you've already learned," and "As you well know . . ."

They did know. That is, all of them except Linnea. Just the day before Kelgarries had taken Ross and Eveleen aside and said, "Your archaeological expert is a first-class academic, and you can rely on her for information. But she only sat through training tapes. There wasn't time for anything else. Watch out for her."

Eveleen sighed. Of course they would watch out for one another. And, so Linnea Edel hadn't had the full course of training? Neither had Ross, once upon a time. And Linnea seemed a lot more sensible than a very young Ross probably had been.

At the inward image of a very young, and impetuous, Ross, she grinned. Stavros flashed her a smile, raised a hand, and then restated in the language they'd all been drilling as hard as they could, day and night: "Sit along the keel."

Ashe, Eveleen and Ross settled along the benches running down the middle of the narrow deck, under a very plain awning. The great engines of the cargo ship thrummed through the wood of the boat, making Eveleen's bones thrum in vibration.

The boat slid, at first slowly, then faster and faster down a ramp, until it shot out onto the choppy waters of the Aegean, reflecting lights from the three ships now steaming in an exact parallel.

Water sprayed up, cooling their faces with shocking suddenness. The boat shuddered and wallowed, and Eveleen clasped her hands tightly together, determined to show no nervousness. She so much preferred to be taking action herself, but this was not part of her job: she could do nothing.

As she forced herself into the steady breathing she'd made second nature during her long studies in martial arts, the boat settled into the rhythm of the waves. Stavros and Konstantin efficiently deployed the single sail, and then sheeted it home.

Now the little boat came alive, lifting the prow up and over the waves. The wind was little more than a gentle breeze, but these shallow craft had been designed for the trickish zephyrs of the Mediterranean climate, and the cargo ship fell away with surprising speed behind them, until it was just running lights against the black horizon.

Eveleen tipped her head back and looked up at the full moon, the Pleiades stretched across the sky like a broken necklace.

The two Russian ships ahead on either side were black silhouettes against a sky barely lit by a gibbous moon. Then a sheath of blue light flickered over their hulls. The air seemed to tighten, and Eveleen thought she heard, deep below the range of human hearing, a vast bell toll, rolling like an irresistible tide through her body. Ahead the sea glowed, a line of bluish light drawn through the chop between the two ships. She heard the slap of flying fish on either side of their small craft as sea life fled the sudden tension in the fabric of the world. Now light billowed up from the sea, diaphanous waves of mist, like a sea-level aurora.

The ship surged forward as a wind began to blow toward the gates, and as the glowing mist surrounded them, Eveleen's skin prickled, but not from the power being deployed around them to wrench a 3,600-year-deep hole in the universe. There were shapes in the mist, wraiths moving, reaching, supplicating, fleeing her direct glance and seen only in the corner of her vision. No one spoke, but everyone was alert and scarcely breathing.

Stavros reached down, pushing on something in one of the storage chests on either side of the keel. The water around their craft suddenly boiled without heat as the series of portal rods carefully spaced along both sides of the ship pulled power from the field now building between the Russian ships. A faint, keening note of power leashed to an extreme degree made Eveleen grit her teeth as the mist began to flow inward toward a bright point of light. It was not a vortex, but straight lines converging on an infinity that flowed hungrily forward to engulf the boat, as though her blind spot was expanding to fill her vision. She saw the prow vanish, wrenched away in a direction her eyes couldn't follow; then nothingness slid forward toward the group huddled in the middle of the boat. There was now no sense of motion, only a sense of a physical violation so great it made nausea seem pleasure by comparison. It seemed endless—

But only for a moment. Her blind spot filled the world and dwindled behind her, giving her for a moment the feeling of eyes in the back of her head, and they were through, sailing into ancient waters.

CHAPTER 5

THE FIRST THING to hit Ross was the acrid odor. No smoggy New York day smelled as bad as this. His hindbrain gibbered with warning at that invidious, pervasive whiff of smoke and the stench of brimstone.

There was no fire, of course. But on previous missions, when Ross transferred into human prehistory, one of the first things he noted was how the stars in the night sky were astonishingly bright: clearer, much clearer, than the clearest night in his own time. This time they were just as faint as the stars over New York City, but there was no kilowattage of civilization to blame.

The haze was volcanic ash.

When are we, exactly? he thought. And then shrugged. Useless to think in terms of exact correlation between dates. When they returned up-time, they'd emerge from the gates whenever they were next energized—probably only moments after they'd entered, no matter how long they spent here. What mattered was when they were in relation to the day of the eruption. That had been the computer jockeys' job. If they hadn't done it right, if there wasn't enough time to make sure the volcanic explosion happened, there'd be no second chance, for a kind of exclusion principle governed time travel: their presence here excluded their earlier presence. Research, and bitter experience, had shown that only inanimate objects could bilocate, like Eveleen's earring. Sentient beings could not. If they tried to jump up-time and then back here again to gain more time to figure things out, the boat would arrive intact but empty of life, like the *Marie Celeste,* the famous half-brig that'd run afoul of the natural time-fold in the Bermuda Triangle. Seventy years later, that story, and others like it, had inspired the research that led to time travel. Had led to Ross and Eveleen, and the other agents, being here, days? weeks? away from an explosion of unimaginable magnitude. He wondered briefly what happened to that crew, then dismissed the thought. If they didn't succeed here, there'd never be a *Marie Celeste,* and . . . No time for that. He wrenched his thoughts away before he got a headache, feeling a grin twitch at his lips at the inadvertent double meaning of "time."

Almost at once Ross turned his head from the silent stars to the hatch to the below-deck area, where golden light glowed.

Stavros had jumped down as soon as they were through. He popped up now. "We came through fine," he said, in the Ancient Greek they must all speak now.

Ross felt Eveleen relax beside him. He said nothing, of course. She'd hate him noticing. He also saw Ashe's grim profile ease slightly.

"Good," Ashe said, as though aware of attention turning his way. "It is night in both worlds. Much to do on the morrow. Let's get some sleep while we can."

They nodded, and trooped below, ducking under the narrow roof. Hammocks woven of net had been provided, and they had all practiced sleeping in them. Ross climbed into his, aware of the breathing of the others, and the balmy air that was just this side of being stuffy and too warm. The day would be blistering, unfortunately. No help for that. Air conditioning was now three thousand years in the future.

The steady lap-lap of the water along the sides, and the gentle rocking, sent him into a deep sleep that only broke when he heard voices.

It wasn't just the voices of his team, either, he realized. Bright sunlight shafted down into the crowded hold, golden rays that fired thousands of dust motes.

On deck was comparative silence; the voices came from beyond the ship. Ross looked around, realized he was alone.

He tumbled out of his hammock and ran up the short ladder to find Eveleen, Ashe, and Linnea gathered under the awning, eating some bread from the stores Stavros and Konstantin had stashed below. Stavros worked as helmsman with a great paddled tiller; Konstantin tended the sail.

The air was hot, still, and hazy with faint smoke. It made the brightness into a fierce glare. Ross squinted against the fierce light, shading his hand against the splashes of fiery sun on the harbor waters.

They had reached Akrotiri, he realized. They were in the midst of what seemed to be hundreds of craft, all more or less like theirs: high of prow, low aft, narrow, and built for speed over relatively mild waters. The main characteristic of one set of boats was the single square sail on a mast. Some of those sails were made of what looked like rough-woven linen, others of matting; the masts varied from single pieces rough-carved from trees to poles lashed together. These little boats would never last an hour in an Atlantic storm, but they were fast to make and easy to sail in the Mediterranean and Aegean waters.

Most of those with the masts were hauling their wind, drifting southward and away.

Eveleen gasped. "Have we arrived just at the departure of the fleet?" she murmured, staring.

Ross heard Linnea respond in a low voice, "Departure of *a* fleet, perhaps. I do not believe the entire island vacated overnight."

The other boats, the ones remaining in the harbor, were an astonishing variety. Some were long and narrow, with twenty and more rowers on each side. A few were so low that the rowers sat, visible, working with the sun broiling their dark heads and bronzed necks. Others had the galley slaves hidden below, in decks probably hot and noisome but at least out of the sun.

Most of the craft had no sails; they were local transportation. And a great many of them were spectacularly painted along the sides, with figures of birds, dolphins, even lions, and the awnings above the passengers were decorated with crocuses and lilies.

At first no one from these bravely decorated boats gave their own plain, modest craft a second glance.

The crowd of voices resolved into individuals. Ross, listening closely, was somewhat relieved to hear a mix of languages: there was Ancient Egyptian and Ancient Greek as well as one that was incomprehensible. People seemed to switch back and forth between tongues, calling greetings, complaining about the heat, demanding space to unload goods, starting in on trade negotiations. Requesting news of friends and relations since the "rock rain." Exchanging gossip. Human relations, in short, exactly like those of their unknown descendants thousands of years up the time-line.

"Rock rain," Linnea Edel repeated, staring out intently. Ross watched the woman continually turning her head, scanning, listening, and figured she probably would give an arm or a leg for a tape recorder, if not a video cam.

Rock rain: one of the falls of pumice that the scientists had talked about, resulting from a preliminary eruption. Ross felt a pang of trepidation inside. The science brains had guessed pretty close, then.

Eveleen sat on the railing, earrings swinging, as she watched a lowlying fishing smack ease up to the beach. No one looked her way as she observed the crew splash overboard, anchoring the ship with netbound rocks on either side and then beginning unloading.

Ross looked about. The crew of the fishing boat seemed to be mostly comprised of men, but not completely. Lithe young girls in their teens and maybe a bit older scrambled about in some of the fishing boats, obviously experienced at their work.

"Yah!" An insistent shout, followed by a quick stream of words, brought all their attention around.

Eveleen exchanged looks with Linnea Edel, who leaned forward, as if to take notes.

Damn it anyway, were they already to be exposed?

Ross turned, to see a man about his own age standing with one foot propped on the side of his boat, calling through cupped hands. An official of some sort, something they couldn't plan for?

But before Ross could say anything, the man switched to Ancient Egyptian of his own accord, and cried, "You there. What are you carrying?" His accent was strange, not at all like that of Jonathan and his team. Slurry, too quick. But Ross had encountered that syndrome before: language was always slower and more tentative in the lab. Here, it was real, living communication.

He mentally framed his response, then said: "Marble and a few other items."

"Then why are you here, where the foods are landed and brought to market?"

"It is our first journey to Kalliste."

"Ah. I thought you were Kemtiu." *Kemtiu*—the word the Egyptians used for themselves.

"Yes."

"There is always place for Kemtiu," the man called, and he bent down to talk to someone below his deck, and then straightened up. "And marble. Just as long as you bear no fruits."

So this man was just nosing out the competition.

"Our only food is for here," Ross said, striking his stomach.

The man laughed, and Ross laughed with him, then said, "Where is the best warehouse for us to unload our goods?"

"You'll want to sail down to that warehouse there with the dolphins painted on the side. We only have two left standing. Temo here is cousin to the owner and says he is honest enough, and speaks Kemt."

"We shall do so. Thank you, and may the gods smile on you."

"And on you." The two boats parted.

The setup made sense: perishables would be unloaded closest to Akrotiri and the market. Other things could be brought by cart.

Stav and Kosta expertly turned the boat, angling parallel to the coast. They made their way through the tangle of craft, sailing parallel to the shore.

Ross and the others studied the buildings dotting the mountainside. And it was a mountain, too, he realized, squinting against the bright haze. Present-day Thera had high cliffs, but here those cliffs were a small part of a sizable mountain, the top of which was obscured in a grayish-brown cloud of smoke. Much of the lower slopes looked adrift with something resembling dirty snow.

"Looks quite threatening, doesn't it?" Linnea Edel murmured, staring up.

"But no one else seems to notice," Eveleen replied.

"It's business as usual for these particular Kallistans," Ashe said. "And so should it be for us as well," he added with meaning.

The rest took the hint, and began to busy themselves about the little ship as Stavros and Konstantin, at yard and tiller, respectively, angled the boat toward a bare patch of beach near great buildings with tiled roofs. One had sun-faded dolphins painted on one wall. Konstantin lowered the sail and vanished below, and then the two men let out the heavy anchors with a splash.

The water was quite shallow, but so were the boats. Ross jumped overboard, turning to extend a hand to Linnea. They waited for the slight surge of water to diminish, and then she jumped in, her hem getting wet. The water was warm, though, Ross noted as they waded ashore.

For a time they all remained busy, as Stav and Kosta negotiated with the warehouse owner for space, and then hired harbor laborers to unload the pieces of pink and salmon and golden marble that the science techs back home had determined would be appropriate trade items from Egypt. They also unloaded the linen bolts that the women would use as trade samples in order to talk to any local merchants they might find.

Then they all oriented themselves, noting where the boat was anchored with reference to the harbor. If necessary they had radio contact, but they wanted to use it as little as possible. The Kallistans would never notice, but what was sent out via EM might be intercepted by other high-tech listeners—like the Baldies.

Ashe was the last to step onto the pumice-spattered white sands. He opened his mouth to speak, but then paused, his brow puckered.

Ross realized the ground was still undulating beneath his feet. An effect of just getting off the water?

Before his mind could frame the question, other sensory details sparked his sense of danger: an explosion of swallows skyrocketing upward, scolding; the rumble of stone grating in walls and buildings of the city just half a mile away.

Earthquake!

The Time Agents all looked up, hands out. Ross realized he was safest right where he was, out in the open. Somewhere in the harbor city, just right of the great gates next to which sacred horns trembled, a sudden white cloud of dust shot upward: either a wall, or a building, had collapsed.

But the city did not change. Far too many of the great buildings, some three stories, had already fallen some time ago. The people who had not evacuated the city appeared to have moved into the smaller buildings, patching them in makeshift ways and carrying on with business as usual. The only damage that the Time Agents could see was bits of carvings falling to the streets below and smashing a row of hanging plants that had been set along a roof edge.

Before anyone could speak, the quake's rolling diminished to a shiver and then stopped.

Ross met Eveleen's eyes. She glanced toward the city, and he knew what she was thinking: their first task lay there, in those narrow streets, under stone buildings.

Linnea Edel had turned her eyes upward toward the portion of the volcano visible here. She licked her lips, then said, "I guess I'd better get busy looking for signs of nasty bald bad guys. The first order of business would be the local gossip center: AKA the oracle." She spoke in English, but no one corrected her.

Ashe only extended a hand, and the two started toward the steep trail zigzagging up the great mountain around the back of the city.

Ross extended a hand, using the same gesture, and Eveleen smiled at his irony. She unpacked one of the sample bolts of the linen that would be her entry to talk to people in the market.

Together they started up the shore toward the city, to begin investigating there. As he walked, Ross wondered who was the greater enemy, the Baldies or Nature.

CHAPTER 6

AS ALWAYS, THE Time Agents were to interact on a personal level as little as possible. Gordon Ashe had kept himself alive by learning to blend in, and to keep his own counsel. His partners, on most runs, had been men; in most parts of the world during prehistory, women had not had the freedom of movement that the Time Agents required.

Of course there were female agents as well, and they'd been successfully deployed in places where they were needed. All those women, like Eveleen, had gone through training, and they, too, had learned to blend in, and to keep their own counsel.

So he watched, uncomfortable, when Linnea held out a hand to stop an older woman. She gestured, then said the ancient Hittite word that Jonathan's team had decided meant "oracle."

The older woman shook her head, looking puzzled. So Linnea repeated the word, only in Ancient Greek.

The woman's face cleared, and she let out a voluble stream, her hands swooping up the path behind her and gesturing to indicate what Ashe thought meant a cave.

"Please! More slow," Linnea said.

"We have only the one oracle who speaks to us from the Earth Goddess, through the Priestesses of the Serpent," the woman replied, enunciating very clearly and slowly. "Where are you from?"

"I come with traders, from Kemt." She gave the correct form for "the Black Land," the Nile Valley, which Egyptians differentiated from "the Red Land," the desert.

"Ah! Well, then. That explains it." The woman adjusted her robe, and wiped her forehead. "I have heard that you have many great oracles over the sea. Well, but here we have the one, and even the islanders come to our mountain to consult." She pointed up the steep cliffs behind Akrotiri.

"Has the oracle told people to go away from the island?" Linnea asked in a careful voice.

"Our goddess foretold the battle of the Great Snakes the season my daughter bore her first son, and many have gone to the far islands, including my daughter." The woman opened her hands, an age-old gesture of acceptance. "Me? It is my home here, for too many seasons to change, just because the earth spirits cannot rest, and the snake clouds form. They are distant, not here in our city."

"Many thanks, and blessings." Linnea's language was correct, but her body language was self-conscious, unnatural, as if she were very much aware of playing a part—as if she felt silly.

Ashe was relieved when the woman smiled sympathetically, repeated in a slow voice her directions, and added a wish for blessings in a soft voice. Sympathy, not suspicion.

His relief was short-lived.

They started at once up the path. Linnea seemed to relax now that they were alone. So did Ashe, but when his old and admired friend looked around and smiled and made exclamations from time to time in English, at first Ashe did not know what to do.

They began trudging up the sharply angled path that zigzagged up the side of the great mountain. Their going was slow, partly because it would not do to go jogging straight up the mountain in what was going to be a very hot, humid day, partly because just ahead of them on the trail was a woman leading a laden donkey, and also because Linnea kept stopping in order to gaze at the half-ruined city of Akrotiri, which spread grandly along the base of the mountain.

"Oh, to explore every building!" she murmured softly.

Ashe did not answer. He kept moving.

Linnea turned her head, saw him a ways along the trail, and bustled to catch up.

Again they walked in silence, Ashe from time to time glancing up the mountain. From this angle he could see at least one great vent, from which smoke rose in lazy curls to join the thick haze higher up. He was not sure if there were others within his view, or if what seemed to be smoke was just air currents moving what had already risen.

"Oh! Here comes someone," Linnea whispered—again in English.

Ashe said nothing. He increased his pace slightly, to narrow the gap between them and the woman with the donkey.

An older man escorting two young girls came round the trail, the girls' earrings and skirts swinging. The younger one was chattering, apparently not noticing the looks of concern on the older girl's and the man's faces.

As they neared the woman on the donkey, they pressed into single file.

The woman looked up at the sky, as if noting the time, then said—in Ancient Greek—what sounded like, "You are today's first seeker, no? Did the goddess speak?"

"Not in a way I understand," the man said slowly, sighing. "And the priestesses only shake their heads and repeat what I was told by the goddess: that a shadow flies across the sun, and another shadow flies beyond that, silencing the earth spirits. She can hear nothing."

The younger girl looked up at the bright blue sky with a fearful glance and then they passed.

Ashe glanced once at Linnea. She had slipped behind him, her lips compressed, her eyes excited.

When the people were safely around the curve below, she murmured in a voice of delight, "Did you hear them? Just like that old lady. I understood! I comprehended! The accent we have learned for the Ancient Greek is not so very far off, no more than, say, BBC English is from a Texas accent." She smiled at Ashe, the old smile of discovery.

But mostly he was annoyed. So much so that he hesitated to speak.

Now the trail leveled out for a time, and even widened for what had to be a little rest stop under the shade of three scrabbled, pumice-dusted olive trees. Just behind them was a cracked basin, carved from the same lovely marblelike rock that most of the city was built of, with dolphins carved above it. They paused to look at it, saw the reddish marks of oxidation, realized it was there to catch runoff during the rainy season.

Ashe glanced down into the bottom of it, saw a wet layer of sediment mixed with the gray pebbly pumice they had seen everywhere else. It had rained, and fairly recently.

A shudder underfoot, and a low rumble, so low it was almost off the scale of human perception, startled them both. Tiny rocks came clattering down from above. One stung Ashe's cheek, and he saw Linnea bat at something and then turn her back.

The quake subsided, though the noise didn't. More people came down the trail, this time two older women.

And again the woman with the laden donkey said, "The goddess, did she speak to you?"

"Only of silence, a silence of shadows," one of the women said, and the other pursed her lips, looking out at the sea. "The same we have been hearing this three moons and past."

Twice more they encountered people coming down the trail, one of them riding a donkey, and with each the woman ahead asked her question, though with those she spoke a language that Ashe couldn't comprehend. But to her questions the people responded with headshakes and shrugs, age-old gestures.

Finally, just after the last one had vanished on the trail below, Linnea said—in English—"The 'oracle' seems to have nothing to say."

And Ashe said, in Ancient Greek, emulating the accent they had been hearing, "I do not understand you."

Linnea looked up with a brief smile that faded when she saw his expression. Her eyes narrowed, her expression now reflective.

She looked down at her sandals winking in and out below the hem of her bravely colored garment, and at last she said, in Greek this time, "I was wrong. It is not real to me."

To which Ashe replied, "It must become real. There is no record of a woman speaking a foreign tongue, surprising people with things that never have been."

Linnea's cheeks reddened. Again she ducked her head, and Ashe's irritation vanished. It wasn't as if she were the first to think of their guises as mere playacting.

Linnea Edel was a superb archaeologist whose specialty was volcanic sites. She'd been cramming, during their own training period, with all the new technology used by vulcanists.

She said, in a low voice, "I did not think about being a woman of the time, only seeing others of the time." A pause, and then, "I envisioned myself invisible to the people now, but I am not, am I?"

Ashe said, "You will be invisible, that is, leave no memory, if you behave as they expect."

Linnea nodded once.

Up ahead, the woman with the donkey said to a family starting down the trail, "Did the goddess speak to you?"

"No," said the family, even the children. The wife added, with a sour glance back, "We even offered our very best fish, fresh caught. But all she spoke of was silence and shadows. She did not forewarn us of the rock rain three moons ago." And, with a sidelong glance at her husband, she said, "I think the goddess has gone away, with the snake fires. I think we ought to hire a boat and go south with my family."

The husband did not respond, and the family moved on down the trail.

Ashe and Linnea kept walking. Not long after, they arrived at the top of a long shelf. A whisper of breeze came off the sea, cooling to their damp faces, but not quite diminishing the whiff of sulfur.

A small number of people stood before a great crack in the rock above the cliff, from which floated the faint sounds of young girls' voices rising and falling in a chant.

Striations of multicolored stone outlined the cave, whose mouth was dark. At the apex of this triangular cave faint wisps of vapor puffed out, swiftly dispersing; inside the cave somewhere had to be a hot stream.

That explained why the unseen oracle, or at least the oracle's attendants, had chosen that place. Water year-round in this climate, hot for cold days, plentiful (if slightly sulfuric) for the long rainless summers, would be important.

Ashe and Linnea edged round the back of the crowd waiting patiently. The woman with the donkey was, for the moment, the only one besides them moving. She plodded straight into the cave as one who had the right.

For a moment Ashe glimpsed robes dyed a robin's egg blue: a priestess. Then the woman had vanished inside, with the first of the waiting people.

Ashe stood in the lee of a great piece of sun-bleached pumice, probably from a blast a million years before, and glanced around. Ah. The smoke came from over there.

He touched Linnea's arm, and tipped his chin.

Her glance of longing was unmistakable, but she turned with no apparent resentment. Ashe felt a surge of relief, even gratitude. He had not wanted to admonish her; the risk was that the assumption of superiority would somehow cross professional lines into the personal. And maybe with a very young agent, it would have. They tended to take things personally, even if it was inadvertent.

Linnea just cast back one last glance of yearning. The archaeologist in her was intensely curious about the living ritual concerning an oracle. But now was not the time to witness it.

They edged along a narrow goat trail and began climbing up along the mountainside, away from the cliffside cave. They were very quickly out of sight of anyone below.

Up and up. The smell of sulfur got considerably stronger. Ashe stopped, holding his breath. Linnea, who had climbed behind him, winced, and mimed putting their breathing masks on.

It was a question. Ashe looked about and saw no one. He nodded, taking out his mask, and said in English, "There is nothing up here but rock and volcanic ash. I think the hydrogen sulfide would drive even the hardiest away—and the locals must know by now how swiftly death can come from these vents."

Linnea nodded, passed a hand inside her robes, and pulled out the cloth-disguised breather that the scientific team had fashioned for her.

Ashe had on his own. The air smelled of plastic, and slightly stale, but the mask successfully absorbed the potentially deadly gases. A small strip of chemplast, visible from the corner of his vision, would change color if the concentration became too much for the mask to handle; another indicated the mask's remaining capacity. Both were green.

They climbed on, easing around a crumbling rock, and felt intense heat. The hardy little tufts of grass and weed that they had seen here and there, more evidence that the rainy season had begun, had long since withered away.

Another ten paces and air shimmered from escaping heat. Ashe paused to glance out toward the sea. Tiny boats and single-masted ships dotted the horizon.

"Go ahead," he said. "I'll do a visual scan."

Linnea nodded once, her intense investigative expression widening her eyes again, She opened her robe, revealing plain cotton shorts and a fine cotton-silk undershirt beneath. Round her waist she wore a sturdy belt, onto which, like a superhero of the comic books, she'd attached pouches and holders.

She unclipped several vulcanology instruments—infrared thermosensor, a sensitive sniffer to measure gas types and concentrations, and other devices Ashe didn't recognize—then edged closer to the vent in order to start recording.

Ashe turned in the other direction, pulled out the mini–field glasses the science team had furnished him, and shaded them with one hand so the glass wouldn't glint in the sun as he closely and minutely swept the bay.

Bravely decorated boats circled about, some hung with decorations from prow to stern, others painted along the sides with leaping dolphins and swarming octopi, some with stylized lilies and crocuses. The people, flattened by the distance, talked back and forth or rowed, or sailed, or fished, or gazed off into the distance. These, then, were the people the scientists called "the squatters"—the people who remained behind after the first great quake that destroyed parts of the city and who had begun to rebuild.

What exactly was he seeking? Some anomaly, some sign that there were others here, perhaps in disguise as well, from the future.

A sigh made him turn around. Linnea was holding one of the instruments he hadn't recognized, a flattened ovoid with a pistol grip. He saw the tendons in her hand flex as she pulled the trigger: a click, a whirr, and several sets of antennae uncurled from the front and fanned out rigidly. She stared down at the instruments and then pulled the trigger again, and the antennae curled back into the casing.

Linnea crossed to his side. "Well, the brains at home will love these readings," she said. "Isotope concentrations and types, gas readings, just about everything is either off the scale or close as makes no difference." She hefted the odd instrument. "The piezo-EM strain detector, too— and it's not terribly sensitive."

"Meaning?" Ashe asked, though he knew.

"Even without strain readings from fixed laser interferometers, which we didn't bring because we don't have time for them, everything points to a big blow, bigger than anything recorded in modern times. Far bigger," she added seriously.

So it was time for Ashe's own test.

He unclipped from his belt a flat meter that was about the size of a video cam. Inside it, though, was a little of the strange tech that had come from the future by way of the past, about which they were still learning. The materials, how they produced their strange effects, including their signature temporal distortion, were still largely a mystery, but scientists, patiently experimenting for twenty-five years, had learned to use the tech for several applications useful to Project Star.

He tabbed the power on and watched the little LED screen light up. Then it was his turn to brave the ferocious heat of the vent, as close as he could get, holding out his meter.

The graph bar on it trembled but did not move.

They looked at each other. Despite the danger, he'd have to get closer.

Ashe edged closer, hearing a whooshing rumble deep below, as if air were being forced through inconceivably big compressors.

Suddenly the graph bar flickered and then leaped halfway across the little screen.

Ashe moved the meter in a slow half circle, just to make certain. The graph bar held . . . held . . . diminished down to nothing when he moved it away from the vent.

Back again. And again, it snapped into a long rectangle, which meant only one thing.

He edged back down to where Linnea waited. He did not know what his face showed, but she seemed to read something there, for she said, "You found it?"

He nodded once. "Somewhere in that vent is Baldy tech."

CHAPTER 7

THE ENTIRE WESTERN horizon was a deep crimson, the bottoms of the approaching march of sheep-backed clouds bluish, the tops the gold of fire. It was a spectacular sunset, almost garish and almost sinister in its intensity.

A volcanic sunset. But none of the six Time Agents noticed it; they were all staring in grim dismay at the destruction of their campsite. Destruction and disappearance: their tents, bedrolls, and the food that the Greek agents had unloaded were all gone. Everything else lay scattered about—broken open by violent hands, rifled through, and then discarded.

"Everything?" Ross asked finally, turning over a pottery fragment with his sandaled foot. He recognized that pot: it had held their oatmeal mix, carefully made to look like regular oats, but vitamin and protein fortified.

"Everything," Stavros said. "Except the last load from the ship." He jerked a thumb behind him at the cloth-wrapped burdens he and Kosta had set down when they discovered the ruined site. "Our gear." He said the words in a low voice, in English: their radio and recording equipment, which would never be left alone.

Ashe, Ross, and Eveleen spontaneously turned, looking outward for signs of incipient attack. Linnea Edel stood, hands cradling her elbows, looking apprehensive.

There was nothing to be seen except the smoke-pall over the sky, the greenish choppy sea, and the barren land stretching in folds toward the sudden, dramatic cliffs along which was built Akrotiri. Behind the warehouse, the desolate land stretched away, dotted with quake-cracked hills and falls of rock, as seabirds circled overhead.

"Baldies," Ross stated. "And one of them is probably lying up on one of those cliffs somewhere now, watching our reaction through a high-tech field glass and gloating. Damn."

"We can't know that," Ashe said. And, to Kosta, "What exactly happened? Did you see or speak with anyone?"

"No," Kosta said. "We chose this empty warehouse, cleared out recently from the looks of things, because it was the very last, the farthest from the city. No people around. Those over there—" he indicated one of the other warehouses, the closest about five hundred yards away, the others lying along the gentle hills in the direction of the city "—we kept them in sight most of the time. The people in that one were all busy with their fish. That was another reason we chose this location." He smiled grimly; when the sluggish air moved, it carried a strong smell of fish. "We did not think this place would be watched."

Ashe nodded. "Baldies might assume that time travelers might come here first and hide equipment. We probably ought to have foreseen that."

"With all our things disguised?" Eveleen asked.

No one answered. She looked around, then sighed. "Yes, we probably would have been on the watch here, too—if we expected unwanted visitors showing up from the past."

"We had just finished unloading the camp gear, and had started setting it up," Kosta said. "Then went back together so we could make the last trip in one session."

"Told you I should have stayed," Stavros muttered in Modern Greek, his big hands tight on the hilt of the knife he wore at his side, his brows a single furrowed line.

"We don't know how many any more than we know who," Ashe reminded everyone. "All right. Then we go immediately to our fallback plan: the men will sleep on the boat with the gear." He pointed to their disguised equipment. "Eveleen, you are in charge of finding us an observation base within the safety of the city."

Eveleen nodded.

"Then let's eat," Ashe said, "and get moving."

SHORTLY AFTERWARD THEY sat on a grassy crag overlooking Akrotiri, eating the barley-and-lentil flatbread that Eveleen had bought hot from the oven, crumbled goat cheese on the top, and for dessert fresh-picked grapes. Ross and Kosta had carried the precious gear back to the boat, where Kosta stayed on guard.

The setting was pretty, a green little shelter carved by runoff, the view spectacular, the food actually quite tasty, but no one was in a good mood.

"So they're here." Ross spoke finally, surprised he felt more satisfaction than any other emotion.

Of course. It was because the presence of the Baldies gave them a purpose, a direction, a goal. Something definite to aim for, accomplish— and then get out.

Stavros grinned, a brief, somewhat martial flash of teeth that was easy enough for Ross to interpret: Stav, and Kosta as well, welcomed more than feared the prospect of the Baldies trying to find and get aboard their ship.

Ashe, noting Stav's reaction, did not hide his snort of amusement. He said, "Just as well you'll be working off some of that hotheadedness with me up on the mountain."

Stavros and Ross both grinned. Ashe gave Ross a wry look, then turned back to Stavros. "And you can begin working it off by getting the gear up there."

Stavros laughed. "With all respect, I shall permit a donkey to bear it instead."

"And you get to coax the donkey. My guess is that'll be work enough," Ashe retorted.

Stavros opened his palm. "Ah, it is true enough. Even 3,600 years up-time, the beasts have wicked tempers. I do not expect them to be sweeter now."

"So would I if my existence was defined as 'beast of burden,' " Eveleen put in. "Well, I'm ready to go."

Ashe said, "Let's get back to the ship and get a good night's rest. Tomorrow will be rough."

TOMORROW'S ROUGHNESS BEGAN shortly after midnight, when blue lightning ripped through the stifling heat. With the first crack of thunder came hail. It drummed on the canopy, which was made of treated cloth indistinguishable from contemporary material—except that it was quite waterproof. Stavros, on current watch, could just be heard swearing as he hastily got under cover.

As abruptly as it had started, the hail turned into rain, a gritty, eye-stinging rain full of volcanic ash. Despite the canopy's shelter the normal working of the boat let the water seep in, and some dripped down onto Ross's face. In the reflected blue glare of more lightning he saw the others in their hammocks, eyes open, faces bespattered with dirty, stinging drips of rain.

No one spoke. At least the hail and rain flattened the sea down substantially; the boat had been rocking fretfully since they'd retired.

The rain continued, a dull, steady roar, and Ross closed his eyes again. He was on the edge of chill; he reached for the fake fur rolled up on a tiny shelf above his hammock, cast it over himself, and as warmth returned, so did drowsiness. Despite the fury of the storm, he was soon asleep.

WHEN THEY WOKE up, the air was washed clean, the breeze from the west pure and brisk.

Konstantin had prepared breakfast for them before coming below to retire. Fresh-caught fish, grilled over an open fire, and more of the flatbread constituted the meal. Smelling it, Eveleen felt her mouth water. Her head felt clear, and she smiled at the clean blue sky in the west.

A glance eastward, though, diminished her good mood. There was the ubiquitous smoke, slowly drifting westward as the breeze died. The volcanic smog was making a comeback.

As Eveleen ate in silence, she listened to Ross and Ashe talk in low voices with Stavros, planning how they would get the heat resistant suits up the mountain without calling attention to themselves. The proof that the Baldies were definitely here had caused the first rule to be implemented: their cautionary radio silence was now, except for dire emergency, total.

The Baldies were here.

Linnea voiced a worry when the women waded ashore and started up the trail toward the city. "Do you think that attack on our camp was the Baldies, then? If so, why?"

Eveleen gave her head a shake. Of course Linnea had been fully briefed on what little they knew of the Baldies. It was so little, missing any hint of motivation, that Eveleen knew that personal experience would be more convincing than mere reference to old reports. "I can't guess. So far, the Baldies have not exactly been subtle when they see us. If that was them, it could have been a test, or a warning, even. They obviously didn't want to risk being seen, for they could easily have waited and attacked Stav and Kosta. Seen or heard: the men would have set up a shout, and maybe those fishers would have come running. The camp attack was probably done fast and silent."

Linnea nodded and blanched slightly. Eveleen wondered if she was thinking of the Baldies' efforts in human mind control, which had worked with unpredictable results. Ross's scarred hand was one result, though admittedly he had been wearing one of their shimmery-fabric suits when it occurred. "I don't think the Baldies could do their mind tricks with a whole crowd of determined fishers. I think they have to concentrate on us one at a time. And as for the ship being attacked next, Stav and Kosta have it well protected. They won't get it as easily as they got that camp."

"All right, then," Linnea said, in a determinedly bright voice. "So let's see if we can find anything that might answer some of our questions." She smiled. "And at the same time regard this as a shopping opportunity of a lifetime."

Eveleen laughed. When they reached the spot where the trail joined a bigger road, packed hard from years of pounding by biped and quadruped feet, they fell silent, melding into the crowd heading toward Akrotiri.

The clatter of voices rose around them. Eveleen listened to everyday chatter as they neared the great gates. The sacred horns rose up against the sky, silhouetted against the milky blue. Already the volcanic haze was spoiling the pure brilliance of morning.

Linnea clutched her basket protectively against her. It was an ordinary basket heaped with small packages wrapped in cloth and leather. The ones on top were indeed the food they were meant to suggest; her equipment nestled underneath. Eveleen preferred wearing hers under her clothing, to keep her hands free.

Not that there was any overt threat here. Eveleen realized that Linnea had stopped, and alarm flared briefly through her until she saw Linnea resting her basket on a low wall as she watched a group of magnificently dressed young women parading down the street, their arms full of crocus flowers. Somehow, somewhere, someone had managed to grow flowers, despite the increasingly cruel slaps of Nature all around them.

Eveleen, staring after them, remembered how often she'd read statements about human adaptability. Here was living proof. She realized she'd expected furtive sneaking about, or outright fear, and not people laughing, talking, carrying on with their lives.

A group of younger girls, sudden as starlings, danced around them, singing, their voices high and birdlike in the open air.

Linnea drew a deep breath.

"The saffron makers," Eveleen guessed, remembering her research.

A single nod.

The procession wound its way past them, making for one of the great buildings in which religious ceremonies took place. As they wound their way along the narrow street, they could still hear singing coming from the open windows of a low building that was still left standing.

Pungent smells assailed them: fish, goat, the pervasive stink of burning rock. Dyers stirred great pots, the fires beneath pale in the glary light. Strong herbal odors drifted on the thick, dusty air. At the sides of the street rubble had been piled neatly; men of various ages swarmed about the bigger piles, some putting down big jagged pieces of stone, others taking them to carts and hauling them away—instant recycling.

Eveleen realized that Linnea had become so mesmerized watching the cloth makers, the potters, the seed grinders and bakers, she'd forgotten about their orders to watch for signs of Baldies' presence before the bedazzlement of seeing living, breathing people performing the homey, everyday activities that scholars far on the other side of the mists of time would spend hours speculating about.

Eveleen didn't remind her. Experience had taught her that this sort of academic reverie was actually trustworthy: an expert would see an anomaly at least as fast as, maybe even faster than, the more mission-focused observer. It was just very slow going. After a time, Eveleen got tired of watching bartering and looked around for signs of rebuilding. She wondered why Linnea seemed so intent on these little exchanges of goods for goods, until she finally realized that what Linnea was looking for was evidence of someone writing.

A flare of humor almost caused Eveleen to laugh. Linnea Edel was an unreconstructed academic, even after their hasty training: she was not looking for Baldies; she was on the lookout for someone carving Linear A hieroglyphs into clay, so that she could confirm or refute recent scholarship on its decoding!

Ought she to say something? No. Her instinct was good. If Linnea was watching people that closely, she might notice something Eveleen wouldn't.

On they walked, back and forth up the hill, along narrow streets with hot sun reflecting heat waves in almost visible sheets. Twice minor tremors caused people to halt, to shift their eyes anxiously up, or down, to pause in conversation, but when the earthquake died, work and talk resumed, in several languages.

". . . I heard the goddess has still not spoken," an old woman told another in Ancient Greek, as they portioned out water in tiny red-clay cups from a great urn.

"Not for three moons. It is why my sister and her family decided to sail. I believe we must wait and be patient. She has always spoken to us before."

"True, true. She will speak when speech becomes necessary. So I tell my son, who fears for the children. He says times have become so strange, with both fire and water rising from the earth, and rocks falling from the sky, he fears the goddess has departed, leaving us to the fire spirits."

A long sigh was the answer, and the two women turned away.

Eveleen and Linnea walked on, Eveleen watching the movements of the people. Un-self-conscious, busy, socializing as they worked, they all appeared to be genuine Kallistans. Eveleen knew that she must look for anything out of place, but she kept envisioning Baldies shrouded in cloth, lurking about on the edges of crowds. Watching for them? Surely they would not interact with the people any more than she and Linnea must, except in the most superficial manner. *We must not stand out,* Eveleen thought. *We are aliens to the Baldies, which is a kind of protection if we are careful not to make any mistakes. If they are searching for us, we must remain indistinguishable from all these others.*

"Grapes?" A gentle hand nudged her arm. "Grapes? Grown well away from the smoke, tasting sweet?"

A young girl looked up into Eveleen's face, gold earrings very much like her own swinging next to dusky-colored cheeks. Candid brown eyes assessed her, and then the girl repeated her question in two other tongues.

Eveleen wet her lips, and then said in Ancient Greek, "I have been thinking about grapes."

The dark brows arched in surprise. "Ah! You will find that mine are sweetest. Here. Taste one." Nimble fingers twisted at a plump grape at the top of the basket.

Eveleen smiled as she glimpsed the older, slightly withered ones beneath. *The girl's sales wiles would probably work better on those young men over there, building the ship,* she thought. But she tasted the grape, which had the same slightly bitter tang as those she'd bought the day before.

"Eh," she said.

The girl's face altered into intent: now it was time to bargain.

As they embarked on their exchange, Eveleen was peripherally aware of Linnea looking in one direction, a slight frown between her brows.

She finished her bargain more hastily than she'd intended, and held out her hand. The girl glanced down at the little bits of lapis lazuli the scientists three thousand years into the future had furnished for everyday trade, scrupulously took two of the smallest, and stashed them in her skirt.

Then with a cheery wave she was gone, and a moment later Eveleen was vaguely aware of her sweet voice again, "Grapes! Sweet grapes?"

Eveleen dropped the bright blue bits of lapis into the pocket in her skirt, aware of Linnea sighing with regret as she watched the young woman walk away.

"What is it?" she murmured in Ancient Greek.

"If I could just hear repeated, slowly, her words in all those tongues, I could find Ancient Greek cognates in whatever it is these people talk among themselves when traders from the other Cyclades Islands are not around."

Linear A again, Eveleen thought with a spurt of amusement. *Detectives on a murder case have nothing on archaeologists for single-mindedness!*

But then she realized Linnea was frowning back in the other direction. "What is it?" she murmured, looking at some brightly woven rugs hanging over a dusty stone wall that ended abruptly just above a landslide.

"Is there something odd about that little square over there?" Linnea asked, her chin lifting slightly off to the right.

Eveleen helped herself to one of the grapes she'd stashed in a shawl sling she'd fashioned from extra fabric, and as she chewed she glanced casually up, sweeping the right.

Nothing looked out of place. In booths marked by low stone walls, built round a tiny side square with mats fixed up as temporary shelter, a man was busy beating bronze sheets into tools; several cheerfully naked small children played a game with smooth pebbles; an old, toothless woman expertly spun thread through her fingers. On the other side, several young girls were busy winnowing fava seeds from beans, singing quietly and without much joy.

Distracted, Eveleen watched the girls tossing aside black-spotted, withered beans, their gestures expressive of reluctance, of worry: clearly a poor harvest. The older women watched, one singing. Another was getting the shelled seeds ready for sun drying, her lips pressed together in a tight line. Others ground dried beans with round stone mills, their song soft and soothing.

What else was there to notice? Eveleen looked more closely at the people as she and Linnea moved slowly along. Linnea stooped to examine bronze tools being made, then straightened up, shaking her head. The artisan, seeing her, turned his shoulder, and Linnea breathed, "House. Next to the monkeys."

Eveleen did another casual sweep, this time scanning behind the people and along the buildings. The primary building near them was a house with three low windows and one door around which were painted dancing monkeys in a graceful pattern. Above each window there was a long-tailed swallow painted, bright blue, each bird flying upward.

The front of the house looked intact, but one could see through the gaping windows that the roof had fallen in, and no one was inside.

Those swallows definitely caught the eye, Eveleen thought, glancing at the women going in and out of a smaller jury-rigged building adjacent. Next to that was a smaller house, somewhat tucked back, very plain—like so many along the streets. No one went in, no one came out, and there was no one visible in the one window.

Linnea walked on and examined fabric draped over a low window adjacent to the two houses. Eveleen bent over the rough cloth, brightly dyed blue and red in lovely patterns that would appeal to people in modern times, but she forced herself to observe beyond the heads of the spinners sitting inside the window. Now she was looking across the little court.

Then she saw it: people walked in and out of all the few whole buildings along the street, in and out of shacks, lean-tos, tents draped from old walls, and mat-covered awnings—every structure, in short, except that one.

As she watched, one of the pebbles from the children's game bounced in the direction of the mystery house. A child ran to get it, his steps faltered, though there was no apparent barrier, then he reached down and snatched up his stone and retreated in haste.

"Force field?" Eveleen whispered. And, with an inward pang, "I should have seen that."

Linnea turned away from the fabric and murmured as she rummaged in her basket, "You were watching the people, as is right. But we archaeologists . . . we are trained to observe the negative spaces, you might say."

Such as no one going in and out of a specific building—something Eveleen had not considered.

"What now?" Linnea asked, bending to look at urns full of dried lentils, all dusted with ash.

"Mark the place, report to the others. Keep looking."

"How do we mark it?" Linnea asked.

Eveleen fingered a rug. "Make a mental map. I'll do that."

They kept moving, Eveleen itching to get back and investigate that mysterious little house. But she forced herself to keep moving along the narrow little streets, though now her observations were at best perfunctory.

Nothing. Nothing. No sign of Baldies . . . no signs at all.

At the very top, they stood in a faint breeze and looked down at the jumble of ruins, hide and reed-mat roofs, and rubble piles below them. "All right, now we try it, just to see how far we get, and what happens," Eveleen whispered.

Linnea nodded once, swallowing visibly.

They bought more cheese on the way down, and fresh bread, all piled into Linnea's basket. Eveleen led the way to their little court. The children were all eating now, except for two of them asleep on rugs next to walls that cast a bit of shade. The women with the fava beans still worked. The spinner leaned out a window, talking in a low voice to a man who held a donkey by a rope, the animal still except for the switching of its tail to chase flies away.

No one was near the plain building.

Eveleen rummaged at her pouch, closed her hands round lapis rocks, pretended to stumble, and cast the blue stones that way. Only one rolled in the right direction. She gave a cry of dismay and chased after them, Linnea with her.

One, two, three, and there was the fourth, over by that empty door. She started over and faltered when danger prickled down the back of her neck, tightening her shoulder blades. She glanced behind her: no one there. No one paid her the least attention.

A step, another, and her fingers closed around the stone.

It wasn't a force field, then; it was some kind of mental impulse or even just subsonics. She permitted herself one glance inside that open door.

Nothing.

She turned away, put her lapis lazuli into her pouch, and fought the instinct to look back.

"All right, we know there's something weird there," she murmured.

Linnea nodded once. "And now we have to find a market spot or at least an apartment. Do you want to negotiate or shall I?"

Her tone of voice, so polite, indicated she wanted to try. From what Eveleen had seen, the older women commanded the most authority, if not respect. So she shook her head. "You do it. I want to watch some more."

They continued on, Linnea now seeking the best vantage. Eveleen's mind was back on that strange room.

The place Linnea chose was next to the building that evidently belonged to the Priestesses of the Serpent, which showed the most signs of repair of any. Not just young women about to embark on religious duties stayed there, but it seemed to be a kind of hotel, or hostel, for women from the harbor. Linnea successfully negotiated a little room, and no one gave them any false reaction, any strange questions, any sign of trouble. Eveleen stood at the one window and looked down at the sweep of market and the edge of the harbor. It was a prime spot for observation.

Yet her shoulder blades stayed tight all the rest of the day.

CHAPTER 8

"IT WASN'T THERE. At least, that's what our instruments tell us now."

Silence.

Ross braced himself for the stupid questions. They didn't come. Linnea Edel, who had been with Ashe when they had discovered the alien tech in the vent, looked surprised, but then she sat back, folded her hands, and waited.

"So we tested again, with Ross's equipment, and it came up as negative as mine."

Silence again. Eveleen rubbed her thumbnail along her bottom lip, then said, "So, what, they have detectors on their device that registers pings?"

"It would appear so," Ashe said.

"Then they definitely know we're here," Linnea murmured, looking about in question.

"That makes it more convincing that it was a Baldy welcome committee that tossed our camp," Ross stated.

They sat in the boat, under cover of truly inky darkness. Thick clouds, mixed with smoke, obscured the sky. The water was fretful, with little shivering rows of choppy waves—the result of several minor quakes all through the evening. There was a sharp smell in the air, a combination of hot rock, ozone, and sulfur that mixed unpleasantly with brine.

Ashe finally stretched out his feet tiredly and said, "Yet we still haven't seen them. Well, to the rest of our report. We put on the flame suits and our breathing masks and went down as far as we could, doing infrared scans as well as Baldy-tech pings, but of course we had no idea what to expect. We didn't know if it had been moved, turned off, or cloaked; whether or not it would be buried or in plain sight; how big it would be." He sat back and reached for one of the disguised flagons of pure water.

Ross said, "What 'looking around' really means is we slipped and sweated in the darkness until it was too damn hot to do anything but broil. The coolers on those suits don't have enough capacity for really long searches; they need a lot more. I wish we could score a few of the Baldy suits."

Their suits used the same technique as space suits: tubes running throughout the thick insulated fabric carried cooling fluid all over the body. He recalled that shimmering blue-green fabric that the Baldies used not just as clothing but also as insulation, filters, and conduits for their mysterious mental radar. Its insulation function actually included refrigeration, preventing heat from entering while exhausting heat from the interior as needed, operating on the same strange power source as all the Baldy tech. Which was why they couldn't bring the stuff they'd captured: the Baldies would have known they were there the moment they pushed through the time-gate.

Ashe said, "So what did you women find, besides a base for observation?"

Linnea opened her hand in a little gesture toward Eveleen, who said, "A house, seems to be empty, with some kind of mental repulsion field or subsonics. No other sign."

Ross frowned. "Could be a trap. To see who pokes around."

Eveleen nodded once. "I thought of that while we were waiting for you. In any case, we only checked it once, and didn't go back."

Ashe said, "Why don't we investigate the buildings around it, then, and see what we find?" He nodded at Linnea. "Eveleen can take one of the suits and my gear and help Ross up on the mountain."

Ross knew what that meant: a long, dreary day of trudging up, searching for vents, and checking them, in case the mysterious device had been put into another vent. Having Eveleen come along was his way of acknowledging a spectacularly dangerous and tiring day's work.

"Oh, thanks," Eveleen said, and the others chuckled. She turned Linnea's way. "At least one of us will get a thrill, eh?"

"Oh, it seems to me that there might be potential thrills enough in exploring volcanic vents," Linnea said, smiling. "But I confess: to see the spectacular frescoes inside those buildings still standing when the paintings are still relatively fresh and new, and not crumbled and age-ruined, would be a joy I'd never forget."

Ashe nodded and then turned to Stavros. "Any suspicious activity to report on the waterfront?"

"No sign of Baldies—no attempted attacks, overt or covert. The fishermen are upset about the numbers of dead fish," Stavros said. "The water temperature is several degrees higher than it ought to be, which would be devastating for many types of fish. It's apparently worse closer to the pre–Kameni Island."

The pre–Kameni Island did not even exist up the time-line. Ross mentally examined the map of the island complex: Kalliste and its appendages looked, to him, like nothing so much as a blob of dough floating in the middle of a donut with a bite out of it. The mountain up behind them was, of course, only a small part of the biggest, crescent-shaped island on which they now stood. The caldera would be about eighty miles in diameter; its center—the dough blob—was, according to the scientists' models, the island that Ross could see lying north of them. This little island, which would be blasted into nothingness during the Big Blow, had been termed *pre-Kameni* by the scientists.

Ross remembered watching it earlier, through field glasses, from one of the western cliffs. They could just make out buildings there, most of them ruins, with some little boats plying round it. Squatters there, too, but very few of them.

Kosta said, in his heavy accent, "The people are worried that the oracle does not speak. The harvest is worse than anyone remembers, the quakes worse, the biggest one three months ago sending up serpents of fire-spewing smoke and bringing down a rain of pumice. Abruptly the quakes have eased since then, but the smoke is worse. Fish dead. They are afraid the gods are angry and won't talk to them through their oracle anymore."

Ashe looked over at Linnea. "Can we become a new oracle, as a last resort, to save lives? There are far too many people here. I do not want to see them incinerated without at least trying to get them to flee."

She shook her head. "You cannot just 'be' a new oracle, not here where there is only one, and that one sanctioned by the local governing body. Perhaps we could come down the mountain wailing about the oracle speaking at last and trust to the grapevine to spread the news."

"Will they listen?" Ross asked, skeptical.

Linnea's considering gaze turned his way. "They have no reason not to believe. The question involves community, though. People might want to question more closely who we are."

"That's right," Ashe said. "We are known as Egyptian traders, but we still are not identified with any kinship group. I don't know if that will suffice to get them to evacuate their homes."

Ross said with grim humor, "Right. There is no Red Cross waiting to help them, no friendly government wanting to aid refugees."

Ashe turned back to Linnea. "You or Eveleen might have to try to get inside the oracle caves, if the priestesses will talk to you."

"Better than the alternative," Ross muttered, but under his breath.

"Let's keep that as a backup plan, then," Ashe said, and no one disagreed.

They finished eating dinner, and as everyone was tired, their heads slightly aching from the oppressive heat and the polluted air, the men camped out on the deck of the ship under the stars, and Eveleen and Linnea used oil-soaked torches to light their way back to their rented room, Eveleen sleeping near the open window, where the slightest sound would waken her instantly.

JUST BEFORE DAWN the women hiked back down to the boat.

"The way I see it," Ross said to Eveleen a couple hours later, as they trudged up the long switchback trail toward the oracle, "is that it was too easy. A vent right around the corner from the oracle? We should have seen that as a setup."

Eveleen said, "What I'm afraid of is that they have put some kind of thingie in a whole slew of vents. What the heck do we do then?"

"Gordon said the same thing when we were thumping our way back down the mountain yesterday, nearly quaking off the trail once or twice."

"Then he thinks it probable." Eveleen heaved a sharp sigh and paused at a turning in the trail. She looked out at the blue-green ocean, deceptively placid in the hazy early morning light. "Vents. Does that mean—"

"Already thought of it," Ross said, grinning. "While you were in the sweatbox, Gordon told Stav to do some diving and exploring. The boys are taking the boat out to pre–Kameni Island today to do just that."

Sweatbox: their unfond name for the tiny shower cubicle the scientists had built into the stern of the boat. Ross thought of that cramped space—the banged elbows and knees as he tried to manipulate the spray hose and the lukewarm water—and laid himself a hundred-buck bet none of the science jockeys back home actually had test-driven the blasted thing.

"Here's the goat trail we marked yesterday," Ross said. "We may's well start here."

The two of them checked the pathway in both directions and then quickly eased off down the narrow little trail. There was very little brush behind which to hide. They would have to trust to the haze and to their neutral clothing—Eveleen had forgone her bright kilt-skirt and jacket-underdress for a plain robe of dusty brown—to avoid notice.

Ross squinted against the fierce glare of the sun, looking for the thin thread of smoke he'd seen wisping out of the mountain in this direction. These things could be deceptive, depending on air currents and wind.

Up, up, pausing for sips of water in the sparse shade of smoke-withered olive trees. Eveleen bent once to touch one of the lovely red lilies. Ross grimaced, thinking of the report he'd seen three thousand years up-time: these plants were totally wiped out. Some life-forms came back. The red lilies didn't.

They came upon the vent suddenly, feeling it first as an oven blast of sulfuric air.

After consultation with Ashe and Linnea over breakfast, they had agreed no longer to use the Baldy-tech device. They would scan with their own equipment, which used only pulses of sonic energy and heavy-duty computing power to filter out the returns from seismic noise. There was a lot of that on Kalliste, unfortunately, the upside being that their little pings were unlikely to be detected by the Baldies amidst the stew of heat, sonics, and piezo-EM emitted by the volcano.

Ross held his breath against the hot gases, knowing he should slip on his breathing mask. But the tests ought to take only a moment, and it didn't smell as bad as it had the other day. Then he remembered the basic vulcanology training all the agents had gotten: *By the time you stop smelling it, it's already too late. Hydrogen sulfide is fifty times more poisonous than hydrogen cyanide, and far more insidious. It just takes one sudden puff from a vent.*

He put on his mask and motioned Eveleen to do the same. Theoretically, if there was another of those devices, the sonics would reveal it, and since it had to be manipulating the ferocious energy output of the vents in some way, the strains and currents that it produced in rocks and lava would help disclose its shape.

They each took a reading, looked, but were not really sure what they had. There were patterns, but nothing suggested an actual object. Ross motioned to Eveleen and she held up her instrument to reveal the IR port. Ross triggered the link, and the two machines compared and manipulated the stored sonic patterns. Now a shadowy shape emerged, too regular to be natural. But the devices still couldn't nail down its distance or size well enough. "Well, now we know that they didn't move it."

"Why can't the detectors resolve it better?"

"Maybe there's too much seismic noise and it's turned off, or maybe it's still running cloaked but emitting sonics as part of its operation. That would scramble things. Let's find another and give the computers more to compare," Ross suggested. "Maybe then they can zero in on it."

"Right."

First to locate another vent.

"There." Eveleen knocked against his arm and pointed upward, almost straight into the sun, which was burning down through thick haze just behind the mountaintop.

"Oh, hell," Ross snarled.

"Yeah, looks like my idea of it, too," his wife retorted.

Ross cracked a smile, and they got busy toiling upward along tiny goat trails, often slipping and sliding in fresh rockfalls. They removed their masks once they were a good distance from the vent; it was a hot, exceedingly dangerous climb, made worse by the weather.

They stopped at noon to eat their bread and cheese and rest in the shade of a spectacular slab of volcanic rock thrusting up from some age-old eruption.

Out over the ocean a thin line of thunderheads marched, their outline ragged. The sea was a sick green, the sunny glare at its worst, glinting off bits of rock. Far below they could see a steady procession of folk making their way slowly up the pathway to the oracle.

"Why would people do that to themselves?" Ross said, shaking his head.

"Why do people in our day read weather reports, or even check the astrology predictions in the paper, much as they laugh?"

"Eveleen, it's too hot to even pretend that's the same as gambling their lives against whatever this 'oracle' might say."

"But I think it's the same impulse. We don't like going into the unknown. So we use whatever tools we have. The weather reports generally work. The astrology predictions speak so generally you can always translate them to match your experience. And these people—" She waved her hand up the trail. "Well, who knows? Linnea told me that one theory holds that the priestesses who served the oracle had the best gossip network going and knew everything about everyone. I guess you could do that with a small population. Remember, even modern market research relies on something called the Delphi effect—you can get information out of large groups of people even if none of them know the actual, exact answer."

Ross raised an eyebrow, but Eveleen's face was serious. Well, there were a lot of things he'd never heard of; evidently the Delphi effect was one of them. He sighed. "It makes sense if people are asking whether or not they should marry some person with a rotten rep, or even about crops and other information based on collective experience and knowledge, but what about this couple we saw yesterday, with a sick kid? They wanted to know if the wasting fever would go away."

Eveleen rested her hands on her knees. "Of course they couldn't really answer something like that, but they probably told the people to make a flower offering to the gods, which at least would give them comfort."

"Some comfort."

"About as much comfort as 'We shall have to do more tests,' gives parents in our time, when their kid has some disease the medical field can't identify."

Ross wiped sweat off his forehead. "Hah."

Eveleen grinned. "You're just grumpy because it's hot, and there's thunder in the air, and no enemy to shoot at."

"Add in a mountain-size nuclear bomb under our feet or, knowing the Baldies, something even worse, ready to blow at any moment, and you've got that right."

Somehow that seemed the right moment to get to their feet, stash their flagons at their waists, and get moving.

The climb was long, hot, and increasingly steep. Rock slides were common, making the ground unstable. Tiny tremors sent pebbles skittering down the mountain, bouncing crazily. They both were stung on hands and faces by tiny bits of rock.

They worked their way steadily upward, the trail carrying them northward over the spectacular cliffs and great, violent upthrusts of rock, until they were able to get glimpses of the northern segment of the crescent-shaped island, with the doomed little pre–Kameni Island hazily lying to the west. Smoke rose slowly from distant vents, adding to the brownish-gray pall.

Conversation became impossible. The thick air was made thicker by sulfurous stenches. They realized at about the same time that their increasingly intense headaches were not caused by the heat and slipped on their breathing masks, which indicated that they were being exposed to dangerous gases, hydrogen sulfide foremost among them. And though no one was around to see them, they still followed orders, both swathing their heads and lower faces with lengths of rough cloth to hide the masks.

Their headaches faded away slowly as the breathing masks removed the dangerous gases from the air. The relief gave them both energy, and they picked up their pace again. As they climbed toward what appeared to be the summit, the thunderheads sailed inexorably toward them, lightning occasionally flashing down to stab the sea.

They were high enough now to look directly down into the clear, blue-green water. Now they could see some of the underwater vents releasing vapors that heated the water within the ring: these were discolored silver-green in some places, and in one or two an ominous rusty-tinged green, like an old bruise. Above the sea hung strange palls of dust and smoke tinged with a sinister orange.

Ross nodded, and Eveleen took out her palm-sized video cam, sweeping the scene with care. "I wish I could see Akrotiri from here," she murmured.

"Maybe higher up," Ross said. "Though the distance will make it look like a toy city."

Eveleen nodded, tucking the cam securely into her belt-pouch. "Let's go."

They trudged up the last distance to what had to be a gigantic vent. Ross, ceaselessly watching for signs of Baldies standing guard, kept his hand near his side, where he wore a weapon. Memories of his hand burning, of helping Ashe cross-country with a bullet wound in his shoulder, made him wary.

At last they reached the vent.

Whose instinct reacted first?

Before he saw anything except swirling smoke and vapor, Ross knew there was someone in that vent. Eveleen let out a startled exclamation about the same moment he palmed his weapon and aimed it, flicking the safety off.

A figure slowly emerged, hands out-held.

They waited, not speaking, as the figure resolved in a humanoid form.

But the Baldy Ross expected failed to materialize. Instead, he stared at a being he'd only glimpsed once before, years ago on his very first run, at a station buried in ice: A triangular face, sharply pointed chin, angled jaw, small mouth, hooked nose. Dark skin covered with long, silky down, crest over the head, and below that two round eyes. Intelligent eyes.

The being slowly brought a furry hand to its chest and squawked in its high voice, using a language full of trills and clicks.

Moments later passable Greek emerged.

"You must come within, for I do not wish to cause you damage."

A small device glinted at them from the other hand and Ross realized it was some kind of weapon.

CHAPTER 9

"YOU NEVER MARRIED?" It was early—Eveleen and Ross were just past the oracle. The place was mostly empty but for the fallen greater buildings of Akrotiri, built haphazardly all along an axis, with the small rooms furnished with benches and bins and cubicles of stone.

Men did not have access to the buildings identified with the priestesses, only those that were made for general use or for men's concerns. Religion here was an integral as well as natural part of everyday life, as one could tell from the rise and fall of voices in song, the processions, the stylized clothing of various members of the religious callings. Women's rooms were not open to men, and Linnea went there alone, leaving Ashe to investigate those belonging to men only.

She had just emerged from one, wherein some local women were singing a lilting song as they decorated a young girl with flowers and a bright kilt, and last clasped a necklace of stylized serpents around her neck. On the walls was the famous fresco of the ladies, the flowers bright and fresh, the perspective breathtakingly graceful. A golden glow from oil lamps made the colors seem real.

Linnea had had to blink away tears. She had known what to expect, yet still she had not been really prepared for the effect of such free, bright, and generous beauty, and the corresponding claw of loss.

So she put her question about marriage to Ashe when she emerged, and he glanced at her, looking amused, and said, "No."

Just that word seemed bald, ungracious. She knew she had trespassed, even though she had taken care to use the Ancient Greek, not just to protect them, though no one paid them the least attention, but because its wording was necessarily quaint and distant from their habitual English, and so it created its own borders of finesse.

Then he added, as though he realized that he had sounded ungracious, "Though it was not an easy choice. But it seemed the best one. My absences would put a burden on a family."

She nodded. She had a brother in the military, and she knew what his wife had suffered when he would be gone one year, two, often without any communication. For twenty years she had spent holidays alone with their children, and birthdays, except for last-minute surprises; he had almost missed their daughter's wedding.

"You did not think to marry within the Project?"

"In the very early days there were few women. And I am, unfortunately, a member of the last generation. A wife with me would take my mind from the work to her, to protecting her. Though I know it's not fair, or right. But instinct is hard to argue with."

Linnea nodded. "Ross and Eveleen have managed."

"Many of the younger agents have paired off successfully, though not all the marriages last. They did not find it easy to adjust. Though they are much alike, and I believe they have an excellent chance of going the distance."

"Adventurers," Linnea said, the noun she chose calling to mind Homer and his tales.

They had emerged from one building and had tried another, but it was all fallen in, destroyed so badly that no one had even excavated the rubble yet. Either that or it had fallen relatively recently.

On to the next one, much smaller, roofed with woven mats. They peered in windows, watching people come and go. Though they could not examine every room, at least they could watch for anomalies.

The noon sun beat down, the air breathlessly hot, drifting with faint ash-fall. One of the tremors froze everyone for a moment into a tableau, a still life backlit by garish sun, while hissings of little stones sifted down from cracks in the walls.

Then songs rose again, donkeys brayed, children laughed, adults' voices exclaimed in question, concern, annoyance, worry, with many glances skyward up the mountain.

Linnea had just looked over to say something when the communicator Ashe wore next to his skin pulsed just once.

It was from the boat.

"An attack?" she spoke without thinking, but at least she'd used Ancient Greek.

He said nothing, of course, but nodded his head upward when they reached one of the narrow intersections. They toiled up a steep street, with a cliff to one side, looking down at roofs, some with withered gardens. Behind them were more buildings. As he left it to Linnea to peer in the windows and go into what buildings she could, he found a tiny join where one wall did not quite meet another, shaded by a very straggly wild palm. Trusting to its protection, Ashe raised to his eyes a slim pair of field glasses, shading them by his palm.

Linnea, seeing what he was about, backed out of his field of vision, instead watching the occasional passerby to draw attention away from Ashe if necessary.

She waited until his hand lowered.

"Baldies on the beach," he murmured.

Linnea felt her heart lurch.

They eased into a crowd moving down toward the shoreline, where the early morning fishers were just arriving in with fresh catch.

Linnea peered up along the sand, which seemed to shimmer in the heat. A thunderstorm was on the way, she realized, though judging from the faint, acid-tangy breeze and the slowness of those clouds, it would not arrive until sundown.

Ashe drew in a breath. He stepped aside from the street into an angle of the low wall that guarded the street from the sheer fall to the next level below. He leaned over, looking down, concealing his actions as he raised the glasses again, mostly covering them with his palm so it looked as if he were shading his eyes.

"I should have expected that," he murmured. "Right out in sight. Of course. People will see what they expect to see."

Silently he handed Linnea his glasses, and she copied his movement, covering them with her palm to shade her eyes as she scanned.

The shoreline seemed curiously flattened, colors muted. But there, not far from their anchorage (was that chance?), where the road from the city to the harbor passed close to the shore, there stood a group of slender hairless humanoids, all dressed alike in rich, glimmering fabric that changed from blue to green to purple depending on how the wearer moved.

The Kallistans walking past looked at them but did not linger or approach them. It was as though an invisible line were inscribed in the sand around them.

"I wonder if they have the same effect going as at that apparently abandoned building?" said Linnea in a bare whisper. "But what are they doing?"

For much of the time the Baldies did nothing, standing in silence, watching, as people streamed by. But occasionally, more often when the crowds moving between the city and the harbor were thickest, one of their number would step forward and stop a group of people. As they watched, the alien stopped a pair of young men.

The men looked up at the Baldy, their body language, even flattened by the distance, eloquent of fear and respect. The Baldy spoke, gestured; the men nodded and replied, then hurried away at a dismissive motion by the alien. The other Baldies paid no attention to the exchange, instead watching intently the people all around.

"They're looking for us."

"Or, if not us, anomalies among the people walking about?"

"They must know we won't expose ourselves in any way that the locals would notice," Ashe murmured, as around them, people exclaimed in worry about the poor catch and fishermen in approaching boats tried to gather crowds to them by calling out what was in their nets.

"How will we eat if the fish all die?" a woman exclaimed in Ancient Greek.

"No, they're probably not so much interested in the answers they get from people as in their reactions and those of the people around them," Ashe murmured. "We're not really clear on the capabilities and limitations of their suits, but I wouldn't be surprised if they could detect our subliminal awareness of who they are, the way we focus on them in a way different from the locals, who just think they're priests from some strange country."

Linnea nodded. That would certainly be true of an entrepôt like Kalliste, where people were used to strangers and wont to assume that any out-of-the-ordinary behavior could be ascribed to foreignness.

The women around them, waiting for the fishermen to unload their nets on the sand and spread out the fish, paid the two of them no attention.

"I think we are being punished," an older woman said.

"For what?" exclaimed the first. "I am a good wife; my husband is a good artisan; my children sing to the gods."

"But I think we'd have to be a lot closer," Ashe continued. "The Baldies cannot really control minds, or send messages, unless you wear their fabric, which has some sort of communication built in," Ashe murmured. "But they can certainly influence people, probably the more so when they're grouped together, as now. I'm sure there're some advanced statistics that guide the way they search. After all, time is on their side, no matter what they intend."

"It is the gods who fight one another," a third woman said, pointing up at the mountain.

"If they cast fiery stones at one another, it is we who are struck," said the first woman in a sour voice.

The older woman laughed. "It is always thus, in war."

Linnea sighed, cramping her fingers together in her robe. "What do we do?"

"Watch, wait, and keep a respectful distance."

ASHE AND LINNEA spent most of the afternoon on or near the last set of stairs before the beach, watching. The Baldies remained where they were, somewhat down the road on the seaside, waiting with inhuman patience for the trace of an anachronistic mind.

Ashe watched them. Though he'd had many encounters with them over the years, this was the first sustained observation he had ever been able to make.

Linnea was quiet, obviously watching the volcano, the city, listening to the people, as Ashe walked and watched by turns. Late afternoon, after another of those long tremors, they followed a small boy herding baby goats up onto the rocky low hills adjacent to Akrotiri. The recent rains had brought up tufts of tough, brown-edged grasses through the ash and pumice drifts. The goats did not appear to like this grass and kept frolicking with one another as they sought green farther along.

Thus they passed up beyond the waiting Baldies, below on the shoreline, and then to the other side.

At last, as the oncoming clouds began to block the sinking sun, Linnea said, "They must think we are stupid."

Ashe shrugged. "Stupid? Ignorant is more like it. Remember, they know we have interfered with them, but they believe it is by accident. And they do not know where or when the humans who have opposed them come from. So as yet they have not interfered with us in our own time; we have managed to keep the time-lines safe."

Linnea frowned. Beyond her shoulder, over the edge of the headland, the sun was a crimson ball of fire underlighting the sky with spectacular, faintly sinister color. "So they think we're like the monkey with the typewriter, then?"

"I think so. We've worked hard to keep it that way. And to keep our encounters here in the past, where we originally found them."

"How strange, that beings who appear to be from the far future would be consistently discovered mucking about in the past."

"A mystery I've almost given up solving. It's enough to fend them off, to keep them from destroying us by tampering with the past," Ashe said. "Although, of course, that might be enough reason. Sort of flattering, really."

"What do you mean?"

"Well, maybe we're too strong, up in the future, and the only way they can attack us is in the past. But that begs the question: why attack us in the first place?"

Linnea shaded her eyes against the slanting ruddy glow of sunset, peering out through the forest of prows and masts of the incoming boats. "Do you suppose we'll ever know?"

Ashe shrugged.

Linnea sighed. "It was fortunate that Stav and Kosta went out hunting vents."

"I don't think the Baldies can find our boat, as long as they don't see anything to cause them to attack and investigate more closely," Ashe said.

Did he sound as doubtful as he felt?

"Our lab rats at home shielded the equipment fairly well in that boat; I doubt there's enough EM escaping to bring down alarms."

"Not over what must be emitting from there," Linnea said, looking up at the volcano.

"True—"

Ashe's words died when he saw the Baldies go tense and alert, their faces raised. Though no apparent signal was received, as one they set out at a fast pace, uphill, directly north.

Ashe thought of the attack on their camp, then looked at small Linnea, who had not had the time to get any sort of defense training. "Go on to your room and watch. Brief the others when they turn up," he said tersely. "I'm going to try to find the Baldies' base."

She did not argue. "Good luck."

LINNEA HURRIED BACK toward the city gates by the lurid red light still glowing in the west. She still had plenty of lapis lazuli, but she did not want to waste one on a smelly, scarcely functional torch.

She was not the only person running to beat the oncoming darkness. Akrotiri at night glowed with dim but welcoming golden light, tiny pinpricks from uncounted lamps. She passed through the gates and ran the short way across the first market area toward her house.

By the light of the lamps many were still lingering over business; the day's heat was now just a stuffy sort of warmth and far more bearable. Linnea paused to trade for some grapes, more because she delighted in speaking with the people than for any other reason, and then bought a big bucket of water.

The bucket pulled at her shoulder joints, making her feel hotter than ever, and some sploshed out until she got the right rhythm for walking with it. Never again, she vowed, would she take for granted the infinite blessing of running water.

Of course some of the buildings had their own running water, even now, despite the quake destruction. She could hear and even smell it, a faintly sulfuric odor coming from an underground hot spring, but she had none in her little room.

And so she withdrew to it, and by the light of a swinging lamp coming weakly through the window opposite, she gave in to—oh, don't just call it temptation. The smell, the itchiness, of her underclothes had become so repulsive that washing them was now the first priority of her life.

She undressed under her robe, keeping well into the shadows of her room, though no one glanced in as people walked by. All the windows were open, and on the still, warm night air she could hear voices. She purified the water first, then drank. After that she washed her face and hands, and then her body as well as she could without completely undressing. And then she scrubbed her underthings. Since she had no soap, she scrubbed and rescrubbed until her hands felt red and tender, and the cloth smelled just like damp cloth. But where to put them?

She took the bucket out and splashed it into the gutter that ran downhill along the outer edge of the street. The bucket was to be returned in the morning. Until then, it was hers.

She draped the underclothes over the bucket, set it in the corner, and then lay down on the woven straw pallet that Eveleen had bought for them the night before. The dampness of her robe cooled her enough so that the very faint breeze felt pleasant.

Cooking smells wafted in, and the sounds of voices, so few now each was distinct: low laughter from across the way, a fretful child, a couple having an argument, all the more fierce for being whispered.

In the distance, far away, some voices began singing a song, the melody strange and yet curiously familiar, too. It pulled at the heart: a lament?

Linnea drifted into sleep.

When she woke, it was to the awareness of movement, of breathing. She looked up in dismay and amazement. Four women had crowded into her room, one of them being the bucket's owner.

One, a young woman in the tight jacket and flounced skirt of the prosperous, held up her camisole and underwear—the good cotton, machine-stitched underwear, and the fine cotton-silk camisole—and shook it at Linnea. She then made a demand in a language that was only vaguely familiar.

CHAPTER 10

LINNEA STARED UP at the women, her brain at first refusing to work. Was she dreaming? No, her neck was gritty, her mouth dry, and she realized she knew this language; the woman had spoken in Egyptian.

And now the women all looked at her with expressions ranging from curious to wary.

Wary.

What was it Gordon had said? *There is no record of a woman speaking a foreign tongue, surprising people with things that never have been.*

The woman frowned a little, then said again in her rough, stilted Egyptian, "Where got you these?"

Linnea thought rapidly, but another of the women forestalled her, saying in better Egyptian, "Why do you not trade this? You and the young one brought that old cloth from Kemt to trade, but our young girls make better." She turned her chin over her shoulder, making a spitting motion.

Curiosity was swiftly turning into hostility. *I am the stranger here,* Linnea thought, and she cleared her throat. "I wish we had such cloth to sell," she said. "Oh, how I have searched."

The women listened, the one's hostility easing slightly. "You tell us, then, that this is the only such things you have?"

"Yes," Linnea responded. "They were brought back for me by my man, from the Land of the Dragon, far, far in the direction of the morning sun."

"Ah," said the older women, all nodding.

"I have heard of that place," said the one with the jacket. "Some of the sailors have spoken of it. And the fine things that come from there, rare and precious. Precious enough for only the great families to trade precious artifacts of gold or very fine pearls."

Linnea, following instinct, said, "It is really for younger women, these fine things. You may have them, if you like."

The one with the jacket gaped in surprise and then pleasure. The youngest one gasped, running her fingers with reverence along the seams. "How tiny the threads are, how even. They must have looms the size of a cricket!"

"It is far too great a gift," said the older woman, and the one with the jacket flushed. "What can we offer you as a trade?"

In other words, why are you really here?

Linnea licked her lips, and because instinct had gotten her this far, she said tentatively, "I have come with my family to trade, but I myself have . . . questions . . . for your oracle. I know the priestesses where I live, and they said that I should consult over the seas," she added randomly.

The three older women nodded again, one with pursed lips. The youngest was still marveling over the machine stitching, holding the cloth only an inch or two from her eyes. Her big golden hoop earrings swung against her cheeks as she studied the seams.

"Ah yes, our oracle is renowned for her communion with the goddess; this we know. But we have troubled times, you can see," the oldest said, pointing toward the sky.

"I could ask about that, too," Linnea ventured, greatly daring.

"We do ask. Many ask each day, but there has been no answer."

"Perhaps it is for the far-sailing Kemtiu to break the silence?" asked the one with the jacket.

"Perhaps," agreed the oldest. And she made a gesture of decision. "I shall send you to the priestesses. My sister's girl is with them. Her name is Ela. Tell her that Theti sent you. She will gain you entrance on the mountain."

"That is a fair trade, is it not?" asked the one with the jacket.

There was no mistaking her anxious look. Linnea nodded. "I think it very fair."

The one with the jacket then plucked the garments from the younger woman, and vanished with a triumphant smile and a flounce of triply layered skirts.

Linnea was left to find her way to the communal toilets, under which ran a stream. She went straight out, bought some fresh flatbread and cheese, and then started up the mountain to find Ela, and the oracle.

AT THE SAME time, Ross and Eveleen woke up, surrounded by complete darkness.

Ross fought the instinct to panic and forced himself to lie still, to mentally review.

He remembered reaching the summit. Remembered the great vent and Eveleen taking pictures of the inner waters, before stashing her camera back in her clothing. He remembered turning around, and there was the Fur Face.

It used some kind of translator to gabble some idiocy about not damaging them while holding a weapon pointed their way.

So they'd gone within, into the heat and dangerous fumes. A smoothed passage then, made by very high-tech means, after which they were motioned into this chamber and the door shut, cutting off all light.

Eveleen had not reacted at all, other than to hold his hand. He'd squeezed her hand in warning, and she'd squeezed back: *I know what to do.*

What to do? Locking people up in a room to wait was a standard scare tactic, meant to soften up prisoners, make them really sweat about their fate. Darkness made it worse. What's more: if there were two, they were only left together in hopes that someone, unseen, would get to overhear talk.

So they'd stayed silent, after a time stretching out on the stone floor and catching up on their rest.

Now Ross was awake, and from the sound of her changed breathing, Eveleen was as well. He groped about and found her hand. He spelled into her palm, *See or hear anything?*

Not a thing. It feels like morning.

I think so, too. I'll bet we'll see action soon.

He didn't want to speculate what kind.

WHILE ROSS AND Eveleen waited, and Linnea Edel slowly trudged up the mountain path, on the northern shore of the peninsula that formed one end of their island-crescent, Gordon Ashe woke up, bleary-eyed and headachy.

He looked around. No sign of the Baldies—of course.

Damn.

Down in a little gully to his left he saw some goats drinking from a small stream. He swallowed convulsively. The stream appeared to be bubbling up from underground, which meant it was probably sanitary. He had certainly risked worse during his many runs; he did have massive antibiotic doses back at the ship, but meantime his canteen was empty, and he had to get some water. He worked his way down the rocky incline. The goats scattered, the older ones scolding him with an insistent *"Na-ha-ha-ha!"*

The water tasted faintly metallic. It had to be rich in minerals, but there was no dangerous flatness as of rotting matter or other pollutants. He drank his fill, and then sat down to think.

He'd followed the Baldies at a respectable distance, not knowing how far their supposed detection might range. But they had not once looked back as they sped in a group northward over the hills. Ashe had followed, using all his years of experience at outdoor trail-craft to stay silent and out of sight but still keep them within his vision. Yet even so, just as the moon rose, he lost them.

He could hardly be blamed. He been edging along a crumbling section of the trail, the Baldies just ahead around a turn, when a sudden quake sent the trail underfoot hurtling down toward the dry creek bed far below.

The next ninety or so nearly vertical feet were like surfing on dirt; Ashe frantically pedaled his feet, keeping himself on top of the swirling dirt and rocks as the mass slid ever faster downward. He was successful until just a couple of feet from the bottom, when a larger rock banged into the back of his knee and sent him sprawling. The impact knocked the breath out of him; he grayed out for a moment. The agent was dimly aware of more rocks hitting him, then silence broken only by random slippages of pebbles.

When he scrambled back to the trail, he hurried forward, limping, finally catching a glimpse of the Baldies far ahead. But only once. He soon was forced to conclude that he'd lost them. The trail was hard and stony there, and he could find no footprints.

By the light of the low-hanging moon he had grimly worked his way from that spot in ever widening circles, but not a trail, or cave, or door did he find. So he'd finally laid himself down on a grassy little hillock to sleep.

Now that it was daylight, he was determined to do another search, and if he did not find any suspicious anomalies like indications of spaceship burn, evidence of vehicle tracks, or flattened vegetation in the case of something air cushioned, he'd be forced to give up and return to the ship empty-handed.

He got to his feet, pulled the stale remains of his flatbread from the leather pouch at his waist, and chewed as he started his search.

IT DID NOT surprise Eveleen that Ross's instincts were right.

With a hiss of muted hydraulics a crack of light appeared, rapidly widening into a doorway. Ross and Eveleen blinked, trying to adjust to the light. She put her hands up to her face, discovered her breathing mask. Panic! With a few more exchanges spelled out on each other's palms, they'd decided to stick to their covers. They hastily adjusted the cloth covering their faces and heads, so only their eyes showed and the breathing masks stayed hidden.

She cast a look Ross's way, and he gave his head a tiny shake.

The doorway darkened. One of the Fur Faces appeared, gesturing for them to come out. Another was in view behind. They slowly rose to their feet. Eveleen watched Ross look around as though totally mesmerized. His gaze, she saw with a bleak spurt of amusement, lingered on how the door retracted into the rock and the mechanism that controlled it.

Out they walked. The two Fur Faces closed in behind them, tall, dressed in shapeless robes, each carrying something short and tubular in a clawed, double-jointed hand. Another Fur Face stepped in front of them, blocking off what had to be some kind of computer console, an egg of shimmering metal and misty bars of light, shapes that trembled in constant motion.

She and Ross were guided into another room, this one light, with another partially blocked off console. The Fur Faces prodded them not ungently back toward the wall and then lined up behind the console.

A Fur Face did something; they could not see what from their angle. The machine hummed, then spoke in a metallic, flat voice: "Who are you, and what seek you on the mountain?" The language was Ancient Greek.

Ross cleared his throat. "We are Timos and Hesti, and we came in search of our missing goat."

One of the Fur Faces spoke softly into what had to be their equivalent of a pin mike. This time the question came out in what sounded very much like Ancient Egyptian.

Eveleen felt a flare of danger. So the Fur Faces did not believe their pose? Would they rip off the breathing masks, then? The virtual overlay in her mask indicated that the chamber was filled with dangerous levels of hydrogen sulfides—natural to volcanoes and also, apparently, to Fur Faces.

They stayed silent, and a moment later, the machine spoke again, in a guttural language that sounded vaguely like Ancient Norse. Then once more, this time in some prehistoric form of Goth or Visigoth.

Eveleen did her best to seem bewildered, though inside she felt a spurt of relief. Even if the Fur Faces did not believe that they were bona fide Kallistans, at least they appeared to believe that she and Ross were from the ancient world.

Her relief was short-lived. The next language to emerge from that machine was Classical Latin. And then the machine proceeded through a remarkable, no, an intimidating number of languages, Eastern and Western, right up until modern times. When it spat out the same question in English—*Who are you? Why are you here?*—and then in German, French, Russian, Japanese, and Chinese, Eveleen had time to consider the fact that modern times were not, as they had comfortably surmised, unknown to these aliens.

After that the machine went on to speak in strange amalgams of what might be English and other languages. Eveleen thought that these would be a linguist's joy to hear, but they were so much gibberish to her, familiar yet not.

She'd just finished that thought when the Fur Face halted the stream of questions.

Silence, as the Fur Face fumbled at the console.

Eveleen was distracted by a warning pressure on her hand, which Ross still held. He pinched her little finger, tugging it to the right.

The right?

She looked up, just as the Fur Face's machine said, again in Ancient Greek, "There are two tongues here that make your blood-organ speed its rate of pumping—"

And before it could identify English, Ross drew in a sharp breath. That was the only warning Eveleen had. As Ross launched himself to the left, she whirled to the right, launching a high kick, a snap to the Fur Face's narrow jaw. As it staggered off balance she gave it a knuckle blow to what would be the solar plexus on a human, and the being crumpled soundlessly to the stone floor. She bent, relieved that she had judged right: the Fur Face was still breathing.

Ross's groaned, but then subsided into unconsciousness.

Eveleen held her hands up, waiting for the other two to attack, and then stared: they stood, impassive, their sight focused on the wall where the two Time Agents had been standing.

Then it dawned on her. "Holographs?" she whispered.

He nodded, raised a finger to his lips.

Of course. The machine had to be recording whatever was said.

They both sprang to the console, which was of course totally incomprehensible. Ross scanned it and then began pressing pads and lights, and when the machine responded with flickers and streams of glyphs, he pressed more pads and lights, then stepped back and delivered a vicious chopping kick down onto the console. There was a musical jangling from within the egg, and several indicators changed color or went dark. Ross kept at it, obviously hoping to at least confuse things.

Then they moved to the door. Eveleen reached for the control mechanism; the door slid open, and they were in the outer room. No one around.

She chanced a word. "Weapon?" She used Ancient Greek.

Ross shook his head. "Useless." He answered in the same tongue.

He paused long enough to do the same thing to the console out there, and then they ran to what had to be the outer door. Again it slid open almost silently, and the two ran up the smoky stone vent to the surface.

"Let's get out of here," Ross said, and they plunged down the path.

CHAPTER 11

BY THE TIME Ross and Eveleen reached the harbor, the day was ending. Four rolling quakes and a brief, fierce thunderstorm full of stinging acid rain had slowed them, but at last they arrived just as the boat sailed up and dropped anchor.

Ross looked around and saw Gordon Ashe coming down the hard-packed trail from Akrotiri.

"Looks like we all had the same idea," Gordon greeted Ross.

"I wish we didn't have to stick with radio silence," Ross said.

Gordon gave his head a shake.

Before he could speak, Ross said, "I know; I know. Baldies could listen in, and identify our time-frame as well as where we are. But you didn't know this. The Baldies are not our only problem."

And, as Stavros and Kosta came up to join them, Ross gave a swift report on his and Eveleen's experiences inside the volcano.

The others listened in tense silence.

Ross finished, ". . . I watched the Fur Faces while the language test was going on and realized that two of them were damn still for supposedly live beings. Only two of them reacted. Then I watched those weapons, or what we thought were weapons. No firing stud or trigger or anything made me wonder if they were just pointing a handy piece of tech at us, their equivalent of a camera or something, and letting us provide the imaginary firepower. So when they started to tell us that our heart rates had given us away, I figured it was time for do or die. Signaled to Eveleen, and we jumped them."

Ashe turned Eveleen's way. She obviously interpreted his look before Ross could, and said, "We left them unconscious."

"We also did our best to mess up their computer setup, which looked field-rigged; then we hightailed out."

"Holographs," Ashe said, looking grim. "I didn't think of that. And I thought the trail they were leaving was a little thin."

Everyone looked at him.

Ashe sighed, and said, "Linnea and I spent most of yesterday watching a group of Baldies standing right out in the open, occasionally interrogating people. That is, only a couple of them did; the rest just watched. When they suddenly took off, I followed them. A quake knocked me over a bit of a cliff, and when I was able to follow, they had gotten too far ahead, and I lost them. But I realize now their trail didn't look right, so maybe some of them were holos and I ended up following a bunch of phantoms."

"*Moving* holos?" Ross asked, scratching his itchy scalp.

Ashe shrugged a shoulder. "Considering the sophisticated level of the rest of their tech, it's entirely possible. A moving projector should be easy enough, if they have a strong enough power source."

Eveleen said soberly, "If you're right, it would indicate that they don't have huge numbers. Not if they have to go to the trouble of falsifying their head count."

"Exactly," Ashe said. "Might even the odds a bit."

"You think they knew you were following them?" asked Eveleen.

"No." He shook his head. "They would have tried to capture me; even with holos they had me outnumbered. I think it was standard procedure to throw off anyone following them. I'll bet they can hide behind holos of the surroundings as well—a perfect way to hide the opening to their base."

"So we can't find it that way."

"Probably not, and anyone poking around that far out from the city would automatically alert them."

"They'll be back," Ross said. "After all, what they're trying to do is flush us out."

"At least, so we guess," Stavros put in. "So far, we ascribe human motivations and reactions to them."

"Oh, they've been human enough in some of their reactions in the past," Ross stated in a grim voice. "Those boys don't play nice, not at all."

"No, they don't," Ashe said. "But we still do not know what game they are playing. Not really."

"My question," Kosta said, wiping back dark curly hair from his brow, "is, are these *Younoprosopoi* their allies, or enemies?"

"A good question, one I'd like an answer to myself," Ashe said.

Eveleen smiled. "I like that. *'Younoprosopoi.'* Is that Modern Greek? It sounds a little like our present Kallistan Greek."

Kosta flashed a grin. "Means 'Fur Faces.' "

Ross said, "Since I was until now the only one who'd ever seen one of these guys, and that was during an attack that we decided later was some sort of triple cross involving the Russians, the Baldies, and at least one Fur Face, what they're doing here is anybody's guess."

"Then let's continue to gather facts. Stav, Kosta. What did you find over at the pre–Kameni Island?"

"Evidence of at least six of those devices, all buried very deeply."

"Did you mark them?"

"We have got markers floating over each," Kosta said.

"Good. Then tomorrow we need to find out if they are in the nearer vents."

"More area to cover," Stav said.

"Start today, then. Take all night."

"I'll go with them," Eveleen offered. "I haven't been on a dive for, oh, a whole six months. I hate to get out of practice."

"An excellent idea." Ashe smiled a little.

Then he turned to Ross, who said first, "You thinking what I'm thinking?"

Ashe shrugged. "I think it's time for some desperate measures. I do not condone undue violence, but perhaps our *Younoprosopoi* friends will not resist our invitation for a little talk."

Stav looked a little confused.

Eveleen said, "Where is Linnea?"

"I was just looking for her," Ashe said. "Before I spotted you coming down the trail and hiked down to meet you here. Answer: I don't know. She was not at that little room you two rented."

"Invitation?" Stav murmured, still looking confused. "Invitation? Is this an idiom with which I am not familiar?"

"No," Eveleen said, casting him a distracted look. "Linnea must be off investigating something," she said. "I can go check, just in case. Maybe one of those women there saw her."

"A good idea," Ashe said, still studying the volcano under its pall of smoke, as if he could see a small figure toiling up and down the trail. "In case whatever she's on the track of requires backup."

"What is this 'invitation'?" Stav asked Ross.

Ross sent a tight grin Ashe's way and then said to the Greek agent, "We're going to do a little alien-napping."

CHAPTER 12

LINNEA HEARD THE singing first.

She emerged onto the cliff outside the oracle's cave, tired and sweaty, to the faint smell of sulfur and the sound of young girls' voices.

The voices rose and fell in a strange chant. It wasn't music, not to a modern, Western-trained ear, but nor was it totally dissonant.

Mesmerizing, Linnea thought, already mentally writing her monograph . . . except where could she publish it? Project Star was totally secret. She then realized something she had, so far, avoided looking at: that Gordon Ashe, with his fine mind and eternal curiosity, had never published anything. Yet how many fabulous secrets of the human past had he seen?

What does he do? Linnea thought as she crossed the cliff and stood with the little cluster of waiting people. Does he plant clues so that other archaeologists can find them the customary way? Or does he live with the knowledge of treasures of knowledge permanently suppressed?

Or is the word *permanently* an arrogant assumption? One thing for certain, he had long ago accepted that fame would not be his. (Never mind fortune. Archaeologists don't get rich, even if they are lucky enough to uncover vast quantities of gold and precious gems in rich tombs; governments then thud in with their heavy feet, waving official papers right and left, leaving archaeologists with little but their dwindling stipend and the hopes that they can get credit for their find.)

So, if a trained mind like his had given up the idea of fame, what was the payoff? The satisfaction of a job well done?

That sounds noble but not quite human, Linnea thought, smiling.

A teenage girl dressed in a brightly colored robe, with a golden necklace of stylized serpents, looked up into Linnea's face. She said something—asked a question.

Linnea suppressed the urge to write down the girl's speech and compare it to Greek as the girl then restated in careful Ancient Greek, "Your quest?"

"I seek Ela," Linnea said in the same Ancient Greek, trying to match accents. "Theti sent me."

"Sent you? Why?"

"I met her in Akrotiri," Linnea explained, and then she offered the cover she'd invented on the long walk uphill. "I am a priestess of the Earth Goddess, only from Kemt. I was sent by the goddess to witness here."

And the girl took it without a blink. "You must come within," she said, gesturing. "We are still finishing the purification, so—" She touched a forefinger to her lips and led the way past the waiting petitioners, who watched with patient attitudes, and curious eyes.

Linnea followed, feeling morally queasy at how easily her lie had been believed. She had always assumed that those who lived around oracles made their living by listening to gossip. Did they really accept directives from outside, just on the word of someone claiming to be sent by their deity?

At least I intend no harm, Linnea thought. *I will do nothing but observe and learn what I may. And my mission is to save these people from a really horrible fate.*

The smell of sulfur intensified as they eased past a great crack between two massive rocks. Short as she was, Linnea had to duck and walk sideways for several yards, until cool air suddenly ruffled against her face and they emerged into a wide cavern with a sudden drop at the left. Linnea did not have to look down to see the rushing water. Above the stream, far above, was another great crack. A shaft of faint golden light, widening slowly, filtered in.

A circle of young girls, all in brightly colored robes with red jackets edged with blue, walked with deliberate step in a circle round what looked like an ancient tree stump, their arms upraised, fingers brought to a point like a beak—or like the head of a serpent, Linnea realized, as she watched the sinuous, dancelike swayings and pouncings of those young arms and hands.

Linnea transferred her gaze to the center of the circle. Had a tree really once grown here? Well, there was light, and below ran water. All that was needed was some bird to drop a seed while flying over that crack.

As the thin shaft of light crept closer to the great tree, Linnea perceived movement in the shadows at the other end of the cave, beyond the circle of the girls and the tree.

Ching! Ching! A girl clashed little copper cymbals, and the chant began again. Between the young bodies, swaying in unison as the girls' voices rose, faintly echoing, Linnea glimpsed a shadowy form all in red.

Two steps, three, and the form resolved into a woman, an older woman, spare of build, her sparse hair bound up in a golden serpent-fillet like those of the girls, her eyes dark and surrounded by wrinkles.

Two older women assisted her. When she neared the circle the young girls did not break their step, only amended it, creating a gap, through which the old woman came on alone.

She approached the great tree stump and climbed up onto it. Linnea couldn't quite see the cut portion, as it was about five feet from the rocky floor, but there seemed to be a seat carved in it, for the priestess sat, just as a thin finger of sunlight touched her hair, lighting the gray to molten silver and shrouding her face in shadow.

The girls finished their chant on a triumphant note and filed back down the narrow crevasse through which Linnea had come. Moments later the sound of the voices floated back: now, apparently, the purification ritual included the petitioners outside.

The priestess sat in her tree-stump throne, breathing slowly, her eyes closed, her hands lying palms up and open on her knees.

Presently a woman walked in, looking about a little fearfully. Her eyes lifted to the great shaft of light, which now fully illuminated the priestess on the throne.

Good theater, Linnea thought, but the skin along her outer arms felt rough.

"Mother Goddess," the woman said in Ancient Greek, as she mounted the gnarled tree roots and joined the seer on the stump. "O Mother Goddess, why do the crops fail, and the sky fill with smoke, and the ground growl at us like a beast hunting prey? What can we do?"

The priestess did not answer. Her eyes stayed closed. A soft hissing sound emerged from the cone of brilliant sunlight, and Linnea realized it was the seer's breathing. Those breaths were long, each slightly louder than the one before, a hiss that sounded very like a snake.

A snake. Just as Linnea identified the sound, the seer straightened up. She seemed to grow, to expand a little, as she lifted her face up toward the sunlight. Still the hissed breathing, in and out, and Linnea became aware of the older priestesses standing along the perimeter of the chamber breathing in the same slow rhythm.

Then, slowly, the seer began to sway, reminding Linnea of the snakelike swayings of the girls during the purification chants. Her head turned from side to side, almost like a blinded snake looking, seeking, reaching. Listening.

Linnea, realizing that, felt prickles again, but she caught herself up, thinking, *This is just theater. It's good theater—the very best—but it's all showmanship.*

Still, it was three-thousand-year-old showmanship, and as such, it was very well worth watching. And she forced herself to divert from the hindbrain's awe by counting up the elements, one by one, that made the whole seem so unnervingly . . . *real*.

The far-off girls' voices, chanting in a mesmerizing pattern; the light; the great aged tree stump that had grown so unlikely in this cavern; the rushing water; even the faint whiffs of sulfur. And then the old seer's rhythmic writhing: despite her evident age, she moved now, graceful and supple as one of those young acolytes out front.

At last she spoke, in a voice that startled Linnea. It was a guttural voice, harsh, loud, and because it was in the local language (or was it?) she could not understand a word.

But the petitioner appeared to understand, for she bowed her head, and her tense shoulders slumped.

A priestess moved forward to help her down, and she walked out slowly, her face drawn and worried.

Linnea turned to the nearest priestess, who saw her movement and touched her fingertips to her lips.

One by one the rest of the petitioners came in, and again and again the seer breathed that hissing breath and writhed, her eyes wide open but blind-looking. Again she cried out something in that guttural voice that clawed at Linnea's viscera, and the petitioners departed in silence, not one of them looking happy with the answers that they got.

There were seven of them. If others waited outside, they had been dismissed. The sun had moved, in the meantime, and the golden shaft now left the seer on her throne and painted the rocky floor instead. The seer, in shadow, seemed to shrink in on herself, and without any words spoken two sturdy middle-aged priestesses moved to the sides of the great tree to help her down.

Her eyes were open, but she seemed to be blind. Her hands, once graceful, now fumbled, looking frail and aged.

The priestesses all moved around the empty tree and followed the seer into that back area. Linnea hesitated, and then joined them, moving tentatively, but no one shooed her away or otherwise paid attention to her.

They each ducked under a triangular archway made by two slabs of pumice cracked and shifted apart by unimaginable forces, and Linnea found herself in a back chamber. It was stuffy here; there was no sky-crack to let in air. Reflected light from the tree chamber was dim, re-vealing rugs on the ground.

The seer was gently helped onto one of these. Everyone stood in silence as she stretched out, breathing slowly again, but without that awful hiss.

After a time she stirred, made a motion to sit, and again two priest-esses sprang to help her, their movements tender with unspoken love and respect.

Someone brought in a little oil lamp and set it down before the seer. Its tiny tongue of flame painted golden color on a worn face that now looked sweet, grandmotherly, and very, very weary.

"Thirst," she murmured—in Ancient Greek.

Someone brought her a cup of water, probably from the stream. Someone else brought dried fish and crumbled goat cheese, and a tiny bunch of withered grapes.

The seer munched her way through these foods with no apparent enjoyment. Her brow was slightly puckered, as if she had a massive headache, and she chewed and swallowed as one performing a duty.

At last the food was gone, and all of the water. She sighed, and one of the women gently massaged her temples.

No one spoke, not until one of the girls came in and said, "Maestra, they are all gone."

The woman who had brought the water turned her head. "Thank you, child. Tell the others they are free to eat their meal."

Others among the priestesses stirred now, some passing out fava-seed bread, cheese, grapes. The priestesses talked in low murmurs as the seer had her head rubbed, her eyes closed now. She was surrounded by quiet now, as before she'd been surrounded by that fierce shaft of bright sunlight, the more fierce, Linnea realized, because of all the par-ticulate matter in the air. The sun here before the volcano began smok-ing and rumbling must have been pure and clear, as clear as the ocean waters.

At last the seer looked up. Her question was the last thing Linnea expected: "What did I say?"

And the chief priestess shook her head sadly. "Nothing. The spirits are still silent."

CHAPTER 13

"UP THIS WAY," Ross said, pointing.

He paused, gazing up the mountain path. A wisp of smoke haze drifted by, borne on the strengthening breeze. The smoke seemed to leech all the color out of the sparse hillside, rendering it unfamiliar, almost alien.

"Or was it?"

"Can you orient on the peninsula?" Ashe asked, after a time.

Ross felt a hot zap of annoyance at his own stupidity. Yes, the smoke had given him a fairly nasty headache, making it difficult to think, but Ashe probably had one as well.

Ross turned around, staring down through the haze toward the peninsula that stretched westward from below Akrotiri. The pre–Kameni Island was barely visible through the murk of smoke and steam, but one thing he could see was the purple clouds headed their way. Even if he hadn't felt fitful puffs of cooler, moisture-laden air pushing through the hot, humid haze, he would have sensed a major storm on the way. From the tightness at the base of his skull, the way the hairs on his arms prickled, it was a storm that carried a full load of artillery in the form of lightning and hail.

"We're going to have to find cover," he said to Ashe.

The man shrugged. "Let's get as high as we can. Maybe dive into some crevasse if we don't find your vent first."

Ross nodded once, ignoring the corresponding pang in his head, and turned around again. He remembered orienting himself several times on that previous journey. "Yes. That way," he said, pointing up to the left. They trudged on.

THE STORM CAME on with energetic rapidity.

Eveleen and Kosta dropped over the side of the boat away from the coast, so that no one who happened to have field glasses, or the alien equivalent, would see their scuba gear. Stav had erected a tent onboard, which was common enough, especially when the weather was as fierce as it was now.

They unclipped the sled from the hull of the boat and hung on as the small but powerful electric motor pulled them away and down. A strong sense of relief shot through Eveleen as they moved steadily downward. The wind had been getting up, and the water had formed little whitecaps; though they couldn't see beyond the mountain blocking the northern sky, Stav had said with Greek stoicism, "Storm on the way. I'll batten down once you two get under the surface."

Out this far from any others they could speak English, which was a relief. Though the Greek agents still called the mysterious Fur Faces *Younoprosopoi,* and they also called the Baldies *Falakri,* or *Exoyinii.* Eveleen found these nicknames more elegant, even though the first one simply meant "bald ones" and the second "aliens." The sobriquet "Baldies" for the hairless aliens of the future sounded kind of silly, but it had stuck over decades. *Rather like the way we still call Native Americans "Indians,"* Eveleen thought as she swam downward, laughing inside. *Which probably thoroughly confuses any aliens who spy in our time.*

The light changed abruptly. They'd reached the level where shafts shifted and changed, but suddenly they faded and vanished. Eveleen flipped over, holding on to the sled with one hand, and saw the remarkable effect of hail and rain pockmarking the surface. It was a beautiful sight, but she forced herself to turn back. *Some day,* she resolved, *if we get back all right, I will have time to watch a storm from below.*

Next to her Kosta turned on his forehead lamp and started surveying the depths in its beam.

Eveleen turned hers on as well and then pulled out the device that Ashe had given her. They couldn't use sonics for this search; there was too much area to be covered and the returns were confused by the water. Ashe's device wasn't much better, but it worked underwater. About all it could do was detect the presence of alien tech within a range of twenty yards; as one might expect when dealing with a technology far beyond most theories contemporary scientists could come up with, it could tell little more. But after much research, and the invention of a different way of looking at quantum mechanics, the brain boys had realized that the power source for Baldie tech involved some sort of temporal distortion, and some smart lab jockey had figured a way to use a piece of the Baldies' own tech to home in on its brethren via that signature. Unfortunately, it was active detection, so they were announcing themselves to the Baldies by using it. But that couldn't be helped. At least they knew where they were—and maybe their actions were causing the devices to be turned off. That was enough, for now.

She and Kosta reached the cliffs supporting the island. Dramatic striations of rock and great upthrusts of ancient pumice testified to the terrific volcanic activity of the past millions of years.

She flicked her device on and held it out. A faint signal responded, pretty much the same signal the men had gotten on their first preliminary cruise.

Now to get a vector on position.

Kosta took the sled—he was far more practiced in its use, and it was difficult to steer when it was going slowly. Eveleen swam away from him until they were just in sight of each other. She checked the detector: still a good signal, if weak.

She turned Kosta's way and saw him gesture toward his device, confirming that he, too, still had a signal.

By hand signals they divided up the immediate terrain, and Kosta dove down to explore parallel to Eveleen. They would continue to do so until their air ran low, occasionally syncing the machines for a pattern comparison that, they hoped, would locate any Baldie tech.

Curious fish swam slowly by as they proceeded along the silent rock face with its dotting of colorful plants. Eveleen looked at those plants with their astonishing variety of waving fronds, tentacles, and cilia, and frowned, thinking of what was going to happen to them all before long. These were the plants that scientists would eventually find fossilized by burning lava three thousand years up the line.

She shook her head. Plenty of time to brood later.

A faint flash of purple caused her to roll over. Another flash of purple beyond the surface, which was otherwise quite dark, gave evidence of a truly violent storm going on.

Eveleen turned back to work. They proceeded along the rock face for an hour, Kosta zooming over to her every fifteen minutes to link the devices, just to discover that the detectors still couldn't localize the signal. Strange. Eveleen watched her device. Either it was defective or it was insufficiently sensitive.

A faint signal without locale . . . could that mean bits of low-end tech all over? Or was it the opposite? A great concentration of alien tech, but at a remove?

A little while longer, and she started checking her tank every ten minutes. About four checks later, Kosta maneuvered the sled up to her, indicating that this was the place they were to go up. He had the compass, and they'd planned out the exploration with Stav in the boat.

They arrowed up. Eveleen was relieved to see that the color of the sky was once again blue, that the surface was visible.

Her relief was short-lived.

When they popped up and removed their masks, Stav and the boat were nowhere in sight.

LINNEA WATCHED THE water shaft down through the crack in the ceiling as the priestesses went about their business. The girls, given permission, danced about in the waterfall, cooling themselves off. They giggled and splashed water on one another, so much like girls of modern times—like Linnea's own daughter had at that age. The sight smote her heart. *We have to save them,* she thought. And again, *Why am I here?*

So far, she had found out exactly nothing.

The storm had come on fast. As the seer sat in silent meditation, the women finished their meal and set about cleaning up the few remains.

Now some of them took off their robes and washed them in the waterfall from the rain, then stepped into the water. Judging from their reaction, it was cool but not miserable. They gasped, but with delight.

Linnea, itchy, gritty, gave in to impulse. She couldn't bring herself to disrobe completely. Old conditioning was too strong for that. But she could get herself and her robe soaked, and at least wash away most of the sweaty grime.

The women, unconcerned, chattered around her. Linnea turned her face up into the water, which had run long enough to be free of silt. As the refreshing coolness pounded down onto her, she gasped, and then as the aggravating itchy heat dissipated, replaced by a sense of cool cleanliness, her mind ranged freely, and she thought about the day.

It was no longer fair to even think "theater," she had decided. These women were not pulling a scam, however other oracles and cults had worked in other times and places. They sincerely believed in what they were doing; there was no reason to behave the way they did otherwise. They were also obviously not stupid people. In their paradigm, what they believed made sense.

How to speak to them so that she would not disturb their worldview but convince them to listen, perhaps to evacuate?

For a brief time she considered faking her own "seeing," but she thought of the perceptive gaze of that old woman sitting so motionlessly in the stifling inner room, and shook her head. She might not be hearing her "spirits" now, but she'd know a phony when she saw one.

Linnea realized her fingers and toes were slowly growing numb and she stepped out of the waterfall, which was now tapering off in intensity. The storm was passing.

When Linnea was dry again, several of the girls, who had been whispering off to one side, approached her. Some looked timid, others frankly curious.

"Please, tell us about faraway Kemt?" one asked.

"What must the girls do there to become priestesses?" asked a second.

A third, blushing and giggling, said, "Are they permitted to talk to young men?"

The first two gasped and shushed her.

Ela stepped up then, before Linnea could scrape her memory for some likely details of Ancient Egypt. She looked from Linnea to the girls and said, in a kind but firm voice, "Is this the way we treat a guest?"

The girls looked abashed.

"You must permit our visitor to speak of her home and customs in her own time."

The girls murmured, one in disappointment, the rest in apology.

"The people will be gone," said one of the older priestesses, coming to join the group. "We will have some sunlight left in which to dry your things. Take them outside."

The girls vanished toward the plateau, and Linnea walked around the tree-throne, touching the ancient, gnarled wood lightly with her fingers.

A little while later, the girls came trooping back in, chattering, some fussing with their hair, others smoothing sun-dried robes.

The light was fading, Linnea realized. She had tried to form up facts in a logical manner, but the truth was she was here on instinct.

Well, she had wool-gathered too long, unproductive as it had been. The sun was fast vanishing, and she did not want to find herself in total darkness on that narrow path down the mountain, especially after such a rain. She could slip and fall and no one would know.

"Come." Ela was there, smiling. "It is time for the evening meal, and our thanksgiving."

The girls had gathered and began another of their chants as fava breads were passed around, and dried fish that had been cooked in olives, and cheese and dates. Others lit the little oil lamps, which cast a weak but cozy golden glow.

All the women chanted, their voices, old and young, musical and unmusical, blending pleasingly. When they were done the seer began to eat, which was the signal for the others to begin their meal. The younger girls all withdrew to a far corner, whispering in the manner of young adolescent girls the world over. Occasional giggles escaped, skipping back in light echoes.

After she ate, Linnea found a comfortable place in which to sit and observe.

Across the cave two women set up a loom, and Linnea watched the rhythmic motions of their hands. It was oddly soothing; though the light was poor, a faint gold that rendered the scene almost dreamlike, the women were obviously so accustomed to their work that their fingers knew what to do while their eyes gazed, distant, at the little lamps, or the two conversed in soft voices.

Three of the younger girls picked up big fans plaited out of some fibrous plant and waved them, forcing the hot, stuffy air to circulate. Presently a touch of cool breeze, smelling of water, caressed Linnea's damp face.

Her eyelids drifted down, and since no one seemed to object, she stretched out on one of the cloth pads and slept.

ROSS AND ASHE found a cave just before the hail struck with such force it cracked little rocks from the cliffside and sent them tumbling down the mountain into an unseen gully below. Lightning struck all over the mountaintop as the storm roared and thundered.

Finally there was the hiss of rain, and both stepped out to cool themselves off and to drink. The rain was so heavy Ross only had to stand there with his eyes shut and his mouth open, and swallow and swallow.

The storm departed as swiftly as it had come, leaving the pathway up dangerously slippery. Here and there mudslides had peeled away at the path. With a sickening lurch Ross felt his foot start to slide, and leaped back just in time; a portion of the pathway crumbled, sloughing down a sheer cliff face.

Neither man spoke. They stuck closer to the mountain and kept toiling upward, until the light had faded in the west and it was too dangerous to continue.

They found some shelter under a rock overhang, squatted down in the mud, and tried their best to sleep.

Ross was in a vile mood when he woke. He itched all over, and the sight of steam rising gently off the mud outside their overhang promised a day even hotter than the one before.

They toiled up a little farther and presently decided they'd better put on their breathing masks.

They did, feeling much better immediately. They set out at a more energetic pace or at least began to set out.

Ross froze when he saw the tall figure standing near a familiar outcropping of rock, a patient stance, as if the being had long been waiting and watching.

"You seek me?" it said, in English.

CHAPTER 14

ROSS HAD JUST enough presence of mind not to answer.

A long pause ensued, during which no one moved, or spoke, and then the being said in Ancient Greek, "You seek me?"

Ross turned to Gordon in question: do we take this guy prisoner or not? And Gordon looked back, brows raised.

The alien's hands were empty. The other one of its kind was nowhere in sight.

"Let's talk," Ross said, indicating slightly higher ground. Neutral ground, away from caves full of mysterious tech.

In answer the being walked round smoke-withered shrubs, rocks crunching underfoot. Ross, feeling uneasy, followed that long robe with its dusty hem, and Gordon fell in behind him.

For a short time the alien looked out over the vista. Smoke and haze diffused the horizon, but Ross, scanning fast, made out smoke plumes issuing from the mountain maybe a mile or two to the north and a twin plume lazily rising from the pre–Kameni Island out in the great lagoon. The island was just barely a silhouette in the yellow-tinged murk.

"Who are you?" Ross demanded.

Gordon half-raised a hand, and Ross clamped his mouth shut, folding his arms across his chest. *Shut up,* he thought. *They've already half-guessed what time we really come from. Don't hand them any more clues.*

The alien's speech was tenor and softly sibilant, almost whistling; though the face and body were vaguely humanoid, its palate sounded like it was constructed differently.

"Call uss Kayu."

Gordon replied, "Why are you here?"

"We are here to halt our old enemiess, if we can. We are now two only. Time," the Kayu added, as a hot, stinging breeze ruffled through its silky hair, "iss dessperate and short."

HIDDEN BY BANKS of fog, the ship bounced through greenish waves. Eveleen leaned against the side, feeling the wind on her face. She listened, with her eyes closed, to the rapid conversation in Modern Greek between Kosta and Stavros coming from belowdecks.

She was glad to be passive for a time. She and Kosta had been forced to spend the night on a little patch of shore, no food, no water, dressed in their wetsuits. Cold had not been the problem, but heat and thirst; they'd resorted to swimming just to get rid of body heat, but of course they couldn't drink the water that surrounded them.

But just after dawn they'd seen the ship emerge from drifting smoke-tinged fog, and by the time they'd swum out, fastened the sled to the underside of the hull, and climbed aboard, Stavros had hot food and coffee waiting.

Finally she heard Kosta's step, and she looked up. He swiped his curly hair back, squinting against the furious glare of the sun, and then he sneezed violently.

"Smoke is worse," he said as Stavros appeared behind him.

Unanswerable. Eveleen just nodded.

"Stav was blown out through the opening to sea during the storm, as we thought. He used the motor to come back in to retrieve us, and stayed close to the cliffs below the main island in order to stay unseen. Very close, or he would not have found it."

Stavros's lips thinned in a smile of triumph, and Eveleen felt her own heart give a jolt.

"So Stavros located a signal?"

"Yes. A strong one, too. It should be almost right underneath the city, along the cliff faces below it."

"We're on our way to investigate now, or ought we to return?"

Kosta turned to Stavros, who rubbed the heels of his hands over his eyes. He'd obviously been up all night, keeping the bow of the ship pointed into the storm so that it wouldn't broach to and sink.

"Let us see now," Stavros said, his accent heavier, his voice raspy. "It is close. The marker might shift if another storm comes."

Kosta grinned. "Get your gear back on," Kosta said, rubbing his hands. "By the time we're ready, Stavo will get us there."

Eveleen set down her empty mug and reached for her mask.

LINNEA WOKE TO the sweet sounds of the girls singing.

Another day. It was time for the long purification ritual. All around her, women rose, shook themselves out, and busied themselves with the little tasks, both sacred and homely, that measured out their lives.

I will stay for one more session, Linnea thought. *And then I'll return to Akrotiri and tell them I failed.*

She was thirsty; her stomach growled; her head ached. There seemed to be smoke in the air.

She shut her eyes and turned her attention to the rise and fall of the chanting voices.

ON THE OTHER side of the great mountain, the Kayu said to Ross and Gordon, "It iss long sstory. I musst breathe. We go?"

Gordon looked Ross's way, leaving the decision to him. Ross remembered the underground cave. It could be that the two Fur Faces had prepared some kind of trap, but why?

No, to get data they were willing to take risks. The particular risk required now was just different than expected.

Ross looked around at the barren rock, the sky full of smoky haze, and just then another tremor rumbled deep underground, sending birds skyward and cascades of small stones clattering down the hillside. Dust rose, hanging suspended in the air.

Ross squinted against the sunlight, watching two swallows fly down into a haze-hidden valley, forked tails streaming after.

"Let's go," he murmured.

Gordon nodded.

The Kayu led the way.

EVELEEN DROPPED BELOW the surface of the water. It was a relief to get her eyes out of the stinging, smoke-laden air. She looked around, expecting the underwater world to snap into focus, blue and clear. But it, too, was turbid, the lighting a faintly sinister brownish green.

Eveleen looked around past waving fronds and tight schools of tiny fishes running with what seemed to her frantic haste. The fish turned about, flicked, and darted downward at an oblique angle.

She looked up and saw not the sky but a brownish layer. She realized that she'd gotten used to the haze, but it was gradually getting worse.

Kosta tapped her on the shoulder, caught her attention. She turned his way, nodded, and held on as he triggered the sled.

Stavros had been quite firm about the location. He had repeated that the signal was very strong, the device might even be stuck right on the surface of the rock.

Waving sea life indicated turbulent currents; here and there eyes peered out between fronds. The underwater world was so very strange, like another planet, she thought, looking around. Even one's sense of time altered.

But anxiety still remained: that sense of impending disaster, of events about to overtake them. *Get busy and search,* she scolded herself. *Explore later.*

She faced downward, her hand hovering over her forehead, when the sled's steady progress slowed, then stopped. Had he found it already? They both flicked on their lights. And then gazed in surprise.

No device: what they'd found was a great cavern. Kosta swept a hand toward it, an ironic *Shall we?*

In answer Eveleen let go of the sled and swam forward, scanning methodically as she drifted. Kosta joined her; they anchored the sled, and with a few short gestures they divided the territory.

It didn't help that they had no idea what they were looking for. Large? Small? Camouflaged? Out in the open? Eveleen had expected to see something sticking out, some sort of futuristic tech nestled among the weird plants and mossy rocks, right in the open. Stavros had said that the signal was strong, and that meant they had to be right near whatever it was.

But although the variety of rocks, fish, and plants was both rich and amazing, nothing futuristic or tech-made was in sight.

Kosta's entire body was expressive of frustration. He gave one great kick and lunged back to the mouth of the cavern, and then he began feeling over the rock.

Eveleen floated up to the other side and did the same, looking past her bubbles. She had to be careful. There were several kinds of coral, brilliant in color, but sharp and deadly; she did not need a cut in her gloves.

They felt over the rock, and she bent close and examined some of the weirder sea plants. They all looked real enough, but if the aliens were clever enough, she might be fooled. She wasn't any kind of an expert on undersea life, especially in the Mediterranean.

Slowly they worked their way inward, and after a time gave up the tactile exploration. Kosta dove down to sift through the fine sand at the bottom of the cavern. Eveleen kept looking at the vast dark hole. Just how deep was this cave, anyway?

She was strongly tempted to go exploring but forced herself to join Kosta and work over the seafloor.

They'd kicked up quite a bit of sand when Kosta finally sat back, his hands clenched into fists.

Eveleen gestured toward the inner part of the cave. He shrugged: *Why not?* It took him only minutes to cross back to the opening of the cavern and return with the sled.

So they pushed off, relieved to be doing something, at least. Eveleen could feel the coarser hum of the sled's engine, now at its lowest speed.

The lancing blue and yellow sunbeams from the surface very swiftly vanished. They could still see the cave mouth behind them, but light did not penetrate far. Eveleen reached over and turned up the intensity on the sled's headlamp, then turned her own down a bit; her battery power was now reading just above half. She knew there was an emergency supply, but she didn't want to have to rely on that if they had to do another search by feel.

The cave bent suddenly and angled up. Strange. Was the rock smoother?

She turned to Kosta at the same moment he faced her, and pointed. There were no sea plants here, just smooth rock. It was a slab. Could it have been made by a great shifting of land, a quake?

They proceeded at a slow pace, Eveleen watching to her side and Kosta to his, with the sled illumining the way ahead to give maximum visibility.

On and on, and then another sharp turn. The sled banged against the rock as Kosta maneuvered it around.

And then they stopped, staring.

The cave widened; there, settled on the seafloor, rested one of the great globe ships.

CHAPTER 15

DOWN IN THE cave with the machinery, the two Kayu faced the Time Agents. One of them manipulated the computer, or whatever that egg thing was. Ross noted sourly that if his attempt to crash it had been successful, there was no sign of it.

One of the Fur Faces signed something to the other, adding a low comment in its clicking, trilling language, and then from the machine came a voice—in English.

"Our previous study indicates that you respond to this tongue."

Neither man moved.

"We use it in preference to the style of Greek the traders bring here because the vocabulary is easier to adapt to what must be discussed. But first we must reveal to you the fact that we have been waiting for you to appear, that everything is in readiness; it remains for you to make the decision what must occur next."

Who can resist an opening like that?

Ross knew that if he were alone, he'd ride with the wave and see what happened, but he deferred to Ashe, the more senior agent—and the one who made fewer mistakes.

Ashe looked up at Ross, his head canted in question.

If you're asking me, Ross thought, *I say let's go for it.*

Besides, trying to interrogate someone in a language he understood as superficially as he did Ancient Greek was no picnic.

Ashe said, in English, "Proceed."

The Kayu responded with a swift exchange in their own tongue. Though it's usually a mistake to ascribe human emotions to nonhumans, Ross suspected they were excited. And why not? It wasn't just a matter of guessing the right language. These furry guys now had a vector on not just where but when Ross and Ashe had really come from.

"There are devices in place at crucial locations in the volcanic caldera," the machine-translation went on, in a perfectly enunciated, dispassionate tone.

"These devices are not ours but belong to the ****—" The machine failed to translate here, instead giving a name in a humming sort of language. "That is their name for themselves; we call them the !!!."

This time the machine provided some trills and whistles.

Ross, giving in to impulse, said, "If you mean the guys in the blue suits, we call 'em Baldies."

"Baldies." The machine repeated the word in English and then in the clicking tongue, and the two Kayu looked at each other, one of them making asthmatic noises that might have been laughter.

The other touched a control and trilled something.

The machine said, "It is a most appropriate term, for it differentiates between us, does it not?"

A little alien humor there? Ross thought.

He said, feeling weirder by the second, "You definitely aren't bald. And neither am I," he added. "So what's the story on these devices?"

If humor there had been, it was now gone. "They are . . . even your language does not have the precise concepts, although your physicists could describe them mathematically. Call them . . . 'entropy adjusters,' and you will be close enough."

"Entropy adjusters," Ross repeated, resisting the impulse to wipe his sweaty palms down the sides of his fake-hide skirt.

"Yes," the Kayu stated through the machine. "In effect they transform the energy of the rising magma into a massive gravitational knot rather than allowing it to build up as heat. The effect has been to cool the magma, thus preventing the explosion."

Ross stared, his heart slamming behind his ribs. They were too late? Was the world, now set on a pastoral path of low tech, doomed to Baldy conquest up-time? Then he thought of the found earring . . . of Eveleen down somewhere in the city . . . and felt momentary relief, until he realized that if the Baldies managed to change history, Eveleen would never even have existed, and he snapped, "You mean the magma has already cooled off too much?"

"No, there is still time, but we are approaching a point of no return. To complete the process, the devices must discharge the energy harmlessly, in one burst of temporal distortion. That is what brought us here; it is detectable across many centuries."

Something tickled at the back of Ross's mind, but before he could grasp it the other alien trilled something. The first one hesitated.

"My companion would note that this distortion, which affects suitably sensitive minds across a wide span of time, may account for the prevalence of prophecy on your world; I would merely add that this is but one way . . . you might say *Nemesis* . . . speaks to sentient beings."

Ross felt momentarily disoriented by the strangeness of the situation. Here he and Ashe were, standing on top of a volcano that was about to blow up with a force that would make a hydrogen bomb look like a mere special effect, and having a metaphysical discussion with aliens.

The alien continued. "The adjusters are still building toward discharge, and if they are destroyed before they complete the discharge, the energy will be released all at once as heat, creating an explosion equivalent to what would have happened without interference."

Ross whistled under his breath—or started to. Remembering the whistling language spoken by the others, he didn't want to inadvertently be saying something he'd get into trouble for.

So the brain boys at home had been right!

Ashe said, "Why have you not acted to destroy these devices? Or don't you know where they are?"

"We know the location of each," one of the Kayu replied. "But we cannot act. It is not our mandate. We have been here, in place, observing, and waiting until you should appear. 'You' being, in this context, someone of your somewhat mysterious people, who appear and then vanish again after violent encounters."

Well, that about sums us up, Ross thought.

Ashe said, "So our guesses are correct, then, that if this volcano does not go off, then up the time-line our civilization will not have advanced much past what it is now?"

"This is correct."

"Thus rendering it easier for someone, like the Baldies, say, to take over," Ross stated. He didn't say out loud, but mentally he added: *Or you.*

The second Kayu said, "It is a logical surmise, but it is not correct. The !!!—the Furless Ones, as you would say—are committed to maximizing the biodiversity of the galaxy by protecting aboriginal lifeforms."

"Protecting!" Ross's expostulation was almost a snort. "These are the same friendly types who shoot on sight? Don't we count as aboriginal?"

"They protect life, not lives," replied the Kayu. "When they find a space-traveling culture, such as yours is becoming, they locate the original world and search its past for critical points. Then they intervene as necessary to eliminate space flight, so as to contain that life-form and prevent it from contaminating the biosphere of other planets."

"So they are self-constituted galactic ecologists, then?" Ashe asked, brows aslant.

"It is a close enough designation, yes."

Silence.

Ross chewed on that, and Ashe said, "So let's get this straight, then. If we don't mess with their devices, the volcano doesn't blast, things are fine, and we never reach space in our future."

"It is so."

Ross burst out, "But if it hadn't gone off, then we wouldn't exist—and how would you know? For that matter, you said you detected the time explosion, or whatever you would call it, but it hasn't happened yet. And if we decide to destroy the devices, it won't, so how could you detect it?"

The two Kayu held a discussion that intensified into trills, with gestures and quick exchanges. Ross glanced over at Ashe to see him frowning. It was fairly clear that the Kayu, however much they looked alike, did not think alike: one seemed to want to say one thing, and the other something else.

At last one stepped back, permitting the other to address the machine, which stated in its precise English, "This choice you will make creates a major bifurcation in the probability wave that represents your world-line. Two futures so different that it is easy to detect the two states, both of which exist until your decision is carried out. In one, a pastoral planet, little or no EM emissions, the major pollutant being methane from cows; in the other, a technological civilization, heavy EM emissions detectable light years away, with heavy pollution from fossil carbon combustion. Those are but two ways of detecting the two states."

"Schroedinger's cat," said Ashe. "Alive and dead at the same time."

There was a long pause. One of the Kayu did something to the machine, and then both exclaimed softly. Looking up Schroedinger, and his cat? The Kayu trilled, and the machine stated: "Yes, according to your physics texts. You would say, superposition."

"But we've already decided," said Ross. "If we don't stop the explosion, we'll cease to exist—cease to ever have existed. And you still haven't explained how you could detect the time explosion if we prevent it. Or will detect it . . ."

"There are still courses of action open to the Baldies," replied the Kayu. "Only when these are all eliminated—or carried out—will the waveform collapse and seal your reality. At that point, one way or the other, the result will not be reversible. But all our actions will have been part of that reality, including the detection of the superposition that includes the time explosion. That is always pastward from your decision, and thus always exists."

"My head hurts," muttered Ross.

Perhaps the alien heard him. "Your people have not had time travel long enough to develop the language and concepts to deal with it— although there are hints in various of your . . . philosophical texts, one might say, and among some cultures, of the proper approach."

"So what do we do? Destroy the machines?"

"No. Not only would that be almost impossible—they are not entirely material—since their mode of operation is timelike, but even if it were, the consequences would be catastrophic. The uncontrolled release of the energy they contain might unravel space-time itself, unmaking your world and all within it."

Ashe let out his breath in a short, not quite silent curse.

I knew I was going to hate this mission, Ross thought. *Instinct is right every damn time.*

Ashe said slowly, "So, might the Baldies do that, if they get desperate enough, just to make sure we never become technological?"

"They would never do such a thing by deliberate action. They value life too highly."

Ross waved a hand. "So you say. But where does the difference between life and lives lie for them? One, ten, a million?"

The Kayu trilled and clicked in what seemed to be distress, and Ashe turned to Ross. "Hold on a moment; let's just go with them for now." He turned to the Kayu. "So these devices. We can just turn them off?"

"No, that would be equally disastrous. But we can introduce chaotic oscillations in the gravitational knot, which will eventually cause the machines to fail. But you must then prevent the Baldies from relinearizing them for at least . . . seven rotations of the sun, at which point the Baldies cannot use them to abort the volcanic explosion without causing the same type of temporal disaster that destroying them would cause."

"But turning them off will permit the volcano to go off, right?" Ross asked.

"It is so."

Ross thought, *There's a time for talk, a time for thought, and a time for action. When they hired me on, it was because I took action. And so far I've been right.*

He strolled forward and noted how the Kayu retreated a little. So they were afraid of him. Interesting.

"So where are the controls to these devices?"

"The !!! have the controls proper. We know that they have a ship, but its location is unknown to us." The Kayu indicated the two of them. "There were, when we came to this place in your time-line, two more of us. The others we believe had found their ship, but they are no longer in this life." A trill and some dismal-sounding clicks accompanied this statement, which the Kayu did not have the machine translate.

Ross shook his head. "So my question remains: how many lives?"

The first Kayu said something in their language; the second one spoke into the machine.

"You must understand what their history has been," the machine stated.

"All I need to understand right now is, how do we prevent these—adjusters—from operating?" Ross asked.

One of the slim fur-covered hands touched a thing that looked like a cell-phone with a single button extruded from the computer. "But there is very little time."

Ross didn't understand much about superpositions and gravitational theory, but the concept of time running out was definitely in his ballpark. And the Fur Faces had as much as said it would take seven days for the devices to fail.

He looked at Gordon Ashe, who frowned into the middle distance. Well, it was his job to consider all the angles, to negotiate, to compromise, to find the middle ground.

Ross saw action as his own mandate.

And so he reached forward, and before anyone could say anything more, Ross smacked the cell-phone in the middle of those glowing touch pads.

Its light went out.

"All right, then," Ross said, breathing hard in his sweaty mask. "What's next?"

CHAPTER 16

WHEN THE LIGHT shaft reached the gnarled tree-throne, the chanting women brought their ritual to a close, and the seer stepped once again into her seat.

The voices of the girls out on the plateau could be heard rising and falling in pleasing treble tones. This day was almost exactly like the one before; Linnea wondered how the priestesses perceived time, if their experiences blended into an indistinguishable run of days and years.

But she must not be lulled into thinking time did not matter. It did. The smoke burning her eyes and making the back of her throat feel raw was a reminder of that, as were the little tremors that rumbled through the caverns.

Linnea looked up. Was that crack new? Her thoughts scattered when the newest petitioner sat down and spoke in the old language.

Oh, if only Jonathan were here with us, Linnea thought. She could envision the linguist swathed in robes, pretending to be a woman and hiding a recorder so that he could gather precious words to add to the little known about the language still termed Linear A.

The thought of poor Jonathan being a linguistic spy brought a sad sort of smile to Linnea's lips; the reason the agent was not along for this trip was his wife having recently been killed in a car wreck. He was now coping with two small children.

Why couldn't he go ahead in the time machine and then come back?

Or for that matter, could they use the time machine to go back and save her? Linnea wondered, frowning, as the seer began to writhe, her old woman's form taking on the aspect of the holy serpent. What would it harm? What would it change, besides making a family whole and happy again? Could such an action unravel the world's proper course? What, given the horrors of history, constituted "proper"?

"Assssssssah!"

The seer's hiss turned into a long, gargled shout, her eyes wide and blind.

Everyone stopped, eyes turned toward the seer.

Her hands snaked out, waving. In that strange, hoarse, wailing cry she shouted words, repeating some phrases over and over.

The priestesses looked at one another in bewilderment and in fear. Then the oldest one motioned to the others. "Get the girls. Go down the mountain now. Tell everyone that the goddess has spoken at last: the people, all people, are to live now on the blue water, under the blue sky. Now, at once, before the sun sleeps."

The younger priestesses vanished through the crevasse leading to the plateau.

Linnea lingered, puzzled, confused. Another tremor shook the mountain, a gentle one, but a cascade of little stones poured down through the skylight crack, some of them falling on her.

"Go," Ela urged, touching Linnea's arm. "The goddess has spoken to us all. You must go; everyone must go. The fire spirits have been released, and their battle with the earth is to begin. There will be safety only on the water, in the air, away from rock and earth and fire."

What did that mean?

Linnea knew one thing for certain: she must find the rest of her team.

She bundled up her skirts into her arms and scooted between the rock slabs, her awareness of their weight, of the inexorable press of stone against stone and how it could so easily crush her, driving her headlong in urgency—and fear.

THIS THING ISN'T old, Eveleen thought, looking at the globe ship.

At first she'd assumed it was another find, perhaps a crashed ship from farther back in prehistory. But as she flippered closer, examining the smooth glasslike substance that formed the hull, she realized that there were no barnacles on it, no sea life attached. If the material was somehow impervious to the amazing adaptability of sea life, it would be a first.

No, this thing is new, or at least, it's newly here.

It's the Baldy ship, she thought then, looking at it in amazement.

Just then a puff of dust caught her eye and she turned her head.

The sea life glowing along the cavern walls waved wildly, and rocks tumbled with hypnotizing slowness through the water.

Quake! Another of those little ones.

She turned her attention to Kosta, who waved an arm at the ship.

She looked down. Before, it had been difficult to make out anything, but now, suddenly, the interior of the ship lit with a variety of colors, some of them blinking quickly. Alarms?

What it meant was, someone might just be along to deal with it. Someone with weapons.

A touch on her arm made her recoil. Eveleen realized her heartbeat was up, adrenaline racing through her system. Danger! Only where?

Kosta pointed upward. Eveleen looked, and where there had been darkness before, a smooth cylindrical vertical shaft, made of clear glass, touched down to the top of the globe ship. She had missed it before; they both flippered up and felt it, solid, smooth, airtight.

Kosta pointed down into the ship. Around the equator, lights chased, the same blue-white cold light of the transporter mechanisms.

Kosta jerked his head toward the ship, and inside his mask, she saw him grin. It was his pirate grin, and she gasped, realizing what he wanted to do: steal the globe ship!

Why not?

Both of them now turned their attention to the ship. How to get into it without it flooding?

But Kosta had learned something about the alien tech. He sped upward again, feeling along the outer connection between the tube shaft and the globe ship. She saw him straighten out, manipulating something.

Clank! Whirr! Sounds reverberated, weirdly flattened, through the water: under the shaft something slid shut in the ship, and then the tube retracted a foot or so.

Kosta then motioned to Eveleen. He mimed pushing the ship, waved his hand at the sled. *Pushing?*

Well, why not? It wasn't one of the huge deep-space twelve-crew jobs, like the one that had taken them to the faraway library planet, last mission. This one was small, everything right there: a two- or four-seater scout craft, she'd call it. And under water, it was just mass they had to deal with, which merely took patience.

Kosta ran the sled up to within a few feet of the side of the ship and let it sink slowly while he reached into a pouch and pulled out a brick of some plastic material. He began to mold it into a pancake, then slapped it on the nose of the sled and revved its engine to ram it gently into the ship. He began to pulse the engine, slowly. At first the mass resisted: it was as though nothing was happening. But eventually, the globe began to rock ever so slightly, and then more and more as he timed the engine pulses carefully. Finally, with a puff of mud squirting from underneath, the ship moved up into the water!

Then began a strange ultra-slow-motion bat-and-ball game, with the biggest ball Eveleen had ever seen. They maneuvered the globe ship through the cavern, back to the access tunnel.

Getting out was a lot faster than coming in, now that they didn't have to explore every inch of the walls. They sped as fast as they could, pushing the globe ship faster and faster until it finally shot out of the cavern into the water and dropped slowly down to the seafloor below.

What now? A little beeping noise warned her that *now* was the right time to get to the surface: she was on her emergency air.

Kosta pointed upward. Ah, there was the ship.

As Eveleen grabbed hold of the sled she caught sight of the alien-tech device, and saw that it had gone blank. Batteries? Broken?

They refastened the sled to the ship and surfaced. Her mind was full of questions. Beside her, Kosta shoved back his mask and looked up at Stavros.

"We found one of their ships. Moved it to the seafloor below," he gasped.

Stavros was already reaching over the side to hand them up. "I will put a marker down. But something happened here: the target went dead," he said.

They looked at his alien tech–location device. It was just as blank as the one Kosta had carried.

Rumbling from the cliffs not four hundred yards away brought all three of them around. Strange little waves propagated out and high up a section of cliff gave way, causing a landslide. They watched the slab of rock smash into the water, sending seaweed-veined water shooting up.

When the sound had diminished, Kosta said, "Something has happened. We must get back."

Stavros did not wait for an answer—not that Kosta or Eveleen would have argued.

More tremors shook the cliffs as the ship moved back toward the harbor area. Eveleen, looking up at Akrotiri built into the cliffs overhead, like steps, made mental calculations and looked back again.

That underwater cave, the one that had connected the shaft with the globe ship. Could that perhaps lead up to that mysterious little room high up on the edge of the city?

Another question, she thought grimly, but before she could say anything, Kosta exclaimed, "Look!"

Stavros exclaimed something in idiomatic Greek.

They all turned their attention westward. Streams of people moved down the road at a frantic pace, many of them carrying bulky objects on their backs. Eveleen, squinting against the glaring sunlight, counted at least three looms, several rolled rugs, and uncountable jars and reed-mat bundled objects.

"It's an evacuation," she said.

Stavros thumped a fist onto the rail. "We must find Ashe."

And Ross, Eveleen said, but silently.

"We must first defend the boat," Kosta stated with grim portent. "If this is the big evacuation that the scientists posited, in reality that means people are going to do anything, anything at all, to get themselves a ship."

CHAPTER 17

LINNEA HEARD WOMEN'S voices behind her and halted on the trail. A cluster of older women appeared, huddling around something. Two of them looked up in mute appeal, and Linnea hurried back up the trail to discover that the three women had fashioned a kind of stretcher from two staffs lashed together with lengths of woven fibers of some sort and cloth laid over the whole. On this stretcher lay the seer, her face blanched.

"She cannot walk," Ela gasped. "The goddess departed from her spirit with such speed, she could not at first find her body."

Meaning, she got herself a migraine? Linnea thought, reaching for the end of one of the staffs. Ela paused to tuck the linen shroud more securely around the poor woman; then she picked up her end and they started down the trail.

At first they tried to keep their steps in sync, but the trail narrowed so abruptly in places it became nearly impossible. Added to that was the frustration of stumbling and slipping over stones that one could not see.

Before too long Linnea's hands ached, and her clothing was damp with sweat. *At least I get some exercise*, she thought with bleak humor; how the other women managed, she did not know. But her mind raced on, and she watched it race, amazed at how one's thoughts will catch at any diversion from threatening danger: as a long tremor, one with a sickening jolt in the middle of it, silenced and stilled them all, what flitted through her stream of consciousness was the absurdity of discussing exercise machines with women who had lived three thousand years before she was born.

When the tremor stopped, they picked up their poles and started forward, halting again when an ominous rattling above heralded a land-slide.

Hastening back up the trail, they watched in fear as boulders leaped crazily down, one smashing onto the trail and sending a chunk of it scattering down the hillside below. A hail of rubble followed, ending at last with a pall of choking dust.

"Come. We must push through," Ela cried hoarsely.

They stepped gingerly over the layer of dirt and stones nearly obliterating the trail and hurried on.

Abruptly the trail widened, and they were able to establish a rhythm. If the seer disliked the swinging, jolting stretcher, she said nothing; she gripped the poles at each side, her eyes closed.

The sun began to sink toward the west, and thirst had gone from pestering to agonizing when Linnea realized dully that they were rounding the last hill.

A gasp from Ela brought the stretcher parade to a halt. Her face, weirdly lit, was turned toward the north. Linnea stared in fear and wonder at the pre–Kameni Island, or what she assumed was that island.

The land itself was utterly obscured by a sky-scraping black cloud, one that had to be reaching at least twenty miles into the air. The cloud was not solid: writhing columns of smoke, from which flames of fire darted, reached like the fingers of death into the east.

"The holy snakes," one of the women whispered, in awe.

Without any warning at all the women were flung against the cliff side and then down onto the ground.

Pain lanced through Linnea's shoulder, but she was only peripherally aware of it. Why was the world sideways?

"Ayah," a voice moaned.

Linnea felt something sting her cheek, and who was pushing her so hard?

The ground, air, and sky roared, jolting her so forcefully she could not struggle to her elbows. Tiny stones clattered all around, pinging her face and arms as she tried to see who was moaning. Black surged overhead, darting down flames toward the mountain from which they had just come.

Clack! Something dark flickered across her vision; there was a pain across her temple, and the world went dark.

"WHAT THE — " Stavros never finished his exclamation.

As the three watched, the island seemed to shrug, and then shudders rippled down in rings from the mountain, churning the water into nervous, choppy wavelets.

They had come to a halt maybe a quarter mile from the shoreline, to avoid trouble. From there they watched the swarms of people pouring into every imaginable type of vessel, from the beautifully painted and decorated pleasure boats to the single-masted tradecraft.

As one boat veered near, Stavros shouted in Ancient Greek, "Where does everyone go?"

"The seer has spoken! The goddess says to live on the water, under the sky! The earth and fire demons are going to battle! I go to warn the other towns!" He pulled on the rope controlling his sail, and the little boat glided away toward the pre–Kameni Island.

Stavros turned to the other two, who shrugged. What the heck did that mean, other than "get out of here"? Had the Baldies somehow manipulated the oracle?

Whatever had happened, the entire population of Akrotiri appeared to have taken seriously the command to evacuate.

Even fishing smacks and little rowboats were crowded so dangerously some of them were so low the rails were a hand's breadth above water.

Eveleen watched as the evacuation began in an orderly fashion, turning desperate on the edges: there were, as Kosta had predicted, some fights for some of the boats. She winced, wishing there was something she could do, but they were helpless to interfere.

She watched one small family, consisting of a woman and two children, shoved back away from a skinny little fishing smack. The woman ran, crying, from one boat to another, until at last one of the great, decorated boats of the priests paused, and she and her children were pulled on.

That was when the side of the mountain gave a heave, and quake waves fled outward, flinging people down onto the ground, sending donkeys braying, goats scolding, and every bird on the island winging into the air, squawking in angry protest.

"It's the big quake," Eveleen whispered, appalled, but afraid to look away.

Wave after wave of shaking toppled walls, and cracks spiderwebbed up the few standing higher buildings. Then, with majestic slowness, the three-story buildings came crashing down, walls crumbling in either direction.

From somewhere jugs emerged, rolling down a cliff, some smashing, others hopping, until they fell a hundred yards into the sea below. Flames shot up somewhere else, as up in the sky, great writhing clouds of black sent out deadly jets of burning flame to lick the top of the mountain.

"Oil," Kosta said, pointing.

All it would take was one untended lamp and spilled olive oil; the flames spilled hungrily from the windows of a storehouse, just to be doused by the thunderous rumble and choking dust of a landslide.

On and on the shaking went, the clouds moving eastward raining down black bits of obsidian first in boulders, then in rocks, then pebbles, and finally in small, stinging bits of glass, until at last the firestorm and motion gradually subsided. By now the waves shuddered back and forth, some slapping back up onto the beaches, drenching terrified people, forcing them back up onto land.

But down they came again, from wherever they had been hiding during the deluge of burning rock, carrying children, animals, birds, and household goods, to cram into the boats.

Eveleen turned her head. Already many of the ships and boats were plying southward as fast as they could, oars rising and falling with fear-driven jerks, sails tautened by terror-strengthened hands.

They would get away. Maybe they would even make it to Crete, their beautifully painted jugs and vases to influence the painters there into a new style, a new way of looking at the world.

Eveleen, with a mental shrug, wished them well, and turned her attention back to the shoreline.

Where was Ross?

"Let us land," Stavros said at last. "Over there, out of sight of the evacuation. We must find Murdock, Ashe and Linnea Edel."

CHAPTER 18

AFTER ROSS'S "WHAT'S next?" he stepped back to wait for a reaction.

Ashe shook his head, but before he could speak, the Kayu spoke with clear urgency into the translator.

"This segment of the mountain is unstable. We will have to evacuate at once. The onset of chaos in the gravitational knot is releasing more energy than we expected. Now the Earth must find its balance point again."

Action, reaction.

Ashe said grimly, "It's going to be interesting, getting down the mountain if he means what I think he means."

Ross and Gordon turned their attention to the aliens, who had embarked on a fast exchange.

Gordon muttered under his breath, "I wish I could reverse that damn translator of theirs."

Then the first Kayu beckoned to the two Time Agents. "We shall give you our two wind vessels, though you cannot use our *** for returning to the mountain. But you do not need that."

Wind vessels? Ross mouthed the words to Ashe.

Ashe said under his breath, "Use 'em to spy on the Greeks and Baldies, I'll bet."

"You musst come now," the Kayu said.

Ross and Ashe followed the swaying robes, not back to the surface, but farther inside. Ross noted that they passed the room where he and Eveleen had been imprisoned for a night, and then they were all three enclosed in a cylindrical elevator shaft made of some stonelike white material, with a source of light impossible to detect.

A whoosh of air carrying a faint smell of ozone hit their faces, but they felt no accompanying drop in stomach like one experienced with elevators in their own time. Ross didn't know if they'd gone up, down, or sideways. The opaque door slid open again, and they emerged onto a cliff. Hot, smoky wind teased hair and clothing; the smell of sulfur fingered its way in even past their breathing masks.

The Kayu touched some kind of control that Ross didn't see because of the limited field of vision caused by his mask; a section of what had looked like solid rock flickered out of existence, leaving what at first appeared to be two giant bird shapes.

"Hang gliders," Ashe said.

"Sort of," Ross amended. He'd been hang gliding with Eveleen. These things looked different.

The Kayu said in its hissing speech, "It holdss humanss."

Gordon gave a shrug and bent over the closest one. Ross also bent, but what he tried to spot was the video projector that had projected the holographic rock. He couldn't find anything, even when he ran his hands over the rough pumice.

"Come on," Gordon said.

A tremor growling deep underground underscored the urgency.

He and Ross dragged the gliders out. At once the wind tried to take them, even though the wings were folded down.

Gordon examined them swiftly; from the look on his face he was doing some fast mental calculations.

Ross bent his attention to the controls, which appeared to be simple. Levers controlled the wing struts and the tails: levers for hands up front, for feet at the back. Out beyond the glider platform someone had painted great glassy bird-eyes on either side of a raptor's beak. So the Kayu had used these to glide in the air over the island, then, and to the locals they would look like giant birds. Had the Baldies seen them? If they were just gliding, there would be no energy signature to detect.

His thoughts were broken when Gordon thumped his arm and pointed. "Lie here. Strap in like this. I think we'll need to balance them for weight up front," Gordon said. "I suspect, from the look of these things, that the Kayu are lighter than we are."

"Is this a really stupid idea?" Ross asked Gordon as they dragged the gliders to the back of the cliff, giving themselves maximum running room. The straps, Ross noted, were made from some silky material that had enormous tensile strength. "I mean, where did that Fur Face go?"

"I don't know, but it looks as if this is the only way down," Gordon said. "And if they've used them, well, so can we." His mouth tightened in an ironic smile.

Another tremor shook the mountain, this one with an odd, jolting hop in it. A sudden roar beneath them sent both men to the edge of the cliff. Far down, just barely visible in the haze, they saw a tremendous landslide.

"Right," Ross said. "Let's get out of here."

"Now or never," Gordon agreed.

They gripped the handles of the gliders, flicked up the wings, and began to run.

Almost at once the gliders bucked and sidled as the wings and the wind played tug-of-war. Five, four, three, two—

There was the cliff edge, with a thousand-foot drop beyond. Ross's palms prickled with sweat, his heart thumped in his ears, as he swung himself out and slammed onto the platform.

The straps slapped themselves round him, the nose edged over the cliff, and the glider dropped.

"Whoo-*eeeeeee!*" The sound tore out of Ross as his guts plummeted, then the wind current caught the glider and tossed it up back toward the cliff.

"Bank! Bank!" Gordon roared from fifty feet away and out.

Ross turned his head, saw the cliff zooming toward him. He jammed his feet against the tail controls and the right wing; the glider banked sharply, sailing with amazing smoothness within a yard of the rocky face of the cliff, then outward and away.

There below was the entire island ring, visible between gouts of smoke rising to join the sheep-backed clouds flocking eastward from the south. *Storm coming,* Ross thought as he lifted his head and gazed to the north. There, beyond the north shore of Akrotiri's peninsula, were the green waters surrounding the pre–Kameni Island. Weird whitish water spoiled the emerald perfection of that vast lagoon. Steam vents?

Not a storm, Ross thought in slow, chilling shock as his wing moved and he could see past it to the huge, black, tentacled plume thrusting up from the island. It was not a storm, but something far worse: an eruption from what would very soon—maybe even now—be the center of the entire caldera.

Are we too late?

That question, too, was swept away when the quake hit.

Afterward, Ross could never pinpoint where the fault slipped. What he became aware of first was the sound, a great, roaring, grinding growl deeper and more terrifying than mere thunder, which was just air. This sound was far more powerful, the restless shifting of immeasurable strata as magma began forcing its way upward. What Ross saw were rings chasing outward, and then reverberating back, through both land and water.

The gliders emerged round a great fold in the mountain just in time for Ross and Gordon to look down and see Akrotiri trembling, like a toy city when children stomp on the floor all around. With excruciating slowness the remaining roofs toppled inward as walls fell outward, sending rubble, broken furnishings and jars, and clouds and clouds of reddish gold dust spewing into the air.

"Up," Gordon shouted. "Under the cliff, as close as you can!"

Ross didn't need the order. He already had his wings spread to the maximum, riding the updraft. Overhead the snaking tunnels of fire-laden smoke reached out, burning everything they touched. The two Time Agents would be barbecued in midair unless they used the quaking mountain as protection.

A terrifying rain of black stone smashed down behind Ross into the sea, sending up hissing steam columns, some of them high enough to mix in with the smoke overhead.

Hot air whooshed round the cliffs, followed by cold drafts. Both men fought to keep their craft within the lee of relative protection. It was the hot steamy drafts that kept them airborne. They circled round and round, the wings sometimes rattling and trembling as occasional shots of fine glassy black rock rained over them and then fell to the sea below, until, at last, the worst of the fiery smoke began to subside.

They could not stay up forever; already they were circling lower and lower.

It was time to try to land. They did not want to fall on the still-shaking ground anywhere near that city, or on the slipping cliffs that slid down here and there on the mountainsides.

They arced away from their cliff shelter and flew out over the ocean, both looking back, trying to see past the great stretches of their wings.

"What's that?" Gordon cried, peering down through the drifting smoke.

They had emerged far enough around the goat-tracked cliffs to see the harbor, which was filled with little craft, most of them with handkerchief-size sails luffing in the wind.

"Evacuation, looks like!"

"Our people must have found something out," Gordon shouted back.

Ross frowned, looking down there. *Eveleen, where are you?* he called silently.

Now they were out beyond the city, which mostly lay in ruins. Not all the buildings had fallen, but most. They did not see any bodies on those rubble-filled narrow streets. Still, Ross felt his guts tighten. Just because they couldn't see past all the rubble and the smoke didn't mean things weren't really bad.

A fretful gust of wind shook the glider, making the wings clatter, and the nose dove down. Ross tightened his grip on the controls and managed to get the craft to straighten out.

Ross stilled the trembling in his fingers, renewed his grip on the handholds, and urged the glider upward again, trying to gain altitude and time. He glanced over. Gordon was about twenty feet above him, maybe fifty feet away. Ross could see Gordon squinting through the smoke and dust haze to the shores.

Ross turned his attention downward. Would they see Baldies even if they were there? He remembered the business about holographic images. Both the Baldies and the Kayu had them. They definitely had the tech edge; the Time Agents hadn't even dared use their radios.

That would have to change, Ross thought. *Meanwhile, what's to keep them from shooting at us up here?*

Yet they drifted on, and nothing happened. As they emerged from one dust cloud, they could see the crumbled remains of tiny villages dotting the lower peninsula of the crescent-shaped island. *I hope the people got out,* Ross thought.

Reminded of the evacuation, Ross craned his neck and looked directly below. They were nearly past the harbor now. On the shore chaotic scrambling resolved into some desperate fights to gain ships: as he watched a line of men emerged from one of the rocky hills behind the farthest warehouses and ran down to the shore, where they attacked a family trying to load household items onto a fishing boat. Ross watched in growing but impotent anger as the burly men struck down family members; his fists tightened unconsciously on the controls, momentarily sending his glider bucketing dangerously in the wind. He shifted his attention to fighting for stability, and when the craft had smoothed out, though the wings hummed and rattled, he looked back. He was relieved to see that two parties of fisher folk had come to the aid of the family. Ross's last glimpse of the altercation was of the attackers, now tiny dots, retreating into the hills.

The hills. He frowned, thinking—

"There's our ship," Gordon shouted.

Ross whipped his head around and saw Gordon pointing downward. Well beyond the mass of boats drifting south lay their own craft. As Ross stared into the sunlight, he thought he caught a brief glint from field glasses.

"Let's aim for 'em," he called, pointing with his chin.

"After you," Gordon answered.

Ross banked his glider. Now that the flight was nearly over, he discovered he was almost sorry.

He realized they were going to have to crash-land on the water and wondered if the gliders would survive. He wondered if he would survive.

The air currents buffeted them hard, cold, hot, sulfur-and-hot-rock-smelling, dust-laden, cold again. Their speed increased as they spiraled downward. The horizon tipped up crazily; for a moment all Ross could see was dark green.

Then the ship revolved into view, passing again. Ross caught a glimpse of Eveleen's pale face. She stood on the taffrail, poised to dive.

Down, and he spread the wings in a desperate attempt to flatten out. Splash! That was Gordon, hitting the water.

Ross skimmed just above the waves. White water splashed up, making him gasp. Then he hit, and would have been wrenched badly had the straps not retracted with efficient, alien speed. He rolled off the platform and plunged into water.

After that nearly effortless flight, he felt heavy, clumsy. He splashed, kicking up his feet, and then struck out swimming.

A moment later an arm appeared, and there was Eveleen. Hands closed around his neck, and lips met his, warm/cold, in a trembling, salty kiss.

CHAPTER 19

"ALL RIGHT," GORDON Ashe said at last. "What have we got?"

Eveleen scooted closer to Ross. She was not the least bit cold—if anything, the air was more sultry than it had been during the day—but the amount of EM in the air, left over from the extraordinary fire the day before and the lightning now, and the subsonic rumblings that came ever more frequently, put her flight-or-fight instincts on overdrive.

Rain hammered down on the canopy overhead, a drenching, stinging rain full of grit and dust. The fleet had vanished southward during a fierce, blood-crimson sunset, the last sails tiny dots on the horizon as the limb of the sun vanished in a sinister purple haze.

For a time the outriding storm clouds had paraded on to the east, underlit like a villain's face in an old movie. There was nothing subtle in that spectacular sunset; the colors were brilliant, as if the sky had been painted by all the ancient gods with their elemental passions.

Lightning flaring from time to time promised no mercy during the night, either; before they'd exchanged stories, Ashe and Stavros both insisted everyone get the ship battened down.

Because of that quake the island was no longer safe at night, not without a thorough exploration. One thing for certain about major quakes: you never get just one. There are always aftershocks, and some of these can be as bad as the original event.

So they'd all worked to get equipment locked down, and Stavros had used the engines to move the ship eastward to a little cove that might afford some protection from the oncoming weather. There was no one around to hear the growl of the engines, not with the continuous rumble of thunder across the sky.

While Stavros had directed the battening down, Kosta had fired up the microwave and brought out some frozen food from the emergency rations cache. They all had earned a good meal, and it was quite unlikely they would be able to forage on the island anymore. As they ate, each took turns talking about their experiences since the last time they'd met—a time that seemed to Eveleen at least a week ago.

Now they sat crowded on the half-deck below the canopy, Eveleen and Ross together on a hammock, the Greeks perched on barrels that masked advanced tech, and Gordon Ashe on the only fold-down chair.

"What have we got?" Ashe asked again, looking around at the four faces.

Eveleen sipped gratefully from her mug of hot coffee and said, "Nobody saw Linnea, so she's still missing."

"And we will make searching for her top priority," Ashe responded. "Next?"

Ross said, "If we can believe the Kayu, we have a week to make certain the entropy device is not reversed. The Baldies have to know that."

"And will be acting accordingly. We'll get back to them," Ashe said.

"Do you believe the Kayu?" Eveleen asked.

"Yes, I believe them. At least, I can perceive no benefit to be gained from their going to all the trouble to contact us just to lie."

The others nodded, looking tired and strained.

"So we will say we have seven days to keep the Baldies busy. After that, the blow could happen anytime; both sides will be scrambling to leave."

Eveleen winced, thinking of the many threats implied in his flat statement.

"We have the globe ship," Kosta said.

"A globe ship," said Ross. "Could be there were only two Baldies and the rest holos, or maybe there's another?"

"There's rarely been more than one in any other encounter, has there? I mean with Baldies real-time?" asked Eveleen. "If I remember right, the science team decided they were spread really thin; otherwise, with their tech advantages, they'd have taken over long ago."

"If you believe the Kayu, the Baldies aren't interested in conquest, just stopping space flight. But I still believe they are indeed spread thin, so I'm betting your undersea globe ship is the only one in this time/space. So here are our three main areas of action, as I see it," Ashe said, holding up his hand. "We have to keep the globe ship out of the Baldies' hands to prevent them from damping the oscillations and again shunting off the energy building up to the big blow."

"We're going to have to stay out of their mitts," Ross said. "That won't be easy. They have the seek-and-find tech, and what little we've got is easy for them to detect."

"And we're alone on the island now, or nearly," Eveleen said. "And I'm including Linnea. The Kallistans have evacuated, as the archaeologists predicted. That leaves just us and the Baldies—"

"And the Kayu," Ashe put in.

"Right," she said. "And the Kayu. But the Baldies are the ones who are going to know that anything that moves and isn't them is a target."

Ross shook his head. "I still wonder about that 'they value life' talk that the Kayu tried to hand us."

Eveleen said, "Perhaps the Baldies warned the oracle. After all, someone had to, or how did they know to get the people out?"

Ross shrugged. "Gordon and I were with the Kayu, so they certainly didn't. But maybe one or the other of them had some way of warning those priestesses." He frowned, then recalled his flight down. "At any rate, there's one more gang out there, unless they did manage to get the boat. Out from the brush behind the warehouses came a slew of guys . . ." He went on to describe the attack on the fishing boat.

Eveleen rubbed her forehead. "Wait a minute. Behind the warehouse?"

"Yes," Ross said. "I was just wondering whether these might have been responsible for the attack on our camp, and not the Baldies, when we first landed."

"We will have to keep these men in mind, but there is nothing to be done about them now." Ashe sat back, cradling his coffee in his hands. "To return to our first dilemma, it makes sense that either or both sets of aliens had that cave wired. If they were studying the Kallistans at all, it seems to me that the first place you'd go is where all of them go, to their oracle. Listening to what went on there must have given them the local languages, at least, and clues to customs as well."

Eveleen snapped her fingers. "So their egg-computer has what Linnea wanted so badly: a full dictionary of words corresponding to Linear A!"

Ross nodded once. "Ah. And what can be wired for sound can go both ways. Maybe they broadcast 'voices' for the Kallistan priestesses to hear."

"Well, if the Baldies tried to save the Kallistans, and I hope they did, why have they shot at us in the past?" Eveleen asked.

"Well, if they're hyperecologists of some sort, as the Kayu said, maybe they think of it as pruning," Ashe replied, finishing off his coffee. "We're spinning out in guesswork. Too much of that without facts is just a waste of time. I suggest we all get some shut-eye while we can. At least this storm ought to mask searches, giving us some time for rest. As soon as it's light, you two had better secure that globe ship." He nodded at the Greek agents. "Once we have it, we can explore it on our time, and maybe figure out a way to permanently disable their entropy adjusters."

Kosta grunted in agreement and tossed the dregs of his coffee overboard.

They all settled down then. Eveleen realized her head ached. Trying to keep quiet she reached into the pouch she wore under her flaring skirt, pulled out some sinus tabs.

Now what? The prospect of trying to swallow them in a dry mouth made her stomach churn.

Lightning flared, a vivid purple slash across the sky. She saw a hand reach toward her from one of the other hammocks, holding out a cup of purified water. In grateful silence she took it, swallowed the tabs. Thunder banged and crashed, dying away in a ragged grumble; she heard someone else popping tabs from a seal-pac.

She passed the cup on, felt fingers take it.

Then she lay back down, and despite the storm doing its best to battle the volcano for mastery of sky, earth, and water, she fell deeply asleep.

JUST ABOUT THE time Eveleen fell asleep, Linnea woke up, gasping. Rain slashed down out of the sky, a pitiless downpour. By the flare of lightning Linnea saw that all the priestesses were now awake, two of them bending over a third.

What could they do? Where could they go? At least the air was not cold. They would not freeze. But as a fairly severe aftershock rumbled below the ground, louder than the thunder, Linnea worried about landslides. Mudslides, caused by those frightening steam vents.

A hot, sharp smell brought her head around. Fire, the most ancient threat of all, made her scrabble back in the mud. Moments later vague shapes appeared. Lightning flared again, and then lights snapped into being. Linnea blinked, dazzled.

"Come. Rise and come this way." The voice was tenor, flat, the accent in the Ancient Greek impossible to guess at.

The lights shifted to a trail that steamed, despite the pouring rain. *Am I hallucinating?* Linnea thought.

"Ah!" A woman's voice gave a soft cry of anguish, and Linnea turned again.

The lights snapped over to the priestesses, revealing Ela and one other holding up the older woman who Linnea had decided was second in command to the seer. The seer herself was on her feet, her clothing sodden with mud. She looked old and frail and very unhappy.

"Her arm," Ela said in a frightened voice. "She fell, and hurt her arm, when the ground shook."

"She must walk," came one of those flat tenor voices.

That's not Ross, or Stavros, or Kosta, and it certainly isn't Gordon, Linnea thought. She said in tentative Ancient Greek, "Who is it?"

The figures remained behind the lights, perceptible as no more than shadows. Lightning flared again, but Linnea had been looking at the ground. She turned her head, too late.

Thunder crashed right overhead, making her teeth ache. Another lightning bolt illuminated the scene. Linnea watched the ground again, the abnormally flat ground: someone, she realized, had cleared a new path. But the ground was smoking. Was it some freak of the volcano? No, the edges were straight, as though a beam of heat had cut through the rock and soil.

She stepped tentatively forward onto the steaming soil. The soles of her sandals did not burn, so she led the way, the priestesses coming slowly behind. Behind them were the rescuers, shining their lights ahead, down the path that they had made.

For a long time they walked, as the warm, dust-laden acid rain washed the mud from their clothing, stinging their eyes.

The world revolved gently, and Linnea staggered once or twice, trying to breathe deeply against the dizziness. The playing lights, the rain thrumming against nose and mouth, didn't help. Every time the poor woman behind her gasped in pain, Linnea's insides tightened.

Crazy hopes ran through her mind. Were their rescuers perhaps from the Project? Maybe the Project of the future? Linnea couldn't recall anyone talking about weapons that burned away landslides, creating a flat pathway. But she was sure they hadn't told her anything they didn't think she needed to know.

Only now she did need to know.

On and on.

The entire trip was conducted in silence, until at last a cliff loomed, blacker than the surrounding night. One moment rain pattered, loud, in their ears, and then it withdrew into a hissing curtain behind them, and Linnea could breathe. She realized that they had entered a cave of some sort. Faint bluish light glowed at one end, through a rough archway.

A hand touched the back of her shoulder, urging her toward their light. She obeyed the unspoken command, and was glad to do so. Light, shelter, maybe food? Oh, and clean, dry clothing?

But . . . what about these women? Linnea thought, her expectations withering away. The Project would surely not permit anyone to see modern technical gear, electric lights, and machine-stitched towels and clothes?

Through another archway, into a round room that was again lit by bluish light. Linnea had just enough time to see that there was nothing in it but shapeless cloth of some sort on the floor, and then she turned around as the others entered.

The last priestess walked in, and Ela and the others eased the wounded woman down. Linnea ignored them, trying to empty her mind, staring at the two figures in the doorway: two figures who were slim, of medium height, their fine features quite hairless, their clothing a shimmery suit of bluish purple.

Baldies.

They had not been rescued; they had been captured, by the Baldies.

Then a door slid soundlessly shut, locking them in. She released her breath; they hadn't singled her out. She remembered the warnings about those blue suits and telepathy. Perhaps the fear of the women around her had masked her own thoughts; perhaps their suits couldn't distinguish thoughts in people close together, especially when all of them had to be radiating fear quite powerfully.

"Where are we?" someone asked softly.

"I do not recognize this place," the seer replied, her voice tremulous. "I very much fear that our own house might have fallen in the shaking."

Linnea hesitated, unsure about speaking. What could she say?

CHAPTER 20

"I THINK," ASHE said, "we'll just have to assume that the Kayu are either dead or in hiding. There is no way to get back up that mountain to the cave where we met them, and even if we did, what would we do or say?"

"We might get them to explain how they think the Baldies are respectful of life," Ross muttered.

Ashe's mouth twitched. "You just can't leave that alone, can you? I admit that the same question has crossed my mind as well. But we'll have to leave that one for leisure moments. Right now, let's go down today's checklist."

It was morning, the full glare of morning. Steam rose from shingle on the beach and from the ruins of Akrotiri, drying in the sunlight half a mile away. They had been shaken awake by a quake sharp enough to rock the boat.

Still, they had landed directly below the ruins of the city. There was no human sound beyond what they made; the harbor, so busy the day before, was empty, the only life the cawing seabirds overhead. Farther up the mountain, swallows darted and chased, their tails streaming.

Ross clipped his radio to the outside of his belt. Now that the need for disguise was over, he wore baggy work pants with sturdy pockets. Eveleen and Stavros stood there in diving gear, Stav with a foot propped on the taffrail. Kosta had changed to a rough linen work shirt and baggy pants.

"Do we all understand the codes?" Ashe went on, tapping his radio.

"Understood," Kosta stated.

"Got it," Ross said.

Eveleen nodded once, biting her lip. Behind her, Stavros half-raised a hand in agreement.

Ashe looked around. "We transmit only when we have to, and we transmit only the codes, and only on the move. If we discover we need to refine the codes, they can wait until tomorrow. Got it?"

Again a round of nods.

"All right, then. Stavros, will you issue the weapons?"

In silence Stavros removed three modified energy weapons from the locker below. These weapons were the reason Eveleen was on the diving team and not on the search team. She would defend herself with the expertise of the martial artist, but she was not certain she could bring herself to use one of these energy weapons and had said so up front.

Ashe turned to her now. "You two know what to do, right?"

"Get the globe ship into a hidden cove, camouflage it, and if we have time, try to get inside."

"Good. Just be back here by sunset, so we can gather with no lights showing. If this place becomes unsafe, we'll let one another know," Ashe repeated, looking from one to another.

Again they nodded, and that was it. Ashe and Ross maneuvered the smaller rowboat out and splashed it into the water. Then they and Kosta climbed over, Ross settling into the stern, the others sitting side by side and manning the oars as Ross kept lookout.

No one spoke. Ross sent a private glance at his wife, to catch a smile in return and a tiny wave of her hand. Then she turned away, reaching for her scuba gear. Stav said something to her in a voice too low for him to hear.

Ross shifted his gaze to the coastline stretching away to the west. It was quite a sight: the shore was lined with an unappetizing tangle of sea brack and dead fish. Unappetizing to humans, at least. An astonishing variety of birds dove and cried and cawed, each flap or peck sending up dark clouds of flies. The smell of sulfur, brine, and rotting fish made Ross breathe through his mouth.

━━━━━━━━━━━━━━━━   ━━━━━━━━━━━━━━━━━━

ASHE AND KOSTA rowed swiftly. Ross kept scanning the coast, not just for slim hairless figures but for suspicious blurs: over breakfast they'd discussed the possibility of holographic "stealthing." If the Baldies could project false images, they might be able to hide themselves from plain sight. He also watched for any revealing gleams or glitters.

As they dragged their boat up onto the shingle and covered it with a layer of seaweed, nothing was in evidence but birds and fish and flies.

Then the three separated, Ashe to investigate over the hills to the north, Kosta up the road to the city and as far as he felt safe, and Ross to try the pathway to the oracle, again as far as it was feasible to do so.

Ross set out at a quick pace, despite the steamy heat radiating from rain-washed stones scattered about. An aftershock caused him to pause, watchful. He could hear the shifting of the earth below ground; it sounded a lot like a train racing along a subway line one level below, only somehow more sinister—a grim reminder of the magma explosion building toward zero hour.

Up ahead he spotted at least two major landslides. The trail still could be picked out, but he was going to have to do some detouring.

"I can make it," he muttered, shading his eyes. "But if anyone is under those tons of mud, it's not going to be me who finds them."

He grimaced, shook his head to clear it of such thoughts, and set out at a faster pace.

STAVROS AND EVELEEN stayed silent as the ship plied its way parallel to the cliffs, heading east. His job was to keep as close to the rocks as he could without crashing into unseen ones below the surface; hers was to use the field glasses and scan constantly for Baldies. Close as they were—sometimes she could have reached out and touched the rough rock, stippled with the remains of shells from millions of years in the past—she still felt horribly exposed.

Stavros kept the engines at low to muffle the thrumming. They glided past birds' nests and crabs scuttling over wave-washed stones, past little beaches with discolored foam and dead fish piled high from the storm surf of the night before.

Nothing disturbed them, and at last Stavros cut the engine and put down the anchor.

Eveleen, sweating profusely by now, pulled on her mask; her scuba gear was already on, in case she'd have to make a fast dive.

It was such a relief to slide into the water that Eveleen permitted herself to shut her eyes and just float for a moment. The air was already unbearably hot outside and would only get hotter.

She opened her eyes, flippered over and grabbed the sled, then looked around. Ah. The cave was still there. She pointed and tried not to let herself think about quakes and rockfalls as they arrowed down, down, as she directed Stavros along the seafloor, heading for where they had left the globe ship.

They flicked on their lamps. The water was unusually turbid, masking their vision. An occasional fish flicked in and out of view, its darting seeming nervous, furtive. The light did not penetrate in shafts, but seemed to come from everywhere, a sinister, nasty reddish color.

Eveleen swam quite close to the cliff wall before she saw it. She nearly ran into the dangerous protuberances before her lamp caught suddenly on the glitter of stone newly sheered, amid wildly waving little plants of unimaginable types, colors, and variations.

Sheered rock?

Eveleen's guts clenched as she felt her way down, down, Stavros no more than a vague silhouette nearby. She remembered about how far down the ocean floor ought to be, and so once again nearly ran into a sharp, upthrust rock.

Landslide. Her breathing sounded harsh and the sharp scent of sweat filled her mask as she flippered back and forth, hands out, lamp beam moving constantly, until she was sure.

At last she sighed and for a time floated, suspended in the warm water, like the clouds of dust particles around her. Their marker had, of course, disappeared, probably buried. So, it seemed, was the globe ship.

Stavros shaped his hands into a ball and then pointed down.

Yes, it's under the landslide, blast and damn, Eveleen thought, pointing. *It's got to be buried under all that rock.*

Stav gave a shrug and then backed the sled up and anchored it a safe distance away. He flippered back and set his hands to the topmost rock. He braced his flippers against another stone and then started pushing and shoving, pushing and shoving, bubbles exploding with furious energy from his release valve.

Eveleen swam down in two strokes, set her hands to the opposite side of the stone, and pushed with all her strength.

The stone shifted; a plume of reddish dirt billowed up, obscuring their faces. Eveleen resisted the temptation to wipe her eyes—as if that would clear her vision!—and watched in satisfaction as the rock tumbled down to the seafloor.

Again they chose a big stone, worked at loosening it, and sent it tumbling with lazy slowness to the seafloor. Eveleen dug at the silt beneath, sending billows out into the water.

They kept digging, tossing stones and shifting mud, finding nothing underneath but more stones, more mud, and tangles of sea creatures and plants.

When Eveleen realized that they had uncovered perhaps six feet of area, and that the seafloor was maybe six feet below that, she had to face the fact that she'd chosen the wrong place. Oh, that was, as far as she could tell, where they had left the globe ship. But it could have rolled away and then been buried, and how would they ever know?

They kept searching until the warning lights on their air packs sent them up again, empty handed.

CHAPTER 21

THE SUN, AN angry-looking scarlet ball of fire, dissolved into the purple murk stretching along the western horizon, leaving Ross in thickening shadows. He had a flashlight now, along with his radio and a canteen, but—mindful of Baldies and those scavenger attackers lurking about somewhere in the hills—he didn't want to advertise his presence unless he had to.

Having found absolutely nothing on his long, hot, dangerous and thoroughly miserable climb, he now discovered he'd miscalculated how long it would take to climb down.

The trail was all but obliterated. He'd had to pick his way up shifting rubble and shale, twice setting off minor slides.

Getting down was far more difficult than he'd surmised. He'd counted on following his own tracks, but the tremors after he'd started up must have set off more minor rock slides, because his prints vanished with irritating frequency.

He paused, wiping gritty sweat from his face, and stared out at the horizon. The sun was gone, leaving a faintly glowing purple bruise smearing the west, its faint glow reflected in the ocean, vanishing swiftly.

Overhead, clouds of dust and smoke obscured the starlight; the pre–Kameni Island was smoking steadily now, preparing for the next, and biggest, blast.

Meanwhile the strange, violet light would totally vanish very soon. Get moving.

He forced himself to clamber down, glad at least he didn't have to do this climb in sandals tied on with thin leather thongs. *That's right; think of the positive,* he told himself with sour humor. Well, he'd found no bodies, except for a goat. The poor beast at least hadn't suffered; a bouncing stone appeared to have broken its neck before it knew what hit it.

No bodies, no sign of anything human. *Not that people of the past were given to litter on the scale of modern times,* he thought as he leaped over a flat stone precariously balanced on two others and came down on sand. He slipped a little, caught his balance, and sneezed from the ever-present dust. He'd had to resort to the breathing mask higher up, because of dust and smoke, a lethal combination; now its particulate filters desperately needed changing.

No, no sign of anything, animal, human—or Kayu. And what about those guys, anyway?

His question, of course, winged out into the universe unanswered, but he'd already forgotten it when he realized that the faint lights groping about down to the left were not hallucinatory flickers due to exhaustion, hunger, and miserable heat, but they were actual lights.

The landscape had changed so much he had only a general sense of his bearings. Straight ahead was the peninsula, thrusting directly west. That meant Akrotiri was to the left, though of course there were no more buildings jutting squarely up, forming a skyline.

Ross crossed a cliff face, picking his way with care mostly by feel, not by sight, until he was maybe a thousand yards above the northern end of the town. Yes. Lights. Was it his team? Should he radio?

No. If they were chasing someone, they wouldn't want to respond and give away their position. Meanwhile, he wasn't moving fast enough to get away from his own.

So he started to run, awkwardly leaping and sliding downward, until some unseen flaw in the rubble brought him down hard.

He sat up, wincing. Nothing wrenched, nothing broken—thanks to countless drills with Eveleen on how to fall without breaking your neck.

Lights again.

He filled his lungs, ready to yell, but caution made him blow the air out again and frown into the murky darkness that had so quickly descended. Yellow light, very faint yellow light. The distances weren't right for those to be flashlight beams.

Therefore . . . lamps?

Ah. He spotted a sturdy outcropping of ancient volcanic rock, exposed now by the ground around it having slid down toward the city.

He eased down and crept on hands and knees along that rock, staring downward, into where he'd seen those lights. He heard noises: running feet, a grunt. Fighting?

Was it Ashe and Kosta?

Linnea?

Again he filled his lungs to yell, but then a ferocious blue-white light lanced out of nowhere and for a moment lit the entire scene before it vanished.

Ross sat back, stunned by the light, by what he'd seen. The after-image played itself against his retinas: the two obviously male silhouettes, one short, stocky, with a wild beard, the other thin and wiry, the first with a knife upraised—the blue-white light gleaming on greenish, unpolished bronze—the other clutching an armful of loot, and then the one with the knife falling, soundlessly, burned by the laser-strike.

Desperate scrabbling sounds skittered up the rock face, echoing slightly against the few still-standing walls below. That would be the second figure, trying to make off with its loot.

Those hill scavengers! But who did the shooting?

Baldies. They were here, just below.

Ross realized he was sitting exposed on this cliff and eased back slowly, looking around. Of course he wouldn't see them. What snoop gear did they have to make searches comfortable and easy? Infrared? Something that detected life-forms? He cursed soundlessly as he eased back and back, away from the cliff, and then ghosted down the side of the great slab of rock.

He was just reaching for his radio to fire off a signal—*Baldies here*—when a voice rose, an angry shout, not in Greek but in the local language.

A moment later again one of those white lights lanced out. Ross heard a thud. It was close—no more than fifty yards—and then silence.

He removed his fingers from the radio at his belt and faded as quietly as he could to the north, away from the ruins. The Baldies, or whoever had those weapons, were obviously on the prowl, and there was more than one.

He'd get to firm ground, preferably with a hill between him and those weapons, and then signal.

CHAPTER 22

LINNEA WOKE UP slowly and reluctantly. Her mouth felt dry and nasty; her joints were stiff; her clothing was impossibly gritty. She felt her scalp prickle, as if all the mud in it had decided to come to life, sprouting many legs.

Is this how human beings always felt before the blessings of running water? Except that the Kallistans had had running water. She thought of that chamber in the priestesses' building, the slightly sulfuric, mineral smell of pure spring water running across stone, and swallowed convulsively.

Did she hear it?

She opened her eyes. Women sat around the rocky chamber in groups. The cell was lit, she realized. Sunlight? Was there a way out?

She sat up, looked around, saw only heavy rock, smoothed unnaturally. *Probably by some terrible laser weapon*, she thought. The light seemed to be sourceless; at least she could not pinpoint a direction in the more roughly carved, uneven ceiling, nor were there shadows to give her a direction.

She rubbed her hands over her face and listened. Below the soft murmurs of female voices she made out an almost subliminal hiss.

"Ah." Ela turned Linnea's way. "The priestess from Kemt has awakened. We feared you took injury, as did Stella." She indicated one who sat against a wall, nursing what was obviously a broken arm.

"Is there water?" Linnea's voice came out a frog croak.

Ela gave her a small smile. "It is through there."

Linnea turned around. She'd had her back to a narrow crevasse. Rising to her feet, she dusted her robe as best she could, and then made her way to the crevasse. She eased through what had once been a wider opening, but was now partially blocked by squares of fallen stone, and then stepped down into what had been a bath chamber.

Running water indeed! A stream had been diverted into two forks; one ran freely down a carved gutter, the other ran beneath a row of stone seats. She was able to relieve herself and then kneel down at the running stream and dip her hands into the water. It was surprisingly warm, and it did not look particularly clear. Her tongue dried in her mouth; she used the water to rinse her face and hands, and then got up. Would she be forced to drink that water? Would thirst finally drive her to it?

Her mind, relieved of immediate cares, fled back in memory, and she realized they were prisoners of the Baldies.

The Baldies—aliens.

Shock smote her. There had been no records of Baldies three thousand years up the time-line. Not that there were many records in Linear A . . . but from what she'd seen, it was mostly merchants who kept track of goods and sales with writing. Histories were orally passed down, to be written much later.

But nowhere had there been any vases painted with slim bald men in strange one-piece suits. So news of the Baldies did not make it to Crete . . . did that mean that these women, and Linnea, would die here?

I must do something. I must think.

She pushed her way back into the main chamber, to be met by Ela again. "The priests gave us this water," she said. "It is good to drink. It does not taste of dust, like the water in the bath chamber." She pointed to a row of three tall jugs, with several of the shallow Greek cups called *kylixes* set neatly next to them.

Thirsty as she was, Linnea paused in the act of pouring water. "Priests?" she asked.

Ela nodded once. "You did not see them, then? We are here. Priests will not let us go; we do not know yet why not. Perhaps they serve the Fire God, who is at war with the Earth Goddess."

"Did they tell you that?" Linnea asked with caution, and finished pouring her water.

"Oh no. They said only 'Water to drink' and shut this door again. It is a strange door, one we cannot open." Ela touched the smooth stone.

Linnea drank greedily and then sighed, frowning at that door. The jugs and kylixes were appropriate to the time, but that door, sliding into a tightly lasered seam, was not. Well, but when the volcano let go, there would be no evidence of this room.

Was that a sentence of death, or not?

She drank again.

Coolness spread thorugh her. She lifted the jug again, looked Ela's way. No one dissuaded her, so she drank another full cup.

Priests. Of course. The Baldies all looked more or less the same, and so the priestesses would define their strange appearance within their own perception of the world. *World.* Linnea sat down on the rocky floor and wearily contemplated the word. Did these people even have the concept of a global community in their language? Not likely.

Linnea leaned her head back. *That means,* she thought with a faint bubbling of hope inside the pit of her stomach, *that there's a chance I might just live through this mess and get back home.*

Home. She thought longingly of her clean bathroom, fresh towels, microwave, stove, her closet full of clothes, her children within reach of the phone, at least hypothetically.

Her children.

What would the Project tell them if something happened? "Your mother was blown up by a volcano three thousand years ago." No, they probably had some smooth way of handling these things. "There was an accident at an archaeological dig, far from hospital services . . ."

Linnea's mind drifted into depressing scenarios: her children finding out she was dead, her house empty—

Stop that.

She sat up, shaking her head. Defeatist mental whining would get her exactly nowhere. All right then, what was the situation? All she knew for certain was that the Baldies had led them to this chamber, wherever it was, and shut them in. They had given them water, and the Kallistan version of plumbing was in the chamber adjacent. That argued for a certain level of humane treatment.

That's all I know. So what do they know? They know that they have a number of Priestesses of the Serpent. They do not know that I am not one of the priestesses, or surely they would have separated me and used me to try to get at the other Time Agents.

Are the others even alive?

Linnea shook her head again. That, too, was unknowable. So what she did know was that she was the only one who had enough awareness of futuristic tech to be on the watch for ways of escape. If she stayed near that door, for example, maybe she'd see how they controlled it. She might see something outside the door that could help them. She might hear something—

The door opened with a low, soft hiss. Linnea looked up, startled, but before she could move, a Baldy slid in a tray. She saw the being's oval-shaped head, the fine skin with a tracery of blue veins under it, reminding her for an unsettling moment of a newborn baby's. Then the being pointed at the nearest priestess, a young woman who stepped back. The Baldy gestured.

The woman did not move.

Linnea's hands rose to her mouth as the Baldy stepped forward, plucked the woman's brightly colored linen sleeve, and drew her forward.

The door slid shut.

"Eat," said the seer. "We shall need our strength."

No one spoke. Several women crowded round the tray, softly exclaiming.

Ela brought the tray to the seer, who sat against the wall opposite from Linnea. All the women stood respectfully back as the old woman touched the stack of flat ceramic dishes, a single round container—a Kallistan jug with lilies painted on the side—the line of flat spoons. Linnea did a rapid count: nine plates and spoons, eight women now in the chamber.

There was one for the woman who had been taken out.

"It appears to be a meal," the seer said in her old, tremulous voice, looking into the container. "It is so finely milled!"

A younger woman turned to Linnea. "Have you such things in Kemt? Or is this priest food?"

Linnea opened her mouth to speak of worlds, aliens, foods that might or might not suit the human digestive system and hesitated. *Your only weapon is your brain,* she told herself. *Use it.* Were the Baldies watching to see if one of the women might be a ringer?

"It is unfamiliar to me," Linnea said only.

"I shall sample it," said the seer. She gave a wry smile. "I am the oldest and the closest to the world of the shades."

So saying she dipped a finger into the serving bowl, tasted. Presently she looked about. "It is a strange food, of a flavor I cannot name, but I do not feel the fires of poison within me."

She signed to the priestess who usually supervised meals, and in silence she served out nine equal portions.

Linnea took hers, waiting until the women had chanted their blessing over the food. Then she tasted it. The consistency was much like pancake batter, the taste not much different. She had no doubt that it was both clean and reasonably nutritious.

"It is not unlike the meal we make with fava seeds, but what herbs set thereto?" someone wondered.

Other comments were offered. Linnea said nothing; the food made her feel energy flowing back into mind and body.

She had just set aside her plate and spoon when a deep rumbling noise caused all the women to go silent, still.

The shaking started then, at first easy, then harder, great jerks and jumps that eventually died away. Fine silt sifted down from new cracks in the ceiling.

Linnea drew in an unsteady breath.

The women began to talk again in low voices, and finally the seer motioned them over, and they began to chant, a steady, soothing rhythm. In their own way, the women were trying to solve the problem, Linnea realized.

The seer shut her eyes and began her breathing.

Linnea shut her own eyes; she no longer felt superior to these women, uneducated and superstitious as they were. She just felt an added sense of responsibility: she could not sleep until she knew what had happened to the woman taken out.

Rescue, she thought bleakly, *is obviously up to me.*

How?

"IF LINNEA IS still alive, she's probably not alone," Ashe said.

Eveleen felt excitement surge through her. "That mysterious room Linnea found that one day, do you remember? I really think the elevator shaft connecting the globe ship's original cave connected to that room. Do you think Linnea might be imprisoned there?"

Everyone turned Kosta's way; he was the one who had searched the ruined city.

"If she is, there's no access I can see," he said. "That entire level of the city has fallen. Not one of those buildings has been left standing. I can't speak for any underground chambers, of course."

"The Baldies obviously didn't want anyone around there, not with the shootings," Ashe said. "But they might have been trying to protect themselves against the hill scavengers."

"One of those scavenger guys was about to jump another," Ross pointed out. He made a wry face. "Though I find it hard to believe the Baldies shot the guy with the knife out of some weird sense of justice."

Ashe shook his head. "More likely he found something of theirs while looting."

They were all sitting in the boat directly under a cliff, so that they could not be seen except from the cliffs directly overhead. They'd met at dawn, as planned, rowing back under a sky streaked with brownish-stained clouds, the sea an ominous green.

Now they finished breakfast. Eveleen, glancing at the others, thought that they looked as weary as she felt.

"I found nothing on the northern shore except collapsed huts and landslides," Ashe said presently. "Ross found nothing but landslides up the mountain. I think, therefore, we should confine tonight's search to the city."

"All right with me," Ross said, drumming his fingers on the ship's rail.

Eveleen swallowed. "I would really like to search for Linnea," she said.

Stavros glanced up. He was busy with a welter of wires and plastic; Eveleen saw dark smudges under his eyes. He had not slept at all for over thirty-six hours. "I am trying here to rig some kind of a location device, using the strain meters," he said. "If we use their tech, we give ourselves away." He shrugged, his mouth tight.

Kosta sat back, his hands cradling his coffee mug. "I did not cover all the areas I would have liked. With all of us working, perhaps we can either identify sections to focus on, or else rule out the area entirely."

"What about the Kayu?" Eveleen asked. "Ought we to look for them—for rescue, if for nothing else?"

Ashe sighed. "The only location we know of for them is on top of the mountain. We'll have to assume they have taken care of themselves. We definitely can assume that they are, for whatever reason, incommunicado."

No one spoke.

Ashe nodded once. "Then all five of us will search the city area tonight, and cover it as closely as we can. We'll use infrared scanners, and a new set of radio codes. Get some sleep: as soon as the sun sets we'll outline our specific search goals, and we'll land under cover of night."

CHAPTER 23

NIGHT. FAR IN the north, lightning pricked the sea; the delayed rumble of thunder stayed in the distance, no more than a low, fretful threat. The air was thick with dust, still, and hot. It smelled of burned rock to Ross, who occasionally spared a glance to that storm moving eastward. It did not seem that the edge of it would brush Kalliste. Too bad. Getting soaked would be a relief.

Ross turned his head and made out Eveleen's silhouette against the soft light of the southern stars, just barely visible through the slowly drifting haze of volcanic steam and smoke.

Ross glanced down at the infrared reader in his hand. He held it out, moving horizontally from left to right. Then, when distant lightning briefly lit the rubble around him, he moved forward another thirty feet.

Slight scrabbling sounds to his right indicated that Eveleen, too, was performing a sweep-and-move.

Ross and Eveleen spent another immeasurable time working across the landscape in a rough zigzag. They could not see Ashe, Kosta, or Stavros, but Ross sensed them strung out along the face of the mountain.

So far, no one had used the radio. Could the Baldies sense them?

No sign. The infrared reader showed blurps and blobs that had to belong to birds or small animals. Some moved in hops; others jetted upward.

Sweep, pause, move. It became a pattern, almost a drill. Ross, tired from too many nights of interrupted (or skipped) sleep, was just feeling his brain settle into a kind of routine when he became aware of noise to the left.

He whipped up the reader, and at first saw nothing. But he heard harsh breathing and rubble clattering.

Lightning flared. Ross smelled the attacker a split second before he saw the stocky figure with something upraised, a sharp, nasty smell of unwashed body and badly cured goat skin. The attacker vaulted around the side of a massive slab of stone, which explained the lack of a reading.

Grunting with effort, the man heaved something directly at Ross's head. He sidestepped, and a huge jar smashed down where he'd been. The scavenger uttered a low growl and flung himself onto Ross.

An angry, desperate battle ensued, the two men teetering on loose rubble, each trying to get a purchase. The scavenger was short but enormously strong, fighting to kill; Ross was still in self-defense mode, which flared, quick as the distant lightning, when a second attacker appeared behind, a stone upraised.

Then came a sound not unlike the whirring of a great owl's wings, and Eveleen leaped up, turning midair, using her velocity to arc out her foot in a perfect side-kick. The edge of her shoe caught the second guy right across the bridge of his nose, and he howled, dropping the stone, and then launched himself at her, arms swinging.

Ross's adversary made the mistake of turning his head to see. Ross used an ankle-sweep to knock him off balance, and two solid punches, one to the face and one to the gut, sent the man crashing down the hill amid a shower of little rocks.

A palm-heel strike to the solar plexus from Eveleen sent the second one to his knees, fighting miserably for breath.

Ross picked up his infrared scanner. His heart raced, his hands trembled, but all his senses were heightened; in a weak, easterly flare of lightning he made out maybe six others, all converging.

"It's a gang," he whispered to Eveleen.

She nodded—he sensed it rather than saw it—and pulled her weapon, holding it in her hand as they eased back down to the south.

They dodged round a broken building and crouched down beside a well, both peering out, their scanners up. By these they watched the gang's progress to the southwest, downhill. Shouts, thuds, and the clatter of stones broke the summer stillness at one point.

By the faint reflected glare of the dim LED light on the scanner, Ross saw Eveleen grimace. "Took care of their two guys, is my guess."

Ross nodded. Her tone in "took care" made it clear that she didn't believe any more than he did that the scavengers dealt out first aid. Well, he had no sympathy, none at all; he flexed his hand, feeling tingles run up his arm to his neck. Probably broke a couple fingers, damn it all. Jammed, anyway.

They waited until the scavengers had moved southward in a clump; then Ross radioed the signal for DANGER: MOVING SOUTH.

He clicked off the radio and he and Eveleen scooted straight uphill, scanners constantly moving.

The rubble altered abruptly from treacherous landslides to jumbles of jutting stone, forcing them to proceed slowly.

"Something's going on," Eveleen breathed, barely loud enough to hear.

Ross saw her facing southeast. He held up his scanner. Indeterminate flickers registered on the very edge. Whatever was going on was on the other side of the ruined city.

Smash! A shower of stones and a scrabbling noise caused Eveleen to gasp. Ross crouched, weapon up.

"Na-a-a-ah!" A very bad-tempered goat plunged right between them, head low, horns butting the air.

The animal leaped, struggled for purchase, and then trotted downhill, scolding the night.

Eveleen breathed a laugh of relief. "I guess we must have stumbled onto its hiding place."

Ross risked a quick glimpse from his flashlight, shielding it with his palm. Sure enough, there was a pocket cave underneath a great fallen wall. Again, the stone was too thick for the infrared to have sensed the animal.

Ross sighed. "You know, this is a waste of time. Unless our targets are right on the surface, we're not going to get anything; these sensors just don't have the penetration we need."

Eveleen nodded. Ross saw her profile outlined against the slightly softer darkness of the sea, the water touched with reflected glimmers of starlight.

"Hear that?" she murmured.

Ross turned his head. Faint echoes of shouts rose from somewhere toward the coastline.

"Let's go see if they need help," she suggested.

"Right."

Their progress was slow, until they found a relatively undisturbed stretch of pathway. But then that, too, ended abruptly at another great landslide. They picked their way over carefully, forced to test every step, lest they be carried downhill with another slide, some two hundred yards.

But just before dawn eased the darkness to a faint, orange-tinged smear, they found the others, all except Kosta.

Ross said, "Scavengers are roaming around in a gang."

Ashe nodded. "They clearly think this city is their territory. We had to fight them off twice. Kosta went chasing after them," he added. "I searched a little more, until a landslide forced me back."

"Any sign of the Baldies?"

"Nothing found, though I thought at one point that I saw an artificial light."

"Was it just a lamp?" Ross asked.

Ashe shrugged, a gesture that looked to Eveleen almost Gallic. For some reason it made her smile. "Landslide, and then a fight, prevented us from going up there. Maybe it's nothing."

"Nothing on our end, either," Eveleen said. "Except a crabby goat."

Ashe breathed a short laugh, and then the swift crunch of footsteps brought all them alert and ready.

They relaxed when the strengthening light shone on Kosta's tired face, his stubble pronounced. He grinned.

"Find the Baldy hideout?" Ross asked.

"No. These scavengers—" Kosta shook his head, muttered in Greek, then forced himself to say in English, "After they tangled with us, several of them retreated in one direction."

Ashe rasped his hand over his chin. "So you followed them?"

Kosta's white teeth gleamed in the morning light. "Yes. And I discovered they have a ship."

CHAPTER 24

"THREE JOURNEYS OF the sun."

Linnea sighed, trying to rest her aching head. There was no rest, not in a chamber made of stone, with only a thin blanket of some synthetic material for cushion.

How absurd, she thought restlessly. As if the seer could distinguish such irrelevant matters as day and night. "The battle will begin in three journeys of the sun." That's what she'd said, and that's what the priestesses believed.

They also apparently believed that the priests kept them here for some grand purpose, because in their culture, no one maltreated the oracle or her Sisters of the Serpent. And Linnea could not bring herself to shake the old woman and scream, "Wake up! These are aliens who hate human beings, and you're just mouthing out a lot of superstitious nonsense that will be nothing but matters for scholars of antiquity and children's comic books in my time!"

But she couldn't. She could see herself doing it—felt the words forming behind her lips, her hands aching to grab and shake, and then she could envision the result: hurt, anger perhaps, but above all, flat disbelief.

They were sure the priests were kindly people, if strange, because so far, none of the women had been hurt.

The first one had returned after an immeasurable time, to speak of being given a beautiful cloth woven of wondrous stuff that had moon- and starlight threaded through.

And when she wore the priestly garment, why, she could hear the inner voices of the priests, just as if she were a seer!

The others had listened in fascination as the priestess described how the "priests" invited her to talk about her life, and about what the seer saw and when she saw it, and how the people responded. At first it was difficult to shape the words in her head, but she learned to do it, and finally they took away the priestly cloth, and she no longer heard the spirit voices, and they brought her back.

Linnea, feeling sicker by the moment, translated that into real terms: the Baldies had thrown one of their shimmery blue cloths over her, which enabled them to hear the thoughts of the wearer, and the wearer to hear theirs. One of those blue suits had nearly cost Ross Murdock his life, when he first became a Time Agent.

Another woman had been taken, this one gone a much shorter time. Then another, but after her, they had not taken a fourth for a very long time.

The fourth had just disappeared; the women, unafraid, now had chosen among themselves who would go next to visit the spirit voices.

Linnea could not tell them why she would resist as long as possible. She would not tell the priestesses who she was because they wouldn't believe her. But revealing her real identity to the Baldies, who would believe her, would put not just her in danger, but also the priestesses and the Time Agents.

She glanced at the women now. The one with the broken arm was asleep but moaning softly. The seer was also asleep, a faint snore escaping her open mouth. The others sat, either meditating or talking in low voices so as not to disturb the sleepers.

All right, Linnea thought. *So that means I have to do something—*

A tremor seized them, and the women went silent, looking up. Yes, more silt drifted down, and more cracks appeared overhead, and especially in the walls. Two in the floor. In the far chamber, Linnea heard the water splashing up over the rock, just like her children used to splash water out of the tub when they played, lunging from side to side to make waves.

She frowned at the crack. The quakes were more frequent now, and Linnea thought they were getting steadily more violent, though that might just be her fear, that and the widening of the cracks.

"Oh, her fever worsens." A voice penetrated Linnea's thoughts.

At once several women crowded around the one with the broken arm. Linnea edged near, glancing down. The others had set the arm, as far as she could tell, well enough, and had wrapped it in strips torn from their robes.

The woman cried, and then turned her head away in shame, biting her lip, as Ela carefully unwrapped the last layer, exposing purple dotted flesh. Linnea's guts churned as she stared at the swollen skin, the greenish tone. Infection. The bone had probably shattered, and there was no way of knowing whether or not the setting had gotten it all back together, or not. But one thing for certain: major infection had set in.

Linnea backed away, moved to the front for one of the empty cups stacked neatly for the next appearance of the Baldies, and took the top cup. Useless worrying about who drank from which: germs were not even remotely in this worldview.

Linnea ran to the far chamber and dipped the cup into the running water. It, too, was running turbid, probably carrying dust and debris from the latest quake. Couldn't be helped.

With her back firmly turned to the crevasse that gave access, Linnea dug under her robe for her pouch. Down at the bottom was the plastic packet of super-powerful antibiotics that the Project doctor had issued each Time Agent. She pulled open the package, pulled out one of her four pills, and crumbled it into the cup, stirring with her finger.

Then she set the cup down to permit the drug to finish dissolving, and stashed the rest of the medicine in her pocket. She straightened her robe, her mind running through explanations: just as she was unwilling to thrust a modern view of hopelessness onto these women, even less was she willing to pose as a miracle worker.

She picked up the cup, stirred it once more with her finger, and then carried it carefully into the other room.

"I have herbs from Kemt," she said.

The others all looked up at her. She realized she had become isolated from them. Not ignored, precisely, but because she did not participate in their rituals, or their conversations, she had closed herself in with her thoughts, and they had slowly closed her out of their awareness.

Now several pairs of dark eyes, all expressive of hope, tracked the cup she carried. Ela helped the sick woman raise her head as Linnea murmured, "It is bitter. But all must be drunk."

The seer, who had woken, smiled very faintly. "Are not all herbs bitter?"

The sick woman sipped, winced, and then, at Ela's soft murmur in the unknown tongue, drank the antibiotic-laced water very quickly, leaving nothing but a trace of powdery, chalky-looking residue at the bottom.

"I shall save it," Ela murmured, pointing. "Stella can drink it later, if this eases the fire within her."

Linnea nodded, backed away, and then the door opened, and the absent priestess came back in.

She smiled. "It is just as you say! Spirits speak when you wear the priest cloth. They are very powerful priests, and very blessed, it would seem."

The seer turned to face Linnea. "There is only me, and Stella, and she is so ill." The old woman narrowed her eyes. Her expression was impossible to interpret, but it seemed to Linnea that she was doing her best to descry some sign from Linnea. "Shall you go, then?"

Linnea shook her head once. "It is not my time, Maestra," she said, hoping she sounded oracular, and not merely sulky—or sinister.

But the seer only bowed her head in acquiescence, and slowly walked through the open doorway.

Linnea could not see the Baldy outside, but she sensed its presence. The door closed.

CHAPTER 25

NIGHT AGAIN.

Or what seemed to be night.

When Eveleen woke up, her sinuses clogged, her mouth dry, she sat up blearily. The late afternoon light was weird orange. The sky was covered with what looked like gray rubble: a mixture of cloud and smoke that appeared dirty and threatening.

A faint whiff of civilization resolved into fresh, steaming coffee. A mug pressed into her fingers, and she sipped, her eyes closed.

When she opened them, Ross was hunkered down on the deck next to her hammock, looking like a movie-land wild man with his long, curling hair bound back by a bandana, his fatigues, and his fake-fur pouch still worn around his waist. He had no shirt on. None of the men wore shirts; the weather was oppressively hot and still. Eveleen resolved mentally that, if she couldn't rightly go shirtless, she could at least make her thin robe work for her instead of against: she would soak it thoroughly with water before she did anything else. Her scalp, too.

"When we get done," Ross began, and Eveleen mentally added the "if" that Ross would never say out loud, "they're gonna owe us a paid vacation. A big one. Where do you want to go? Paris? San Francisco, where it's foggy and cool?"

"I want to go to a spa and soak for a week," Eveleen said.

"I want a prime-rib dinner," Ross said, "and all night to eat it."

Eveleen cudgeled her aching brain to top that, but the urge to be silly for a blessed time was all too brief: there was Gordon Ashe, patiently waiting for them to finish. He didn't interrupt, or frown. He simply sat on his hammock, half a sandwich in his hand, his expression blank.

Ross glanced up at his chief, gave a sour smile, and said, "More good news?"

Ashe shook his head. "No news. Kosta took off at about ten this morning. Went down to find that globe ship. Said he thought about it all last night, and insisted he knew just where to look."

Eveleen shook her head. "Isn't he ever going to sleep?"

Ashe quirked his lips in a grim semblance of a smile. "He said he'll either sleep for eternity, if we're caught here, or else he'll sleep for a week when we get safely home, but either way he won't get any rest running around on top of a fifty-thousand-megaton bomb that stinks of burning rotten eggs."

Eveleen laughed, then got to her feet. "Who can resist a call to arms like that?"

As she spoke, she studied Ashe. He'd lost that restless, angry nervousness she'd sensed earlier, and he seemed to have come to some sort of decision. Not that anyone could really read him, of course, but she lingered for a moment or two, waiting to hear how that decision would translate out into a plan.

After a little more chat about the technicalities of the dive, she said, "Well, I'll get cleaned up and ready, if you'll tell us what's next."

"I don't know," Ashe replied. "Depends on what Kosta comes up with—"

"Here he is, if I'm not mistaken," Ross said, poking his head up through the hatchway.

A lot of splashing and some gasped curses in Modern Greek resolved into a dripping Kosta.

Everyone swarmed up on the deck, waiting in silence as he pulled his breathing mask off. He blinked away sweat, then said, "It's gone."

Eveleen, stunned, said, "The globe ship?"

Kosta glanced her way. "I shifted the rest of that debris we found. It's gone."

Ross let out an expletive that seemed to sum up everyone's feelings.

"Gone like taken?" Ashe asked.

Kosta shook his head, dropping down wearily onto a bench. "It's buried, so deep it's impossible to get to." He looked up at Eveleen. "I believe there was not just a massive landslide, but a fissure of some sort opened, the ship fell into it, and a slide occurred. The landscape down there changed, some of it shifting about twenty yards west, and then dropping."

Everyone looked stunned, considering what that meant.

"Well," said Ross, "at least that means the Baldies can't get to it, either. I hope."

"We'll have to make certain," Ashe said. "But not yet. Everyone get ready: we'll meet back here in ten minutes. First we search, and then we'll plan further."

Eveleen went down to the sweatbox. As she untangled the sweaty mass of her hair, she yanked impatiently at one of her earrings, as usual caught in a mat. The other wasn't, for once; she felt, and then jerked her face up to the tiny mirror.

The other earring wasn't caught; it was gone.

She touched the hole, saw a tiny scab, and vaguely remembered a sting there during the fight the night before. So she *had* lost an earring in Akrotiri! She'd lost the earring—but was still alive. So far . . . She grimaced, knowing that up the line in the future, she and her remaining earring might still be buried elsewhere.

"It's not a good sign, or a bad," she whispered to the shower. But would anyone else, such as Ross, take it badly?

She hustled through a quick semblance of a cleanup and dressed, her mind racing. When she stepped out, she quietly removed the other earring and stowed it with her gear. There. Either it, and she, made it back, or they . . . didn't.

Then she straightened up, refusing to think about it anymore. But that was no comfort. Her mind promptly reverted to Ashe and that look of resolve, of a decision having been reached. Whatever Ashe's decision had been, he hadn't shared.

Or was she just imagining things?

She got one of the dried-looking sandwiches that Stav had put out and sat down to wait for the others.

━━━

A STRONG QUAKE sent the surf crashing out and then in again in strong waves, nearly sinking their rowboat.

Once again the entire team was there.

No one quite wanted to say it, but this was their last search for Linnea. The silent testimony to the north lit the sky like a vision of hell: the plume of smoke from the pre–Kameni Island had widened gradually into a wide, glowing red. Between wind-torn flaws in the smoke they could see veins of lava shooting up into the sky.

They were far too close to the point of no return, and they still did not know for certain that the main controls to the devices were on the globe ship. Ugly as the sky looked, the constant quakes might still bleed off just enough energy to prevent the great eruption if the Baldies could reactivate their devices.

One more search for Linnea, then, and after that, they had to put all their effort into finding out if the Baldies' tech was elsewhere besides the missing globe ship.

Meanwhile, their boat floated, unguarded, at anchor, its only protection a crumbling cliff.

They rode a mini-tsunami that deposited their rowboat high on the beach. They landed with a jarring smack. At least it was above the fly-covered sea wrack. Ross could smell the rotting fish and seaweed, and he could hear the buzzing of great clouds of flies, but at least he didn't have to see the revolting mess.

He helped the others drag the rowboat up farther, and then they did their best to camouflage it with a reed mat.

After that came the grueling climb to where Ashe had seen the light. This time, the last time, they would all look.

Ross bided his time as the others began walking. When his wife fell into low-voiced conversation with Kosta about the scavengers' ship, Ross took a long step and fetched up next to Ashe.

In the dim red glow from the north, Ashe looked grim but amused. "And your objection is . . . ?"

"I haven't known you all these years not to smell a dead rat when the stink hits me," Ross said.

Ashe breathed a soft laugh.

"You're going to find those damned Baldies and offer to trade yourself for that woman, aren't you?"

"What makes you think that?"

"The fact that you didn't outline it as a possible plan—one that you know we'd all veto. I'll bet you Linnea Edel would, too, if she were listening in."

Ashe shook his head. "I should not have let her come. This mission was not the right one for a beginner, and—" He paused, looked north, then said only, "I owe it to her children to send their mother back alive."

They're grown up, Ross wanted to say, but he knew it would sound wrong. Just because he'd been abandoned at an early age, had never had a family bond, didn't mean it didn't exist for other people. He'd learned that much from marriage.

So he said, "You don't know that she's alive, or that they have her."

"No. But it makes sense that they'd take hostages, if she were alive. After all, we got their ship—we had it—and time is running out."

"But we still don't really know that the globe ship vanished. They could possibly have gotten it back. We still don't know if there's another ship, or not. Maybe there is, with high-tech recovery equipment. Or maybe they've solved the exclusion principle and can slip back in time, get it, and then move it somehow."

"Or maybe they don't have it," Ashe retorted. "It could be so buried they can't get at it. All I know is, if I find them and we can't break her out any other way, then I have to try."

There's going to be another way, Ross resolved, tightening his hand on his weapon. *Watch me find it.*

WHEN AT LAST they came for Linnea, it was almost an anticlimax.

The seer had returned, peaceful in her conviction that she spoke with spirits through the blue priests. They had said that when they finished talking to the women, they would send them on their way.

"Stella cannot take her turn," the seer said, looking down at the sick woman. "And yet the priests need to bring us all before their spirits. But there is still this problem, that time is short."

Moral suasion, then. The seer wouldn't tell Linnea to go, but it was clear that she, and all of them, except the sleeping Stella, expected her to go. Linnea looked at the expectant faces, the innocent trust there, and bit her lip hard.

She heard the step of the Baldy behind her.

She filed out behind the alien, knowing that she could do nothing else, as the seer stood looking down at the woman who slept peacefully for the first time since she'd broken her arm.

CHAPTER 26

HERE IT IS, Linnea thought, trying to walk steadily on legs that trembled. She gripped her hands beneath her robe, sidling her eyes here and there. *Should I run? But then they will know I'm a ringer before anything else happens. The others did not run.* And besides, her knees were so watery she was afraid she wouldn't make it five steps.

Well, she thought, trying to steel herself, *then I must think only in the old language, and* be *a priestess from Kemt, just as Gordon told me to be.*

That conversation on the road to the oracle now seems a hundred years ago, she thought sadly as she followed the silent Baldy up a rough rock corridor.

At least the walk was not long, just around a rough stone corridor into another room, a small one, with plain local furnishings and a jumble of unrecognizable objects on a central table made of olive wood.

Behind the table waited several Baldies, one holding an armful of shimmering blue-green cloth. "Baldies." Now that she was face to face with them, the old nickname seemed more inappropriate than ever. Not that they weren't bald; they were, indeed, hairless, at least in terms of what was visible, and the absence of eyebrows and even eyelashes made their faces very hard to read.

Yet she made out individual characteristics as one held out the cloth, shook it slightly, and then cast it over her head. One whose light-colored eyes were wider spaced than the others, another with a narrower jaw, one whose ears protruded, just a bit.

A hole had been slit into the fabric, through which her head emerged. As the cool weight settled on her shoulders, she held her breath, trying hard to think in complete sentences in Egyptian, but when the telepathic augmentation opened a sense she had never known she possessed, she gasped, staring around.

Wonder and delight and fear flashed like silver eels amid the stream of tumbled images and words that, she realized with an internal wail, were all in English.

Mentally she reached, trying to snatch it all back, but of course her thoughts were gone, as thoughts do vanish, only this time she felt the stream wash over her listeners, for their reactions in turn splashed back on her.

No anger, no leaps to kill, no growls of vengeance—that much was clear but little else. Outside of surprise, their reactions were too complex for her to comprehend.

A whisper of communication, too quick for her to catch, zapped among all the Baldies.

They, in turn, caught the word *Baldies* from her. Again, she knew this from their reaction and from the riffle of humor that streamed through her mind and vanished, but afterward she sensed recognition, the assembling of clues, and the name *Ross Murdock*. To which she, inadvertently, responded with a vivid mental image.

Another exchange between the Baldies, even faster than the previous; all she perceived this time was relief, a sense of "at last!" and then resolve, as if an order had been given and received somewhere else.

And then one "spoke"—if shaping words into sentences and sending them by thought can be termed speaking. In English, of course.

You are another from the hidden Time.

The mental images with the words were fast flickers, well controlled: a very young Ross, wearing a dirty blue-green outfit, launching across a fire at someone; what looked like a laser battle around a great globe ship; men speaking Russian; and some other images that she could not identify, but which she guessed were other Time Agents, encountered in prehistory.

Linnea perceived the statement not as a question but as an interrogative, and she braced herself. They already had her identity, and probably her purpose, and of course they held her life: what had she to lose?

She frowned, trying to shape her emotions into clear sentences, when quick and facile as a swift in the sky came the thought: *Say it aloud, if you like.*

"Why are you forcing your way into my mind? Why not just talk to me, since I'm already here as a prisoner?"

It is that your words and the motivations and meanings behind them so often contradict. And with those words came the unsettling sense of being made dizzy, as if trying to listen to two conversations at once, or to watch two scenes at once.

"All right, then. As for my own time, let me say this, too, and you'll 'hear' it as truth: I resent being kept a prisoner," she stated. "On my own planet. I, and the others, came back to this time to save our civilization. Our actions are those of rescue, not destruction. Can you possibly say the same?"

Yes, said the Baldy with the narrow jaw. He (she realized she chose "he" as a default, though there were no signs of gender that he could perceive, other than the slender shoulders being somewhat broader than slender hips; again, she felt a riffle of humor, but no information, from them) spoke aloud.

We must protect the galaxy's diversity of life. Only that way can it attain the full consciousness that is its goal and its flowering. With the words came images, many of them incomprehensible to Linnea. But from them she identified a problem that was very real in her own time: the extinction of hundreds or thousands of species by a technological race.

What you do on your own world is not for us to decide. But we will not permit you to do it to other worlds.

Linnea was discovering that their mind voices were individual, too.

Another Baldy, somewhat taller than the others, mind-spoke in cooler terms: *We seek the minimum interference that will prevent you from developing space flight until you are mature enough not to want it, or not to misuse it,* the alien said. *We do not destroy worlds. As ours was.*

And with the words came images of possibilities, what the Baldies could have done, such as destroying Australopithecus with a tailored plague, or sending asteroids to detonate in Earth's atmosphere.

But beneath the explanation—and they waited for her to perceive it—lay the specific memories of these specific individuals: arriving in their own time, not distant from the now of Kalliste and its volcano, to find that their own sun had been detonated.

She saw, and felt, their reaction of shock, disbelief, terror, grief, anger, all emotions human enough to strike deeply into her heart.

"Who?" she shaped the thought, and the reply was an echo from them all:

The Kayu.

"HERE," GORDON ASHE said, pointing.

Eveleen paused, wiped her stinging eyes, and surveyed the scene. It looked more alien than the alien landscapes she had visited in her travels away from Earth: rubble, fragments of jars painted with stylized seed pods, stacked reed-matting beds, and all around landslides, lit by the glowing-coal smolder from the north.

It was the glimpse of dancing monkeys that snapped the puzzle pieces together, altering the scene from unfamiliar to familiar, just as Kosta said, "I rcmembered those monkeys. It was about here last night that I felt the need to turn away, turn back, and I heard you being attacked." He pointed at Ashe. "And so I ran down that way." He indicated the darkness to the south, toward the harbor.

"I know where this is," Eveleen breathed. "It's that square we told you about. The one with the weird compulsion."

Ross, who had been slowly circling the rubble, looking high and low, paused, hands on his hips, looking back. "I feel it," he said in a short voice.

They all stepped toward the rubble-surrounded walls of the square house. At once Eveleen felt that inner tightening of danger, and she could see, even in the ruddy dim light, that the others were tensing up.

Ross stepped up next to Ashe. His voice was low, but his wife, attuned to his moods, to the softest utterances of his voice, heard him breathe: "Remember what I said."

Ashe did not react. He motioned to the others. "Here's what we do."

LINNEA GASPED. "THE Kayu? Who are they? Some kind of futuristic super-villains?" Though the Baldies had said those words about conflicting meaning and statement earlier on, she wondered if it was the seeming-truth of the master liar: if she were being manipulated not just through words, but mentally.

"They believe in noninterference."

"Blowing up a sun is not noninterference," Linnea answered back, before the Baldies could organize and send to her the mental images that they wished to accompany their words.

You must wait, one responded mentally. *You cannot communicate with our speed in this way, and you are forming false understandings.*

Linnea paused and received a series of images: the Kayu with their furry appearances and their warm robes, creatures of a very cold world, an old world. Not all thought alike, as one would expect from a race that did not share a common mental plane, but they did believe in leaving life to progress as it would toward eventual reunification in Telos.

Telos? Linnea thought, fighting for comprehension. That simply meant "goal" in Greek, but underlying the word were feelings or images of light and energy and awesome power. Were they talking about the Big Bang? Or the Big Crunch at the end of time? Everything was coming far too fast, though she could feel the Baldies' efforts to slow down, to keep their images simple.

"When they discovered that we had learned how to travel across time as well as distance, they began to follow. They are here now, having perceived across several centuries our efforts on this island."

Linnea struggled now not to comprehend the *what* but the *when*. Of all the tenses in English, the future perfect progressive is the most clumsy: "by [future date] we will have been making . . ." Now she realized that the Baldies could not possibly share their language, that they had several modes and conditionals within that single tense that she couldn't understand any more than she understood quantum physics.

"Most of our people are gone, except those who were on missions," the Baldy stated. "Many do not know yet what has occurred at home. We are here to complete our mission because it would guarantee a peaceful world here. And when you do reach space, you will not go as a plague."

"We are also here to find Kayu and eradicate them, that our time might restore our world," another said.

But we do not know which of their individuals carried out that mission; many of the others are also travelers like you, and have been forbidden to interfere except by truthful exchange of information.

Linnea struggled, and struggled, and finally burst out, "When is your time? Is it now? Is it in my time? Is it beyond my time? Because if it's not beyond my time, how do you know that our world takes destruction to the stars? And if it is . . ." She faltered in a welter of conditional verbs.

"The time-line we give to you with our interference here does not kill a whole people," the Baldy stated. *It gives your world a future of peace.*

"But it also takes me out of it, or if I were stuck here, it takes my children out of it," Linnea said, fighting against tears. But they clogged her throat anyway, making her voice quiver like an old woman's and her eyes sting and blur, so that the Baldies became mere forms standing before her. "My children have a right to their existence. Everyone who is born has a right to existence, everyone, including you. I am sorry for your world, but don't destroy mine. My children want to make a better world, as do all the people I know and value—"

It was right then that the sizzling crackle of laser fire sheered into the doorway.

The Baldies turned as one, their mouths open in consternation. Swiftly they withdrew in the other direction, leaving Linnea standing there.

She heard a shout. "Linnea! Are you in there?"

It was Ashe.

She moved to rip the cloth from over her head, but paused. The Baldies were disappearing, some of them taking some oddments she realized hazily must be part of their technology.

Dark figures entered, bringing a sharp smell of smoke and sweat and hot, burning metal. Lasers lanced out again, not at anything living, but at the few bits of Baldy tech left in the room.

She slapped her hands over her eyes, bewildered, confused, but above all desperate for answers. She flung out the mental cry: *You talked about my time and time now but not our future time. Which future is it?*

No answer.

Are you us?

No answer.

Then someone pulled the cloth from her head and flung it away, and the world slammed round her again, imprisoning her thoughts inside her skull.

She was still standing there, her hands over her face, and tears smearing down her palms, when she heard Eveleen's soothing voice: "It's okay. We're here now. The Baldies hightailed. They can't do anything to you."

CHAPTER 27

"IT'S GOING TO blow!"

Who shouted that? Eveleen couldn't tell; the roar of groaning, cracking rock was louder than the biggest thunderstorm she had ever experienced.

The violent red glow all across the northern horizon had visibly increased during the short time they'd stormed the Baldy hideout.

Eveleen watched Ross gape at it and then force his eyes away. She knew what he was thinking: he would deal with what it meant later. Right now, that spectacular lava fountain cast enough light for them to see by.

They began picking their way down the landslide. Ross and Eveleen had just reached a wall and were about to vault it when Stav let out a shout and raised his weapon.

All of them stopped, ready. Down the trail from them was a cluster of figures. But the figures turned, none of them yelling or fighting, and in the weird red light they recognized that they were all women.

Linnea Edel gave a gasp. "The priestesses! They have let them go."

"We've got to get them off the island," Ashe stated.

Yes, but how? Eveleen had an unpleasant inward vision of their ship crowded with women who belonged in a world three thousand years in the past, but then Kosta smacked his hands together. "The scavengers' ship."

Ashe grinned. His teeth glinted in the bloody light.

"We might have to scuffle for it," Ross warned.

"Then all four of us can go," Ashe said. "The scavengers can see to themselves. These women deserve a chance to get away from the blow, but if they don't do it soon, they might not make it." He turned to Eveleen. "You get them some supplies off our ship. Stuff they'll understand," he added. And to Linnea, "I take it you know how to communicate with them?"

She nodded.

"Then explain that they need to get going, now, fast, either south to Crete, or if they're afraid of missing the island, then northwest to Greece. Anywhere but east."

She nodded again, and started speaking to the women.

Eveleen, after the first few sentences, stopped listening. Linnea was talking in Kallistan terms, making it all simple. Eveleen realized that the preparations for food would be entirely up to her; time was running out, and she'd better hurry.

When Linnea paused, Eveleen whispered, "I'm going to run ahead and row myself to our ship. Take them to the beach and wait. We have radio," she added. "Here. Take mine. If I need to, I'll contact you with a spare from the ship. If the guys beep a signal, beep back four quick ones, which is the emergency code." She sighed. "At this point, I suspect Gordon will break silence and come on in the clear and talk to you."

The older woman looked tired and worn in the terrible red light. Her eyes were puffy, but her gaze was alert and focused. "All right," she said in a soft voice. "I will meet you on the beach, then."

Eveleen ran the rest of the way down, or rather slid, skipped, hopped, and once rolled. Even with the roll—a painful one, over what seemed to be every pointy stone on the island—she was glad to be going down, not up. The air was hotter than ever and filled with smoke that smelled of hot rock.

She found the rowboat, cast off the covering, and was about to jump in it when two figures emerged from the shadows under an outcropping of rock.

A guttural-sounding roar from one gave her enough advance warning that this was no friend and to pull out her weapon. She aimed at his feet and fired.

Hot, smoking sand blasted up.

"Ow!"

A gargling howl of anger from the other presaged a berserker attack. She jerked up the weapon, realized she still couldn't bring herself to fire, and reversed it, dodging the flying fist that came at her head, and pistoled the man across the mastoid bone. He went down like a felled tree, stinking of years-old sweat, stale wine, and uncured goat skin.

Gagging, she turned around to deal with the second one, to see him running westward down the beach, his pumping legs flinging sand up behind him.

Using her breathing techniques, she tried to calm her jangled nerves and forced her watery legs to function as she shoved the rowboat down to the water.

Having learned the hard way about rowing, she wrapped some old seaweed around her palms before picking up the oars. A few good, hard pulls, and she launched into choppy waves. The water looked as black as ink, except for the oily reflections of the distant lava shining an unpleasant red in spilled ripples of color.

She reached the boat, guided by a faintly glowing buoy bobbing around in the water, tied the rowboat to the stern, and clambered aboard.

There, she hesitated. For the past few days they'd moved the boat right into the harbor at sunset, trusting to darkness to hide it, and then they'd returned to their little cove, sheltered by crumbling cliffs, at dawn.

But Linnea had clear orders, and she couldn't see to execute them without lights.

Maybe the danger is over, she thought, and went ahead and turned on the lights. Not the ones she knew would light the deck, if needed, just the ones below.

Then, trusting to the murk outside to hide any cracks of light, she got busy.

LINNEA FORCED HERSELF to concentrate on walking, which was a challenge perilous enough. The terrible red light from the north was bright enough to distract one but not bright enough to highlight the many places on the walk down where the foot could get stuck in a hole or cause one to slide.

The priestesses had given Eveleen mildly curious looks, though in the darkness her mixture of modern clothing (khaki trousers) and Kallistan (her knee-length thin linen robe) had barely been visible. Linnea did not worry. She knew by now that what you expect to see you see. The priestesses were not looking for visitors from the future any more than they had recognized the Baldies as beings from another world.

Their only conversation was about the strangeness of the blue priests. Between the time Linnea had been taken away and their subsequent freeing, they had managed to convince themselves that the priests had sought someone from Kemt.

"Perhaps," Ela said as they trod in single file, except for the two helping Stella, "they wish to go there, as our island is where the spirits have chosen to battle."

"Yes," several of the other women said.

"Our island is no longer a place for the living." The seer's old, cracked voice was wry.

Stella stumbled; the other two caught her up but necessarily jarred her arm. She gave a hiss of pain but made no protest. The others fell silent, the youngest two smoothing the road with their sandaled feet so that Stella would not trip.

In this manner they made their way slowly down to the beach. Out on the water, Linnea saw a tiny row of golden lights. That had to be their ship. She felt a surge of relief at the idea of settling down into her hammock once again.

The others exclaimed in mild voices and then sat down above the line of sea wrack to wait. Linnea was thus left alone with her thoughts, which arrowed straight back to her conversation with the Baldies.

What could she think? Her mind reeled with questions, with emotional responses to the questions, and of course no answers. She longed to sit down with Gordon, except she suspected he would have as few real answers as she did. He'd fought against the Baldies but did not know them.

Were they the enemy—or not?

She was just wondering when the sound of shouting voices carried, faint as the cry of distant seabirds, from the ruined city behind. She turned. The priestesses all turned. The thick, still air carried the sharpness of male shouts but no words.

Then, out of the darkness lanced three or four bright blue points of light. They arced across the ruins, and one angled down past the cliff at the water, hitting the boat!

Their boat!

She sank down onto the sand and covered her eyes.

CHAPTER 28

THE MEN HAD just climbed, dripping, aboard the scavenger ship when they saw lights lance out of the darkness, pierce the thick smoke obscuring the sky, and then stab across the harbor.

Ross squinted against the eternal haze. He saw a brief, reddish flare of burning wood. Their ship! Someone had blasted their ship!

He grabbed the field glasses away from Stav, cursing steadily as he slammed them to his eyes. Eveleen was on that ship . . .

But when he brought it into focus, he saw a shadowy figure moving around on the deck. It had to be his wife. Or . . . ?

"Come on, let's move," he snapped.

"No wind. We'll have to use the oars," Kosta replied.

Ashe was at the other side, watching the ruins through his glasses. Stav, Ross, and Kosta each picked up oars. Ross was glad that the galley wasn't belowdecks; the surface of the deck stank bad enough. Whoever those scavengers were, it was abundantly clear that basic hygiene was not remotely a part of their paradigm.

At last Ashe closed up his glasses and sat down to pick up his oar. He matched rhythm with the others, and then said, "It's difficult to be sure, but I believe the scavengers regrouped and tried to rush the Baldies."

Kosta said, "They might have been drawn by the noise we made in our raid."

"It's possible," Ashe said. "It's also possible that the Baldies think they're part of our group, or that we're allied."

Stav snorted. "They might not even know the difference."

Ross sighed, trying not to worry about Eveleen. "I wonder what the hell they did, or said, to Linnea."

"I expect we shall soon find out," Gordon said, and then they fell silent, putting their backs into lift, push, lift, push.

The scavenger ship had a very light draft and skimmed along the water, which was alive with little waves. *Nervous little waves,* Ross thought. The sort you'd expect to see after a whole lot of earthquakes.

They rounded the last point and angled in toward the harbor. Out on the water, which reflected glitters of crimson from the increasing glow northward, they perceived a small black lump.

Ross's heart gave a lift when the lump resolved into a rowboat with a single occupant: Eveleen.

As they drew abreast of the figures waiting on the shoreline, Kosta sounded the bottom with his oar. They maneuvered in as close as they could, and there followed a couple hours of very hard work.

It was especially hard in that murderous light, with the possibility of being fired upon by more weapons. No one knew where the Baldies were, or why they'd fired, or where the scavenger gang was, for that matter. So they worked as quickly as they could, helping Eveleen unload the barrels of water and the sacks of grain and beans and lentils that she'd selected for the priestesses.

"You're giving away all our camouflage," Ross whispered to his wife as they passed the sacks up into the scavenger ship.

She snickered. Then said, "If we need camouflage anymore, then we're in serious trouble."

Ashe gave them a grim smile as he passed up a big hard round of goat cheese that Kosta had traded for in the harbor the day before the big quake.

"I put some purifier in the water," Eveleen added in a murmur. "It might not last their entire journey, but I figure their systems have to be used to whatever biota will develop by the time they reach Crete."

"That's the last barrel," Ashe said. "Let's get them aboard."

Among those on the first trip was a woman whose family had been fisher folk. She understood the basic principles underlying hauling wind. Through Linnea (the women did not talk directly to men, they discovered, though Ross noticed a couple of the younger ones taking peeps at the four male Time Agents, Kosta and Stav especially), Kosta gave some quick lessons.

The woman nodded, obviously listening carefully. She seemed to comprehend that their lives were in her hands.

Ashe said, at the end, "Tell her that it's important not to go anywhere east."

Linnea looked up. "We discussed it while we rowed over. She says she'll take them northwest, if the gods of the winds will smile on them. It's easier to find land than it is to find islands."

"A wise choice," Ashe said.

All this in Ancient Greek, of course.

Ross and Ashe then bent to help the last woman up, the one with the broken arm. They waited while Linnea gave her a cup of something to drink that she said was more Kemtish herbs. From the bitter smell, Ross guessed she was dosing the woman with antibiotics. Good idea.

And then they climbed down, the five of them balancing in the little rowboat. Linnea crouched down into a ball in the stern sheets, and off they went.

Ross watched the women take control of their new home. Some of them were already cleaning, throwing garbage and filth over the side, others busy settling the sick one. The pilot was handling the sail as if she knew what she was doing, and the narrow little craft picked up speed, sailing away westward on the faint, fitful breeze stirring off the water.

I hope they get away, Ross thought, and then turned his attention back to the others.

"I think it's safe to talk," Ashe said, as the oars lifted and splashed. "Our boat first. What happened?"

"I don't know," Eveleen replied. Ross could hear her regret and self-blame in her voice. "I turned on the lights below in order to see what I was doing. Did that make us a target? I didn't think the light carried."

"I could see tiny pinpoints of light," Linnea murmured.

Ashe said, "The contrast with the total darkness in the south was apparently enough to guide their aim. Did you see how much damage was done?"

"No, I just turned on the fire extinguisher, and left the foam all over, then got back to the last of the flour sacks. I didn't know what else to do, outside of getting that food to Linnea's group," Eveleen replied.

Various nods of acquiescence from the others were the only response.

Ashe said, "Linnea? Are you ready to brief us on your experiences? Or do you require some recovery time?"

"No, I can talk," the woman said. She sounded at first as if she'd aged ten years, but as she spoke her voice gained firmness.

As Linnea outlined what had happened to her, they finished crossing to the ship.

Kosta was the first one up. He dashed below, then returned, and in the reddish light from behind them, Ross and the others saw his relief.

They didn't nail the engine, then, Ross thought, and sat down on deck. The air was miserably hot, smelled worse than ever, and faint sounds, a rushing rumble, emanated from the distance. Hairs prickled on the back of his neck. Yeah, they'd said a whole week, but his body thrummed with fight-or-flight adrenaline. It sensed danger now.

". . . and that is when you came in," Linnea finished. "I was not able to ask any more questions, nor clarify any of theirs to me."

Ashe rubbed his hands over his face.

Ross said, "Well, look on the bright side. At least we fritzed out any tech they had there. I shot it all myself. So they can't come after us, especially if the globe ship is gone."

While the others talked, Eveleen and Stav went down to the little galley area, and the homey smell of freshly ground coffee added its blessed, and unlikely, scent to the terrible odors of a volcano preparing to blast.

Kosta had gone down again to clear away the mess that Eveleen had made with the extinguisher foam and repair any holes he found.

So it was Linnea who looked from one to another, and at last back to Gordon Ashe, before saying, "It changes everything, does it not, if it's true?"

Ashe sighed. "I think we might take it as true. Let me brief you, and you tell me what you think."

So he told her what the Kayu had said and recounted everything else that had occurred since she'd gone. He also told her what the big quake was, how it had been set off.

She pressed her knuckles against her mouth once or twice but otherwise stayed silent.

When Ashe was done, her first question took Ross by surprise. "Did they say they had somehow monitored the Priestesses of the Serpent? Perhaps radioed suggestions to them, as part of their policy?"

"They didn't say anything like that, but it's not out of the realm of the possible," Ashe admitted. "Why?"

"It's just so strange that the seer predicted that quake just before it happened, sending the people to evacuate. And you say that most of the city had gotten out of the buildings and down to the shore before it struck. That is an astounding coincidence, if the Kayu, or even the Baldies, were not manipulating the priestesses without their knowing."

Ashe stirred as Eveleen and Stav passed out mugs. For a time no one spoke, and the only sounds were those of the water lapping against the sides of their boat, the creak of wood in hull and mast, the distant, harsh cry of seabirds, and farther off that hydraulic whumble that promised violent action soon.

Then Ashe said, "I really believe that those questions are, for now, academic. The thought I cannot get away from is that we're going to have to go back up into that ruined city and rescue the Baldies."

"What?" Ross nearly dropped his coffee.

"Huh?" Eveleen stopped in the act of pouring more.

Stav said something under his breath, and down below, Kosta cursed in Greek.

Only Linnea nodded, a slow nod. She'd expected just that, Ross realized. "It changes everything, doesn't it?" she said. "That they have a . . . a moral directive? Each of them? The Kayu saw behind the Baldies' mandate a genocidal logic, and killed their sun in order to save other worlds, and the Baldies were changing worlds in order to protect some future that we are not permitted to see, lest we change it even from here and somehow destroy our fulfillment?"

Ashe laughed. "You put it better than I would have. I was going to say, 'Damn it; it's the right thing to do.' "

"But they shot at us! They shot at our boat!" Ross protested.

Linnea looked his way. "But we don't know that. Did you not all agree that the Baldies might not be able to tell the difference between you and the scavengers? That it's possible they thought this boat theirs?"

"What a nasty judgment on us," Eveleen muttered. "Not to see a difference."

"Yet that could have been true all along," Ashe said. "We've encountered them in the past. We don't know if different groups of them are ones who've just discovered their murdered world or if they've mixed us up with people of our prehistory, but either way, we probably haven't looked too good to them."

"Is this rescue plan a voting thing, or not?" Ross asked.

Ashe turned his way. "Do you think we need to vote on it?"

"No, I think we need to act, and fast. I don't care what the Kayu said about having a week. That damn island in the north is blowing bigger by the minute. If we're going in, let's go and get the hell out. Remember, where we're sitting is part of the caldera."

Ashe nodded. "Let's get in, then, and do what we must."

He turned to direct Kosta to start the engines, but then the radios at everyone's belts gave a brief, high burst of static and then lit.

Ross and the others grabbed their radios.

From them, in wide-spectrum stereo, came the mellifluous voice of the Kayu translation computer. "We shall take the !!! with us. But departure must be immediate, if you are to successfully translate both space and time."

The seabirds shrieked, unheeding, and the water lapped against the sides, a subtly faster pattern. The only human sound was Kosta's voice, still cursing.

"The seven days we spoke of was predicated on certain energy figures at the time, but those have considerably altered," the voice went on. "There is no safety here for finite beings; only the entity can remain. You must go, and so shall both our races, the !!! having failed to destroy your time-line and we having failed to hear the entity we sensed cross time."

"Entity?" Ashe said, looking puzzled.

"The entity that only the serpent woman could sometimes hear. And it would not speak when the !!! placed their devices in the temporal world."

"Wait," Linnea said, taking Ashe's radio from his hand and kneeling on the deck to speak into it. "Tell us! What have we done in our future to make them so desperate to destroy us in our time?"

There was no answer.

Ross realized that Kosta's cursing had gotten louder.

Ashe said, "Kosta? The engines?"

"Are fine," Kosta called.

"Then fire them up and get us out of here. Unless there's another problem?"

Everyone now got to his or her feet, crowding around the hatchway.

Kosta stood there looking up, his face gleaming with a sheen of sweat, his eyes black, his mouth tight with anger and tension.

Stav gasped, and said something in Greek. Kosta shrugged one shoulder and then said, "The onboard damage is not too bad, just some splinters and melted plastic—but the time-gate is compromised."

"Compromised? How?" Eveleen asked.

"The Baldies' laser fire damaged the portal rods. If we can't fix them in time we won't be able to sync up with the gate."

He gestured at the violence behind them. "And then we shall see, up close, Kalliste become Thera—"

He stopped, but they all knew what came next: *before we die.*

CHAPTER 29

—FEAR. EVELEEN STOOD there on the deck, trying to think.

The mission was over. They were done. In fact, they had to leave. But the time-gate was broken.

None of these facts caused the least reaction in her. She felt unreal, as if the red sky and the black sea and the never-ending smell of burning rock had replaced reality.

Her eyes turned Ross's way. In the ugly red light he, too, looked stunned.

Then Gordon Ashe moved. "Let's get down to the fixed point as fast as we can; we have spare rods." A rattling roar from the disintegrating island punctuated his words.

Stav shook his head. "Yes, we shall, but it will be a close thing. And even with the new rods, can we recalibrate it well enough in the time we have left?"

"What does that mean?" came a whisper at Eveleen's shoulder. Eveleen cast back a distracted look and saw Linnea.

"All speed. Set the sail to help," Ashe added, as the wind had been flowing out of the west—and they knew that the wind would carry the volcanic detritus east—but no sailing ship could sail into the eye of the wind. Bracing the sail round to catch that west wind might aid the struggling motors and help propel them southward just a bit faster.

Eveleen said to Linnea, "Whether or not we manage to fix our side of the time-gate, we still have to get to the same spot the Russians are waiting at." She paused. "Good news and bad news: it's probably close enough to reach before the volcano blows but too close to survive if the gate fails us."

"But what did Stavros mean about recalibration?" Linnea asked.

"Our signal, which emanates from the portal rods, allows the Russians to calibrate the gate at their end. I don't understand the details, but the science types all agree that it's dangerous to linger when passing through a time-gate—and no one knows, or wants to know, what happens if you try to back up. There's some indication that that's what happened to a big Russian time-base that blew up a while back. At the time we thought it was the Baldies. Now—"

Linnea nodded. "So passing through on a boat sounds dangerous."

Eveleen nodded. "The scientists were afraid of that, so they put those engines in so we could get through at what they figured was a safe speed. But now, if the Russians don't get an accurate reading and open the gate at the wrong moment, well, I suppose the resulting bang will be lost in the Thera explosion, but we won't know."

Linnea winced.

Ross and Stavros were already busy at the simple sheet-ropes and braces that controlled the single sail. And there was a breeze, if a fitful one, stirred by the hot air coming south meeting the western flow. The water currents were also fitful, probably due to steam vents opening in the ground below the sea.

As Linnea watched, the men finished sheeting the sail home, and the ship began to pick up life. She realized she could not hear the engine adding its contribution to their speed; she could only feel its vibration.

"Now," Ashe said, his voice rasping with evident exhaustion. "Konstantin. Tell us what to do to help fix that time-gate, if you can."

"We must generate light on deck," the man replied, making motions with his hands. "I must disassemble the rods and lay out the pieces so that I can examine the damage."

"That's a clear order," Eveleen murmured. "Our part is to clean up the deck, then." She sent a humorous look Linnea's way, hoping to ease the woman's stricken expression.

Linnea nodded, gave her a perfunctory smile, but it was a polite smile, and did not mask the inner turmoil that Eveleen could so plainly see.

They worked quickly, and in silence, shifting all the decorative "trade goods" belowdecks—those that they'd gotten for the scientists, that is. The fake things they threw over the side, figuring every bit that lightened the boat's load increased speed. And in the blast to come, no one was ever going to find those floating plastic jars or fake furs.

The blast to come—maybe it had even started. Eveleen saw that she was not the only one glancing often over her shoulder at the north. The scary thing was, they didn't seem to be moving at all, yet she was able to feel the wind and saw little rippling waves slapping up the bow and passing, with oily-looking foam, down the sides. The current did not seem to be setting north, so what was the problem?

When they got the last items clear, and the men began bringing up the big metal rods that were the frame of their time-gate, she stood on the taffrail and stared northward.

No, the familiar outline of Kalliste had diminished. But what had steadily grown was that red glare in the north. In fact, it had grown so much that it seemed to have come closer; the red now climbed high into the sky, tentacles of glowing smoke straining toward the horizon. Dawn was near: a greater light glowed in the east, but underneath it spread the violent reddish-brown cloud, reaching horribly outward in snaking fingers. Some even stretched westward, writhing upward like a monster out of the worst nightmare. Eveleen made out house-size chunks of matter spewing high into the sky and coming down with fiery force into the sea.

The sound, she realized, had grown steadily, a rumbling, rushing roar.

"It's as I thought," Kosta said.

Eveleen turned around and saw that he had laid out the portal rods on the deck. She'd thought of them, from the name, as being simple rods of metal; instead, they were hollow cylinders, now open like elongated clam shells and packed with circuitry and bizarre metallic shapes.

"The shunts in several rods were overloaded somehow by the Baldy weapons. I suspect they actually are a combination of laser and plasma fire, carrying quite an electrical punch."

"Did we pack enough replacements?" Ashe asked in an equally loud voice, his tone superficially calm, but there was a hard snap to his consonants, the question that is not quite an order.

"Of course, a full set," Stav shouted. "More than we need."

Everyone heard that, and Eveleen saw the hope in their faces.

Ashe said, "But will it take longer to replace the bad ones and test them all, or just replace them all? I assume we'll have to check the calibration of every one of them, whether or not we replace them."

"Exactly, especially under these circumstances," Stav said, after a short colloquy with Kosta during which they both glanced at the island slowly falling away behind them.

"Then let us not risk any weakened ones. Let's replace all the shunts. That, any of us can handle," Ashe said. "Stav and Kosta are the only ones who can handle the calibration; that leaves two rods for each of us remaining."

Stav nodded once and then knelt down to explain how to install the shunt cradled in his hands.

But before he could speak, a deep, ripping clap spun them all around. As they watched in horror, flame jetted upward from that distant island far into the sky, followed by a cloud of hot steam.

Moments later heat smashed at them, and the boat surged over the top of a big, warm, green wave that raced outward at unimaginable speed.

"Come on!" Ashe shouted. "Get to work!"

Eveleen saw everyone force his or her attention forward again.

They listened, with desperate focus, to Stav's explanation and demonstration—the process a simple mechanical one—and a brief systems check. Then the rest of them began work on the other rods while Stav and Kosta installed and began to calibrate the first one.

Soon there were fewer rods unrepaired than waiting, freeing some of them to assist.

Stav motioned Eveleen into the bow, where she crouched, looking back along the length of the ship. She couldn't help herself. She had never been able to turn her back on danger, and this was the worst danger she had ever confronted in her life. Thick globular shapes rose high into the morning sky, spreading out; as yet most of the eruption pushed into the east, carried by the higher streams of wind. In those globes incandescent ash could be seen darting about like gigantic fireflies from hell.

Eveleen hoped the fleet had not gone east; any of those clouds of burning ash touching ships would convert them into instant gas.

"Is that it?" Linnea cried, working next to Eveleen, who could only shake her head. The noise pounded her ears, her skull, her teeth, her bones.

Stav appeared next to them, handing a completed rod to Linnea and motioning so they put their heads close to his. His breath smelled absurdly of coffee, Eveleen realized, which added to the surreal aspect of the terror gripping them all. One part of her gibbered in weird laughter; the other apparently took in his rapid flow of instructions, though when she looked down, her hands lay there like a pair of spiders, unconnected to her, unable to move.

"Here, help me push it down," came Linnea's urgent voice, her lips just next to Eveleen's ear. She'd already placed the portal rod in its bracket. "This one first, and then that one," she said, motioning to the wire harnesses and jacks.

Ah. This thing first and then that.

Simple directions seemed to be what she needed. Another clap, even louder than the first, caused them all to jump, but everyone worked fast. Eveleen knew that the unmeasured tons of rock being spewed into the sky would be coming down soon, bringing with it a killing downblast that would send out lateral shock waves of volcanic glass shards to shred whatever wasn't being burned by the ash clouds.

They were running out of time . . .

"Next."

They moved along the hull to the next position. Linnea again settled the rod. Now Eveleen's hands worked quickly, independent of her mind; her eyes tracked Linnea's small hands, with their thin skin stretched over tendons and age spots, but fast hands, expressive hands.

Yellow light, weird yellow light, cutting weakly through the red-shot darkness slowly enveloping them, made Eveleen realize that the day had been banished by a volcanic night.

The air was hot; another surge lifted the ship, passed beneath, and set them down, bringing even hotter, thicker air, more difficult to breathe . . .

Someone slapped a mask over her face. She did not look up, but kept working. As she breathed in gratefully, she realized how close she had come to fainting.

But they were done. She looked up, her head pounding, her thoughts thick as the lava spewing into the stratosphere overhead.

Linnea motioned; no one could hear voices anymore. The roaring had taken over the world.

Eveleen crouched where she was as Stav, with a face of pain, reached down and triggered the gate. She looked over the side of the boat, but the sea was so frothy and filthy with ash that she couldn't tell if it was boiling along the portal rods, as it had when they had first passed through the gate. How would they know when they were synced?

A third clap, this one so loud they could only feel it as it tried to scour their bones, and Kosta smacked the engine into high. Hot wind blew into their faces as the ship shuddered, racing fast over the churning water.

Eveleen's imagination jammed into overdrive as well. As vividly as though she were somehow there, like a god proof against the violence, she saw the magma exploding upward, vaporizing the pre–Kameni Island, billions of tons of white-hot rock and searing gas punching up through the atmosphere almost to the edge of space, spreading out in a choking cloud that would bring killing winters to the Earth for years to come. And below, the sea racing in, exploding into superpressurized steam as it raged against the liquid rock.

Another surge, the greatest one yet, raced under them; they braced for the murderous shock wave of steam that they knew would be following behind—

And air and earth and sky began to rip apart in an explosion of noise and light and power. Her bones shuddered as the night around them flared with light and ahead the strange straight-line vortex of the gate manifested, sucking in the violence rushing past them.

Eveleen felt hands seize her roughly, throwing her violently down on the deck, and Ross's body on top of her. Moments later the gunwales burst into flame sleeting violently forward under the impetus of the hell wind chasing them; the sail vanished in a flare of light and the mast burst into flaming splinters. A thunderclap smashed at her ears, clamping her skull in a vise of silence while the devil played his organ music through her bones. Eveleen squeezed her eyes shut and shouted with pain as a whip of fire flayed her and the nausea of the transition was lost in a world of pain—

—and the shaking roar ceased abruptly, the fire cooled. The boat rocked violently for a moment, then calmed.

She squirmed out from under Ross and slapped at her smoldering clothing and then at Ross's. He'd been more exposed than she. She barely noticed the pain of her burns; what she did notice was the pressure in her ears and a total absence of sound.

Around her the others did the same. It appeared that everyone had come through. They were alive.

After a moment she stood up and looked around. The still-smoldering gunwales of the boat were burnt almost to the deck; all around them, she could see sparks falling gently down upon the sea like a benediction.

Eveleen ripped off her half-burned mask, and sucked in the cold air, still tainted with the breath of hell that seemingly had tried to follow them through the gate. She wondered what it had looked like from the Russian ships, now faithfully veering in toward them.

They were alive, and *home*.

She turned her face into Ross's shoulder and wept.

CHAPTER 30

IT WAS JUST over a week before Ross heard his wife's voice.

Until then, he could see her lips move, and he could see her changes of expression, and feel her arms around him, but his ears seemed stuffed with cotton batting. That was all right. Cotton batting was far preferable to that head-slamming blast back in the past.

Then sounds started coming in. Their first conversation was about their hearing; Eveleen complained that a bosun's twee had been set off in her brain, and she couldn't find the off switch.

They joked; they rested aboard the unmarked ship the Project had had standing by. They slept a lot. When they were awake, doctors ministered to them, at first patching up their burns, clearing out their lungs and sinuses, prescribing food, rest, and lots of water. Ross had no arguments with that.

Milliard came in by helicopter; Ross woke up one night to the *whup-whup-whup* of the blades, which he could feel more than hear, and next morning at breakfast there was the big boss, looking like the CEO of a *Fortune 500* company, except maybe tougher.

His lips moved, but Ross couldn't hear him. So they began communicating on-line; there were terminals all over the ship.

At first Ross didn't want anything to do with their questions, with debriefing, even with remembering. But the memory will not be denied: if one fought hard enough against it all day, it popped out again at night, taking control of one's dreams with such a vengeance one awoke, sweating, thinking they were all back in Kalliste again, and the pre–Kameni Island was going up maybe a hundred yards away.

So Ross gave in, answered one or two questions, then Eveleen started sending him playful e-mails, and before he knew it he spent those soft, summery days sitting out on the deck with a keyboard in his lap, typing away.

When he could hear again, the interviews started: Milliard, Project heads from various departments, and of course the medical teams, including psychologists.

They were interviewed separately, though no one made any attempt to keep them apart. Their own hearing functioned well enough to do that, had there been any urgent need for individual testimony.

Memory gave way to thought, and thought eventually produced questions—the foremost ones fueled by anger.

It was some time after the main battery of interviews was over that the entire group found themselves sitting out on the deck under an awning. All around them the sky softly wept, clear, clean rain, sky, air, and sea all a silvery gray.

The gentle drumming of raindrops on the roof merely served to make it seem warmer somehow underneath, as they helped themselves to a fresh pot of coffee brought out by the steward.

Gordon Ashe sat forward and gave them what Ross recognized as his scan look. "So, any thoughts?" he asked, sipping coffee.

They obviously weren't going to hear his thoughts first. Ross had no problem with that. He had no problem with leading off, either.

"I'll tell you what fries my butt," he said.

Linnea Edel's eyes crinkled. Kosta grinned his pirate grin. "What's yours?" he asked.

Ross laughed. "You, too, huh? Well, mine is this: those damned Kayu guys had the gall to judge us! I mean, look at it. They came on the radio like that, without us connecting in or anything. They obviously were listening to every stinking word we said while we sweated out those last few days. Every word. So they only speak up and tip us the clue that the whole damn island was about to blow *after* Gordon got his harebrained idea of rescuing the Baldies."

"That makes you mad?" Eveleen said, her brown eyes going round.

"Of course it makes me mad! That they could set themselves up in judgment like that, without letting us know. And if what the Baldies told Linnea is true, they don't exactly have clean hands."

"Irrelevant," Ashe said—*at his most maddening,* Ross thought with unrepentant grumpiness.

"Game playing," Kosta said. "I hate that." He grinned. "Unless I make the rules."

The others laughed, and Kosta went on, "We never perceived the rules with those ones. They had rules as far outside our ken as automobiles, computers, and TV shows are outside of the Kallistans'."

"In other words," Gordon said, "they made us feel stupid. Granted."

"Not stupid," Linnea Edel murmured, looking around at them earnestly. "Stupid is ignorant and doesn't care. We knew we were ignorant and we did care. We cared passionately."

Murmurs of agreement rippled round the group as the rain kept drumming overhead and far in the distance gulls screeched. *It is good to be home, in our own time, if not our own place,* Ross thought, swallowing down his coffee.

Stavros spoke up, taking the others by surprise. He'd been so quiet during the mission, like many engineers, living mostly inside his head. "I want to know," he stated, his English very accented. "I want to know what is this entity to which they referred."

"So did the brain boys," Ross said. "At least during my turn on the hot seat."

Nods of agreement from everyone.

"Well, I want to know, too," Ashe said.

Ross shrugged. "I think they went nuts. I mean, don't try to tell me those guys suddenly started believing in fire gods." He snorted, reaching for the coffee pot to pour out some more. "Or do they mean there's some kind of mysterious alien force living in the volcano? Give me a break—that's almost as bad."

"One thing I learned while I was so briefly a prisoner," Linnea said in a slow voice, "is that, even if I were to have told the other women about my time, what vocabulary would I have used? These women were not stupid. They were thinking beings, aware of their world, involved, several of them wise—much wiser, I think, than I will ever be—about certain kinds of things. Yet I'd be forced to use the language of childhood to describe a pair of nylon stockings."

Eveleen nodded. "That's what I thought. *Entity* could mean almost anything, and our mistake would be to assign our old rules to it, especially old rules we automatically distrust."

"I figured it had to be another sort of alien, at first," Kosta said. "From what I understood on that last radio transmission, the 'entity' couldn't 'talk' to the oracle woman while the device was in place."

Stavros nodded. "That argues for physical limitations of a sort that we can understand."

"Unless the noncommunication was not related to physical limitations but to some other set of rules, some we can't possibly imagine," Ashe said.

"Like what? Gods playing chess with us and the Baldies?" Ross scoffed. "If you're going to start gassing about gods then I'm going back to sleep."

"I'm playing devil's advocate," Ashe said, with a faint grin. "Probably a more comfortable post, at least in today's deterministic paradigm."

Ross knew that Ashe was joking—and he was the butt. He sighed. "Look. I just don't know, and none of you do, either, about that kind of question. So why get into it, since we can't really know?"

"Because it's interesting, trying to apprehend the infinite," Linnea said. "I, too, scoffed and thought myself so superior to those poor benighted women with their snake dances and their oracle, there in the dirty cave with stuffy air. But by the end, I began to see that in certain ways, I was the ignorant savage, and not they. Their perception of the universe was clear, it had moral rightness, and for all my superiority in realizing that they couldn't see the Baldies as aliens, only as priests, how many things were around me that I could not see, that they could? There is always the chance that at least Maestra, their seer, had in some way glimpsed past the shadows on the cave wall."

"Then you think there's a fire," Ashe said, looking across at her.

"I think that there are times when we feel the heat of it and see things reflected from the light of it," she said, even more slowly than before. "Don't you?"

Ashe sat there, staring out at the open sea. "I didn't, when I was young, but now, after years of seeing strange things, unexplainable things, I can only safely admit to my own ignorance."

Eveleen said, "Well, those Kayu knew there was something there. And so did that priestess. We found out too late to make our own investigations."

"And who knows if we would have found anything? We might still be too ignorant: all our tools are the wrong tools, our questions the wrong questions, because we so often have, if unconsciously, preformed conclusions," Linnea said. "It seems to be the curse of our modern times: we think we know enough to strip the meaning from all the past paradigms, without replacing it with anything."

"And without really comprehending the underlying meaning that made those paradigms work in the first place," Ashe put in. "Well, it ought to be interesting, the future. The Kayu and Baldies both know not only where we are but *when* we are."

"Do you think they will show up here, then?" Linnea asked.

Ashe shrugged. "It wouldn't surprise me."

"But we don't really know that they are from our own future. It could be that they cannot go forward, only backward," Kosta stated.

Stavros pursed his lips. If he had thoughts about time travel and aliens, he wasn't speaking.

Ross sighed. "Back to the speculation."

"Ah, but we're so good at it," Ashe said, smiling. "Why not indulge ourselves?"

"Because to me it's running in circles. Give me a clear goal and the tools to take action, and let me at it. I hate palaver that can't go anywhere," Ross said. "If that puts me in the ignorant camp, I think I can live with it."

Linnea smiled over her coffee cup at him. "It puts you in the camp of those who act. I am in the camp of those who react. There is, I believe, a place for both."

Ashe turned to her. "Does that mean you want to stick with the Project, then? Despite a fairly harrowing first trip?"

"Oh, yes," Linnea said. "Oh, at first I thought that I would never even be able to look back, and then I started looking back, and then I thought I would only stay on to consult on others' experience—Milliard specifically invited me to do that—but these past few days, I find myself thinking of things I would do differently next time. And that means I want there to be a next time."

Eveleen grinned. "So you got bitten, too, eh?"

Linnea turned to her. "Yes. So I told the bosses that I'll go home, revisit my children, as I promised myself, but I'm going to design my life differently, I think. Even the briefest glimpses of our past are treasures, and I want to be the treasure hunter."

"She's bitten," Ashe said.

They all laughed, and presently they got up and separated, all to various tasks.

THE SHIP WOULD dock in two days, the bosses having decided that they had enough preliminary material and that the agents were rested, had no mystery viruses or diseases, and were due some extended leave time.

Stavros headed straight back down to the labs, where all the instruments on the boat that hadn't been broken in those last few desperate hours were being evaluated. Kosta was up on the bridge. Gordon and Linnea went off to talk to some of the archaeologists that the Project had on staff.

Ross lingered longest, standing at the rail, trying not to think, but thinking anyway. When he finished his coffee, he went down below, and sure enough, there was Eveleen, in the midst of a workout.

He waited until she was done, then said, "We did talk about what to do when we got out, but we didn't decide. Or don't you want to think about the future yet?"

Eveleen gave him a too-innocent grin. "Oh, I think we should visit Hawaii—and go tour the big volcano!"

He chased her halfway around the ship before he caught her.

ABOUT THE AUTHORS

FOR MORE THAN sixty years, Andre Norton, "one of the most distinguished living SF and fantasy writers" (*Booklist*), has been penning bestselling novels that have earned her a unique place in the hearts and minds of millions of readers worldwide. She has been honored with a Life Achievement award by the World Fantasy Convention and with the Grand Master Nebula award by her peers in the Science Fiction Writers of America. Works set in her fabled Witch World, as well as others, such as *The Elvenbane* (with Mercedes Lackey) and *Black Trillium* (with Marion Zimmer Bradley and Julian May), have made her "one of the most popular authors of our time" (*Publishers Weekly*). She lives in Murfreesboro, Tennessee.

Sherwood Smith is the author of more than a dozen novels, including *Wren to the Rescue* and two other Wren adventures. She is also the coauthor, with Dave Trowbridge, of the Exordium series of SF adventures. Smith lives in Southern California.

Together, Andre Norton and Sherwood Smith have also written also two Solar Queen novels, *Derelict for Trade* and *A Mind for Trade*.